SARAH'S CHALLENGE

SARAH'S CHALLENGE

G C Millroy

ATHENA PRESS
LONDON

SARAH'S CHALLENGE
Copyright © G C Millroy 2007

All Rights Reserved

No part of this book may be reproduced in any form
by photocopying or by any electronic or mechanical means,
including information storage or retrieval systems,
without permission in writing from both the copyright
owner and the publisher of this book.

ISBN 10-digit: 1 84748 006 3
ISBN 13-digit: 978 1 84748 006 4

First Published 2007 by
ATHENA PRESS
Queen's House, 2 Holly Road
Twickenham TW1 4EG
United Kingdom

Printed for Athena Press

Hazardous Shopping

For most people, life hinges on a single extraordinary event, which in the course of things might never happen, but it is there, and just around the corner – if only they could turn the corner. But while they wait for that moment to come they degin to tread the path of life, happy with the simple things around them. For those – and they remain the lucky few – it might be winning a lottery, or for some it might be winning a talent competition. For others it can be the feeling that comes from being offered a job that leads to undreamed of wealth; but ask anyone just why the hand of fate should have reached out and granted them instant promotion in life and they will say it is a mystery. They all wonder why it has happened to them and not to the person standing beside them, and which attribute of their character was responsible. But there is never an answer.

For Sarah Levine it was a the trivial event that changed her life. She had all that a woman of twenty-eight years of age could possibly want, having pursued a career in publishing that had brought her a well-paid job with apparently excellent prospects. It allowed her to fraternise with her many friends, and to spend her time indulging in the wild pursuits of the young. These took the form of drinking with her mates most nights of the week and rushing off at the weekend to some party that started on the Friday and finished on the Sunday morning. She enjoyed her holidays undertaken with a group of like-minded girls, indulging in a frenzied round of drinking followed by burning in the sun. She had few regrets, for none of her contemporaries had regrets; had she lived in a past era then she might have the regrets of her sex, who could only look and yearn for the freedom of their brothers. No longer did the quirk of birth deny a woman the life she wanted; indeed, life seemed tilted to their advantage.

It was one lunch hour when she was shopping in Oxford Street when the event that changed her happened. In reality it was

5

nothing. As she went through the new plate glass doors of the department store, a small boy moved to the inside of the door and put his hands flat on the smooth glass surface. He had found a moment of freedom as his mother had taken her eyes away from him and, fuelled with curiosity, the small lad set out to sample the wonders of life that he had yet to experience. He had no sense of danger for he still relied on his parents for protection. His mother, drawn by the delights of the store, remained ignorant of his actions. As far as she was concerned, provided the lad was inside the doors he was safe. Possibly she wanted some minutes to herself, as all children make demands on a parent's time and patience, and for that reason she had ignored her son. And what sort of a small boy, when let off the leash, follows his mother obediently? Any lad left to himself would look for adventure. The door was his aim for it fascinated him with its large sheet of glass and the feverish world beyond in Oxford Street.

Without moving quickly, like most children he had turned and went determinedly to the door. He could not discern the glass, and his hands became his sensors. Sliding them over the surface he could feel the solidity of the glass and yet that did not satisfy his curiosity. Perhaps he could see the area that reflected the light and knew there was a limit to the glass, for his hand reached for the edge at the pivot end; his fingers slid around the edge allowing him to grasp it, and to all intents and purposes he looked as if he were trying to hold the ponderous door open. But inexorably the door was closing and he could not see the danger. Sarah, coming in through the other door noted the cheeky grin in his upturned face and in an instant saw the danger. In three strides she was round the door and pulling the lad away.

She set him down with a great sense of relief and she found a certain pleasure knowing that she had been able to help. And that was where the matter should have ended. Indeed, had it ended there Sarah would have thought little more about it and it would have become one of those mundane events in life that occur regularly along the way making up the full picture of one's experiences. But the boy, feeling that he had been roughly treated, burst into tears and screamed for his mother who, on hearing his anguished tones, turned to look at him. She summed up the situation, and, like a mother hen with all her feathers fluffed out, strutted over to do battle with enemy. Sarah was trying to console the lad and expected nothing but thanks for her actions. She was completely taken aback by the vehemence of the mother's reaction. To her astonishment, Sarah found herself being berated for daring to take hold of the little boy. It was as if she was being accused of attempting to abduct him. Under such a tirade it was impossible for Sarah to defend herself. The mother was not the sort of woman who cared to listen, and despite Sarah telling her that her son had been in danger of having his fingers at least badly squashed, the mother refused to listen; to her Sarah had committed a dreadful social solecism. She had no claims to heroism; she was some kind of criminal or pervert.

In desperation, Sarah looked around for someone who had witnessed the whole scene to come to her aid but the foyer had strangely emptied. People who had one moment been following her in, or milling around the nearest counters, seemed to have vanished. A male member of staff who had earlier been behind the nearest counter was peering anxiously from behind a distant pillar, and another was walking away from her at the far end of the corridor, presumably called to something far more important. It compounded her sense of injustice to see them scuttling away.

After much finger waving from the mother, Sarah was able to make her escape, and it was hardly surprising that she felt a grievous sense of injustice over the affair. The pleasure of shopping had evaporated and Sarah could only return to her office. It annoyed her, for the store was twenty-five minutes' walk from the office, which left her with only ten minutes of her lunch break for shopping. This woman had wasted five minutes of her precious time and given her a conscience over the advisability of her recent course of action. And if Sarah continued into the store now, what would happen were they to meet? Sarah couldn't face another confrontation. She wished she had joined her office colleagues for a light lunch. Instead, she was standing in the street outside the store feeling very deflated, and that made her feel hungry. She had expected to have some shopping to compensate for her lack of food, and that would have seen her through the afternoon. But the incident had taken much of her time and she

7

would now be late back to the office unless she really hurried.

Sarah toyed with the idea of being late back but she was a conscientious person and placed a high value on her job. She knew that she should have taken a taxi but she saw no point in bargain hunting if she spent the savings on the travel. She turned and walked as fast as she could, but halfway back she knew that hunger pains would overtake her during the afternoon and she had to satisfy her stomach. A short distance along was a sandwich bar and she joined the queue of three people waiting to be served. Sarah debated with herself whether or not she could actually afford the time but she felt that she was ahead of schedule and stood her place in the short queue. Her reward was to see the man at the head move away after what seemed to be only a few seconds. The woman who was next clearly was in no hurry but her purchase was simply and efficiently handled, and then the man in front of her was at the counter. It seemed a shame, but he knew the girl who was serving and Sarah had a premonition that it was going to take longer than it ought, for it seemed he was the boyfriend. She was right and felt the anger of someone being ignored. Suddenly the man turned to the door and it was her chance at the counter.

'Have you a cheese and tomato sandwich?' asked Sarah.

'What we've got is all in front of you,' was the uncompromising reply. To Sarah's annoyance the girl moved away and served the man behind her. Then she was back.

'Have you made your mind up, then?' said the girl.

'I would like a cheese and tomato sandwich,' said Sarah.

The boyfriend returned, gained the girl's attention, and they resumed their conversation; it seemed that they had forgotten to make a date for the evening. Sarah stood and wished she were the type of person who had the nerve to speak out and demand to be served. She ought to have made her point by leaving but knew that she would feel defeated and hungry; she would have to be patient and wait. It still took too long, and Sarah again asked herself if she shouldn't leave. But the girl behind the counter was a professional, and just at the moment Sarah determined to make her exit the girl turned to her.

'I don't know that we've got any... cheese and tomato, wasn't it?' she said, and proceeded to go through what was behind the glass counter. 'Oh, look,' she said, 'there's one!' She pulled it out and plonked the sandwich unceremoniously on the top of the counter. 'That will be two pounds.'

Sarah handed her the money and wished she could say that she thought she was being ripped off. She cursed her politeness as she automatically said, 'Thank you.' Then she fled from the shop back to the office, stuffing the sandwich in her mouth as she went. Her mind was now in a turmoil.

The office where she worked was on the edge of Mayfair and situated above a bar. The door was hidden at the side, and on entering there was a flight of stairs leading upwards. Despite the fact that it all needed new paint, it felt safe and Sarah was glad to dash in. At the top of the stairs was a small landing and to the left was the main office where she worked. But first she had to pass Ms Marchbank's desk, situated ominously near the door. Sarah hoped that it was not occupied, but to her dismay she could see that Ms Marchbank was standing beside her own desk. Since her wrist was stuck out, giving her a clear view of her watch, it required no imagination to see that the martinet was waiting for her.

'Ten minutes late again, Sarah, I see,' she remarked. 'What have you to say for yourself?'

'I'm sorry,' said Sarah as sweetly as possible and walked past her tormentor to her own desk.

'Sorry is not good enough,' said Ms Marchbank following her. 'I have no option but to tell Mr Deakin of your tardiness.'

'I've had a bad time and hurried back,' said Sarah. 'I need to get my breath back.'

'Then you'll have to do it in Mr Deakin's office,' she said and turned on her heel. She did not stop at her desk and hurried out of the door. Mr Deakin's office was at the other end of the landing.

One of Sarah's office colleagues, Michael Rending, came over. 'I'm sure she has it in for you,' he said.

'I'm not sure,' said Sarah, 'I'm absolutely certain! If it were left to her I wouldn't have a job here.'

Michael laughed and said, 'She's gone to have a go at Deakin.'

'Let her!'

'Do you think he'll humour her?'

'No, despite everything said about him he's fair chap.'

'What makes you say that? In my opinion he's nothing more than a sad middle-aged man who really by any definition shouldn't be running a business.'

'But he is...' Sarah began to protest.

'Yes, but he never smiles at anyone. He seems perpetually depressed.'

'I expect he has his reasons. At least he rarely comes round the office.'

'I suppose so. And we have only to see him once a week for the progress meeting.'

'In my last job they were always at us – "Where's this?" and, "Where's that?" They never stopped! But whatever you say about Deakin, he trusts you. If you say you'll be finished by the end of the week he accepts your word and he's not hovering around on Friday afternoon waiting for it.'

'If you keep that up he'll start to appear very easy-going! Oh, she's coming back!' said Michael. He moved swiftly to his desk and sat down.

Ms Marchbank was no fool and threw him a look of disgust but she had no time for him at that moment.

'Sarah – Mr Deakin will see you now!' She spat the words out.

'Fine,' said Sarah, rising from her seat. She wanted to say that she would be along in a minute but did not dare.

They went through to the back office, where Ms Marchbank ushered Sarah into the presence of Mr Deakin. It reminded Sarah of being ushered into the headmistress's office back in her school days, rather than into the office of a well-established publisher. She was stood in front of Mr Deakin, who remained seated at his desk still perusing a piece of paper, which was without a doubt a letter from an author bringing more problems. Sarah looked at his balding head; she thought she should be scared but she felt truculent and wanted to laugh out loud.

'You can go, Ms Marchbank,' said Mr Deakin at length, without actually looking up to see if she was there. 'I will deal with this.'

Ms Marchbank glared at him. She had been determined to see justice done and now she knew that her boss, faced with a pretty face in front of him, would fudge the issue. She wanted to say so and kept opening and closing her mouth. Finally she thought better of it and petulantly left the office, closing the door noisily behind her.

'Now, Miss Levine, what do you have to say for yourself?' Deakin's voice was deep and he sounded uninterested in whatever was going on. But then he always gave the impression of being elsewhere. Sarah knew of no one who liked him, and included herself on that list; but she had reason to be grateful to him for he had given her the job together with an enhanced salary that had always been paid on time. But there her thoughts about him ended, for he was nothing more than a dour, uninteresting man.

'I was late back from lunch, apparently,' she said, and was conscious that his indifference annoyed her intensely. For despite the fact that she felt truculent and wanted to be thoroughly rude to him, his tone, without being demanding, required the truth.

'Ms Marchbank tells me that you are making a habit of being late back from lunch.'

'It's the first time this week,' said Sarah, 'and I was only late once last week.'

'Ms Marchbank has a considerable list of your infractions.'

Sarah thought about his words. 'Is there something wrong with my work?' she asked at length.

'No.'

'Am I behind with my work?'

'I'm not aware of any slackness.'

'Then I don't understand why I'm being treated like a schoolgirl.'

'I only asked you why you were late.'

'Yes, but it's just like being in the headmistress's office: "Now, Miss Sarah, why did you throw a paper dart at Miss Jones?"' said Sarah sarcastically.

'And why did you?'

Sarah looked at him in surprise but his expression did not alter. 'Do you really want to know?' she asked.

'No, but you saying that does arouse a certain sense of curiosity.'

'We were all making paper darts, and I made one that flew the length of the room and hit Miss Jones just as she walked in through the door.'

'Were you punished?'

'Yes, I received a double detention. I thought it very unfair, as nearly everyone else was throwing darts; but mine was the best, and because it hit her they all had the chance destroying the evidence that would have incriminated them as well.'

'It was always the way at school. I remember being taken before the headmaster because we had had a pillow fight one night. Six of us were caned, one after the other. Only a complete idiot made the same mistake twice.'

'Anyway, do you want to give me a detention for lateness?' She wished he would smile but he seemed to have totally lost his sense of humour.

'Ms Marchbank wants me to give you the severest warning that I can about your tardiness. Please go and get on with your work.'

Sarah stared down at her boss and remembered that she had judged him as a fair man, and suddenly she felt glad that she did not work for Ms Marchbank. She left the office under the piercing gaze of the waiting worthy, who promptly discerned what had happened and clicked her heels before marching resolutely back to Mr Deakin's office. Sarah paused on the landing to listen, for the office door was still open.

'Shall I issue Miss Levine with a written warning?'

'No. I admonished her, and that's the end of it.'

'You're too soft on these people, especially if it's a pretty face.'

'Is Miss Levine's work below standard?'

'That's not the point! She sets a bad example to the rest of the office.'

'In my opinion she's one of the best people we've ever employed.'

'In my opinion you men just like having a nice bit of cleavage around.'

'If we are to swap niceties of a sexual nature,' said Mr Deakin ominously, 'then I can only presume that you are jealous of the younger girls.'

'Oh, you men can never see reason!'

'We can, Ms Marchbank, we can see reason and I see it this way. For ten minutes of lateness, and it is now half past, three of us have wasted twenty minutes, which is an hour and a half; and now you're proposing to spend more time on typing out a letter of warning. Further, the letter before it is given to Miss Levine, should be looked at by our solicitors to ensure that it's within the scope of the present laws on employment. Finally, to replace her will cost me a lot of money in advertising and interviews. Indeed, the same goes for anyone here, including you.'

'But that's a licence to be always late!'

'Please get me a cup of coffee.'

Ms Marchbank flounced out of the office and Sarah, with great presence of mind, had time to get back to her desk before she was observed. The pillar of indignation in the stout form of Ms Marchbank arrived in the front office and, after throwing a murderous look across the room at Sarah, subsided onto the seat behind her desk.

Across the office sat Emma and Clementine. They were both striking girls in their early twenties who wore blouses and dresses to show their ample bosoms to perfection. It was they who were responsible for the jibes about cleavages, for both of them had no compunction about displaying their assets. It hurt Sarah at times, for she had a very flat chest, and whether or not she wanted to display her cleavage, it simply did not have the same effect. It left her feeling very self-conscious when anyone looked at her, especially men; she felt that they were curious about her lack of feminine adornment and laughed amongst themselves, joking that they had larger pectorals.

As a teenager, Sarah had sensed her lack of bosom acutely and it had seemed that everyone knew about it, even to the point where some would comment on it to their friends. She had done all the usual things such as putting padding into her bras, sometimes handkerchiefs and at other times the paper variety. Her mother for some reason never saw that she could have used a padded bra. So she had made do, and one day had suffered the mortification of jumping into a swimming pool at a party in front of a crowd of people and seeing supporting paper tissues disintegrate in the water.

13

It took a long time for her to get over the humiliation. But she had more pressing things on her mind than to sit and ponder her lack of cleavage.

Her glance at Emma and Clementine had not gone unnoticed and now they were darting looks in her direction and then putting their heads together. It was clear from their grins that she was the butt of their joke. Sarah hated their furtive conversations, especially when she was the main topic. A glance round the rest of the office showed that they too were out of sympathy with her, and the lowered looks and the sly grins showed that they were enjoying her misery.

Normally Sarah would be upset at such behaviour and sit at her desk with her eyes down, blushing furiously. To counter that, she began arranging her desk so that she could hide behind the computer screen and give the impression that she was working, for she badly wanted to sort out her thoughts. She moved the blocks of print around her screen. Should anyone ask her what she was doing, then she was trying to find the best layout for that page. Now she felt secure from both the smirking faces around her and the relentless glare of Ms Marchbank, and she turned her mind to the incident in the store that had so bothered her. She creased her brow at the screen and in her mind's eye she saw the hand of the small boy come around the rear edge of the plate glass door.

It took no imagination to see that within a few seconds the door would have automatically closed and the boy's fingers would have been badly injured. And, as Sarah thought about it, it revolted her. Was it possible that the door had been designed that it would not have hurt the fingers, or at worse merely have bruised them? There did not seem to be anything that came under the heading of a safety device, though she was not someone who would know if there was one. What she was certain about was that in the absence of any safety device the fingers would have been badly lacerated and the boy disfigured for life, leaving him unable to express any talent that he might have with that hand. Suppose he was destined to be a talented musician! What would have happened to Mozart if the little Wolfgang had rushed into to his father to inform him that he could play the piano; then as the rushed back to the piano, a conscientious servant had slammed the door shut smashing his fingers? Would destiny have raised another Mozart?

Sarah smiled at the philosophical undertones and wished she knew people with whom she could discuss the finer points of life, but as a topic amongst her friends it would be greeted with yawns and murmurs of 'Boring!' Then someone would go and buy the next round of drinks. Somehow such things did not bother them and even to discuss the effects on the little boy would have been dismissed by them on the grounds that it did not bear thinking of.

But she, Sarah, had saved the little boy's hand, and for that she deserved at least thanks from the parent who, though she might not appreciate it, had been preserved from much aggravation. There would have been the heartrending cries of a boy being taken to a casualty unit. Without doubt the child would have been elevated to the top of the list for treatment, but even so there would be hours of waiting around and the continuing anguish of the boy. Other members of the family would have been put out by having to share the anguish and drive to the hospital and back, involving needless cost. Life would have changed for the boy, and his mother would have had to bear it. Was his mother so shorn of compassion that she wanted that!

But Michael was now standing beside Sarah and she could no longer ignore him.

'You seem miles away,' he said amiably.

'Yes, I was,' she replied, recollecting herself. She glanced at Ms Marchbank's desk. Michael noticed the movement of her head and understood.

'She's had to pop out for a minute, so I felt I could come over for a chat.'

'Fine.' She wished he would go away, for the others were taking an interest in their conversation and she wanted to be left to her thoughts.

'You've spent rather a long time on that screen, and it doesn't look that difficult to me.'

'I imagine it's quite simple, but as you can see this photograph is larger than the others. Should I keep the size the author wants, or reduce it to fit the page – which is incidentally more in keeping

15

with the rest of the book. If I reduce it as it ought to be, then there will be insufficient text on the page.'

'Why don't you just write another sentence?'

'Because it's not my work.'

'Yes, but the guy's so verbose he'll never know.'

'But *I* will!'

'But you'll never read the book – you're sick and tired of it already!'

'Well, maybe I am, but I'm paid to do a job.'

'Then you shouldn't be sitting there dreaming.'

'What I was doing was none of your business.'

'But Ms Marchbank will make it her business if she spots you.'

'I've taken precautions.'

'How?'

'With this problem page.'

'She'll see through you.'

'I doubt that.'

'She really dislikes you, you know.'

'I was not unaware of it.'

'Mind you, she hates all of us!'

'I was also aware of that, and I sometimes wonder why she has a job here.'

'Because old Deakin employed her before anyone else.'

'She does her job well enough.'

'But her management is out of the Victorian era.'

'It gives us something to talk about and adds a bit of colour to the office.'

'I don't call grey a colour, even when it comes in a variety of shades. But do you think you could run the place better?' Michael asked, changing the subject suddenly.

'It has crossed my mind.'

'It has crossed everyone's mind.'

'It's down to Deakin though. He's so stuck in a rut that an atom bomb wouldn't change his direction.'

'Yes, he's a sour old puss, isn't he? Never smiles! One wonders where he gets his pleasures in life.'

'I don't think about such things as it's not my business.'

'Don't give me that rubbish, Sarah! You women think about these things more than men.'

'We might, but we claim the higher moral ground in that we don't talk about it so much.'

'Since when? You women are always exchanging tittle-tattle. Those two over there…' he nodded in the direction of Emma and Clementine, 'never stop chinwagging.'

'They do when Ms Marchbank is watching.'

'But they don't stop yakking all day. I reckon that they don't listen, so that when one has had her say the other can repeat it.'

'Here comes Ms Marchbank!' Sarah hissed. But Michael had seen her and resumed his seat.

Ms Marchbank entered the office and her first assignment was to cast a look of disapprobation at Sarah. Sarah looked up at the same moment as if it were possible to reflect her looks back. Their eyes met and seemed to agree an uneasy truce.

Sarah turned back to the browser and with as little thought as possible she did the obvious and moved on to the next page. For the sake of it she did six pages and rose to get a cup of coffee. It pleased her that the office still had a kitchen with an electric kettle and a fridge. Nothing could be worse than shoving money in a machine and receiving back a concoction of chemicals dubiously called 'coffee'. Somehow the use of fresh milk was very pleasurable. It was a point in Ms Marchbank's favour that she had resisted the entreaties of vending machine salesmen. Emma joined her to make two cups.

'She's on the prowl today, isn't she?' she whispered to Sarah.

'You shouldn't talk about your employer in such terms,' replied Sarah in more moderate tones.

'You're a fine one to talk! It didn't take much to work out what you and Michael were on about.'

'You have no idea what we were discussing.'

'With all your nods and looks in that direction, and the body language, you can't kid me that you weren't talking about her – and Clemmie agrees with me!'

'Clemmie would agree with you as a matter of course.'

'No, she wouldn't! We have lots of differences of opinion.'

'Name one!'

The kettle boiled, and Emma was able to use it as an excuse for not supplying an answer by filling Sarah's cup first.

'Well, we do have lots of differences,' she assured Sarah at length, 'it's just that none springs to mind at the moment.'

Sarah took her coffee back to her desk. She was annoyed with herself for venting her feelings on Emma. It was an act of meanness to sound superior and it was intellectual cowardice to trap the girl with words; she resolved to make it up to her sometime. But it would have to wait, for Emma and Clementine were deep in conversation, and the looks in her direction left no doubt that she continued to be the subject matter of their discussion.

Sarah could not avoid reflecting on the little boy and his mother and she made no effort to think of anything else. It rankled badly that the mother had rebuked her so soundly for daring to touch her child. It had been as if she had tried to abduct him! Of course, there was insufficient proof to make the charge stick. But it was total nonsense and probably explained why people had disappeared. Had they come to her aid they would have been dragged into the conspiracy, and the resulting scene would have done no credit to the store at all. That explained their reticence for they were simply no match for a strident woman like her, and they were aware that justice today actually worked against them. The mother could have accused them of conspiracy in an attempted abduction and made such a fuss that the store would have had to pay out money just to keep her quiet.

Was that the woman's motive? Did she want money? Was she so determined to get money that she actually *wanted* the child to catch his hand in the door? No mother could be that mean, surely. But if her son had lost the use of his hand she could have sued not just for thousands but for hundreds of thousands. For the woman it would like a lottery win! And she could live a life of continuing luxury… but wouldn't the store resist such claims? Those standing nearby had seen nothing! Yet the woman could have sued the architects or the company who installed the door, or even the manufacturers. Could any of those parties defend the claim if their insurance company was willing to pay up? How dreadful of the mother to have worked out life so cynically! Had she no responsibility towards her son? Could she really have watched him go through life severely disabled when it was quite unnecessary? And how was the son to feel when he found out the truth…?

No, the woman had to have been mistaken, and could not have realised what she had done for the boy. One wanted her to be mistaken. One wanted to make excuses for her because one wanted her behaviour to be normal and human; except that her anger was real and one could not make excuses for that. Her face was that of an angry person. Every muscle was tensed in a determined effort to get her way, and her whole being shrieked of self. Her motivation only concerned herself – no one else. She was quite without compassion or gratitude, and somehow she, Sarah, had got in the way of her greater designs; and for that she had to be verbally punished.

But deep down in her heart Sarah knew that it was none of these things that shocked her. For no one was completely immune to irrational anger, and there must be many times in people's lives when they appear to have no compassion or charity for others, even though most people would be shocked to discover that they had given that impression. The injustice hurt her profoundly, but she could bear it, knowing that the boy was uninjured. Nor was it so much that the woman was a thoroughly bad mother that upset her, for she was sure that anyone must be a better mother. It was her own maternal instincts that Sarah could not come to terms with.

Never before had she seen herself wanting to be in that position, and never before had she wanted to be so. She was certain that she was not broody but she could not rid herself of the notion that she had been challenged. She had mapped out her life for herself and she saw it as a straight line – any deviation would deflect her from her ultimate goal. Nowhere in her plans were children. She had long ago in her teens been through the arguments for having a child and she rejected them easily, finding great pleasure in the decision. And in the fullness of time she had never questioned the decision. Yet this woman had caused her to deviate from her chosen path.

Despite her natural inclinations, Sarah determined to get back on the road she had chosen for herself.

The Rapist

It was just before six when Sarah arrived at the flat that she shared with two other woman of about her age. Usually she was the first home, as the other two girls left their places of work after her and had longer journeys back to the flat. But that evening Gerrie was already in and it made Sarah feel that she had left late. It was irksome, as she had wanted to get home and shower and generally make herself feel able to meet the others, for her mood had not left her.

'Had a good day?' called out Gerrie gaily from the kitchen area. She was a well-built woman for her twenty-seven years of age, though she was not overweight. She had a pleasing face but made no secret that she resented her nose; she felt that it was too large and somewhat stubby. Most people assured her that it wasn't and that she had a well-proportioned face, but she did not accept it. Her hair was blonde, thanks to the hair colouring that was regularly applied to her natural light brown hair. She had a regular boyfriend, but like most woman of her age had no thoughts of getting married. Occasionally they would talk about living together, and the flatmates all knew about it because it resulted in hints being dropped that the boyfriend ought to move in with the three of them. It was easy to resist, on the grounds that the flat was not large enough for cohabiting couples. It was generally agreed that when either one of the women decided to cohabit elsewhere, then it was the end of the flat that they were renting between the three of them. None of them wanted to be the one to break up the flat-sharing arrangement, and it was one of the reasons for not wanting to move out.

Having to answer Gerrie in her present distress was just what Sarah had wanted to avoid, since she would have to reply, and however she framed her reply it would, at best, sound forced.

'Oh, it was all right,' she called out.

Gerrie came out of the kitchen and accosted her in the passage. 'So, how bad a day was it then?' she asked.

'Dreadful!' said Sarah, unable to meet her friend's eye.

'Don't tell me you've been given the boot!'

'That wouldn't be so bad... and I came close to getting the boot, as it happens.'

'Well, don't worry; our solicitors are red hot on getting compensation for dismissal.'

'Thanks, but it won't come to that.'

'Are you going to tell me all about it?'

'No, I'm going for a shower.'

'But you can't make people curious and then leave them in suspense.'

'Why not?'

'Because you can't – it's dreadful not knowing.

'Tough! But what are you doing home so early?'

'Oh, we finished everything and they let us go early. It was only half an hour, but the fuss they made about it you'd have thought that they were giving us the whole afternoon off.'

'What's on the agenda tonight?'

'We're meeting the guys at nine and then we're onto a nightclub at eleven.'

'Oh,' said Sarah doubtfully.

'You can't let us down now! You know Ted's cousin, Gareth, wants to meet us.'

'No, correction: he's been *inveigled* into meeting *me*. Anyway, who is he?'

'He lives in Canada and he's making his first visit here.'

'Do I really have to go out with him?'

'Well, of course. I can't let Ted down, and Cathy's going out with Charles. You're always the odd one out, but tonight we can be three couples.'

'Thrilling,' said Sarah with as much enthusiasm as one would have for a visit to the dentist.

'Do you want a cup of coffee?'

'Might as well. I want that shower though.'

'I'll bring it in.'

'No, you leave by my bed.'

'You really are a prude, Sarah. Anyone would think there were great differences between our bodies!'

21

'I don't agree with you that we need to share the data concerning our bodies!'

'We're all women, after all, so what does it matter?'

Sarah had reached her room and closed the door on her flatmate. She had never been one to share a shower with other girls. There had come a point at school where one no longer enjoyed a communal shower or even the changing rooms, and she was not going to start now, whatever Gerrie thought about it. Perhaps it was a symptom of having breasts that she could not feel proud of. She had been tempted to have implants, but to do so would have meant that she would have to show them off and she had been avoiding doing that for too long. And the truth was that she hated her body, despite the fact that people told her that she looked good in a bikini. The men wanted her to go topless and she was certain that they were fascinated by the smallness of her breasts; it was almost as if they were bored with the fulsome assets of her flatmates and friends...

She cared little for her shower and was soon dressed again. Cathy, the third member of their trio, had arrived home. Though Sarah didn't really want to join them she had to make a meal for herself. As she opened her door to go to the kitchen she could hear them talking in low voices about her.

'Sarah's in a mood again.'

'Doesn't she get on your nerves?'

'Life can never be plain sailing for some people.'

'Truth is, she needs a bloke to give her a good shag.'

'That's about it...'

Sarah retreated back to her bedroom and closed the door. It was the second time that day she had listened at a door to what other people were saying about her! It seemed to mark her out as some kind of weird person, but she had always considered herself to be perfectly normal! But why did she need a man? Why was having a man so necessary to having a good time? Perhaps she would think differently about men if there was actually one who she liked. But neither Cathy nor Gerrie had a particularly high opinion of men. Both of them slept around whenever they felt like it and, like Sarah, they were all for women's liberation; but unlike her they needed the services of men. The real truth was that because she abstained from sex, it gave them a conscience about what they were doing. But she never advertised her celibacy by talking about it, nor did she make snide remarks about their sexuality. Yet she was aware that by remaining silent she had given them tacit approval to their behaviour. She gave them no cause to feel intimidated by her resolve, and they clearly assumed that it was only a matter of time before she took the plunge.

She sat on her bed and pulled out some nail varnish. First she attended to her toes and wondered why she bothered, but after going through a number of trivial reasons she decided that it was because she liked the smell of pear drops. Then she did her fingers and lay on the bed to dry them. Then she noticed the cup of coffee and cursed her stupidity in not drinking first. Still, there was time for at least another cup. It was quite idiotic to be lying there with her arms and legs outstretched waving them around to harden the varnish. And all for what? Just so to look good for men! In many respects, Sarah felt, women look good without all the make-up, posh hair-dos and fashionable clothes. And what do the men do in return? If you were lucky, they would have had a shower. But their clothes would look as if they were dragged out from under the bed. So who were the more stupid? It had to be women, for they cared too much about something that was not worth caring for!

Given a choice, she would not be going out, but her flatmates had expected her to and it seemed only politic to bow to their wishes occasionally. The varnish was dry, and the next decision was what to wear. She decided on grey trousers with a white blouse. She would have liked to wear a scarf round her neck and hide her lack of bosom but she felt it would catch the attention of her flatmates and she would end up being humiliated. She went to the kitchen for a fresh cup of coffee.

Cathy was there and looked up as Sarah entered and said in a shocked voice, 'You can't wear trousers this evening!'

'Why not?'

'Because you're meeting a fellow.'

'If I really *wanted* to attract a man I might possibly invest in feminine clothes.'

'I've got a nice slinky skirt and we're the same size – why don't you try that?'

23

'I don't want to.'

'But you should be trying to attract a man.'

'I thought it had something to do with personality.'

'Are you kidding? It's got everything to do with looks and sticking your tits out so they that all go weak at the knees. Oh sorry you've only got little ones...'

'If you were really sorry you wouldn't mention my breasts at all.'

'Oh come on, grow up!'

'Look at sexy Sarah,' said Cathy to Gerrie, who had just come back into the room. 'She's going in trousers!'

'What's wrong with them?' asked Gerrie, who was conscious that she had an ample figure to contend with and was well versed in the art of covering much of it up.

'But out of the three of us she's got by far the best figure – and she won't show it off.'

'Well, I'm quite happy to lessen the competition, especially when it's to my advantage,' responded Gerrie.

'What competition?' said Sarah. 'You're both going out with steadies, or are you hoping to dump them halfway through the evening?'

'Now that's an idea, Sarah! I hadn't thought of that one... and we could leave you to console the jilted.'

'Thanks a bundle!'

'No problem. Have you got any deodorant, Cathy?'

'No, you had all mine the other day. Sar will lend you hers.'

'Oh, that's a pity because we're all going to smell the same.'

'It least it won't clash.'

'Don't worry, the guys will never know.'

'That's a little bit spiteful, Sar.'

'I doubt it.'

'Why? Some men are quite sensitive!'

'The only reason I'm wearing deodorant is for my benefit. It might just cover up the smell of the lusty armpits of others.'

'There are times when it's a real turn-on!'

'For the simple-minded.'

'What's got into you Sar? You're a real misery at the moment.'

'She's had a bad day,' Gerrie cut in.

'How's that? You've a doddle of a job and it's darn well paid.'

'I had a very upsetting time! This little boy put his hand behind this door and I pulled him away just before the door closed and crushed his fingers. And then the mother had the cheek to accuse me of trying to abduct her son.'

'But you told her what you were doing.'

'Of course, but she wasn't listening.'

'Oh, come on, she couldn't have been that thick-skinned.'

'Well, she was, and it was embarrassing because she wouldn't shut up and just kept ranting.'

'You should have left her to it.'

'I did in the end, but I felt the injustice of it all.

'And you're still smarting from it.'

'I'd never let any children of mine get in such a position.'

'Oh, hark at that, Gerrie! That from the woman who's said she's never going to have kids.'

'I know! Good, isn't it! I'm so perfect but actually I'm not going to have any,' said Gerrie as mockingly as she could. Sarah wished she had not said anything and felt the blush rising on her cheeks.

'I seem to recall someone saying that only idiots got pregnant!'

'*Complete* idiots,' corrected Gerrie.

'She doesn't think much of the female population who've brought in the next generation.'

Smarting from their words, Sarah returned to her room to finish her hair. She was in totally the wrong frame of mind to be going out and she wanted to find a means of excuse. She finished her hair and sat sadly on the side of her bed waiting for the other two to drag her out. It crossed her mind that they might just forget to take her. But it was not to be, for Gerrie was soon hanging her head round the door and urging her to come.

'I'd really rather not go out tonight.'

'You've got to! You always used to enjoy going to the pub and the nightclub!'

'I'd much rather stay in tonight.'

'Just because you had a bad time today is not an excuse not to go. It will help you put it behind you.'

'I doubt it.'

'No, you're coming with us and that's the end of it! This evening's going to be a good laugh.'

It was difficult to resist the pressure she was under and Sarah meekly gave way.

They walked down to their local pub where they were due to meet the men. The lads had already arrived and had almost finished the pints in front of them. They turned to greet the women.

'Hi,' said Ted, 'what are you drinking?' They all nominated a drink and Ted turned to the barman, who filled the men's pint pots up first.

It did not augur well as far as Sarah was concerned. She knew Ted and Charles, and Gareth, she assumed, was the one at the end whom she had never met. He was tall with light-coloured hair and a sallow complexion. His mouth had a determined look about it; his nose was a size too large, and his eyes were too close together, giving him a piercing look. In some people it might be taken for shrewdness but in others it was surely meanness, and Sarah guessed that in his case it was the latter. Nevertheless, he had an air about him that must have melted many young hearts.

'They do a good pint in here,' said Ted conversationally.

'I like it,' said Charles, and Sarah felt that it was a one-sided conversation as none of the three women were drinking beer.

'It's what marks a good pub out,' said Ted, 'and that's the pint they pull.'

'Yeah,' agreed Charles, 'they pull it really well here, none of that carbon dioxide rubbish.'

'And you guys reckon you can tell the difference,' cut in Sarah.

'Of course,' said Ted, 'it's all to do with the head.'

'That's the bit that gets stuck on your top lip, is it?' asked Sarah, ignoring the pinch on the arm she received from Gerrie.

'Yeah,' continued Ted, 'but if you ever want to run a pub, you have to understand these things.'

'But suppose I never want to run a pub?' said Sarah.

'Well, you still need to know what a good pint is, so that you can recognise it.'

'I don't like beer.'

'Yeah, but your fellow might, and it's no good you saying,

"Oh, I like this pub, let's go there" when you know full well they don't do a good pint.'

'So I have to choose a pub that my fellow likes, is that it?'

'Now you've got the hang of things, lady! Get what your fellow wants and everything will go swimmingly.

'I thought that the boot was on the other foot.

'How can it be? The rubbish you're drinking tastes the same in any pub.'

'Probably, but I think you've missed my point.

'You see that guy over there,' said Charles in a conspiratorial manner. He nodded in such a way that everyone in the bar must have known who he was talking about. 'Well, you should see the wheels he came on.'

'What's he got then?' said Gareth. 'A Harley?'

'No, it's Kawasaki. It does nearly 180.'

'Does he do that on the way to work every morning?' asked Sarah innocently.

'Don't be stupid, the cops would pick him up!'

'What's the point of doing that sort of speed, then?'

'You can't legally, but if you wanted to then you could.'

'Haven't you ever been on a motorbike?' said Ted to Sarah.

'No,' said Sarah, 'it sounds much too dangerous to me.'

'Most women love all that throbbing power between their legs.'

All three men were now laughing, along with Gerrie and Cathy.

'I'm sorry,' said Sarah seriously, 'but I seem to have missed out on this one.'

Ted made an obscene gesture with his body and Sarah wished she had not said anything. She was feeling trapped.

'Hey, I'm only joking,' said Ted. The feeling subsided with his words and she relaxed again. Everyone was laughing, and Sarah felt they were laughing at her.

'Sarah likes to sound innocent,' said Ted. 'Still, don't worry, you're going with Gareth tonight – and you won't be very innocent when you get back! Have you met Gareth, by the way?'

'No, I haven't.'

'Hey, Gareth! This is the woman you're escorting this evening.'

'So you're Sarah… You guys sure are generous letting me take the prettiest face around here.'

'Gareth's a real ladies' man,' said Ted by way of explanation.

'That's me; I've got so many notches on my bow it looks as if I've whittled it away.'

'I doubt that,' said Gerrie.

'Why? Do you want to find out?'

'No, we always believe you fellers. Don't we, girls?'

'Speak for yourself,' said Sarah dourly, and everyone was laughing.

'Lighten up, Sarah,' said Cathy under her breath. 'It's only a bit of fun.'

Everyone continued laughing and Sarah had a strong desire to go home. But Cathy and Gerrie were standing behind her and she doubted that they would let her make an exit.

'Shall we have another pint or shall we get down to the club?'

'Let's get down to the club,' said Ted. And they all agreed.

They went out into the street. Ted had taken Gerrie's hand and Charles was walking beside Cathy. It was left to Gareth to escort Sarah, who fell in beside her and put his arm around her shoulders. Sarah did not like the gesture. She shrugged her shoulders.

'What's up?' complained Gareth.

'Nothing is up,' said Sarah, 'but I don't want you leaning on me.'

'Are you suggesting I'm drunk?'

'No, I would prefer you to hold my hand.' Sarah loathed herself for having to compromise.

'That's all right then.'

They stopped by a bus stop.

'Aren't we going to get a taxi?' asked Sarah.

'You can only get five in a taxi and there are six of us.'

'Well what about two taxis then?'

'Here comes the bus.'

Sarah climbed reluctantly onto the bus. She worried that she was becoming a snob as she rarely took a bus anywhere. But she reasoned that this was one moment in life when a taxi would have been more to the point. She consoled herself that had they taken a

28

taxi they might have had to wait twenty minutes or so, and since the bus came on cue they were going to get to the club sooner. She wished she were at home as the expedition had all the makings of a nightmare.

Sarah sat down in a seat and found Gareth pushing in against her. Twenty minutes later they were in town, with Ted leading the way to the chosen nightclub. Soon they were inside and seated at a table.

'Who's going to buy the drinks?' said Charles.

'It's the girls' turn,' said Ted, looking at Sarah

'Why me?' asked Sarah.

'Well, if you go to the bar and buy the drinks they'll cost less than what I have to pay.'

'Oh, is that reasonable?'

'No, it's sexual discrimination.'

'All right then,' said Sarah, 'what are you having?'

They all said what they wanted and left Sarah to go to the bar. The barman took the order and filled the glasses, putting each one on a tray for her.

'That'll be £44, please,' said the barman.

'*How much?*' said Sarah in a shocked tone, which the barman chose to ignore.

He repeated what he said and Sarah searched her bag for a fifty-pound note.

She carried the tray to their table and everyone took their drink. Sarah tried to protest about the cost of the drinks but no one would talk about it. She resumed her seat and felt that she had been conned into buying the round.

'Cheers, everyone,' said Ted, lifting his drink.

They all lifted the glasses. Sarah, not knowing what they were doing, was slightly behind. She tried to speak again about the price of the drinks but the lights dimmed and the disco started.

Although they were sitting some way from the speakers it was still deafening, with the sound waves seemingly penetrating to one's inner being. No normal conversation was possible and it made even thinking difficult. Ted and Charles, who were sitting in front of Sarah, were both nodding theirs heads extravagantly in time to the music. People started heading for the dance floor.

Spotlights began to flash throwing weird shadows across the room.

'Come on, you lot,' said Ted, 'let's dance!'

Sarah hesitated but she found that she was being almost dragged onto the floor by Gerrie and Cathy.

They started dancing in a large group with nobody dancing with anyone else. Sarah felt very self-conscious. There had been a time when she had found these activities very enjoyable but that night it was different. The music was too loud – but it was always that loud! The flashing lights made one disorientated, as if they were determined to loosen one's grip on reality. No one seemed to be dancing in any particular fashion. It was all so stupid, and Sarah wished she were not there!

The music seemed to go on and, with the only break coming when the disc jockey spoke as he changed the record. It was fully half an hour before they sat down again.

A woman came out onto the floor and began singing in deep tones. Sarah could feel sweat dripping down her back. It annoyed her, for no amount of deodorant would hide it, and worse still, she knew that the efficacy of the deodorant was fast being compromised. When she looked at the men she saw that their shirts were covered with sweat. But the comparative quietness of the singing allowed Sarah to think. There had been a time when she enjoyed these evenings and, though she never went out as often as Cathy and Gerrie, she had once looked forward to them. She appreciated her flatmates, for they were responsible for bringing her out of her shell and showing her something of the world that she would not have bothered with, left to herself; and yet what she had thought of as fun and exhilarating she suddenly found was extremely irksome. Nothing about the evening was stimulating; her friends were there merely to opt out of the worries and cares of life for a time. The men were drinking heavily and moved to the beat like nodding ducks. Her friends were little better, having merely had slightly less to drink. Between them they hadn't uttered one word of real conversation, but she couldn't blame them for that. No, she could only blame herself! She should never have allowed them all to persuade her to go.

Sarah glanced at Gareth and decided that there was nothing about him that she could like. He caught her glance and leered back at her. He really was quite obnoxious! She wished she were at home. Suddenly the singer finished, and amid extended applause she bowed her way back to wherever she came from.

Charles went to buy the next round of drinks. Then they were back to the dance floor for another half-hour sweating session. At the end of it Sarah declared that she had had enough and would like to go home.

'But you can't go home yet,' said Gerrie. 'The evening's only just started!'

'What time do we go home?' asked Sarah, but the singer then appeared with a fresh outfit on and began to sing again. Sarah received no answer.

Gareth was sitting very close to her and she did not like it. She tried to attract Gerrie's attention, but she would have none of it, forcing Sarah to suffer in silence.

She could feel Gareth's breath on her neck. His hands were kneading her shoulders, something which she thought could be quite pleasant; but in Gareth's case she was certain was a prelude to putting his hands elsewhere. Nor was she mistaken, for one hand slipped from her shoulder and down her arm. On reaching her elbow it was transferred to her waist and then slowly it progressed upwards. Sarah froze, for his hand now covered her breast. His other hand moved and she knew that he was going to feel her other breast. Perhaps it was that hand touching her arm that drove her to action but suddenly she swung round, throwing his offending hand away from her and leaving the other somewhere in mid air.

'I'm going home,' she announced, but no one was listening. She fled for the door and was shocked to discover that Gareth was by her side when she reached the road. She would rather that he was not there, but then thought that she was probably safer with an escort than without. She wanted a taxi but there were none about. Gareth walked near her, and without realising it she found herself at a bus stop again.

'Let's take whichever comes first,' said Gareth.

A bus appeared, and to Sarah's consternation a short way behind it was a taxi.

'We'll take the taxi,' said Sarah, and then she saw that it had stopped to pick up some other late-night revellers. Her heart stopped along with the bus. Gareth propelled her aboard and she felt his attitude was almost triumphant.

'We'll take the bus,' he announced.

She decided that he was pathetic.

They boarded the bus together and Sarah sat down in a seat close to the driver. But Gareth pushed his way in beside her.

'Please take your hand from me,' said Sarah.

'It's protection,' said Gareth.

'I don't care what it is,' replied Sarah, 'just keep your hands to yourself.' She felt trapped. She couldn't get off the bus without passing Gareth and she couldn't trust him. He was close to being drunk and was in a state in which he would deny being drunk. He had reached the nasty stage and Sarah was inwardly frightened, though she kept her outward appearance calm.

The bus reached her stop and she told Gareth it was time to get off. He rose from his seat with alacrity and waited for her to go to the door. At first she thought he was going to let her get off on her own, but suddenly she realised that he was going with her. The whole thing looked so natural that she could not appeal to anyone with any conviction – not that there was anyone to appeal to. The driver sat in his cab patiently waiting for them to alight. The couple at the back of the bus had not even noticed them, and the old man with his eyes falling out would be as much help as a dishcloth in a dishwashing machine. Indeed, he was probably more drunk than Gareth. She felt sick with apprehension and blindly allowed herself to be led off the bus.

'You don't have to take me home,' said Sarah evenly.

'You don't like me, do you?' he said suddenly.

'You're a nice enough person in your way,' she temporised, 'but I don't want you to take me home.'

Gareth seemed to take her evasiveness as encouragement and continued to walk along beside Sarah, who now wanted nothing more to do with him. Home, and the bed she wanted, seemed to be receding. He could not understand that he did nothing for her and she found him repugnant, though some women might find him attractive. He might be handsome, but somehow in her mind's eye he came nowhere close to her expectations. She assumed that it was his attitude, and it had not taken her long to see that he was vain and very self-centred. The way he treated her was not right, for he seemed to have possessed her for the evening, yet she had not been put on a pedestal and fêted for herself. She was there to give him pleasure, and yet she was unsure of what she would receive in turn. Her instincts were telling her that it was a negative quantity. Had he been someone who respected her, surely they would have got a taxi home, but he'd had to take a bus. It was annoying. Why did he have to inconvenience her? She would have paid for the taxi, but along came the bus and he dragged her aboard with the silliest set of excuses that he could muster. She was certain that he had very little money on him and that he had sponged off his cousin for the evening and in many respects he had sponged off her. She'd been made to buy a round of drinks for everyone, and though she was not averse to doing that, there seemed too many in their party who had bought nothing. But Gareth followed her home like a pet dog on a leash. The only difference being that the dog she could have left hitched to someone's gatepost!

The closer they got to the house the more Sarah became convinced that he would come in for coffee or some such reason and then attempt to get into bed with her. Her friends had been no help all evening and she felt that they had been egging Gareth on. Hadn't he boasted of his conquests? Doubtless he charmed some women into bed... yet if he did, she had seen nothing about his methods that excited or awakened latent instincts within her. And he seemed to think that by saying so, all the women around him were desperate for his attentions. By not standing up and leaving him he presumed that any of the girls there were fair game and he could take his pick. She had been his choice for the evening and she had committed only the crime of remaining with her friends. Indeed, for her to have left them was difficult at any point throughout the evening, as no one had given her an opportunity to leave. Gareth, they had decided, was the man for Sarah, and that was that. It wouldn't have been so bad if they had seen Gareth as the attentive lover who was desperate for her hand in marriage, but it was not so. The only thing Gareth was desperate

33

for was her body! He might be a most conscientious lover, but she doubted that he was, for she had seen enough of him to know that he was too egotistical for that, and anyway, she was in no mood to find out just how attentive he was.

To Sarah's dismay, the front door was approaching too quickly. She felt safe enough just walking down the street and had hoped that a friend or a neighbour might have passed them by so that she could have appealed to them for help. Perhaps she could have walked to their house with them and left Gareth at their garden gate, but no one she knew moved into view. She began to hope for someone she did not know so that she might appeal to them, but there was no one around. It left her feeling very alone and afraid. Her stomach had become a deep pit and a feeling of desperation swept over her. Her instinct told her that were she to let him in the house then she was lost. She maintained her outward calm knowing that she must not aggravate him.

They reached the doorstep and he stood behind her. She knew that the moment she opened the door he would step in with her and her worse fears would be realised. She dared not tell him to go away again for it would only serve to increase his resolve. At the moment he was pliant and reasonable but once he knew that she did not want him she guessed he would change and become increasingly aggressive. Her fingers trembled as she reached into her bag for the key. It was not visible and she had to look into the pockets of the bag.

She turned, peering into it, and said, 'I've lost the key in my bag. Can you get out of the street lamp light so I can look for it?' She could only hope that her voice did not betray her anxiety. He seemed affable and took a step back.

She found the key and inserted it in the door.

'Let me find a light switch,' she said, calmly pushing the door open just enough to let herself in. But he was off his guard and she was able to turn and slam the door on him. For good measure she put the chain on the door.

'Open up,' he hissed through the letter box.

'Goodnight,' she said, standing back, and the relief brought a smile to her face.

'Let me in, Sarah!' he pleaded. 'You've led me on all evening; I only want a cup of coffee.'

'Is that what it's called now? Then go and boil your head.'

'Open the door,' he said raising his voice.

'No, I won't,' she said, 'and if you don't go away I'll call the police.'

'*You bitch!*' he shouted at her through the letter box. 'I've a good mind to smash the door down.'

Sarah went up the stairs to their part of the maisonette. At the top was another door and the lock on that had broken long ago, but a kitchen chair sufficed to hold the handle shut. She went through and checked the rear door to the fire escape, and having satisfied herself that she was safe put the kettle on and sat down. She felt a sense of victory that was heightened by feelings of relief. After a minute she went back down to the front door. Gareth was still there swearing at her.

She went back upstairs and picked up the phone. Having phoned the police, she sat down with a cup of coffee and waited for her friends to return. It was two hours later that the phone rang to announce that they were outside and could not get in.

Sarah answered slowly, 'Is Gareth there?'

'Of course he is,' said Gerrie, who had used her mobile. 'Come on, Sar, let us in.'

'I'm not letting Gareth in.'

'Why not? He's harmless.'

'Send all the men away and I'll let you in.'

'Oh, be reasonable, Sar.'

'Then I'll phone the police *again*.'

'What do you mean again?'

'I've had them remove Gareth once, and he must have returned.'

Sarah could hear voices in the background.

Then Cathy was on the phone saying, 'Sar, it's our house as much as yours – now let us in.'

'I've told you, I'll only let you in if the men have gone.'

'This is quite unreasonable, Sarah. Now open up and let us in.'

'Not until the men have gone. Phone for a minicab for them.'

'This is really too much, Sar.'

'Then I'll phone for a minicab.'

35

'If you phone for one then you'll have to pay.'

'If I pay then you won't come in.'

Sarah had the phone book out and was shortly phoning the nearest cab company. Fifteen minutes later a cab arrived, closely followed by a police car that had been called by one of the neighbours. Sarah went to the front window and watched the group of people below. Two burly policemen were now in charge, and before the minicab could leave the police wanted to find out what was going on. Then the phone rang. Sarah went back to it and heard Cathy on the line.

'The police will see them off, now let us in.'

'No fear,' replied Sarah. 'I'm not letting anyone in until the men have gone.'

'Then I'll get the police to have a word with you.'

The mobile phone was left on while an argument with one of the policemen ensued. Sarah could not make out what was being said but after some minutes it was clear whom the police supported. They then discovered that Gareth had already created a disturbance that evening at the same address. The minicab driver was getting upset and he drove off.

Cathy was speaking on the phone again. 'This has gone beyond a joke, Sarah, come down and let us in.'

Then one of the policemen was on the phone. 'Are you all right, ma'am?' he asked.

'Yes,' replied Sarah, 'but I'm too scared to let anyone in until all those men have gone.'

'Right, we'll have to take them with us.'

'Tell Cathy and Gerrie I will not open the door until you have taken them away and they are standing alone by the gate where I can see them.'

'Yes, ma'am.'

Sarah watched from the window as the three men were put in the back of the police car. Then it was driven off, leaving Cathy and Gerrie at the gate. When the car was out of sight she left the window and went down to the front door, where she took the chain off.

'Well, open the door,' called Gerrie through the letter box.

'Use your key,' said Sarah and went to the top of the stairs.

Both the women came in, throwing angry looks at Sarah, who was standing at the top of the stairs.

'That has made a wonderful evening about the worst I've ever known,' remarked Cathy.

'What on earth possessed you?' asked Gerrie.

'Possessed me! You set a rapist on me!'

'But what a scene you made of it! Half the neighbourhood has woken up and been watching.'

'Why should I care? I've had a perfectly hateful evening! I've been under siege for the last four hours. What did you care?'

Sarah retired to her bedroom door and watched her flatmates arrive at the top of the stairs. Anger was the predominant emotion.

'I'm not talking to anyone who's such a selfish cow,' said Gerrie and made for the kitchen.

'You've really surpassed yourself tonight,' said Cathy. 'I just hope the guys get home all right.'

Trembling with anger, Sarah glared back and forbore to say anything. Her anger increased, for it seemed that all they were concerned about was the welfare of the men! And that of course was what they had planned! The men were coming back to spend the night with them, and where Gareth fitted into that scheme was quite obvious. She shut her bedroom door and twisted the key in the lock. It was old, and the wood around the latch would not keep a strong man out for long.

The Brother

Despite a reasonably good sleep, Sarah awoke still feeling the anger from the previous evening. She lay in bed for an hour mulling it over and knew that she couldn't face her flatmates. It would be easier if they were in a conciliatory mood and were prepared to talk. But they did not seem to understand how isolated she felt. Where she had once thought that they all looked after each other as women in a common cause, the events of the previous evening had shattered the illusion, leaving her feeling very vulnerable and unable to trust them. She decided that she had to get away from them at least for a day. She rose despite the protestations of her body and made herself some breakfast. It was then that she thought of her brother Matthew. She had not visited him for ages; in fact she felt guilty, for she had only visited once since he married Elaine six years ago. She had managed Christmas cards, and she had kept up with the fact that they had had two children by remembering their birthdays. Indeed, they must have been wondering who Auntie Sarah was; though if they had any sense they would be more concerned about the presents she sent them on both occasions. Still, you could not accuse a four-year-old of having no sense, since he lacked experience. There was one problem that she needed to sort out before she went: what were their names! She went to the drawer beside her bed and drew out her address book. Right, Jason and Chloe. She should have remembered, for they were not long names. She made a note of their address just outside Southampton. Should she ring before she turned up? Why should she? She wasn't a big eater, so they ought to have enough for an extra mouth; and anyway her brother was always exhorting her to go there.

Sarah showered and dressed and was soon at the station where she could catch a train. Despite Southampton being on the same line, she would have to take a train to Woking and change there. Although the ticket stated that it was via Woking, it was quicker to go to Waterloo and catch the fast train from there. It was naughty, but Waterloo was only three stations up the line. She would have to check if the train also stopped at Clapham Junction, for that was only one stop up the line, and would be better on the way back.

Gerrie and Cathy were still asleep and she went down the stairs and into the street. She used her pass to Waterloo and purchased a ticket there. She was pleased, as there was a train to Southampton that only stopped at Woking and Winchester before Southampton Central. And that there was only ten minutes to wait.

An hour and ten minutes later she stepped off the train in Southampton. She hadn't a clue where in the city her brother lived, and took the easy way out by putting the matter in the hands of a cab driver. He knew the address, and twenty minutes later they drew up outside her brother's house. She paid him and then asked him to wait in case they were not in. But the noise of her walking up the gravel drive caused the children to look out of the window. She dismissed the taxi and went up to the front door. She didn't have to knock, as the children had summoned their parents and the door was opening when she reached it.

Her sister-in-law was at the door with two children looking out from around her to see who was coming.

'Sarah,' she said and came and embraced her.

'Hello, Elaine,' said Sarah when she was released.

'Well, this is a surprise! Matthew will be so pleased to see you; he often says that he wishes you would just turn up.'

'Well, I have come at last. Hadn't I better greet my nephew and niece?' Sarah bent and hugged the little boy, but the girl, who was only two, suddenly resorted to shyness and hid behind her mother.

'Did you bring me a present?' asked Jason.

'No,' said Sarah disconcerted by his forthrightness. She found herself feeling upset that she had not even thought to bring them something.

'Let Auntie Sarah in, Jason,' said Elaine.

'I want a present, Mum.'

39

'He can talk, then,' said Sarah.

'Oh yes! He has all the vocabulary for getting what he wants. Chloe would agree with him but she can't speak yet. Matt thought she said "Da" last week, but since she hasn't repeated it, she can't have done! And anyway, she's going to say "Ma" first.'

'I hope she doesn't start too much of a family row.'

'No, she won't – she's such a poppet!' The little girl was swept off her feet and given a massive hug.

'I want a drink.' Jason decided that it was time to change the subject.

'I think,' said Sarah to her sister-in-law, 'Chloe's first words might be "I want"!'

'Yes, if I was a betting person I'd have my money on that as well. Of all the people she listens to, it's Jason more than anyone else. Look, here's your brother.'

Sarah greeted Matthew. Then she took her coat off and found that there was nowhere to put it.

'I'll take it for you,' said Matthew, and in doing so gave his sister the briefest of kisses.

Elaine made drinks and they all went into the lounge.

'To what do we owe the privilege of you visiting us so suddenly?' asked Elaine.

'I don't know really,' said Sarah.

'But something must have prompted you.'

'Conscience, perhaps.'

'Well, if it's only conscience then we're still pleased to see you.'

'No, I needed a change of air.'

'Men trouble?'

'Yes, but not in the way you would imagine.'

'Tell me about it.'

It was clear that Elaine was short of gossip and that nothing was going to buy her silence better than telling her.

'I agreed with my flatmates that I would go out with one of their boyfriend's cousin just to make up numbers. It was one of those diplomatic arrangements, and to not go along with it would be silly. But it turns out he was a real lecher!'

'What do you mean?'

'He was after a one-night stand.'

'So he was the type of man who says "hello" first and then "let's get into bed together" second…'

'That's right. He thinks he's a Lothario or a Casanova but he's not; he's more like a male warthog that's gone berserk.'

'You should not insult warthogs,' said Matthew. 'He was just not your type.'

Sarah glanced at her brother and said, 'What are you implying?'

'Nothing, except that I know you don't like that kind of man.'

'How do you know what kind of man I like? To be honest, I don't like any of them.'

'You sound as if you've been crossed in love,' said Elaine.

'No, let me finish. He took me home and would have forced an entry but I locked him out. He was so persistent that I called the police. Then everyone else arrived back, including this guy, and I wouldn't let them in.'

'Good for you,' said Elaine with feeling.

'The police came back and I made it clear to them that I wouldn't open door until the men had gone.'

'What did the police say?'

'They were on my side!'

'Well, we think you did a very brave thing,' said Elaine, 'and you should not be ashamed of it. Are we to understand that your flatmates didn't see things your way?'

'Quite, they were all for letting the men in.'

'So you had a bad experience,' said Matthew.

'Yes, but the last few days seemed to be full of them.'

'What else happened then?'

As Sarah explained about the little boy with his hand in the door, Jason wandered in wanting something and had approached his mother, shaking her leg.

'Take him in the kitchen and sort him out, Matt, while I talk with Sarah.'

'It was the injustice of it,' said Sarah, 'I couldn't stand by and watch a small boy get his hand crushed; no one in their right mind could.'

'No, of course they wouldn't. I can see the woman's point of view, but she should have given you a chance to explain things before giving you a piece of her mind. If you had been a man it might be different.'

'Why?' asked Sarah.

'Because men are...' Elaine tailed off.

'Men are what?'

'More likely to do odd things where children are concerned.'

'But that implies that a man in that situation should not respond to help the child.'

'He's going to think twice.'

'And by then it might be too late. I concluded that the woman couldn't have cared less about her child. It even crossed my mind that had the boy been injured she would have been keen to sue!'

'It's very upsetting when these things happen.'

'It was pleasing enough to know that I had saved the boy from injury. The barest of thanks would have sufficed.'

'And it leaves you feeling awful.'

'Yes, and because of it, I was late back to the office.'

'And they weren't sympathetic.'

'No. My supervisor, Ms Marchbank, certainly wasn't! She wanted to give me a written warning.'

'Is she actually your boss?'

'No, I was hauled in before him.'

'And did he agree with her?'

'No! He's a right miserable sod, but on this occasion he took my side.'

'Then you have one friend in the world.'

Matthew was back in the room. 'Look,' he said to Elaine, 'you've got to come; Chloe's got a disgusting nappy on.'

'Why don't you change it?'

'If it was only wet, I would! But you know how I hate changing those.'

'Oh, you are men are so helpless!' said Elaine and left the room.

Matthew took her seat and grinned at his sister.

'Mother keeps me up with your news. How's the job going?'

'All right, but I've felt like chucking it in recently.'

'Why's that?'

'It's just the way we're treated.'

'I heard what you said about your boss. He sounds a fair sort of man to me.'

'It's not him so much. He's all right, but he's so melancholy – never smiles. He gives the impression that he hates life.'

'Perhaps he does. What's the pay like?'

Sarah told him. Matthew raised his eyebrows and said, 'Well, meanness is not one of his faults.'

'No, forget what I've just said. It's me really. I thought I knew where I was going and suddenly I don't.'

'The feminist stuff bothering you?'

'No.'

'Why don't you find a nice man and settle down?'

'I don't need a man.'

'Elaine loves being married.'

'As an institution it is designed for some.'

'No, you don't want to look up to a man, do you?'

In most circumstances Sarah would have responded angrily to any man saying such things to her, but she could take it from her brother, and nodded slightly in agreement.

'I've never met a man to whom I could look up to.' Sarah was beginning to feel that she was being interrogated and she wanted to say less. Elaine returned, and hearing the last comment said, 'Oh, I'm sure there must be many.'

'Let's form a picture of the kind of man Sarah would go for,' said her brother.

'That would be fun,' said Elaine. 'He must be taller.'

'How much taller? Just an inch or so, or should he be a lot taller?'

'If he were a lot taller it would be too dominating for Sarah.'

'Then he must only be a little taller.'

'What colour hair?'

'It has to be dark.'

'What about his attitude?'

'Must be friendly and very easy-going.'

'Forgiving?'

'Oh, absolutely.'

Sarah's hackles were rising but she was saved from further

examination by the sound of crashing coming from the kitchen. Matthew was quick to get to his feet and disappeared. He put his head round the door and said, 'I'll take them outside for some fresh air.'

'What was the noise?' asked Elaine.

'Only the saucepans.' Then he was gone.

'It's lovely to see you, Sarah. I hope you don't find us too cloying; you having your ideas and really they are a bit alien to us.'

'But then you don't have the hang-ups about men that I have.'

'No, I always saw myself as being married.'

'You wanted children.'

'Oh yes, I couldn't see life without them.'

'And you enjoyed having them.'

'Of course! There are moments when it's not particularly pleasant but you soon forget them. Do you want another cup of tea?'

There came a crying noise from somewhere in the distance and it got louder. Matthew came in, holding a screaming Chloe.

'What's happened?' said Elaine.

'Chloe's just fallen off the swing – well, actually, Jason pushed her off.'

'But you shouldn't have put her on the swing.'

'She was getting the hang of it.'

'It's too much at her age.'

'But she wanted to get on.'

'You should have directed her elsewhere.'

'That's easier said than done when she's trying to get on.'

The little girl, held high in her mother's arms during this exchange, had stopped crying. Her thumb was stuck hard in her mouth and her eyes were glazing over with sleep.

Sarah could only stare at the couple. It was hardly a scene that commended marital bliss to her. She couldn't see herself with the same patience, nor could she see herself shunting children around. Seeing her sister-in-law holding the child, Sarah noted that she was expecting another.

'Look,' said Elaine to her husband, 'why don't you grab something to eat and take Sarah down to the boat or something. I'll look after the children.' Matthew visibly brightened.

'I'm not really dressed for boating,' said Sarah.

'You'll do,' said Matthew, 'you'll love it.'

Twenty minutes later they reached Hamble, where his boat was moored. Sarah had no idea what sort of boat it was. Matthew had offered no clues and Elaine had said nothing. She had the dreadful feeling that she was letting herself in for something that later she was going to regret.

They parked the car and walked to the harbour. Matthew had a brief word with someone and soon they were walking along one of the jetties. On either side of them were wonderful yachts, the sheets on their aluminium masts slapping back with a pinging metallic sound. Amongst these were some large cruisers looking quite capable of reaching the French coast in a couple of hours. Then Matthew stopped and pointed something out to Sarah.

'There she is,' he said.

Her eyes followed where he pointed and she was agreeably surprised to see a sleek speedboat moored to the jetty. Matthew was soon on it, pulling the covers back.

'Jump on and sit there,' he said. And Sarah obeyed him. He pottered around for a few minutes and then she heard the sound of the engine starting.

'Sounds good,' he said, 'I'm just checking the fuel. Oh, plenty there.' He was round at the bows untying the mooring ropes. Then he was back in the driver's seat.

Sarah watched her brother. His face was shining as he eased the craft away from the moorings. Then they were edging round the marina to find their way onto Southampton Water.

'Brilliant, isn't it,' he enthused. Sarah nodded, though it was not quite her idea of fun; but to say less was to be churlish.

'Tell you something,' he said, 'I've never been allowed to open her up. Shall we try this afternoon?'

'Why's that?'

'Elaine won't let me!'

'So why do you think I might be different?'

'You're my sister!'

He pushed the throttle away from him and the boat surged forward. Sarah had to admit that the effect was exhilarating. Matthew pushed the throttles open more. He was like a small boy with a brand new toy. He was ecstatic, with a huge grin on his face.

'We're doing over thirty knots,' he shouted at Sarah, 'I hope you don't get seasick!'

'There doesn't seem time for that.'

He slowed, for they were now reaching the more turbulent waters of the Solent.

'What do you want to see? Portsmouth or the Needles.'

'The Needles.'

'That's Cowes over there,' said Matthew.

From the angle they were at, Sarah could not see open sea, though she knew where it was. But Matthew seemed determined to get there as quickly as possible and opened the throttle again. To their right were mudflats finishing in a forest of masts, with Lymington beyond them.

'Alum Bay's over there,' said Matthew pointing at the multi-coloured cliffs. The needles could be discerned in the distance. They were almost in the open sea with the waves slapping at the boat and Matthew slowed, as they came up to the Needles.

Matthew backed right off and they glided in towards the huge pillars of chalk.

'We won't go too close,' said Matthew, 'there are some odd currents around.'

'Matt,' said Sarah, glad that they had slowed down and the engine was almost silent, allowing them to have a normal conversation, 'can you not go on about marriage and its advantages? I've come down here for a change of scenery and yet all anyone can speak of is men!'

'Sure.'

'Thanks! I made my mind up years ago to never get married and I've no desire to change my mind.'

'What if the right bloke did come along, though?'

'I can't see that. I've never met anyone I would really like.'

'It's not a case of liking anyone, sis, there comes a point when your eyes follow a person around a room and you hate another person talking to them, and when they touch you it sends little electric shocks up your arm. It's called love!'

Sarah nodded and said, 'I've never experienced that. I think I'm frigid…'

'I doubt that,' he said kindly, 'if you ever met a man you loved you would open up.'

'But let's admire the Needles; I've only ever seen them from a distance before or in photographs.'

'I've been here a couple of times; Elaine won't let me get too close.'

'Massive, aren't they! Yet in the photos they look so small – just appendages on the Isle of Wight.'

'We could go right round the Isle of Wight but it would take too long; let's go back to Cowes. I know a nice bar there.'

It was teatime when they arrived back at the house. The two children were sitting at the table waiting for them. With their arrival, Elaine brought out some food.

'That was well timed,' she said. 'I didn't know whether to wait for you or not.'

'Instinct,' said Matthew.

'Did you like it, Sarah? You didn't get seasick, did you?'

'Just a bit, but it was really quite calm.'

'I hope you don't mind, but it's only beans on toast. Matt and I have supper later.'

The children were eating theirs. Jason sat at the table on a chair with a cushion underneath him and Chloe sat in the high chair that acted as a restraint. Everything was going well until Chloe rubbed her eyes and threw what was left of her food onto the floor, the baked beans scattering over the carpet, bringing a smile to the tot's face. The boy laughed and looked as if he were about to throw his on top of his sister's, but his father restrained him.

'Oh, Chloe,' said her mother, 'don't do such naughty things! Matt, get a cloth from the kitchen.'

Sarah sighed; she found it difficult to cope with the disruptions, and decided that when the meal was finished she would get her brother to take her to the station.

Order was restored, and Elaine started feeding Chloe from her own plate. Jason decided that if his sister could have some help then he ought to have it as well. He pushed his plate away.

'Oh, Matt, give him a hand will you?'

'Have you learnt to drive, Sarah?' asked Elaine.

'No, I've not had any inclination to, and even if I did I couldn't park a car near the house.'

'That's a shame.'

'Not really. It would just sit there and go rusty.'

'Yes,' said Matt, 'just to keep some old banger outside would cost over £600 a year, by the time you've included insurance, tax and MOT.'

'We've both got cars,' said Elaine. 'Well, we need them for work.'

'Do you work then, Elaine?'

'Oh yes, I'm a social worker. My mother comes in on odd days of the week and we have a nanny for the other two. She's good, for she'll step in if Mother can't make it.'

'And what's your house like?' said Matthew.

'It's the first floor of a large house. It's got three bedrooms and a reception room and there is a separate kitchen.'

'That sounds all right. Is it an old house?'

'Edwardian, I think.'

'Any garden?'

'Yes, but it's communal. There's only grass there and we should take it in turns to cut it, but we don't.'

'Do the people downstairs do it?'

'No, the grass is left to grow.'

Sarah had finished her coffee. She wanted to take her leave, but Elaine and Matthew seemed oblivious of her needs and she was forced to wait patiently while the children were put to bed. It annoyed her that they were being put in the bath.

Matthew came back. 'What do you want? Another coffee?'

'Actually I'd like to be going.'

'Oh, right, I'll speak to Elaine.'

It took sometime for Elaine for to come down and make her farewells and then she went back to her children. Matthew returned and they left for the station.

Sarah sat on the train feeling depressed. She had hoped that the change of scenery would snap her out of her mood but she now felt profoundly depressed. Her brother was a man from whom she had fully expected a lively debate on almost any subject under the sun, but it had not happened. He seemed more than happy to find fulfilment in his family and she felt he had become boring. Was it her fault? Should she have started a conversation on the state of the economy? But there never seemed a point in the conversation where she could change the subject. The only thing that concerned Elaine was her family, and she had been at pains to show her that Sarah, too, should be part of a family. What Elaine had not realised was that what she saw as domestic bliss was not Sarah's idea of contentment. Then they had been concerned that she should find a man. Why couldn't they see that she did not want one?

Sarah wished then that she had not gone there, but the other end of the journey had its problems too. Waiting for her were Cathy and Gerrie, with whom she needed to make peace. That alone was a daunting prospect, as it was two against one. Were she to make them all fall out it would be the end of the house, and that she did not want. But it irked her that their actions had betrayed her and she had expected them not just to respect her person but also to protect it. Instead they had treated her as nothing more than a prostitute. Then there was the fact that they couldn't see her side of the argument. Just because they liked sleeping around did not mean that other women did...

It was a wasted day, she concluded. She had hoped to find succour and comfort at her brother's house and she had found the opposite instead. They expected her to find a man, but she was not even looking for a man – and why should she? Surely she was a complete entity in herself! Men were complete entities within themselves and in many respects had no need of women. Did they worry about biological fulfilment? Surely she could be just like that? Did she need to surround herself with children, like Elaine? Did she really want to see an extension of her body running around?

Seeing the little boy's hand in the door of the store in Oxford Street had set off her depression. She had mapped out life for herself and she had been happy with her plan. She sailed along for years without thinking about it and never deviating from her course. But was her brother right about love? If he was right then she had never experienced love... or had she? There was the

French student when she was fourteen whom she'd had a desperate crush on. She remembered her legs going weak, and she had wanted him to speak only to her. When he spoke to others as he had to her she had been consumed with jealousy. She had wanted to give him her whole being and let him run his hands all over her. She had wanted to yield to him. Yet the spring term came and he was gone, being replaced by a starchy French Madame for whom no man could surely have had feelings. It was then that she found out that most of the girls in her year had the hots for the Frenchman, and as one they had blamed the staff, since they were all women.

But it was one of those moments when suddenly she felt clairvoyant. They had all blamed the *teachers* for getting rid of the man! Surely it had been down to the man; he must have felt uncomfortable in the presence of all those nubile girls. He had had no option but to extricate himself from them, simply for his own peace of mind. Did it make him a coward? Really he was very strong-minded not to succumb, for the provocation had been extreme. She marvelled that she had never seen it before.

But it was her reaction to his leaving that she needed to consider. It had hurt her enormously and she had determined never to let a man have such a hold on her emotions again. But was she right to do so? Her flatmates were victims of their emotions, and they enjoyed their bodies! Why did she look askance at their behaviour? She did not think it wrong, but she certainly thought that it was not for her.

Waterloo Station was coming into view and Sarah did not want to go back to the house and meet either Cathy or Gerrie. She would have liked to have gone somewhere else and stayed the night, but standing on the wide concourse of Waterloo looking at the indicator boards she could think of no one that she could go to. She had many friends and acquaintances yet there was no one she wanted to visit. She felt depressed and suddenly very alone. Elaine came to mind and she realised how fortunate she was to have married her brother; but then she had wanted to get married! Reluctantly she walked to the platform to get the next train to Earlsfield.

The house though, when she returned, was empty. Of Cathy

or Gerrie there was no sign – not that she had expected them to leave her a message or anything. In many ways she was glad, for she did not want to meet them yet; that she would have to at some point she was well aware, but she wanted it at sometime in the future.

On Sunday there was still no sign of her flatmates, allowing Sarah to do her chores, and it was late in the evening when they finally came home. Sarah was in bed and still not ready to meet them, and since they did not hammer on her door she assumed that their feelings about her were much the same as hers about them.

In the morning Sarah dressed and went straight out, getting a much earlier train up to town. Despite being the first in and alone in the office, she felt safe at her desk.

Reconciliation

At ten thirty Monday morning Sarah and Michael were called into Mr Deakin's office for the routine weekly meeting. Sarah was slightly ahead of Michael, and arriving in the office on her own she felt rather sheepish. Mr Deakin didn't seem to notice and waved her to a chair. He looked up in his dour way, giving Sarah a long hard stare that made feel uncomfortable.

'Do you have to go around being cross with everyone the whole time?' said Mr Deakin.

Sarah's hackles rose. She did not like his tone.

'Perhaps I'm trying to imitate you,' she retorted, and instantly wished she had kept a still tongue in her head.

Her rudeness produced a haughty look from Deakin and he curled his lips as he said, 'I am the owner of this concern and I employ you. I can act in any manner I like. I do not expect you to tell me how to act.'

'I'm sorry,' said Sarah, 'it just slipped out.'

There was no time to say any more, for Michael came in, followed by Ms Marchbank. Tom and Millie, two of the other staff, joined them. Both of them were doing similar work to Sarah and Michael. Tom was a recent addition to the office, having been with them only three months. He was a tall, languid man with greying hair, though he was only forty or so. His thin face reminded Sarah of a few of her lecturers from her university days. He was a nice enough person, though Sarah had little to do with him, especially as Millie appeared to have taken him under her wing and they had become friends. She felt now that it was Millie who had really crept under his wing, which was surprising, for it was known that Tom was not married but lived with his partner. But Sarah was certain that Millie was one of those people who loved to play office politics, and her hiding behind Tom was to deflect criticism away from herself and onto someone else.

It had not been a good start to the week and Sarah was glad

that Ms Marchbank had not been present to hear what had passed between them. She thought Mr Deakin's rebuke was justified, and was angry with herself for letting her feelings get the better of her. However, it was merely a reflection of her thinking, for she had felt for ages that Mr Deakin actually enjoyed his miserable outlook on life. He gave the impression of having the worries of the world on his shoulders, and there came a time when one no longer wanted to overlook it. But it was not part of her job description to make the man smile. Sarah peered at Ms Marchbank, for she and Mr Deakin seemed to have much in common. She too looked miserable and pursed her lips as if she were thinking of the vengeance she was about to wreak on some poor unsuspecting person.

The meeting followed its usual pattern. Everyone had to give a brief progress report and conclude by saying whether the project they were on was ahead of schedule or not. If the answer was negative, the person concerned had to say why it was so, and what they proposed to do to get it back ahead of schedule. The easy answer was to say that they'd stay behind for a few evenings and work at it. This always produced the query about why it hadn't been done already, together with a lecture on the cost of missing deadlines. Sarah felt that this method of putting people under pressure was somewhat unwarranted and antiquated but few people transgressed twice, and if they did it was with good reason. She had had to admit to it once and her reason was that that on the Friday before the meeting she had reached a lengthy passage which was nonsense, and the only recourse was to go straight back to the author and get it sorted out. It was odd because on that occasion it had been Ms Marchbank who gave her the public lecture in Mr Deakin's office. After that meeting she had been called back, whereupon Mr Deakin told her that she, Sarah, was quite right and the author needed to be informed immediately, and if things were too delayed they would have to put more resources into it. She had wished he had spoken in the meeting.

But as each person gave their report it was patent that everything was going smoothly. It should have been a time of pleasure but the glum remained glum and everyone in the office assumed the same air of glumness. Michael mentioned that the manuscript he was working on contained no reference about who had taken the photographs. He asked if that was usual.

'Does it give you cause for concern?' interjected Ms Marchbank.

'It does worry me a bit,' said Michael. 'One expects to see permissions or the claim that it is all copyrighted.'

'Have you questioned the author about it yet?' asked Mr Deakin.

'I've not questioned him as such, but I alluded to it and tried to make him talk about it. All I got was a cold shoulder.'

'It not your place to worry about such things,' said Ms Marchbank.

'Well, I think I would be remiss not to bring it up.'

'Why do we have to worry about it?' said Tom from the end of the row of seats that faced Mr Deakin.

'Well, this man is a university lecturer, and it crossed my mind that he might have yanked the whole of his book out of someone else's. We'd look jolly stupid if that were the case,' retorted Michael.

'And we'd probably be vulnerable to a lawsuit,' said Mr Deakin dryly. 'Leave it with me, and I'll talk to the chap.'

Everyone nodded in agreement that the right decision had been taken. But it seemed to loosen tongues, and Millie, who was sitting between Ms Marchbank and Tom, spoke up. Soon a lively debate was underway on the direction that publishing would take in the future. Mr Deakin was appealed to first, and he seemed to think that there would be little change in publishing. Ms Marchbank gave it as her opinion that there would be none, since, she believed, people would always read books despite the Internet. Michael rather felt that there would continue to be a dumbing down in literature as a whole. It was an interesting point of view and Sarah determined to speak to him further on the matter. Millie thought that too many outside influences were ruining good literature. Tom then gave his opinion, which Sarah thought was contrived, as if he had had time to think it out. He felt that the Internet would put publishers out of business, though he could only hope not. It was clear that Ms Marchbank thought his view was heretical and she would gladly have led Tom out to the stake and lit the pyre herself. It was then that everyone realised that Sarah had remained silent.

'What's Sarah's opinion?' said Millie, with a hint of bitchiness in her tone.

'Yes,' said Michael, giving Sarah a mischievous sideways glance.

'I think Sarah's sufficiently up to date to support my point of view,' said Tom.

'I think we would all be interested in what Miss Levine has to say,' said Ms Marchbank tartly.

Sarah was blushing at having had attention drawn to her, but deep inside she was drawing her thoughts together.

'Come on,' said Millie, 'we can't wait all day or we'll all get behind on our schedules.'

Tom laughed but quickly stifled it as both Ms Marchbank and Mr Deakin looked at him severely.

'I think,' said Sarah, speaking slowly, 'that there will always be a place for well-written books on any and every subject. I can see that the Internet poses a challenge, for it stifles individuality, as one is at the mercy of the programmers.'

'But we're the programmers of publishers,' complained Tom.

'No we're not. None of us write the books, nor are we required to write over what an author has written. We can *suggest* what should be there, but it's still down to the author.'

'Good point,' said Michael.

'Are you going to say more?' asked Mr Deakin.

'Well, no one took up Michael's point of dumbing down.'

'And have you an opinion on that?'

'I thought that we all might have.'

'Perhaps Michael might like to expand on what he said.' When Mr Deakin spoke it was hard for anyone to butt in, for though he spoke quietly, his deep tones cut across whatever anyone else was saying.

It was Michael's turn to go bright red and demonstrate that he had not thought it out.

'I think the bit about computer programmers goes back to dumbing down. We seem to be stuck with whatever they think, and if they want the English language to be full of Americanisms then all they have to do is to put such words in their spelling checks. But that only touches on the subject. There are many points of view going around where we can say some things but not others.'

'Such as?' said Tom suspecting a good argument.

'Let's say sexism, for a start. It's changing attitudes.'

'So it ought,' said Millie. 'And Sarah would agree with me.'

'I might,' said Sarah, 'but I don't think Michael's finished yet.'

'Well,' said Michael, 'it's all right to make this world more female friendly, but if I suggested something that would only benefit men there would be uproar. Now if the sexes are equal then what goes for one sex ought to go for the other.'

'I can't see how that is dumbing down,' said Ms Marchbank.

'Well, it is,' persisted Michael, 'because you reach a point where free speech has disappeared and we're only allowed to have certain opinions. Any idea of discrimination disappears, for the next thing is that all books must be written so that people of even the lowest intelligence can read them.'

'And so they ought to be,' said Millie.

'I accept that the art of writing is to reach the maximum number of people but there has to be a limit. For instance, how many people would be interested in what happens inside the sun? How does it produce its energy? Do large sections of the population really want to know – and because they don't, should we not write for the intelligence of those who do?'

'But that would be to suggest that there are people of low intelligence,' said Millie.

'And so there are. I know of people who don't have a book in their house, and if I were to write a textbook I would see no point in writing it for them.'

'But your book, if pitched at their intelligence level, might be just the thing to get them reading,' said Tom who enjoyed a rollicking good argument.

'Pigs might fly,' said Michael, giving up the unequal task somewhat bitterly.

'I think we've had enough,' said Mr Deakin. 'Let us get back to the work in hand.'

These were the words of dismissal that everyone was waiting

for, and with a scraping of chairs they all rose except Mr Deakin, who sat in his chair behind his desk as if he were stuck there.

Sarah still could not face her flatmates that evening and she decided to eat out on her own. There were a number of restaurants close to the office that she had never tried and she wanted to try a small one above the Regency Inn public house. The doorway at the street level seemed quite uninviting and she wondered if she ought to go up, but decided she had to try it despite her reservations. At the top one turned left into a small lobby and went through it into the restaurant. A waiter came forward to greet her and finding that she was on her own, he took her to a discreet table set for one person. It gave her a view down the restaurant towards the door.

Having seated her comfortably, he put the menu in her hand. She took a deep breath when she saw the price list and realised why the entrance was so unassuming. The average person could not afford to eat there, and were they to do so they would think they were being mugged when they received the bill. But she steeled herself, for she could actually afford anything there. Were she to eat there every evening she would soon require a large loan, but she reasoned that she could surely indulge herself just once in a while, especially when she felt so unhappy with everyone. She was pleased with her own company and glad that there was no one there to tell her that eating certain foods was unhealthy. For once in her life she could eat anything without having a conscience. Cathy and Gerrie would be scandalised if they knew what she was doing, and she had expected a man like Gareth to have taken her to a slap-up restaurant and a minicab home afterwards.

She shuddered at the thought of the bus that Gareth had preferred. Then there was the meal he wanted in her kitchen, and then, having slummed it, he wanted total access to her body! Would she have given it to him, had he wined and dined her properly? In Gareth's case she had seen early on in the evening that he was not going to spend much if he could help it, so nothing like this had been intended and the question did not arise.

57

She ordered her favourites but only one glass of white wine, for she wanted to go home in full control of her faculties. It took twenty minutes for her meal to come but it seemed a very short time for she had the whole room to take in. The building was late eighteenth century, and the restaurant had been decorated in the Regency style. It allowed her imagination to see some of the figures of the period dining close to where she was sitting, for the streets of Mayfair reeked of that period. Could the restaurant have been a discreet place where dukes and duchesses ate? Could Beau Brummel have dined here with the then Prince of Wales? But then they had a falling-out, which caused the former to end his days living in Calais... What a place to end one's life! Would it not have been better to have apologised to the Prince? Of course, the restaurant might have been a place where no such thing happened. Or could it have been one of those places that had acquired a degree of infamy? Perhaps it was a gaming house, or maybe even a brothel!

Sarah's thoughts were interrupted by her meal arriving. The waiter placed it before her and gave her a little bow, which pleased her to no end. She was in no hurry and ate slowly, savouring her food. Her wine glass was empty and against her better judgement she called the waiter over to get another one. She finished her meal with a dessert followed by coffee and sat back at peace with herself. She concluded that for two hours she had not thought about her problems, and was pleased. The only cloud on the horizon was that shortly she would have to ask for the bill and she would have to leave; but that she decided could be offset by the thought that she could do it all again in a couple of weeks' time. And she returned to her previous mood of euphoria.

She had reached the point when she was trying to catch the waiter's eye to get her bill when she realised that someone was approaching her. A tall, handsome man stood before her.

'Excuse me,' he said, 'we've never met, but I believe your name is Miss Levine.'

'How do you know?' she asked, her mind instantly suspicious

'The gentleman who has just left told me who you were.'

'I see... and who was that?'

The man gave the name of his acquaintance and added, 'He is

an author and I believe that you are about to publish one of his books.'

'I'm not, personally.'

'Of course not, but I thought that in mentioning the name you might have heard of him.'

From past experience Sarah knew that she ought to be wary of strange men but there was an air about the stranger that fascinated her. He was well dressed, with his suit being impeccably cut, and he sported a hand-tied bow tie. That in itself she regarded as a rarity, and in consequence warranted her attention and highest respect. Then there were his manners, which were so unlike those she had seen in Gareth. She sensed that were he to be shut out of a woman's house he would have departed, totally mortified. The way he addressed her left her in no doubt that he would ever force an entry.

'My name,' he said, 'is Clive Brunswick. Perhaps you would do me the honour of dining with me one evening?'

What could she say to such an invitation? It would be impossible to say no, and the man's tone suggested that he did not expect a negative answer.

'That would be very pleasant,' said Sarah hoping that she achieved a fair imitation of the man's deference.

'Shall we say this Saturday week?'

'And where?' asked Sarah.

'Why not outside here at seven o'clock?'

Sarah reached for her bag to find her diary. The man was already fingering his.

'It has been a pleasure making your acquaintance so fortuitously,' he said softly. And then, with a nod of his head, he turned and walked from the restaurant.

The waiter had seen their little chat and had waited for it to finish before he brought the bill over. Sarah glanced over the bill and winced. But she consoled herself that she did not intend to dine so lavishly every day, and she decided that it was money well spent, despite the invitation that she had received. No, the restaurant and her surroundings were worth even the appetiser; the pleasure of dining by herself and feeling so at ease were worth the main course and the invitation was as the dessert, that came with a large dollop of whipped cream topped with a glacé cherry.

With the bill paid she rose to leave. It pleased even more that the waiter remained obsequious to the end. At the door the head waiter wished her good night and offered to find her a taxi, to which Sarah replied in the negative. She had given no thought about how she was going to go home and realised that she had no desire to be simply whisked home. She was enjoying her evening and was looking forward to the walk to the Underground station. The thought crossed her mind that it might be nice to spend some time walking around the West End.

It was nearly two hours later when she arrived back at the flat, and her friends were beginning to get worried about her. The atmosphere was strained.

'Where have you been?' asked Gerrie.

'We have been quite worried about you,' said Cathy.

'You were out yesterday when I got home,' said Sarah.

'But you've not said a word to us.'

'I know. I wanted time to think things over. What did you want? My eternal gratitude?'

'No, but it's made us look very stupid.'

'And so it should.'

'But nothing happened.'

'Perhaps you should ask Gareth,' said Sarah, 'but then you were party to it, and you can hardly claim to be innocent.'

'We haven't done anything,' said Cathy indignantly.

'You only set Gareth on to me.'

'No one set him on to you – don't be so stupid!'

'You both dropped hints that I was up for it.'

'We didn't,' said Cathy without conviction.

'Oh? I imagine things, do I? I imagined Gareth coming home with his tongue hanging out. If I had let him in he'd have raped me!'

'Rubbish! He's a thoroughly nice guy.'

'I had spent all evening trying to tell either one of you that I wanted him off my back, but you wouldn't hear of it.'

'You wanted to go out with him.'

'No, I did not! I only agreed to keep you two happy.'

'But you're the one who spent the past week sending out all the signals that you needed a man.'

60

'I have not! I don't know how you can say such things.'
'Oh, come on! You know full well you're frustrated.'
'I am not.'
'Well, you are, and he was just the man to give you a good time.'
'Rubbish! He was totally self-centred. I would have become just another "notch on his bow", as he so graphically put it.'
'You're a mean one! If I'd have known I'd have had him myself.'
'I wish you had.'
'So what's wrong with just having a bit of sex and a laugh?'
'Nothing if you're that kind of person, and I'm not.'
'You're weird!'
'No I'm not,' said Sarah. 'If you really must know, I've never had sex in my life!'

Cathy and Gerrie looked at her in disbelief.

'*What*! You're a virgin?' said Gerrie in amazement.
'If you want it bluntly, yes!'
'Oh, Sarah, with all that worldliness – and you're actually completely naïve!'
'Thanks,' said Sarah sarcastically, 'and I thought that my two best friends would have supported me, not thrown me to the lions! You don't realise how much you hurt me. If he had come in that night I'd have been raped for sure. You had set him up and made it clear to him that I was some poor cow waiting for the bull. You said nothing that would make him hold back, and you downplayed every reservation that I had. He thought he was on to a winner.'
'All right, so we got it wrong.'
'Yes, and if he'd raped me there'd have been nothing I could have done about it! Everyone would have said that I invited him into the house; it would have been my word against his that he had not forced his way in. Then everyone would say that I had led him on the whole evening, which is palpably untrue: I was trapped by the "niceties" of my friends, I could not get away. And when I made it clear that I did not like his attentions he took that as a sign that I actually did! Had I said I was up for it he would have taken that as a positive statement; I couldn't win, either way!'

'How many times do we have to apologise?'

'I don't know, and I don't see how I can forgive you, because it still hurts me. I went to a restaurant on my own this evening and for the first time since then I was able to forget about it. And then you say you want me to forgive you – but are you asking to be forgiven for everything?'

'What do mean?'

'Are you asking to be forgiven for leading him on and putting me in an awkward situation?'

'Yes.'

'But are you asking to be forgiven for misrepresenting my feelings.'

'Yes,' said Cathy, but there was doubt in her voice.

Sarah pounced on it and said, 'There you are! You hadn't even thought about it, and that is my point! You want a skin-deep forgiveness that you have not even thought about. Had you really thought about it you would be utterly ashamed of what you did.'

'I know I haven't thought it over, Sarah, but I am trying to put it straight. We do have to live together. I can only promise that neither of us will do it again.'

'Then I'll have to accept that as a complete apology and say that I forgive you.'

Cathy flung her arms around Sarah and gave her a hug. 'Thanks,' she said, 'I really have felt bad about it, and Gerrie feels the same.'

Gerrie nodded and said, 'I'm really sorry.' She too hugged Sarah.

'Frankly,' said Sarah, 'you two ought to find better man friends.'

'Too much bother.'

'I thought the hunt was the bit you enjoyed.'

'It is! Coffee?'

'Yes. You don't shake them off because you don't want to hurt their feelings.'

'Oh, it's everything, it requires effort. It's like favourite clothes; you know you should be more fashion conscious but you continue to wear the old stuff because you find it comfortable.'

'I must have misunderstood this women's liberation thing.'

'We do – we're not committed to any guy.'

'But you are! Cathy and Charles, and Gerrie and Ted. You both go around like married people!'

'That's not fair, Sar.'

'Why isn't? In fact I'd go further and say that you're not just a married couple, you're an old married couple! Just look at yourselves. You've got everything but the certificate. If you went around and told everyone that you were Mrs Brown, they would believe you!'

'Brownlee!' said Cathy, correcting Sarah about Charles's surname.

'I have no intention of marrying; so far as I'm concerned it's an outdated institution.'

'So you're going to live in sin like the rest of us.'

'No.'

'But you don't have the qualifications to be a nun.'

'I have *some*...' Sarah replied.

'Well, the obvious one; but when did you last go to church?'

'To my brother's wedding. I rather had to go. That was over six years ago!'

'I wonder that he got married in a church.'

'Oh, his wife came from a pretty little village in Hampshire and it was her parents' wish.'

'More likely hers.'

'Anyway I have no intentions of being a nun. My ambitions are more worldly.'

'And what are they?'

'Well I'd like to run my own publishing business and have the respect that was due only to me and my efforts.'

'The first of those might be possible, but I always thought respect was something that was given, not something that had to be earned.'

'I do meet influential people, you know,' said Sarah.

'But your boss takes all the kudos.'

'Well, I do know he's considering a book written by the wife of a cabinet minister.'

'What's the book about? Romance or thriller? Or is it the next blockbuster that everyone goes out to buy and when they read it, it's as tedious as a dictionary?'

'No, it's about living in stately homes and the contact between the servants and their masters – from the servants' point of view.'

'That'll sell in its millions,' said Cathy sarcastically.

'Perhaps, but I'm off to bed. Goodnight.'

The following day as Sarah busied herself at her computer she became conscious of someone standing close to her. Glancing up, she found Mr Deakin hovering close.

'Good morning,' she managed to say, surprised that he should approach her after she had been so rude to him the day before.

'Morning, Sarah,' he replied. 'How is it coming on?'

This gave Sarah a problem: was he asking her merely out of politeness, or was there a deeper meaning to his words? Had the deadline been changed? Had it been extended? Or, as was more likely, had it been shortened? Had a decision been taken to bin the book? She needed to give a qualified answer!

'It's coming along quite well,' she said.

'Good!'

What did that mean? Deakin did not normally check people's work. What had Ms Marchbank been saying about her? Had the police been round to the office about Friday night? Did he know something about her nearly being raped? What should she reply? She felt a pit open in her stomach. There was nothing one could reply when someone said simply 'good'. It was final and did not require an answer. She stared miserably at her screen waiting for his next words.

'I don't normally ask people this,' said Mr Deakin slowly and Sarah now felt that the worst was coming, 'but the author who's written what you are working on wants to take me out for dinner, and he has specifically asked for you to come as well.'

All he wanted was to ask her out on a dinner date on behalf of a client! The relief flooded through her.

'Of course,' Sarah replied, 'I'd be delighted.'

'Next Monday evening… Will that be all right with you?'

'What time?'

'Say eight o'clock.'

'Where?'

'Come to the office, we'll go from here.'

Sarah wondered if the likely restaurant was to be The Regency, but she hoped not, for she felt that she had found it and it was her retreat and she wanted it to remain that way.

Mr Deakin was walking away.

'Odd,' said Michael, coming over to Sarah's desk, 'I thought he hated taking people out for meals.'

'I think this author is taking both of us,' said Sarah.

'He had a policy of not wining and dining authors. Who's the author of your book?'

'Jonathan French.'

'Nope, I don't know him.'

'I think the author is paying!'

'So that raises the question as to what he wants from the meal!'

'Well, I presume he wants Mr Deakin to push his book.'

'He'd do that anyway. We'd never make money unless we pushed whatever we published. I guess that it's a smokescreen and that he's really after is you!'

'Don't be so stupid, it's a business meal.'

'That's where it all starts. I reckon the author fancies you and his foot touches yours under the table and – bingo!'

'What do you mean, "bingo"?'

'Only that before you realise it he will have swept you off your feet!'

'Then he's going to be very disappointed!'

'What I find most amusing is that Deakin's going to play gooseberry!' He was laughing and Sarah could not resist smiling.

'By the way, on Friday we're all going to the pub after work. I even asked Ms Marchbank.'

'What did she say?'

'That nothing would induce her to condescend to join us.'

'Did you ask Mr Deakin?'

'No, we don't want him to put a damper on things before we start, do we?'

Sarah thought that he might be a bit hard on the man, especially since no one knew how he might react to being invited. She temporised and said, 'Any particular celebration?'

'No, it's just a bit of a booze-up, but do bring your friends.'

The Challenge

Friday evening came in the fullness of time, and at five o'clock everyone left for the Mermaid. It had been chosen as it was a large pub and they could take over one end of the lounge. They arrived and the place had yet to fill up allowing them to select the armchairs and form a circle. Michael went for the drinks and came back with a loaded tray.

He sat down close to Sarah. Turning to her, he said conspiratorially that one should always buy the first round.

'Why?' she asked dutifully.

'Because it's the cheapest,' he replied, grinning, 'and everyone remembers that you bought a drink, whereas if you buy one midway through the evening no one remembers.'

He winked knowingly at Sarah. A short while later Cathy arrived and joined their circle between Millie and Tom.

'Shouldn't you buy Cathy a drink!' said Sarah, leaning over to Michael.

'Do you think so?' he said.

'Oh yes,' said Sarah, 'you wouldn't want to be remembered for buying only part of the first round!'

'No, of course not,' he said and sprang to his feet to ask Cathy what she wanted. As he did so Emma and Clemmie arrived late having been diverted at some point on the way. Brian, who ran the sales side from the firm's Cricklewood warehouse, followed them in. He was a jovial man in his late fifties and he liked his drink, though he was at great pains to deny it.

Emma took her jacket off, revealing that she was wearing a blouse cut indecently low. It made her cleavage look wonderful, and Sarah felt a pang of envy as she saw all the men's eyes stare at the girl. Clemmie then took her jacket off and all eyes swivelled to her, but being plainer than Emma she could not match her friend's effort. Clearly they had stopped off somewhere en route to effect the change. Michael had not reached his seat before he noted the arrival of the two girls. He stood for a few seconds gaping at the sight before him. Flashing a dirty look at Sarah, he asked them what they wanted to drink.

'They do smashing pasties here,' said Emma, deciding that she ought to contribute something to the assembled company. Michael arrived back with their drinks.

'Michael,' she said, 'be a darling and go and get everyone a pasty.'

Michael looked agonisingly at Emma, trying to ask her for the money.

'Please,' said Emma, and Michael, completely out of his depth, returned to the bar to order pasties for those who wanted them. It was not surprising that everyone opted for one.

Michael returned and said, 'The barman will bring them over when they're ready.'

Gerrie arrived with a girlfriend from her office.

'Are you going to buy Gerrie and her friend a drink?' asked Sarah. She had the satisfaction of hearing him swear under his breath. There was one vacant chair and Michael's seat, from which he had just risen. Gerrie sat down in his chair and her friend took the vacant one.

'What's going on?' asked Michael plaintively.

Gerrie looked at him and smiled as if to say that he did not mind.

'You will have to be the gentleman,' said Sarah.

'I thought we were all equal today,' said Michael.

'We are,' said Sarah, 'but we got the chairs first. Who is your friend, Gerrie?'

'This is Anthea,' said Gerrie to the circle of people, and everyone said hello.

The lounge bar was beginning to fill up and the conversation flowed amicably. Only Michael, who now stood between Sarah and Gerrie, looked aggrieved. A group of young men from another office arrived. Seeing the circle of women, they promptly came over and stood around admiring them all. More introductions ensued and one of the men named Bob went and bought the next round of drinks. Other men from the same office joined them, and suddenly there were now about thirty people gathered in the corner of the lounge. With everyone in good spirits, it had all the portents of being a good evening.

'Let's play a game where everyone tells a joke,' said someone.

'You start then.'

And the young man who had made the suggestion began with a joke that everyone had heard. There were loud moans and groans that they all knew it and the onus was passed to the next person.

After some time Sarah turned to Gerrie and said quietly, 'shall we buy a round of drinks?'

'I've got no money,' said Gerrie.

'Don't worry I'll pay, you'll owe me. Do you think Cathy will come in with us?'

'Let's find out.' Gerrie leant over to her flatmate.

'She says yes.'

Sarah pulled a fifty-pound note from her bag and turned to Michael.

'Get Bob and buy another round of drinks.'

The barman dragged a large jug up from beneath the counter and filled it for them to pass around, as they were nearly all drinking the same beer. The joke telling continued for some time, with the men doing the hard work; but it was beginning to flag and one of the men felt there should be a greater effort from the female side.

'Come on, ladies,' he complained, 'the blokes have been doing all the jokes. How about you lot telling us some?'

'Come on, Sarah, you must know some jokes,' said a wit. 'You've been around long enough.'

It was the kind of rudeness that Sarah normally took great exception to, and given a free rein she would have gladly boxed his ears, but she was not in a position to even begin such an act of vengeance. Instead she decided to call his bluff and tell a joke. Some instinct told her that in the sight of the other men she would be elevated and the wit would be on the receiving end from his friends.

'All right,' she said, 'I'll tell a joke.'

'Go on,' said the wit, 'let's hear it.'

'Shut up, you lot,' said someone else, 'we want to hear Sarah.'

There seemed to be a hush in the proceedings and all eyes were turned on her as she started her joke.

'Imagine,' she said, 'that your father dies and your mother remarries. Her husband becomes your stepfather.' Everyone was looking at her, seemingly eager to hear her story. She felt rather pleased to be holding the attention of so many people and noted that none of the other women had dared to do the same.

'Now your mother dies and your stepfather remarries. His wife becomes your stepmother. Now your stepfather dies and your stepmother remarries. What is her husband to you?'

There was considerable chat amongst everyone as to what the answer could be, but finally they prevailed on Sarah to say.

'So you want to know,' she said teasingly.

'Yes,' they all agreed.

'Stairs!' said Sarah triumphantly.

Some of the men saw the joke immediately and burst out laughing. There were a number of people who could not see the joke and had to have it explained to them, but when any joke needs to be explained it tends to lose its impact. It was generally agreed that she had worsted the wit and some of his friends were demanding that he left the assembled company immediately, as he was not worthy to be part of them.

It was then that one of the men told a very sexist joke that was not suitable for mixed company. He had a good demeanour and a voice that carried well and at the end of it all the men were laughing, but the women en bloc denounced him with much booing and hissing. But the gathering had reached the point where nothing was taken seriously. The jug went around the room again, and when anyone put a glass down it was promptly filled again. When the jug was empty it was replenished with equal zest.

'Aren't the ladies lucky,' said someone, 'they could have anyone of us they fancied tonight.'

'They could have a whole selection,' said someone else.

'What, all at once?' said another.

The women complained that they had reduced sex to its lowest common denominator.

'What's this lot then,' said another, 'feminists?'

The party had passed the point where one took no exception to rudeness, anyone could say whatever they liked and no one took umbrage. Sarah realised that she too came in that category, for she couldn't help laughing at what was being said. She tried to rebuke herself, as she made a habit of never letting herself laugh at such bawdy camaraderie. How much she had drunk was anyone's guess.

'Sarah's the feminist here,' said Millie, exerting herself for once.

'You're up for it then, are you, love?' said one of the men across the group to Sarah.

'Not in your condition,' she replied, and the women laughed more.

'So,' said the man whose voice carried so well, 'Sarah's the real feminist among you...'

'I might be,' Sarah countered, and in her inebriated state she blushed, but she was enjoying being the centre of attention.

'Well, I think you're all hypocrites!'

'That's coming at it a bit strong,' replied Sarah.

'No, no,' said the man, 'hear me out first. I bet you're all experienced women.'

'Put some money on it,' said Cathy.

'Fifty quid! No, make it a hundred!'

'Is this an auction?' said someone.

'For one hundred quid, let's put it in blunt terms! There isn't a virgin amongst us.'

'I claim the hundred,' said Cathy, 'there is a virgin here.'

'Really! Oh my gosh, I don't see one!' He looked round the room in mock wonder.

'Sarah's a virgin.'

'Come on, loudmouth! Get your money out.'

'Yes,' said someone else, 'where's your money!'

'Oi, I'm not putting my hand in my pocket that quick! You'll have to prove it!'

'Shut up, John!'

'Well, you tell us, Sarah! Are you a virgin or not?'

'I am,' said Sarah with a degree of pomposity. If she had not been drunk she would never have admitted to such a thing.

'Can we draw lots to see who can make you change your mind?'

'No,' said Sarah with magnificent dignity, 'there is not one among you who can make me change my mind. But if any of you could show me that romance was a better way, then I would have to give myself to him.' She saw in her mind the man who had approached her in The Regency restaurant, and there was no one in the lounge who came remotely close to his manners and dress. She knew that she was on safe ground.

'Oh – a *challenge*.'

The jug was going round for the umpteenth time.

'Yes,' said Sarah belligerently, 'if that's what you want.'

'And who makes the rules?' asked one of the men.

'I do,' replied Sarah suavely.

'But that's unfair; you could change them at any time!'

'Of course I can, it's my prerogative.'

'But we could never win at that rate.'

'If that is so, then clearly your efforts are pathetic.'

'So what sort of evening do you want us to invite you out on?'

'That's down to you, and if I don't like it then I'm not going out with you.'

The men had given to talking amongst themselves. Sarah glanced around and saw that Gerrie was looking as if she had reached the state where she was about to pass out. The party was beginning to break up and some of the men moved away to form a little clique by the bar. Sarah rose unsteadily and went to call for a taxi. Gerrie disappeared towards the toilets and Cathy went after her. Michael caught up with Sarah and seemed to be apologising for the events of the evening.

'Don't bother,' she said.

'But I feel responsible for you.'

'That's sweet of you,' she replied, 'but it's not quite good enough.'

'Then tell me what is good enough?'

'You'll regret what you've just said in the morning. What about your girlfriend Charlotte?'

'Yes, you're right,' he said, looking very chastened and subdued.

'I'll see you Monday morning.'
'Of course. Cheerio.'
'Has Gerrie been sick?' Sarah asked Cathy when the pair emerged from the toilet.
'Most of her stomach.'
'Let's hope she holds the rest in until the taxi gets us home.'
'I think she will.'
'Here's a cab now.'

The day after a heavy drinking session is never the best. It starts with a throbbing head and aching muscles, and the victim goes through a painful metamorphosis until finally he or she feels able to face the day.

Sarah was up first and she decided that she'd had less to drink than the other two. She sat in the kitchen trying to watch the small television that was there. But the sight of people gyrating madly to pulsating music was too much for her and she switched it off. Cathy joined her and Gerrie followed shortly after, saying that if she did not get up she would miss something.

'What a night!' complained Cathy.
'It was a bit over the top,' said Sarah.
'But they were a good laugh,' said Cathy.
'Who were?' asked Gerrie.
'Most of the fellows were bankers,' said Cathy, 'I gave my telephone number to one of them and I'm hoping he phones for a date.'
'Do you reckon he will? And what about Charles?' asked Sarah.
'What about him?'
'Sounds as if you're going to two-time him.'
'And what if I do! He two-times me!'
'What an excellent relationship you have!' said Sarah sarcastically.
'And what do you know about relationships?'
'Nothing, except that if I was dating someone, I would say no to the next person.'
'Perhaps I am saying no to the *previous* person!'
'I doubt that – you keep him hanging around like a little lapdog.'

'I don't!'

'You do,' said Gerrie, butting in, 'and you've said so before. You only keep him around for a bit of sex every now and again.'

'That's not true, and anyway you're a fine one to talk! You keep Ted hanging around for the same reason.'

'My head hurts!'

'I'm not surprised, given the way you were knocking back the booze.'

'Never mind about us, what about Miss Pure-as-the-driven-snow here?'

'Oh yes, Sarah, there are a lot of questions we want to ask you!'

'Well, if you honestly think you can remember last night then I'll try and answer them.'

'What was all this boasting about virginity?'

'I didn't think that I was boasting about it! You were the one claiming the money!'

'Only on your behalf, but then he never paid up.'

'Yes, the cheeky sod, he wanted you to prove it!'

'I had the distinct impression that had any money been handed over I would not have seen a penny of it.'

'That, Sarah, was because you were too slow.'

'But what I really want,' said Cathy, 'is an explanation from Sarah about why she had to challenge the whole damned lot of them.'

Sarah looked a sheepish and said, 'It was only a joke.'

'A *joke*! You had all of them going! It was disgusting; you wanted all those men for yourself.'

'Don't be so stupid – it was nothing of the sort. It seemed reasonable to put them all in their place at once.'

'You are so naïve! It did the complete opposite. To them it was a question of who gets past the winning post first and collects the freebie that's awaiting them.'

'So what! If you had worked it out you'd have done it.'

'You bet I would, but it's never happened to me.'

'Her virginity was her secret weapon, Cathy.'

'Well, it was their big joke for the evening and it'll be forgotten already.'

'That lot will be drinking to your virginity for the next month. And what if someone takes up this challenge?'

'Are they likely to?'

'Well, some of those guys are quite stupid. Who's to say what they might do!'

'And what if they did take up the challenge? It might be rather fun!'

'And that coming from a confirmed man-hater!'

'I don't hate men, I don't need a man, at least not in the way that you do.'

'But it's a bit sick just to wind all those men up simply for the pleasure of kicking at least one of them in the teeth.'

'Maybe it crossed my mind that one of them might actually be worth looking at.'

'Oh, and which one was that?'

'No, I mean in general terms. I haven't told you but I've met this really wonderful man... you know the sort, they make women go weak at the knees just looking at them.'

'I never thought to hear you say such things.'

'He's taking me out to dinner sometime. But he means nothing to me! It's just that he dresses wonderfully and his manners are divine.'

'You're smitten by him.'

'I suppose I could be, but not at the moment. He has a glaring fault.'

'I thought you were making out that he was Mr Perfect.'

'But I'm certain that he treats women as doormats.'

'How much of a doormat?'

'Totally! He's the type of man who loves the hunt. He's absolutely charming until he's got a woman into bed and then he tires of them.'

'So he'd make a rotten husband.'

'The worst, and you end up broken-hearted, broken spirited and utterly dejected.'

'So why are you attracted to him?'

'I'm not, but he asked me out and I couldn't refuse. And then he seems to have an entrée to society, and if nothing else I'd like a peep round the door.'

'No! The truth is, Sar, you know he's dangerous and suddenly you want to live dangerously.'

'I had thought of that and it worries me, I must admit. But he represents a marker! If I've met one man as good as he is why shouldn't I meet a better man?'

'I certainly disagree with your method of getting a man. I reckon it'll merely stir up all the odd bods.'

Sarah shrugged, determined to enjoy what was left of Sunday, and it was only the following morning at the office that Cathy was proved right.

Tom approached and Sarah was surprised to find him standing by her desk wanting to speak to her. She looked round to see where Michael was, but Tom had chosen his moment, for Michael had disappeared.

'I'm sorry to disturb you,' he said in his monotone voice, 'and I hope you don't mind my asking.'

'Asking what?'

'Well, I don't like being the messenger for other people and if you'd rather I went away then I will.'

'Just tell me, Tom, I won't bite your head off.'

'It's my brother, Jason; he was there the other night.'

'He was one of the bankers?'

'Yes, but he's older than them and doesn't see things quite their way.'

'But it was your brother who invited them all along.'

'Probably.'

'There's no probably about it! You told him, he told them and they all came along! Why? Because, I suspect, they wanted a change of venue!'

'Yes, I suppose so.'

'Well, if you've come to apologise then I accept your apology.'

'Thank you, but I've not come for that reason.'

'What have you come for, then?'

'Because Jason asked me to ask you if you would like to go out with him.'

'No, I don't think so, Tom. Last Friday evening is going to prove a big mistake in my life.'

He looked relieved and said, 'I thought you might say that. But at least I've done my bit! I'll get back to my desk.'

Sarah was by nature a generous person but his words made her feel very mean. 'Look, Tom, I'm sorry, I'm just not seeing anyone at the moment,' she said.

'Then you want to go out with him!' He brightened up and Sarah realised that he had misunderstood her.

'No, I don't want to go out with anyone. I don't want a man hanging round me.' Sarah spat the words out and knew that she was slowly digging herself into a hole.

'But he would like to.'

'No, I'm trying to be nice to him; I'm trying not to dent his ego.'

'Then you don't speak very plainly.'

'I just thought that saying no was too blunt and would have hurt him, so I've tried to say it in such a fashion that he can't take umbrage.'

Michael was approaching with two cups of coffee.

'Hello, Tom,' he said breezily, 'you don't often talk to Sarah, what's brought you over?'

'Nothing, I'm just going.'

'Strange bloke,' said Michael when Tom was out of earshot.

'Not really, he doesn't find it easy to talk to women.'

'Then why does he talk to Millie?'

'Because she makes him treat her like a sister.'

'That's true, I hadn't thought of that, but I can see it now. But what did he want?'

'His brother was there Friday night and he wants to take me out.'

'Just tell him you want to go to a very expensive restaurant and sit in the best seats at the theatre afterwards. That will scare him off!'

'But what if it doesn't? He then feels that he some sort of hold over me because he's paid!'

'Pay your way, then. Isn't that what female liberation is all about?'

'It may be, but the quickest thing is to avoid the situation in the first place and have nothing to do with him at all.'

'What if he's a nice bloke?'

'There won't come a day when there's a nice bloke for me! I

don't want a man, not for any reason. Now they're talking about me. It really is too bad! I'm made to feel guilty when I have done nothing.'

'You shouldn't feel guilty.'

'But I do, it seems to be part of being a woman. I'm not allowed a life of my own because some man is always upset when I say no.'

'But about Friday, you said buying the first drink was the cheapest round.'

'No, I didn't, you did, I merely agreed with what you said.'

'It cost me over forty quid.'

'Well don't get bitter about it. Was there any change from the round I bought?'

'What – you bought a round?'

'Yes, it was supposed to be with my flatmates so I only paid a third, but I haven't yet been given any of my money back.'

'Oh, sorry, it all went behind the bar.'

'So you're £40 out of pocket and I'm £50!'

'So everyone was drinking on us.'

'It looks like it. Listen, I've got some work that needs attending to.'

It was half an hour later that Ms Marchbank leant over Sarah's desk.

'There's a telephone call for you from your bank.'

'Oh right, thanks.' Sarah went to the phone.

'Miss Levine speaking.'

'Sarah, it's me, Bob Standish! Remember me from Friday night?'

'No, I couldn't see through my alcoholic haze very clearly.'

He laughed. 'Can I ask you out on a date?'

'No thanks, Bob, it's very kind of you to ask but I don't want to.'

'All I was going to suggest was that we met in a pub somewhere. The Mermaid?'

'I said *no*.'

'Oh, go on, Sarah, anywhere you want…'

'The City Tavern, seven o'clock, Friday evening.'

'What? It's a bit pricey there.'

'Take it or leave it.'

Sarah put the phone down and returned to her desk, conscious that Ms Marchbank had been listening. But she merely glared at Sarah, allowing her to escape to her desk.

'Who was that?' asked Michael.

'Bob from last Friday; he wants a date as well.'

'And?'

'I agreed.'

'What?'

'I agreed.'

'But why not agree to Tom's brother, then?'

'If he's anything like Tom then I don't want to know.'

'He might be the best bloke in the world.'

'Pigs might fly.'

Lunch was a cup of coffee and a sandwich brought in by Clemmie. The phone rang and it was for Sarah again.

'Hi, Sarah, it's me, Jeremy! I'm the one who told the best jokes last Friday evening.'

'Hello.'

'Hi, how are you?'

'Fine.'

'Look, I was wondering if you and I could get together sometime.'

'I don't know.'

'I know you're doubtful, but I'm darned good fun to be with and I'm sure that you won't be disappointed.'

'All right then! The City Tavern, seven o'clock, Friday evening.'

'Great, brilliant – I'll see you there then.'

Sarah returned to her sandwich.

'What on earth are you doing?' asked Michael.

'Sorting out some overzealous male egos.'

'I thought you felt guilty about such things.'

'I do, and I'm going to sort it all out in one go.'

'How do you work that out?'

'It's quite simple. No one has asked me out for a while and suddenly I'm invited out three times in one day. It seems reasonable to suppose that there will be others.'

'I see.'

'I hope you do, because I'm not going to explain it to you.'

Dinner with an Author

Monday evening Sarah was back at the office for the meal to which she been invited out.

Mr Deakin was there on his own waiting for her.

'I have a car waiting for us,' he said and ushered her out. A limousine was at the entrance, and Sarah noted that it had not been there two minutes before. Mr Deakin was left to lock the office up, and the chauffeur came round the car to open the rear door for her. She slipped in and slid across the seat. It was unnecessary as Mr Deakin got into the front passenger seat. Within minutes they were bowling down Piccadilly towards Hyde Park Corner where they rounded the Wellington Arch and proceeded on to Knightsbridge, turning left towards Sloane Square. Suddenly they stopped outside a restaurant. The chauffeur opened the door for Sarah, touching his forehead as he did so. The gesture pleased her. Mr Deakin led the way in and dutifully she followed. A word with a waiter and they were led to a table where a youngish man was seated. On their arrival he rose to his feet. Sarah correctly assumed that it was Jonathan French. He held out his hand first to Mr Deakin and then Sarah, who expected him to simply shake it; but instead he grasped her hand firmly and held it for what was far too long. At last she was released and invited to sit down.

Sarah could not make him out. He seemed rather effeminate and it was odd that he should pay so much attention to her. But he was stylishly dressed and oozed the sharp aroma of someone who used too much cologne. His countenance was florid and enhanced by his crop of blonde hair, which Sarah felt looked a bit silly.

He asked Mr Deakin some questions and she was dismayed that Mr Deakin set about answering them in a lengthy and most boring fashion. Jonathan was forced to listen, and she had the impression that it was far from what he wanted. She wished she had a better cleavage, for she could have flaunted it and both men would have been staring her. Ruefully, she decided that had she been Emma their conversation could never have taken place. But though she was bored by the conversation it gave her ample time to observe both men.

Jonathan, she found, did not improve on knowing. He suddenly pulled a cigarette case from his pocket making a great play of offering them around. Finding that he was with two non-smokers, he gave up and lit a cigarette. He seemed to suck in with great relish and then blew it out in vast clouds. She decided that they had come to this restaurant because it allowed smoking.

He went down in her estimation and she turned her attention to Mr Deakin. She had never had time to observe him to any great degree up until now, which was odd considering the length of time he had employed her. He had receding hair, accentuating his forehead. His face was pleasing and he looked very intelligent, but he never smiled and that annoyed her. She noticed for the first time that he wore a wedding ring on his left hand. It was nothing flashy, just a plain gold ring. She looked at his clothes and because he was close she could see that his shirt was less than perfect. His suit was shiny in certain places. If he had come out in his best then he was just a little bit shabby. She wondered what his wife was like and guessed that she was a fat woman who had become very boring. She would spend his money, putting him under perpetual stress and never leaving him with quite enough to cover all his requirements. She clearly took no pride in how her husband looked, and if she did the ironing she ought to be ashamed of her efforts. Obviously he worked long hours so that he wouldn't have to go home and make small talk to her. That left her wondering what kind of house he lived him. It would have to be a good district and it would be small and very pleasant but not too pretentious.

Their conversation had come to an end and Jonathan turned his attention to her. Mr Deakin sat and watched his efforts at dalliance with a bored expression on his face. Doubtless he had seen many girls chatted up in his time.

'Sarah, isn't it?'

The question hardly needed answering but she acknowledged that it was her Christian name.

'Has anyone ever told you that you have beautiful eyes?'

Sarah reddened slightly for she had not reckoned on such a question for his opening gambit. As to how she answered it she had no idea.

'And I love your smile, Sarah.'

He was becoming embarrassing, and her face deepened in its shade of red. She was thoroughly confused and hoped that Mr Deakin would resume his monologue on publishing.

'I hear,' Jonathan continued, 'that you are not married.'

'N-no,' she stammered. She could not cope with such direct questions.

'Should Miss Levine be married?' asked Mr Deakin.

'Not Miss Levine! No, you can only call her Sarah. But yes, she should be. Indeed every woman should be married.'

'Why?' asked Sarah.

'Because they and they alone can bring the next generation into being.'

'But what if a woman does not want her genes to go into the next generation?'

'No, it's as natural as a man wanting to put his into the future.'

'I don't see much of that happening in the present generation of men, all they seem to want is sex.'

'There's not much left for a man if you remove his sexual function.'

'Who says? And if you believe that, then it makes women no more than toys for the men.'

'Isn't that the desire of women?'

'What, to service their man?'

'Exactly.'

'What dream world have you dropped in from?'

'Only that of one who observes much and who feels therefore that he can pronounce on such matters.'

'Then I have news for you. The world you think everyone should live in is long gone and you ought to join your ancestors – namely, the dodo family!' Sarah felt she had been rather rude, but as she glanced at Mr Deakin and saw a slight smile on his lips, and felt relieved.

Jonathan turned to Mr Deakin.

'What is your opinion?'

'Oddly enough,' said Mr Deakin, 'mine is much like Sarah's. I see people getting married still but I think the emphasis has changed. The partnership today is on a more equal basis with the roles being less well defined. But I am not too enamoured of people cohabiting because I cannot see the benefits for either party, especially the woman. In other words the break-up favours the man.'

'And do you see the selection of partners on the basis of love?' asked Jonathan.

'Oh yes, and I think people should have much greater understanding of love.'

'But you still want to dominate the woman,' said Sarah.

'Not really, but I do feel that at the end of the day one of the partners in marriage must have the last say.'

'You do want to dominate women,' said Sarah disgustedly.

'No, I see the man having to love his wife. Now that emotion should in no way make him do something that his wife would hate. Therefore if a man loved his wife he would be doing the things that pleased her. If women want the power of the casting vote then they would have to do the things that would please their husband.'

'That's I why I don't approve of marriage,' said Sarah, 'if you don't have marriage then neither party has this casting vote.'

'But what have you got in its place?'

'A lot more people who are very happy.'

'No, I mean, what are the benefits to both sexes?'

'Well, they won't have this constant debilitating argument.'

'That's one improvement in life. Are there any more?'

The main course was put in front of them.

'Surely, though,' said Mr Deakin, 'if we throw out marriage with its benefits then whatever we replace it with should have greater benefits not just for a select few but for the vast majority of people and these benefits should not be illusory but real and tangible.'

'Can't things simply be left to evolution?' Sarah asked.

'You are becoming a politician, Sarah; that's not a good enough answer.'

She had the grace to blush, and Deakin added, 'I would go along with what you saying, Sarah, but I think we need to know what those benefits are.'

'But there is so much unhappiness in marriage.'

'The happy marriages far outweigh the unhappy,' said Jonathan, determined to get a word into the conversation.

'I would take issue on that point, Jonathan,' said Sarah. 'Have you ever considered what a woman's lot is like?'

'No.'

'She marries and becomes a man's unpaid servant, unpaid fancy piece, his babysitter and childminder. You name it and she becomes it. And all because of a bit of paper. Before this unpaid work, she has to give birth, which is about the most painful thing in the human world – and all for what? Just for the vanity of men!'

'I always thought that crucifixion was the most painful thing that could happen to a person. History abounds in horror stories. Being burned at the stake was rather gruesome as well, I dare say.'

'To some extent you are right, Sarah,' said Mr Deakin, 'but you forget one thing and that is that woman has needs as well as man. Leave aside the fact that giving birth is painful, it is also a beautiful experience and one that the vast majority of women want.'

'One that is denied men,' added Jonathan eagerly.

'Quite,' said Mr Deakin. 'And women have the same demand on love as men have. It is different because their monthly cycle changes, while men's desires are much more evenly based.'

'I didn't agree to come tonight to have my beliefs ground under by a couple of prejudiced men!'

'Let us be subjective rather than objective, as we have been,' said Jonathan, and he turned to Sarah. 'Have you ever been in love?'

'Only once that I know of, and it makes me embarrassed just to think of it.'

'Who was that then?'

'A student French teacher at school. And that is all I'm saying. Have you been in love?'

'I am always falling in love,' said Jonathan, as if it were some kind of malady.

'Then I doubt if that is love,' said Sarah archly. 'It sounds much more like lust. What about you, Mr Deakin?'

He looked graver than normal but said in very low tones, 'I have known real love once, but I doubt if I'll ever experience it again.'

'Can you tell us why that is?' said Sarah.

He pushed his empty plate away and picked up his wine glass, ignoring her question. Sarah could see that she had touched him on a very raw nerve and she concluded that he ought to divorce his wife yet being trapped, he was obviously unable to do anything about it.

Jonathan had no such perception and continued in a tactless fashion, 'Yes, why is that?'

Sarah saw a look of hurt cross Mr Deakin's face and she felt sorry for him. The waiter crossed and cleared their plates.

Suddenly Jonathan said, 'You must excuse me... call of nature.' He rose and headed towards the toilets close to the exit doors.

'Funny man,' said Sarah. 'Why did you agree to eat with him tonight.'

'I don't know. Perhaps he intrigued me, for he wanted to show me something.'

'Has he shown you yet?'

'No.'

'What is it that he wants to show you?'

'He didn't say.'

'Why am I here?'

'Because he asked me to bring you.'

'So I'm here for his benefit?'

'Apparently, but I'm glad you're here, I have enjoyed your company.'

Sarah was pleased with his compliment.

'He's been a long time in the loo,' she commented.

'Yes, and it's my belief he's no longer in there.'

'What do you mean?'

'I think that man who came out some minutes ago was him.'

'What man?'

'A man came out with a bald head and no glasses. He was fat and in his shirtsleeves.'

'Well, that wasn't him!'

'Of course it was! He was wearing a wig. So he stuffs it in his pocket along with the glasses. He takes his jacket off and rolls it up and hides it carefully under his shirt so that he looks like a fat man.'

'That was very observant of you! If he's gone, what are you going do?'

'Eat the dessert!'

'But he hasn't paid the bill.'

'He might have done, so we'll have the coffee before finding out.'

'But why would he do that?'

'He's that type of person, and presumably that was what he wanted to show me.'

'*Up*,' said Sarah.

'What?'

'Up, he wanted to show you up.'

'Yes, quite.'

Sarah thought he might have smiled at that, and said, 'But what about paying the bill? Are you going to suggest that I do the washing-up?'

'Don't worry about it! Enjoy the evening.'

'I find it very difficult when people do things like that.'

'But if he hasn't paid, when his book finally makes some money I'll deduct what he owes me for the meal from it.'

'Maybe he's writing another book and he did it to see what our reactions would be.'

'Possibly. When I see him again I'll give him a very garbled account of how the evening turned out. You do the same.'

'That's a good idea. It will wreck his book!'

'Unfortunately it won't, because he'll write it anyway and you'll have the embarrassment of seeing all your wrong answers in print.'

'I find it odd that I'm preparing his book for publication.'

'There are people who want others to think that they are strange and for some reason people like it. It is also something the press and television pick up on. If you are odd then they believe it to be synonymous with character.'

'You sound as if you would disagree.'

'I do, because I find it curious that someone would do something odd purely for the sake of doing it.'

'But that would mean that every action that you consider not normal is therefore odd.'

'Yes,' Mr Deakin spoke slowly. 'The question is, what is odd? We can both agree that that Jonathan's behaviour just now was odd.'

'Now you've put it like that, I haven't seen anything else that I would really think was odd. I can think of nothing I would consider odd.'

'Then Jonathan's behaviour must be considered as eccentric.'

'I suppose you do see people walking in an odd fashion.'

'Yes, but one has to be careful because they might be doing so because of some physical disability.'

'I'll give you an example of odd behaviour,' said Sarah suddenly, and told him about the small boy's hand in the plate-glass door, and his mother's reaction.

Mr Deakin thought about it and then said, 'It is odd, but would "not reasonable" describe it better?'

'Yes, it would. Her reaction was irrational.'

'It upset you.'

'Yes it did, for it seemed to be unjust.'

'So for the action to be odd, it must not be unreasonable, irrational or unjust.'

'But unexpected.'

'So odd behaviour must lie outside of normal behaviour, or what can be considered normal by anyone.'

'With the exception of a person who *wants* to be odd.'

'Yes.'

'Have you ever done anything odd?'

'No, Sarah, I don't think so. I think I've spent too much of my life being normal. Do you think I ought to cultivate some oddities?'

Sarah stared at her employer. She felt that the conversation had gone far enough and was reminded of their exchange a few days back.

Mr Deakin was thinking the same and said, 'I don't mind if

you say what is on your mind. You caught me off my guard the other day.'

'No, this has been a pleasant evening...'

'That's very diplomatic of you.'

Sarah sat with her elbows on the table and her hands supporting her chin. She was very relaxed and felt stimulated by the conversation. The meal had been excellent, the wine very good and the dessert had slid down easily, even though she had felt full before partaking of it. A cup of coffee was before her and the pleasantness of its aroma completed her mood of euphoria.

'So you don't think men and women should form attachments,' said Mr Deakin.

'No, I can't see the need for it.'

'Then what's the difference between your position and Jonathan's?'

'There's an ocean of difference.'

'I don't see that. I thought that you were both saying almost the same thing.'

'How's that?' asked Sarah.

'He sees women as a commodity to fall in and out of love with, and you see men and women not bothering to form attachments to each other. He fulfils his need by making love to any woman who presumably welcomes his advances. You presumably see men and women satisfying their needs in the same fashion.'

Sarah felt somewhat cornered and found that she had to admire the man for teasing her. She had not been made to think so deeply for a long time and she was worried that the wine had gone to her head.

'You say "needs",' she said. 'Aren't we simply answering to our animal instincts?'

'Can we exist without answering to our animal needs?'

'I see people rising above a purely animal existence.'

'And laying aside their basic needs?'

'If that is necessary, yes.'

'That suggests that sex has no place in the human psyche.'

'I think it's overrated.'

'Have you had a bad sexual experience, then?'

'No, I have not,' she flashed at him, expecting him to delve further into her sexuality.

'But you must admit that there is a place for the sexual experience.'

'I might for others but I don't see it for myself. I'd rather do without.'

'Is that the way you want to live your life?'

'I think so.'

'I notice an element of doubt in your voice.'

'Well, there has to be, I don't want to be dogmatic. If you want to hold a contrary view that is up to you; it shouldn't be up to me to change you.'

'You mean that if we were to argue then it would spoil our evening.'

'Yes,' she said softly and lifted her coffee cup to her lips. She felt annoyed for she had let it go cold. She glanced up at her employer but he was not looking at her; but feeling her eyes on him, he turned to her.

'It's about time we sorted out the bill.'

'Well, I'm sorry, but it's down to you.'

'Oh, quite.'

Mr Deakin called the waiter over and paid the bill. He rose and looked at Sarah. 'Can I give you a lift home?' he asked.

'If you would, please,' she said and was glad that he had asked, as she did not want to find her way home alone.

The limousine was waiting by the exit and Sarah guessed that Mr Deakin had arranged a time to be picked up, and all he had to do was to watch the clock.

The following evening she joined some of the members of the office in one of the nearby pubs. Tom and Millie were there, but Michael had an engagement with Charlotte. They sat at the bar which when they arrived was almost empty, it being so early in the evening. Sarah was not sure why she joined them for Millie disliked her, being envious of her looks; and as for Tom, she was not sure of his friendship. But she felt she had too many acquaintances and not enough close friends so that it seemed best to keep the pair of them sweet. Then, as the bar filled up, suddenly Tom's brother, Jason, appeared beside her. She flashed Tom a dirty look, for it had to be his doing, and there was little she could do about it except to be pleasant to him.

'I'm glad to see you again, Sarah,' he said.

'Are you?'

'Of course. You are a most beautiful woman.'

'I thank you for the compliment.'

'But you must hear it often.' He paused. 'I heard about last Friday.'

'Friday?'

'Jeremy told me. There were all these fellows in the City Tavern waiting for you. Took them over an hour to put it together that you had stood them all up!'

'It must have been a new experience for them all.'

'You broke some hearts there!'

'I very much doubt that.'

'But it sorts out the serious from the oversexed.'

'Oh, thanks! You really mean that there's a difference?'

'Of course there is.'

'And which category do you come in?'

'The more serious side.'

'Really?'

'Well,' he said, looking around the room to make sure that he was not being overheard by anyone, 'I'm a virgin, like yourself.'

'I'm so pleased to hear it,' said Sarah dryly.

'Well, there are a lot of men who are virgins.'

'Are you having me on?'

'No, I'm serious about this. A lot of men won't touch a woman because of sexually transmitted diseases.'

'So they try other men.'

'No, don't be stupid. Perhaps they missed when they were at school and everyone went and lost it just to find out what sex was like. Maybe they're not the most forthright of people so they never find a woman, but really they want someone who is like them.'

'Really.'

'Well, it's what you want, isn't it?'

'I might, but again I might not want to discuss it with anyone.'

'Fine, but I reckon that you would much prefer to go out with a bloke who is also a virgin.'

'And you're recommending yourself!'

'I feel nothing for you, so the question does not arise. However I will say this: it would be awful to love someone who lacked constancy.'

'Yes.'

'So you do think my way.'

'Probably.'

'I didn't think that I could talk you into a date. Tell you what, though, I think I could get you a job in the City at twice what Deakin pays you.'

'That's very kind of you. Doing what?'

'Something in banking.'

Bob Standish had seen them and was hurrying across the bar towards them.

'There you are, Sarah,' he said, oozing enthusiasm. Jason remained silent.

'Hello,' said Sarah without returning his bonhomie.

Bob reached her side and grasped her hand. Sarah tried to pull it away but his grip was stronger and she yielded for the sake of her dignity.

'What are you two talking about?'

'Jason here was offering me a job in the City.'

'Well, I could get you a job at far more than what Jason can. Mind you, if you had a boob job done then the sky's the limit.'

'So a woman's financial acumen is dependent on the size of her breasts?'

'No.'

'But that's what you said.'

'No, the guys in the City just like women with large ones.'

'It's a very sexist place, then.'

'But it's what life is all about.'

'It may be, in a man's world, but we no longer live in such a place.' Sarah climbed off the barstool. 'I don't care much for your conversation. I'm going home.'

As she made her way to the Underground Sarah felt upset, for she could not go out for drink now without feeling intimidated.

She spent much of the week worrying about the way she dressed. When Jonathan had left her and Deakin together it ceased to be a business meal. As the rest of the evening progressed she had felt that she was wrongly dressed. When they had left she would have liked Mr Deakin to be the complete gentleman and taken her arm, but she realised that from behind it did not look too good for people who were both wearing trousers to be so close. She couldn't decide why she felt that way and chided herself for not living up to her ideals. She was sorry for Mr Deakin, for it could be no fun to married to someone who did not return love and affection. Had she wanted to assure him by letting him take her arm? She did not know but she was determined to wear a skirt on Friday evening and not make the same mistake again. Then she worried that she was compromising her beliefs, and rebuked herself for being so eager to please. But many of the articles she read exhorted women to obtain their ends by any means, and if that meant wearing a skirt then for once she would.

Her wardrobe was deficient in skirts, and she knew she would have to buy one. But having made a purchase and tried it on again in the privacy of her bedroom, she was cross with herself, for it was only then that she realised the extent to which she was compromising her position. Why should she wear a skirt for the man she was meeting on Friday? She didn't even know him, he was a total stranger! What had there been about the man that had attracted her? He had been handsome, well dressed and had wonderful manners, and he was akin to her perfect Adonis coming upon her.

Really, she was dressing for herself, and that was because she wanted to feel good. But that was another argument she hated. No, she wanted to look good because the man she was meeting looked good, and to look much less than him, though she could never compete with his bow tie, would be to demean herself. She would sit there ashamed of herself and feeling at a distinct disadvantage.

Mr Deakin had dressed just slightly shabbily, bringing him down to her level and allowing her to converse on an equal footing. He had enjoyed the conversation as well as she had, though she had to admit that he had had the upper hand in the argument. Had she been arguing with Michael or Tom they would have retired defeated after a matter of minutes.

Friday evening came, and Sarah sat in the kitchen of the flat finishing her meal.

Cathy and Gerrie were getting ready to go out. They were hoping to eat later and had watched Sarah eat with some envy.

'Look, if you're hungry,' said Sarah, 'make yourself a sandwich.'

'But we've only got marmalade to spread on it.'

'Well, it's hardly my fault if you never bother to shop.'

'But haven't you got a date, Sar?'

'I might have.'

'Where are you going?'

'The City Tavern.'

'Don't know it.'

'In the City somewhere.'

'When have you got to be there?'

'Seven o'clock.'

'What are you doing, then? It's ten to seven now!'

'I may go, but on the other hand I may not.'

'What are you playing at, Sar? Who are you going out with?'

'Well let's see now. There's Bob, Jeremy, and Barry. Then on Wednesday Ronnie phoned, and yesterday Malcolm called.'

Cathy looked shocked.

'And James and a couple of others.'

'What are you talking about? You can only go out with one man at a time.'

'Really? I'm trying eight tonight!'

'Just what have you done, Sar?'

'Nothing much, but on Monday I was invited out three times in a couple of hours' time. The first time I refused, but by the second I decided that it was unlikely to be the last. I was right, and there was another call within an hour.'

'So you've sent them all on the same date!'

'Yes, if they've not put their heads together already, then they can do it in a rather expensive pub.'

'You are the limit! Gerrie, have you heard what Sar's just

done?' Gerrie was still in the bathroom and Cathy felt it was sufficiently important to go to the bathroom door and shout the story through it.

Cathy returned to the kitchen. 'You're determined to stay single.'

'I am.'

'And not have sex?'

'Yes, it doesn't bother me.'

'I couldn't live without a bloke.'

'No, you mean that you can't imagine what it would be like to live in a world with no men.'

'I certainly can, and I think it would be horrible! They may only have limited uses, but two of those are important.'

'Wasn't it only one?'

'No, they're just as important for money. Why should I spend my money if they're dumb enough to buy all the drinks?'

'I thought you went halves.'

'No way – not if he wants my favours!'

'That makes it sound like prostitution.'

'Don't be stupid, it's what makes the world go round.'

'You make men sound like real idiots.'

'Anyway, Sar, never mind my problems, what about yours? Suppose the man of your dreams turns up, what are you going to about it?'

'I don't dream about men.'

'Oh, come on, you must have thought about what your ideal man would look like.'

'I might have, but I haven't, and even if I had I wouldn't tell you.'

'OK, so let's assume that you have, then what if he suddenly materialises?'

'Knowing my luck he'd be married already.'

'So you admit then that you have looked out for a certain man.'

'Not at all. You have assumed that. I merely answered you with the obvious rider to remind you that I was not expecting too much.'

Gerrie came in. 'So you've set eight blokes up, have you?'

'Yes, of course she has.'

'I'd have gone out with any one of them – they're all loaded.'

'What makes you think they have money?'

'Stands to reason.'

'But most of them hated the thought of going to an expensive pub. If they've got money then they're heavily committed to something.'

'But that's no reason to make them all feel small.'

'I really hope someone comes and makes a fool of you, Sar.'

'I'm nearly twenty-nine and fought them off for fifteen years, give it about the same time and I'll be into the menopause and it won't be worth bothering about.'

'We're leaving you to it.'

With her flatmates gone, Sarah relaxed in front of the television. She wanted to put things out of mind and watch a satisfying programme but after a quick look through the schedules she became aware that there was nothing that was going to entertain her. Her thoughts took over as she tried to make sense out of a blank screen. She found that she was worried about her life. It was one thing to be casual and toss out the occasional stupid remark, and indeed most of the time one could forget about it. But it was fifteen or sixteen years ago that she'd had her first period, and at her present age she had about that length of time left in which she could conceive. It was a dreadful thought which did not go away merely because she could persuade herself that she liked being single. In many respects, if she was going to do anything about it, now was the right time. Gerrie was right that she had dumped eight men in a pub, and while it was a very clever thing to do, it was in fact the action of a very stupid and insensitive person! Any one of those men might have made a good husband, though none of them had recommended themselves to her in the pub. And she didn't want to put herself out for any of them. So what would her ideal beau look like?

The question was more easily put than answered. What then did she want from a husband? He had to be mentally stimulating; she could not bear a man who had only his hobbies to talk about. She wanted to talk about books, music, the theatre, opera and philosophical subjects, especially those which she had glimpsed at university but never managed to get to grips with. None of the men she had met gave her any sort of conversation. Or was she expecting too much? She just couldn't see herself sitting all evening in front of a mindless television set with a man who had hardly a word to say. At least on her own she could make her own entertainment, and if it was not good enough she had only herself to blame. Her real problem was that she had made no effort to understand what was involved in meeting a man, and as her age progressed she was at more and more of a disadvantage. Flirting with a few men would be the first step toward knowing whether or not she was in love with them and what being in love was about. If she then found a man she really loved she would be able to hang on to him, and if he loved her then there was nothing to worry about. It all led to another big life question, and that was whether or not she was in the right job.

She had been pleased to join Deakin's Publishing, as it seemed a good step up, but she had been left to fester in the same job for two years. There was no prospect of advancement, for that depended solely on Mr Deakin, and he seemed too stuck in his ways to understand the needs of his employees. True, he had taken her on at a higher salary than she had expected, but the euphoric feeling that that had engendered had left her.

She felt depressed, as she ought to be doing something and she did not know what it was. No, she hadn't a clue what she should be doing! She ought to be dressing up and presenting herself somewhere where she could meet the opposite sex. She should have gone with Cathy and Gerrie! But Gareth returned to haunt her and she knew that it was a reason why she did not go out. Still, she had another dinner date to look forward to on the following evening! Did she feel more or less uncertain about the man she had met in The Regency than she had done about socialising with her boss? She had no clear answers to anything.

Dinner with Danger

Having finished dressing she went to the kitchen for a drink. Cathy was ironing some blouses.

'Well, who's looking smart then!' she remarked. 'Who are you meeting then?'

'Just a person I met the other week and he invited me out for dinner.'

'This Mr Nearly Perfect?'

'Yes.'

'But you don't normally dress up, so what's the occasion?'

'There's no occasion; we're going to a swanky restaurant and I don't want to feel at a disadvantage.'

'Pity about your lack of cleavage. With your looks and legs you could have anyone dangling after you.'

'That's all you think about – men!'

'Well, there's not much else to think about, is there!'

Sarah took the train back to Green Park and walked through to The Regency. She noticed a few looks coming in her direction but she was too concerned about the evening to take any notice.

Clive Brunswick was waiting for her outside.

'Hallo, Sarah,' he said urbanely, 'and how are you?'

'Hallo,' she replied, and smiled. 'I'm very well and you?

'In excellent health, and very much looking forward to this evening.'

'Me too.'

'I thought it might be best if we went to my club.'

'Well, all right.' She was somewhat flummoxed, having expected to eat at The Regency. There was a chill in the air and a hint of rain. He led her out towards Green Park and Piccadilly.

'It's only a fifteen-minute walk,' he said, 'but we'll take a taxi.' He waved the next one down and a few minutes later they were outside a club in St James's Square. He ushered her in.

Inside the door was a lobby, and a uniformed doorman hovered ready to take their coats. A clone of the first stepped forward and led them into a lounge. Her host spoke to the man, who went away. Sarah was led to a large armchair where she sat down. Clive joined her, sitting in an adjacent chair.

'I've ordered dinner for us at eight, and we'll have the menu in a minute. I hope you don't mind but we have sherries coming.'

'Not at all,' she responded. It was his party, and he was there to entertain her.

'You like The Regency, do you?'

'Yes I do,' she replied, 'though I've only eaten there the once.'

'Do you normally eat on your own?'

'To tell you the truth I was very much out of sorts with my friends.'

'Your friends – or your acquaintances?'

'My friends.' Sarah sipped her sherry. The waiter appeared and placed menus before them.

Clive had already made up his mind, and pointed out to her what he was going to have.

'The chef excels himself with his *boeuf en croûte*.'

'Then I ought not to refuse it.'

'Can I suggest the asparagus soup, followed by the anchovies?'

Sarah looked down the list and felt she was not in a position to do anything other than agree.

'I'm going to suggest to start with a Château Magence. It's a white Bordeaux and is light and crispy. It's a favourite of mine and I'm positive that you'll love it.'

Wines were a subject that went straight over Sarah's head. Anywhere else but in this man's presence to hear a wine called crispy would have brought her out in peals of laughter but she dutifully bit her lip. This was, after all, a lesson in etiquette! She looked at Clive and saw him smiling. She was glad he was pleased and she was in harmony with his coming here. The Regency was her find and she wanted to keep it to herself as a place where she could escape to when she wanted. But she was slightly miffed with Clive's attitude, for so far she had had no choice in anything and she felt that anyone who invited her out should not be recommending the fare in tones that suggested it was a social solecism to exercise free will. But there was also the hint that other things on the menu might be a disaster. They talked for a while until the waiter appeared to say that their meal was ready and Sarah put her thoughts into abeyance.

Clive was an excellent host and a charming man to be with, and in her general state of euphoria, Sarah entered the dining room without noticing the stares of the surrounding diners.

They ate in silence to begin but finally Clive spoke. 'Do you realise that you are perhaps the most beautiful creature that I have ever had the pleasure of dining with.'

Sarah smiled wryly at his words. She liked the compliment and was happy to wallow around in it, but she could not dismiss the thought that Clive must therefore dine with an awful lot of ugly women. She considered the word 'beautiful' as being a gross exaggeration and she blushed just to think of her small breasts, conscious that her blouse must reveal her lack of cleavage.

'Did you never consider modelling as a career?'

'No,' replied Sarah, keeping her eyes on her food.

'I saw you the other week in your trouser suit, and it really did not flatter you.'

Sarah remained silent. She had worn a skirt because she wanted to feel good, not to gain praise from her companion, and it left her feeling a bit of a hypocrite.

'For you to have dressed specially for me, has made me the happiest of men.'

'I have only wanted to imitate what I saw.' It was meant as a statement of fact not a compliment.

'You do me the greatest of honours,' he said suavely.

Sarah was angry with herself feeling that she had been caught off guard, but she was aware that, like Mr Deakin, here was a man with whom she could bandy words; though she felt that he had so far had the better of the exchange.

'Why have you invited me to dine with you?'

'You have no need to ask, because from my viewpoint no explanation needs to be given.'

'That's not really an answer,' said Sarah.

'My dear, you really cannot expect me to own up to being one whose tongue is hanging out.'

'What I mean is, that when you asked me at The Regency,

there was another reason for it.'

'How could there be, when I was immediately and overwhelmingly smitten?'

'I just had the feeling that you had been sent over to meet me.'

'That my friend and I had talked about you was obvious, but the conversation was only in the context of your beauty.'

'You must have spoken about other things.'

'Not in the presence of one whose attraction is impossible to resist. Tell me about yourself.'

'I didn't think there was much to tell as you seem to know my history.'

'Forgive me for appearing familiar, but I've only had the pleasure of seeing the outward woman; I also desire to meet the inward person.'

His tone was making her more wary of revealing her true feelings about anything. It removed the sharpness of her rapier, giving him the upper hand; she was loath to tell him anything of herself.

'Are you happy with your job?' he asked suddenly.

'Yes,' she managed.

'You don't see yourself at Deakin's in, say, five years' time.'

'No.'

'Where do you see yourself then?'

'I'm not sure; can anyone be certain when they are on a career path?'

'There are uncertainties, of course, but we all have a picture of our future.'

Sarah was aware that her wine glass was being refilled.

'I'm just not sure that I should share such profound thoughts with you.'

'Then let me guess, and you can tell me if I am right or not.'

Sarah looked at him and he took that as her agreement to his suggestion.

'From what I was told your work is not onerous and I think it bores you.' He was looking at her face, from which he seemed to draw inspiration.

'Your face says that that it is true. You have wanted to work in publishing since leaving school, or maybe later when you left university. Either way you did not find yourself by accident in publishing; it was something you had determined on.'

Sarah could only finish the food in front of her. Clive was holding up his wine glass and looking at the distorted image of her that he could see through it.

'Yes,' he said, 'you have got this far, but it is fast becoming a dead end. You know that the time is coming when you must move on.'

Sarah hated people who could see through her so easily but she contented herself with the thought that what he said could have been said about almost anyone in employment.

'That is the question. Deakin is not an option; he would never take on a partner.'

'What makes you say that?'

'My understanding of him is that he is a very difficult man to work alongside. That being so, he would never shed a tear if you were to move on.'

'I couldn't see him indulging in any emotion.'

'No, he's a person who thinks nothing of others! Believe me, behind the facade he is egotistical.'

Sarah wished she had said nothing about Mr Deakin. It was disloyal to him, since he was her employer, and having said what she had about his feelings she knew that she had no idea what his emotional state actually was.

'So you never thought of a career in acting.'

'Oh, no! Wouldn't it have been awful to stand in a line up at an audition and be one of the many who would be rejected?' She wanted a change of subject.

'But think of the triumph if you were the one selected.'

'But I could not see myself as that person. Any girl who gets picked has always got that little something that no one else seems to have.'

'Absolutely, and that is why so many go. They hope that they have the something. But surely you have it.'

'If I have, then I never put it to the test.'

'But with you, surely whatever you turned your hand to you'd not be disappointed.'

'Meaning that I have only to turn up to get a job or position...?'

'If it required nothing more than your presence, then yes! And should they want more they would be doubly impressed!'

It occurred to Sarah that woman must be silly creatures to be taken in by such compliments, for it was all tosh. When men had won their women they installed them at the kitchen sink!

The compliments she had received suggested that never in a month of Sundays was that her destiny, yet without doubt any woman would be hard-pressed to avoid reality. Perhaps she should have been a film star.

'Would you like a dessert?'

'What are you having?'

'I would prefer a coffee and the cheese board.'

'Then let's have that,' said Sarah, knowing that she would have liked to order a dessert, but felt so full that she would look stupid leaving it mostly untouched.

The cheese board arrived with the coffee, together with two glasses of brandy. It was not a drink that Sarah cared much about, and the sight of it reminded her of how much she had drunk that evening already. Between them, they had drunk a bottle of white wine before the main course, and with that course Clive had ordered another Bordeaux, and they had managed to drink that as well. She was not aware that he had drunk more than her and now she was worried about getting home.

'Let's sum up your character,' said Clive.

'If you must,' said Sarah.

'Well, first of all, you're a very self-contained person, as you don't like talking about yourself.'

Sarah nodded.

'You have the normal traits of women, for you make yourself agreeable and you like compliments.'

Sarah nodded for it was not the moment to accuse him of exaggeration.

'You hold opinions which you do not necessarily agree with.'

Sarah smiled wanly.

'You are ambitious – very ambitious.'

Her smile increased.

'You hate being a woman.'

This remark wiped the smile from Sarah's face, for she was

certain that she had never mentioned her sexuality. It was Clive's turn to look very pleased, and Sarah realised that he had been trawling around for something to say on the matter. She regretted allowing her emotions to give her away.

'You have very little time for other women.'

But Sarah had forced her face into an unflinching mask.

'Now that I've given you a résumé of your character, I invite you to do the same for me.'

It was an invitation she would not normally have refused, but she felt that Clive had been toying with her all evening and she feared that he was working up to his coup de grâce. He had won the bout hands down, and that irked her. But she could see much of his character, for he was clearly a ladies' man who thought nothing about bedding them and she was determined not to be his next victim. He probably made some of his living out of them. The rest of his living he surely made from the gaming tables, and he probably didn't play games of chance; it was much more likely he played bridge or whist for so many pounds a point. They would be games from which he would invariably rise the winner. He could hold his own in any company and treated most people very cynically. But undoubtedly his Achilles heel was his pride!

'So, Sarah, having had a few moments to compose yourself, what is your estimation of my character?'

'I think you are very proud,' she said, 'and that it is such a big topic that we'll have to leave it for another evening.'

She watched his face and was sure that for a split second the urbane smile in his eyes had given way to a flash of anger.

'But my dear, you cannot leave me in suspense,' he purred.

'Why not? Does my sex usually let you have your own way? Now, I'd like to go home – it's gone eleven o'clock.'

His good manners made him jump up and call a waiter to get her a taxi.

Ten minutes later she was heading home alone with her thoughts and a certain feeling of relief, which even the cost of the cab fare to Earlsfield failed to dent.

Neither Cathy nor Gerrie were in, to Sarah's surprise, but it allowed her to relax without an inquisition. But her pleasure was short-lived, as Cathy arrived home almost as soon as she had sat down on the sofa. Gerrie was not far behind.

'Thanks for not locking us out,' said Cathy dryly.

'You're home early.'

'Yes, the club was not up to much and the boys decided to go bowling.'

'Why didn't you go along?'

'Um, because we didn't want to, and they didn't seem to want us to go with them.'

'Who was with them?'

'Benny and Ray.'

'Do I know them?'

'You might, they're all part of the pub's football team.'

'Oh, it's a bonding session, then.'

'They only thing they bond with is beer.'

'Anyway, I don't think bowling with them would be much point as they're all a bit over the top. But how did your evening go?'

'Fine.'

'Where did you go, then?'

'A club in St James's.'

'What sort of club?'

'A gentlemen's club.'

'I thought they had got rid of them.'

'Well, ex-gentlemen's club.'

'Not the kind where they do lap dancing?'

'Oh no, it was all very genteel.'

'What's the fellow like?'

'He's terribly handsome. Dresses appallingly well! And has the most wonderful manners.'

'What do you see in him?'

'Nothing, actually. I accepted his invitation out of curiosity and the desire to see what the nobs do.'

'I bet he wasn't really like that.'

'No, he wasn't. He was trying to talk me into bed with him.'

Cathy laughed. 'Fat chance with you!'

'Why do you say that?'

'Oh, come off it! After the way you treated us with Gareth.'

'It might just happen one day that I like a man so much that I'd let him.'

'Well, I'm off to bed,' said Cathy.

'Me too,' agreed Sarah.

The Ticket

The envelope that was lying on the breakfast table was addressed to her: Miss S Levine, 25 Cardinal Mansions, Carnford Road, Earlsfield, SW19; and even with an incomplete postcode, it was clearly meant for her. Maybe, though, it was the early hour of the morning that caused her to stare at it long and hard, not because the writing was difficult to read or the envelope itself was something out of the ordinary, but because her mind and body were functioning with minimal efficiency. And then she was remiss in not responding to the alarm clock. It wasn't so much actual tiredness but the alcoholic haze that she was peering through, and she wished that she hadn't overindulged the previous evening. Why did she allow her friends to take her out on a Sunday night? What on earth did she drink to feel like she did? It would be just like Cathy to toss a vodka into her cocktail. But being a Monday morning, one had one's responsibilities, and that meant being in the office by nine o'clock.

The letter stared up at her from the kitchen table, demanding to be opened. Sarah picked it up, methodically staring at the stamp showing the queen's head. It piqued her curiosity, for usually her mail was pre-franked and contained bills or advertising literature. Normally such letters contained very little, and she found it more satisfying to guess the latest arrival's origin before opening it. Such thoughts did at last penetrate her mind, and she tried to slit the envelope open with her fingernails. But the envelope seemed to have more resistance than Sarah had bargained for, and mindful of her manicure, she picked up the knife which a few minutes ago she had used to spread the butter and marmalade on a piece of toast. She inserted the knife behind the flap. With a practised movement of her wrist she cut along the entire length of the envelope, leaving her feeling pleased with the neatness of her effort.

Again, she spent some minutes staring at the envelope. Her

mind had slipped into gear, shaking off the lethargy and inflaming her sense of curiosity, and she inserted her fingers into the envelope, withdrawing the paper that was within. She had no expectation of what was in the envelope and could only stare at what was before her with a look of total astonishment. She fingered through the contents, which were definitely meant for her as her name was on the letter, but there was no mention of who the sender was.

Cathy had arrived in the kitchen. It was strange that in forty-five minutes they had to be at the station to catch the 8.14, yet Cathy slopped about in her dressing gown pouring out a cup of tea with one hand and bashing the toaster with the other. Her hair was a disaster, the remnants of yesterday's make-up needed to be washed away, and if she had any clean clothes even Cathy herself would be surprised. Yet it was her way every morning, and still they would manage to catch the 8.14.

'Why doesn't this toaster work?' she complained, hitting it again. 'My mother told me that when she first got married they were given *three* toasters!'

She glanced round at Sarah and saw that she was going to get no response.

'I just think that she could have kept one and given it to us.'

Gerrie was watching from the doorway. 'I thought the toaster was one of your mother's and that was why it didn't work!'

'No, it isn't. We inherited it from somewhere and it's got old.'

'Why don't you buy another?'

'Because I shouldn't have to!'

'Anyway, what's up with Sarah? She looks like she's been turned to stone.'

Sarah glanced up and tried to smile but realised that it was wasted gesture as her facial muscles seemed to respond in the wrong order.

'I can tell you had a bad night,' said Gerrie, who had a loud voice. It was not that she turned it up, it was her natural way of speaking, and for anyone with a hangover it brought a grimace to one's face. 'You look as if you've seen a ghost.'

Sarah shook her head and said, 'What do you make of that?'

'What's that?' asked Cathy, turning away from the toaster.

But Gerrie had the envelope and pieces of paper and was already turning them over. Cathy sat down at the table with her back to the toaster, visibly pouting that she had once again been left out, and was only satisfied when Gerrie pushed the papers over to her. Had she not done so at that moment it was likely that Cathy would have snatched them from her.

With the practised eye of a seeming connoisseur she looked through them.

'It's only an airline ticket,' she said baldly, and slapped the pieces of paper down on the table.

'To Paris,' interjected Gerrie, keeping her place in the intelligence stakes, 'and it's the weekend after next.'

'So when did you decide to go there, Sarah?' asked Cathy. 'It's only two weeks later that we're going on holiday!'

'I haven't decided to go.'

'So why buy the tickets?'

'I didn't buy them.'

'Well, tickets don't just fall out of thin air, do they? Who are you going with?'

'You've completely missed the point,' replied Sarah, 'I didn't order any tickets to Paris – or anywhere else, for that matter.'

'Then they did fly in from nowhere. Perhaps they're not for you...'

'But the letter is addressed to me, and the tickets are in my name.'

'Come on, tell us who you're going with!'

'Yes, *do*,' said Gerrie, and, with masterly understatement, added, 'you can trust us to keep a secret.'

'I'd never trust you with a secret.'

'Absolutely,' said Cathy, 'it would be all round the neighbourhood within a day.'

'And scrawled on every wall in the locality!'

'So you've got a secret admirer then!'

'Really, be sensible, Gerrie,' complained Sarah. 'It's news to me.'

'Yes,' agreed Gerrie, 'knowing you, it would be news to you!'

'Why do you always have to speak in those tones about my interest in the opposite sex?'

'Because you don't have an interest in them!'

'Why does life always come down to thinking about what men want from us?'

'Because we enjoy them,' said Cathy, 'and you don't.'

'Don't wander from the point,' said Sarah. 'Someone has sent me a return airline ticket, departing two o'clock Friday afternoon and returning eight o'clock Monday morning.'

'That's very kind of them,' said Gerrie. 'I wish someone would do that for me.'

'Yes, but don't you see, he's left no note or anything as to who he is.'

'Your toast is burning,' said Gerrie.

Cathy jumped to her feet, swearing and cussing the toaster that now refused to release the burnt offering. Picking the toaster up, she shook it violently upside down, causing a mass of burning bread crumbs to cascade over the dresser and floor. Seeing that the toast had refused to budge, she grabbed a knife and looked as if she was about to thrust it inside and lever the toast out. Sarah moved to the plug and switched the appliance off.

'You really do the most stupid of things,' she admonished Cathy.

Gerrie was laughing and managed to splutter that Cathy had always wanted to be a bright spark. The smouldering toast suddenly freed itself and jumped onto the floor. It was not obvious why, with the toast on the floor, Cathy should look at the clock on the windowsill.

'Damn!' she exclaimed. 'We've only got twenty minutes to catch the train!' She then fled the room.

'What's new?' said Gerrie dryly. 'She's late every morning.'

'Yes, she is disgusting. She'll just spray her whole body with deodorant and throw yesterday's clothes on.'

'You've noticed as well.'

'Of course I have! I go with her on the train every day. I get the full benefit as I have to sit with her.'

'Personally I think she does it for other reasons.'

Sarah gave Gerrie a withering look and went to her bedroom to finish getting ready for the day ahead.

She thought no more of the letter until the mid-morning

coffee break, when the office emptied to allow the smokers some respite on the pavement below. At the same time she was struck more by the thought that there had been nothing to remind her of it. But it was most likely because of Cathy, for they were late for the train and had had the dubious pleasure of seeing it pull into the station from the street below. With the best will in the world they had been unable to mount the steps from the pavement to the platform before the sliding doors had closed with a plonk. Gasping at the top, they had endured the chagrin of watching their train pull slowly out of the station.

It was not in Sarah's character to blame others, even when their shortcomings were so obvious. She shouldn't have waited for Cathy that morning! When the next train arrived, only six minutes later, Cathy spent the rest of the journey to Waterloo moaning about her deodorant since her favourite had run out just when she had finished one side of her body and one leg. Naturally, she could not think why she had done that, when she knew it was low. Then it was the question of finding a new one and she had been unable to find another and had resorted to using Charles's, which he had thoughtfully left behind at the weekend. Only later did she realise that she must smell peculiar, with one half of her smelling sweetly of female deodorant while the other half smelt of a musky masculine odour! It was, she opined, akin to forgetting to put one's knickers on.

Sarah, being far more particular, had been unable to see the connection and was left wondering if her flatmate had in fact forgotten her underwear. It would have been unusual, but in Cathy's case not unknown. At Clapham Junction she had turned her attention to the mobile phone users and spent the rest of the journey berating the people for their lack of manners. Sarah could have passed that by, had not Cathy, in full swing, rather obviously – though silently – let off wind, and her embarrassment was compounded by a number of the male occupants noticing and letting their faces develop into broad grins. Cathy had continued as if nothing was amiss and Sarah's face had gone bright red... Waterloo brought relief, as they piled off and headed towards the Underground. At Oxford Circus she split with Cathy, who continued to Baker Street.

Despite the disaster of the beginning of the day, the thoughts of her letter forced their way into Sarah's consciousness. She had not wanted to think about the tickets but she knew that they gave her a certain amount of pleasure. For the letter had come to her and no one else. The return ticket to Paris was for her and, as stated on the ticket it was not transferable, she could not give them away even if she wanted to. Fate it seemed had selected her from millions of other women. It was like winning the lottery or winning a talent competition. Either way, it made one feel unique, which meant that one was precious, and it did a lot for Sarah's self-esteem to feel that she was for once in that category of persons on whom there was a greatly enhanced value.

Sarah could now see herself as someone who had been lifted out of the mundane and appointed to a great office in life. Her halo would shine out as she walked down the street and people would stop and acknowledge her. Mothers would pause and tell their children that they must look at her, for she was a shining example, and that was what they too should strive to achieve. She hoped that men would perceive her on a higher plane than a purely sexual level, and that fathers would show their sons how she had the characteristics of womanhood that men would do well to desire in their future wives.

For fully ten minutes she sat at her desk in vain contemplation until Michael came back into the office. He gave her a look and for an instant caught her eye, but Sarah looked away, her embarrassment palpable. His look had indicated that in that short space of time he had completely read her thoughts and seen through her vanity. She felt enormous shame at having been caught out and pursued her work with increased vigour in the hope that he would not see her blushes.

However, he noisily pulled out his chair and sat down. Then he opened a drawer and scrabbled around for some time until he breathed an audible sigh of relief. Then, pushing his chair back, he applied the toothpick that he had been searching for to his teeth. It wasn't an action that could be ignored. Michael had opened his mouth wide and was contorting his lips like a gargoyle as he scraped away. It became clear to Sarah that his look on entering the room had nothing to do with her thoughts. He had merely been surprised that she had spent the whole coffee break sitting at her desk.

It being Monday morning, they were waiting to be called in for the weekly progress meeting. She had not thought over the conversation she had had with Clive Brunswick, as Sunday had been busy, for it was necessary to clean the flat and wash clothes for the coming week. That had taken the best part of the day, and in the evening Cathy and Gerrie had insisted on watching a long video in the evening, leaving her little time to think.

She had enjoyed the meal and the conversation with Clive. She had found his company agreeable but he had said some things that irked her. Was she someone who, given the choice, would rather have been a man? It seemed ironic that for the first time in many years she had put herself out to look and act as an attractive woman, and yet she'd been accused of being a man dressed as a woman.

Did she exude all the spirit of a man? She had never thought about it and had accepted her lot as a woman, despite men being better plumbed and not having the aggravation of monthly periods. No, she saw men and women on an equal footing in life, without one of the sexes prevailing over the other. If men today felt that they were a threatened species then they had only themselves to blame. For too long they had ruled the roost at the expense of women, and if the latter now felt that they predominated then it was too bad. Women should not bow down to a fragile male ego merely so that men might feel better about themselves.

And what an ego Clive had! That he should imagine that all he had to do was to wine and dine a woman to obtain the right to bed them was surely taking chauvinism to the extreme. He deserved to be put down and have his ego torn to shreds. In fact, he would annoy many men too, as he would make them look pathetic and sexually inadequate. But he certainly had pulling power! And she was thankful her feminist attitude was so deeply entrenched that she was immune. How would a woman feel after being seduced by a man when she awoke the following morning? Would the aftermath be satisfying, or would it leave a residue of guilt? Would she feel used by him? And how about being just another notch on his staff?

Sarah felt pleased with her final remark to Clive, for she felt he had won every round but the last! It was the last comment that would grate with him, and best of all it was his pride that she had wounded. Would he want a rematch? She laughed inwardly with pleasure at the thought.

Then everyone was called to the meeting and they all trooped into Mr Deakin's office, where a line of chairs had been placed facing his desk. Ms Marchbank was last in, as if she needed to herd them, and she took her seat with a rustling that everyone heard in the silence. Mr Deakin got the meeting under way. Sarah watched him, trying to compare him to the picture that Clive had put over to her.

He was shrewd behind his stern countenance. The eyes that appeared so indolent took in the whole room. Yes, his bearing was indolent and suggested that he could be easily fooled, but she doubted that. She was sure that it was a front put up by him to protect himself. Possibly he was bored and needed stimulating. A quick look round the persons sitting around her and she could see no one with the mental capacity to take him on. She thought of the meal she had had with him and how he had twisted her words round so that her attitude appeared to be no different to that of the foppish Jonathan French.

Michael was asked first for his report, followed by Tom. Millie gave hers, offering the opinion that if the author whose book she was working on did not reply to her request then she was likely to get behind. Mr Deakin made notes. Ms Marchbank brought up a number of subjects related to the working of the office. There were too many incoming phone calls and there needed to be some sort of curb on them. Sarah noted that a number of persons shuffled their feet as she spoke. Mr Deakin agreed and suggested that people who phoned in should be told that the company could only accept emergency calls in working hours.

'Sarah has not given a report,' said Millie pettishly.

'No,' said Mr Deakin, 'she's just finished preparing a book and will shortly be starting the next.'

'But that's not fair; she should have given a report.'

'I am the arbiter of fairness,' said Mr Deakin, 'and should you finish your project on a Friday and be awaiting your next on the Monday morning an exemption may be extended you. Does anybody else have anything to say?' His tone made it clear that he expected none. They all shuffled out.

Michael spoke to Sarah when they arrived back at their desks.

'Those two seemed to have ganged up against you.'

'They probably think that you and I are just as thick together as they are.'

'It's a pity, since we all ought to work together.'

'I agree, we don't do ourselves any favours.'

'I was sure that Tom was going to bring up the question of not having the meetings. I wanted to see Deakin's face when he suggested it.'

'He didn't dare.'

'No, he hasn't the heart to take Deakin on; he's just one of those people who says it all behind his back.'

'Even if he did have the nerve, he wouldn't get anywhere.'

'I think Millie was pushing him.'

'She is a bit sly, and it's just the kind of thing she would do.'

'Absolutely! "Sarah has not given a report, it's not fair" – that was a bit pathetic.'

'It was, but that's Millie. You can bet that as a little girl she made the boys do naughty things, and probably got some sort of delight in seeing them punished.'

'How can you remain so calm with such awkward people around?'

'Well, I'm not going to get wound up by her; I wouldn't want to give her the satisfaction.'

Ms Marchbank was on the prowl. Michael sat down, but Sarah remained standing. After a few seconds she walked to the door and without giving Ms Marchbank another look went along the landing to Mr Deakin's office. She knocked, and he called to enter.

Sarah went in and closed the door behind her.

'What is it, Sarah?' he asked, barely looking up at her.

'I want to ask you something that's been worrying me.'

'Does it concern me or yourself?'

'It does not concern you, except that I want your opinion.'

'Sit down and tell me.'

'On Saturday night I was having dinner with someone and he said that I wanted to be a man. When I had dinner with you did you get that impression?'

He was looking at her. 'Why do you ask me?'

'Because I thought that I might get a truthful answer from you.'

'To be honest with you, I did not get that impression. Clearly you want to exist in a man's world as an equal, but I thought you were rather proud of being a woman.'

'Thank you,' she said. 'Do you know I even did him the honour of wearing a skirt.'

Mr Deakin blinked at her. 'Who was this man?' he asked gently.

'Clive, Clive Brunswick. Do you know him?'

'I know of him. Prides himself on never having done a day's proper work in his life. Where did you meet him?'

'In The Regency.'

'What were you doing there?'

'It's a long story, but I was depressed and I cheered myself up with an expensive meal. He came across just as I was leaving and invited me out for a meal.'

'I see… and why did you dress up for him?'

'Because I felt silly when I was with you in a trouser suit, and I did not want to do it again.'

'And I suppose you went to The Regency for this dinner?'

'No, I went to his club. I thought we were going to The Regency because that was where we met.'

Mr Deakin nodded. 'I doubt if he could afford The Regency. When he goes there you can be sure that the other person pays the bill.'

'It crossed my mind that that might be the case.'

'Can I give you some advice?'

'What is it?'

'That you don't make a friend of him. He will do you no favours and at the end of the day you will get hurt.'

He was looking down at the papers on his desk and made it clear that the conversation was at an end. She wondered about asking him for his opinion of her tickets to Paris.

'Thank you,' she said and rose from the chair. She thought he was about to say something but he remained silent and Sarah returned to her desk.

It was two days later when Sarah met Clive again. He was walking slowly along Piccadilly like someone who was just watching the world go by, but she was certain that he was deliberately waiting for her.

'When may I have the honour of taking you to dinner again?' he asked.

'I don't know,' she replied.

'You don't know because you feel you should refuse me, or you don't know because you haven't thought about it?'

'Both,' she responded, since it was the shortest answer she could think of.

'Why are you so reticent?'

'I didn't think I was.'

'You are the expressing the level of enthusiasm towards me of someone who has been warned against me.'

Sarah was unable to hide her blushes and cursed herself for being so honest.

'That may be so, but I might not necessarily agree with that person. I am quite busy at the moment and I had no plans in my mind.'

'Then may I take it that I might once again have the pleasure of dining with you? But better still, I have a friend who is also desirous of making your acquaintance.'

His words pleased her, as she did not want to have a meal with him on his own again. She had beaten him once and she doubted if it were possible to do it again, for he was well versed in toying with people's emotions. He would hardly make the same mistake again and be caught off his guard. Perhaps he had underestimated her. She had been determined not to be charmed by his good looks into making another arrangement, but that he wanted her to meet someone changed the complexion of his invitation. Against her better judgement she decided to make another arrangement.

'There's nothing I can do for at least a fortnight, and soon after I'm going on holiday.'

'Let us agree, then, on Wednesday in two weeks, before you leave on your holidays.'

She felt helpless under his gaze and found herself agreeing to his proposal.

'Until then,' he said, turning away and leaving her to her own thoughts.

Having had the tickets for Paris for over a week, Sarah felt that she had to make a decision on whether or not she used it. If she used them she ought to ask for the time off, since two weeks later she was going on her summer break for a fortnight.

She approached Ms Marchbank who had the authority to give her limited time off.

'This is most unusual, Sarah. If it was the dentist I would agree but to go gallivanting off to Paris for a weekend – I really don't think that it is possible.'

'Could you ask Mr Deakin for me?'

'I certainly could not; it is something you must ask yourself of him.'

'All right then.'

Sarah crossed the landing and knocked on Mr Deakin's office door. She heard him grunt and entered the office.

'Yes, Sarah what can I do for you?'

'I'd like to ask something of you.'

'Then take a seat.'

Sarah sat down. 'It's difficult to know where to start.'

'At the beginning?'

'Yes. Last Monday I received a letter and when I opened it, it contained a return airline ticket to Paris.'

'Yes.'

'Well there was nothing in it to say who sent it.'

'Didn't it come from a travel agent?'

'No, you don't understand. I mean there was nothing there to say who had bought the ticket from the travel agent. It is paid for and everything, but I had nothing to do with the purchase of it.'

'I'm still not with you.'

'I have an airline ticket to Paris which I know nothing about. It has been paid for and is non-transferable and must be used on the days they are made out for.'

'Which days?'

'Fly out this Friday at two o'clock return Monday morning at eight o'clock.'

'So someone is taking you off for the weekend.'

'It would seem that way, but I don't know who.'

'Then I should not bother to go.'

'Seems a shame to waste it.'

'Not really. What happens when you arrive there? Has any accommodation been arranged?'

'Not that I'm aware of. It's just the travel ticket.'

'Then I'd definitely throw it away.'

'The reason I would like to go is that it seems a bit of an adventure… and I lead such a drab life.'

'Well, I have given you my advice and I doubt that what you're saying is a good enough reason to go; but then I'm not up with the minds of women today. Who are you hoping to meet?'

'I don't know! I've been racking my brains as to whom it could be. I thought it was one of the bankers I've met recently, but I don't know.'

'So you want to fly to Paris, have a weekend and fly back. You don't know how you're going to get from the airport to Paris and you don't know where you are going stay. Presumably you don't know what you are going to do when you get there.'

'No, I just thought that if I met no one I could go into Paris and find a room for the weekend and hunt around. Or I could just get the next plane back.'

'Are you hoping to meet this person?'

'Oh yes, I would think that he will be sitting on the plane in the seat beside me.'

'So this is an affair of the heart.'

'No, it's feminine curiosity. You know my views, and I doubt if I'd fall for this guy.'

'Have you have come to tell me this for any particular reason.'

'Yes, to ask you if I can have the time off. I thought it best to take Friday off and I'll try and not be too late in on Monday morning.'

'And by granting you the time off I become a party to this reckless pursuit.'

'No, I'm asking for the time off, that's all.'

'Then I'll do it for the reason that you gave me – which is that you lead a drab life and it needs pepping up! We do tend here to keep our noses to the grindstone. When do you go on holiday, by the way?'

'Three weeks' time.'

'Then I have been too hasty in allowing you to go.'

'No, you haven't! I do want to go to Paris.'

Sarah returned to her desk with a changed impression of her employer. He was sad, but he had not let his problems cloud his judgement so far as she was concerned. Many people in his position would have been upset that a similar opportunity had not befallen them and they would have allowed their envy to deny the younger person their due, but Mr Deakin had not. One of the advantages of working in a small office where your boss also owned the company was that he was able to make better judgements. In her last job at an advertising agency, had she asked her boss if she could do such a thing it would certainly have been denied. For they would have to check with their superior, who would check with theirs and if extra days were available to hand out, they went to those at the top.

Michael was hovering close to Sarah and said, 'Deakin give you the time off?'

Sarah shot him a disapproving look. 'How did you know about it?'

'These things get round. Everyone knows you're going to Paris. Who are you going with?'

'It's none of your business.'

'That tells me a lot of things.'

'It tells you nothing.'

'It tells me that you want to keep it secret, and so it must be romantic!'

Sarah refused to answer.

'I mean, a good-looking woman like you shouldn't remain on the shelf. So which of those bankers is it? Not that loud-mouthed fellow!'

'Michael, get on with your work and leave me alone.'

Paris

Sarah arrived at the check-in at Heathrow to join the milling throng of travellers. She looked around her, studying the many faces of the men standing about, conscious that any of them might be her benefactor. It added a certain piquancy to the trip. It couldn't be the man in front of her, as he was with a woman. She watched them closely and decided that they were husband and wife. Another couple to the right were on their own and she felt they were just partners, since there was a reserve between them. The married couple acted far more naturally. But they were moving away from the check-in and it was now her turn.

Then she moved through customs and the security checks and into the departure lounge. Again she looked around her with something of an air of expectancy, but by her own reasoning it was more likely that she would meet the mystery man on the plane. She had noted that she had a window seat, and that would allow him to slip into the seat beside her just before they took off. So by that logic he was not yet in the lounge and was waiting for the last call.

She had not been so excited for a long time, and chided herself for placing so much store by it. The flight was called and she picked up her holdall and made her way to the boarding gate. It seemed almost commonplace just to walk down a tunnel and onto the plane. In some respects you couldn't be sure when you actually stepped onto the plane. A stewardess showed her to her seat and Sarah slid across next to the window. Her expectancy had reached its peak and she could feel her heart pounding. Her eyes took in the men that walked past, hoping that he might be the man but she found herself being selective and also hoping that others were not him. It could not be that heavily bearded man, unless it was a disguise... nor the sloppy man with the crumpled raincoat, though if one did but know it he was probably a millionaire. A handsome businessman was next, and he came towards her studiously avoiding her gaze. Her heart declared him to be the man, and she anticipated him dropping into the seat beside her. But he passed the seat, continuing down the plane, and Sarah felt a wave of disappointment.

It was time to put one's seat belt on, and she guessed her beau was going to cut it as fine as possible. But suddenly the steward was on the intercom greeting the passengers for the flight and explaining the safety procedures. Then Sarah realised that the plane was rolling backwards and the seat beside her was empty. For a moment she felt like shouting out that they needed to wait but common sense told her not to bother. She was angry with her benefactor, for he had cut it too fine and had missed the flight. But she calmed down and reasoned it out differently. The flight was not full by any means and he could actually be sitting anywhere. So, having taken any seat on the plane he hoped that sometime into the flight he could change and make himself known to her. He was probably sitting behind her, looking at her, smiling at her evident confusion, and waiting to pick his moment. She was back in her expectant mode, knowing that he would not move until they were in the air.

Sarah glanced out of the window. They were moving towards the end of the runway. Then she heard the engines revving up, and suddenly they were gathering pace with the rumble of the undercarriage on the tarmac. Then the nose lifted and suddenly the rumble ceased. The land beneath became fields and was growing more distant. Soon, clouds scudded under them and blotted out the view of the ground. Finally they were allowed to relax and move around. Was this the moment he was going to come to her? But the stewardess appeared instead with a light lunch.

She ate with little conviction. Then a steward was leaning over her with a cup of coffee. Still she waited for the man to make his move but no one came. Another stewardess came to collect the empty packaging. There was a complete cloud covering beneath them. She glanced at her watch and calculated that they were fifty minutes into the one-hour flight. The seat belt sign started flashing at the passengers and Sarah felt the plane slowing. He was not going to sit with her on the flight!

Fields appeared below and the ground was visible passing rapidly beneath them. Then the outskirts of the airport came into view. The ground was approaching fast and suddenly the runway was rushing along underneath them. Then the motion of the plane slowed and they were firmly on the ground. It remained only for them to taxi to the terminal. Sarah wondered why she had not been approached, and for the first time that day she felt lonely.

Reluctantly she followed the rest of the passengers down the plane to the exit to endure another long walk through the terminal building. It could have been anywhere but the signs were mostly in French and so she assumed she was in France. At the carousel she waited disconsolately for her case to appear. The pleasure of the expedition had evaporated. Ahead of her was the unknown, and she had been so sure that her escort would introduce himself that she had given no thought to the consequences of finding herself in Paris alone and with nowhere to go. She began to wish that her case would not appear, but there it was, flowing slowly and inexorably towards her. Just to annoy her even more, a man further down picked it up and checked the label. Finding it was not his, he threw it back on the carousel. Others gave her case a tug to see if they could find an explanation as to why the man had rejected it. But at length it was with her, and she was able to give everyone a reproachful look, though no one took any notice. Then it was out through immigration and into the main hall of the airport.

She passed through the door from immigration that took them into the main hall of the terminal, and thought how fortunate many of the people were to have their friends or relations waiting for them. She wished someone were waiting for her and glanced hopefully down the row of placards with people's names on them. Something made her pause and she stepped back to look at one sign on which was written '*Mlle Levine*'. For a moment she debated whether or not it was for her, and her instincts told her to carry on, but her curiosity made her check it out. Why should there be another Miss Levine on any of the flights?

Sarah turned to the little man who was holding the sign.

'Je m'appelle Mademoiselle Levine.'

'Mais oui.' He gave her flight number and where she had come from.

'Exactement.'

'Alors, permettez-moi de prendre la valise.' She handed him her case, and he added, *'Suivez-moi.'*

Sarah's heart rose, for here was something prepared for her and that meant that someone was orchestrating her weekend. It also meant that at some point he would appear to her and clearly he was going to pick his moment. Perhaps he was watching her now, checking that the little man, who was presumably a chauffeur, was doing his job properly. Ten minutes later they were beside his battered Mercedes. With a flourish he opened the door for her, and with her case in the boot he was in the driver's seat. Soon they were heading out of the airport to do battle with the Parisian traffic.

Sarah had no idea where she was going and watched the short motorway trip into Paris slip past. Then they were into the suburbs. The roads became very crowded and every set of traffic lights seemed to hold them up. But the landmarks of Paris were becoming more apparent with the Eiffel Tower dominating all the buildings. Occasionally it would be obliterated by a large building close at hand, but a block or so later it was back peering over the roofs of the lower buildings, seemingly keeping an eye on them.

They crossed the Seine with Notre Dame Cathedral to the right and onto the north bank. Once again they were swallowed up in narrow streets but suddenly they stopped at a hotel.

'Nous y sommes, Ma'm'selle.'

Sarah looked out of the window at the Hotel Chataillet. It boasted three stars, though the exterior was drab, like most buildings in Paris.

'Excusez-moi, Ma'm'selle.' The chauffeur was handing her his card.

She took it and waited for him to open the car door.

'Ici?' she asked, as he opened the boot.

'Mais oui.'

At least she had a point of contact and looked at the dapper little man.

'*Allez-vous, je vous suiverai.*'

Reluctantly, Sarah entered the hotel to find herself in a brightly lit foyer. It was large, with a flight of stairs facing her. To her left was the reception, and she walked to the desk and gave the bell a smack. A man came running.

'*Oui, Madame?*'

'*Je crois que vous avez une réservation pour Mademoiselle Levine.*'

'Yes, we do,' he replied without a trace of irony, 'I am the manager and may I welcome you to our hotel. I hope you will find your stay to your satisfaction.'

The chauffeur arrived with her case, breathing deeply.

'Monsieur Claude is your chauffeur for your stay; if you wish to go out, just give him a call.' Claude beamed though the manager eyed him severely. Claude took the hint and gave a little bow before departing.

'I will show you to your room and I will have your case brought up directly. Please follow me.'

They climbed the staircase and turned to the left at the top. Sarah was led round the landing to one of the rooms that opened on to it. He unlocked the door and led her in.

Sarah stifled a gasp, for it was obviously one of the best rooms in the hotel.

'You can see the Seine from the window,' said the manager. 'The dining room is at the bottom of the stairs and you turn left and it is the door on the left. Ahead of you is the lounge. If there is anything you want, please ring for service.'

'Thank you,' said Sarah, still awestruck.

'We are here to make your stay comfortable.'

The manager left the room, closing the door behind him. Sarah did another search of her quarters and discovered the shower room. She looked out of the window and wondered how she came to be so close to the Seine, but concluded that the chauffeur had had to drive round some one-way streets to get to the hotel. She found herself very pleased with what she had, and sat down in the armchair.

She had had a mind to think that it was her flatmates who were having her on, but her surroundings dispelled any idea that it could be them. They might have afforded the airfare, but surely not the hotel and the chauffeur. Nor had she merely been given a drive from the airport to the hotel, but the little man was her driver for the weekend, and she was determined to test the point. She was sure that the manager knew what was happening, for he had been so particular about the room service and he knew about the chauffeur. She decided to test the room service first and rang down for a coffee with real milk. She had to spell it out, as the French were likely to use their version of long-life milk and she worried until a tray duly arrived and was put on a little table beside the armchair. On the tray were one cup, a small coffee pot, a pot of sugar and a jug filled with what smelled of fresh milk!

Whoever had sent her the tickets had money. Did that exclude all the bankers who had been in the pub that evening? She hoped it was none of them, but she could not dismiss them on the monetary grounds alone. No, she doubted their taste! But though she wanted to dismiss them en bloc she was aware that it was still possible for one of them to have planned the weekend. But who else could have done it?

There was Clive... Yet he was the kind of man who wanted her to be in his presence, which meant that he might pop out of the woodwork at any moment and demand her body! She suddenly felt uncomfortable and not a little fearful; she rose and checked the door. The lock looked solid enough, but suppose that Clive had stayed here in the last few weeks and taken a pattern of the key, he would then be able to let himself in. She walked round the room and, finding a chair in the bathroom, took it to the door. The door handle was low enough for the chair to be wedged underneath. That would surely frustrate the man's entry!

She returned to her thoughts and the cup of coffee.

What about her boss, Mr Deakin? But why should he do such a thing? He had not been in the pub and heard her ridiculous boast and the ensuing challenge. She had had dinner with him and he had shown no real partiality for her. And when she had been in his office he never gave her those admiring looks which she expected from a man. Had he not told her off one day, leaving her feeling like a little child! And then his advice to her had been not to go! No, he was a workaholic who did not have the imagination for such a scheme.

Then there was Jonathan French. It was right up his street! But if he did not pay for a meal, why should he be forking out for an expensive weekend? Was she the subject of his next book? It was dreadful to think that she might be. It might be some other author. And Sarah could think of a number of possible names.

What about someone in the office? Could they have planned the weekend for her? It surely was not a woman! She discounted Ms Marchbank, for whatever she was she did not have the ability to plan her such a weekend. Millie, Clemmie and Emma would not have done it, leaving Tom, who just did not have the imagination. It surely was not Michael, for he had a girlfriend, and he didn't have the money. So it was no one in the office.

Yet someone had planned her journey, and seemed bent on demonstrating to her that she was a woman who needed a man in her life. She was determined never to be dominated in this way by a man, and wished she had not come.

That thought made Sarah feel very uncomfortable. She had challenged that group of young men and one of them was determined to win! Now she wished that she'd said nothing, and wondered that people should listen to a woman who had had far too much to drink! She tried to picture the men all standing round, and to her annoyance the only one she could see clearly in her mind was the loud-mouthed man who had got everyone going about virginity. Cathy should never have told everyone about her; it had been that which had made her speak out so stupidly. She hoped that it was not him, as she had taken an instant dislike to him, and to have to give him thanks for her weekend was too dreadful to contemplate.

So who did that leave? But another idea came to her. Clive Brunswick had always given her the impression that there was someone behind him was pulling his strings, even though he wanted her body. Probably he would have a little pot made inscribed with the words 'I took Sarah's virginity'! But if Clive wanted sex with her, what did the other person want? And she could think of no reason at all for a complete stranger to take such an interest in her...

So she was left with the loud-mouthed man! Her heart sank at the thought. But then she decided that she had it in her own hands to punish the man. She could make it a really expensive weekend for him!

But wait, there had been another man there in the pub! He was standing to one side, and she could only see him if she turned, but he was the one who kept admonishing the loud-mouthed man. Indeed, when he spoke she had liked his voice, and unlike his friends he had spoken what seemed to be good sense. It had to be him and he was about her age – perhaps a year or two older. She was pleased with that and decided that now she would walk down to the Seine.

First she checked the time that dinner would be served and from the manager she found that she had just over an hour. She stepped outside into a warm early summer evening and made her way to the bank of the river. It was only a few minutes' walk, and she came out where there seemed to be a permanent market with people selling books and paintings against the balustrade of the Seine.

Paris, she felt, was a place of its own. They built everything with high sloping roofs with black slate tiles. On top of some were ornate ridges, often looking like little fences placed around the tops of the roofs. Built into many of the roofs were wonderful secret windows, hiding amongst the tiles. The walls built with grey stone were very unattractive in appearance but the builders had circumvented criticism by putting in elaborate windows. They were windows that went from waist high nearly up to the ceiling of the rooms inside, and the sills and lintels were carved in stone. And none of the stone was carved with simplicity or in the Corinthian fashion, but it was carved fantastically. Everything about their buildings when one looked closely had been done elaborately; even the gutter ends had been finished with ornate gargoyles.

Notre Dame was no exception; indeed it was more likely the leader of the French way. And why did one always think of Notre Dame and hunchbacks? Was it just because Victor Hugo had produced a novel of astounding cruelty and inhumanity? Was it necessary for Esmeralda to die so appallingly, just to ensure the dramatic final scene where the Bishop, standing high on the roof, could be pushed off one of the steep roofs to his death? Indeed, if there was any truth in the book, it did neither history nor humanity any favours. It was certainly a book that Sarah was determined never to read again.

She crossed the bridge and walked around the entire cathedral. Finally she retraced her steps along the bank, pausing to see what books and paintings were for sale. But though the old books were satisfying, just to hold and feel their age, she was able to curb her desire to buy one. At the paintings she paused longer, but decided that art was becoming difficult to buy. Some of it looked as if it was painted to order and perhaps even done mechanically. The rest of the art was muddled in amongst it, and one needed to hunt very carefully to find the genuine article. It left her dissatisfied and out of sympathy with it all. She wanted to see an artist actually doing the painting, and with a magnificent gesture buy his work.

Dinner had started by the time she returned, and she was shown to a table that gave her a good view of the restaurant. Having made her selection for the evening meal she was left to study the other guests in the room. Was her benefactor bold enough to be here eating in front of her? Would he make himself known to her? Most of the people were men, and she guessed that they were on business. Their suits looked as if they travelled a lot and many of them had mobile phones on the table beside them. It was a symbol of the age; long gone was the telephone brought over by a waiter and placed on your table.

She noted that a number of the men were eyeing her up and down. She hoped she looked hard and businesslike so that they would be deterred from coming over. Were she to look soft and feminine they would surely all be making plans to introduce themselves.

The waiters flitted between the tables, never seeming to stand still. Suddenly one of them was coming her way. She thought that the next waiter to her table would come from the kitchen area. She wished she knew from which table he was coming. He was at her table and swiftly placed a piece of folded paper before her. He was gone without waiting for her to look at it. Eagerly she grasped the paper, believing that it must come from her benefactor. She glanced anxiously around the restaurant to see if there was a familiar face that she had missed. But there was none. She unfolded the paper and looked at the neat handwriting. It stated briefly: *Table nineteen, I too am lonely tonight.*

Sarah tried to work out which table was nineteen but it could have been one of a number of tables. There was a chubby faced man at some distance who was staring at her. To his right was a thinner, much older man, who was more careful about how he looked in her direction; but look he did. To his left was a table with two men sitting at it. Both of them looked at her and one had actually moved his seat, for he had started off with his back almost to her and now sat so that he could see her with just a small twist of his head. The note needed a reply and she gave it much thought. The man who had sent it over was presumptuous and disrespectful, especially to women. He needed to be put in his place.

She found a pen and an envelope from her bag and tore out a square piece, making sure that her name and address were not on it, and wrote, *Thank you for the evidence of your adultery. Your wife will now be divorcing you.*

She folded it and, slipping it into the envelope, placed it on a side plate. The waiter appeared suddenly and said, '*Est-ce qu'il y a une message pour la table dix-neuf?*'

'*Oui, prenez-vous celà à dix-neuf. Merci.*'

Sarah pointed to the plate and watched to see which table he went to. He stopped at one table but he did not put down the plate. He walked circumspectly around the room, giving her nervous glances every now and again. She lowered her head to give the appearance that she was not interested, but while her head was down Sarah's eyes followed him. Then she knew that he had put the note down but still she was not certain which of two tables it was, though neither were one of her original choices. She was sure it was the casual looking man next to the two men. He was being very canny, for if he had the note he had not yet looked at it. After what seemed an age his eyes went down and he moved his hand slowly to open the envelope and withdraw the note. Almost nonchalantly he held the note and with his other hand relaxed the fold. She was sure that he was conscious of her looking at him. His eyes were looking down again and he had to be reading the piece of paper. A look of horror went across the man's face, which he quickly suppressed. Had that been the only reaction she got from her note Sarah would have been very pleased; but the man, who was close to finishing his meal, rose from his table and moved swiftly to the door trying not to look in Sarah's direction. The other guests all stared at his abrupt departure, and it caused such a stir that it took some time before the restaurant resumed its calm atmosphere again.

Sarah's meal was put in front of her and she continued to smile while she ate. After her meal, Sarah retired to the lounge, still laughing inwardly at the man's response. A woman was sitting alone at a table. Her husband was talking animatedly with two other men at the bar.

'*Bonsoir, Madame,*' said Sarah. '*Puis-je m'asseoir ici?*'

'*Mais bien sûr, Mademoiselle,*' said the woman, and Sarah joined her for a very satisfying hour speaking only in French. Soon it was time for bed.

In her bedroom, Sarah went about blockading the door. The chair under the handle was not very satisfactory as she felt that a strong man could waggle the handle from the other side and dislodge the chair. She got one of her books out and pushed the chair down hard into the deep pile carpet and forced the book between the handle and the chair. Making sure that the door was locked, she climbed into bed and was soon asleep.

The morning brought some new surprises. It appeared that the chauffeur had turned up for her. The manager knocked on her door. She rose and dragged her dressing gown on before removing the barricade.

'The chauffeur is here to take you out,' he said, coming into the room.

'But I haven't asked him to take me anywhere…'

'He is under orders, Ma'm'selle.'

'Whose orders?'

'I believe he is taking you to Montmartre this morning. At two o'clock this afternoon you are due at the Louvre. At seven thirty this evening you are attending the opera.'

'And tomorrow?'

'That, I believe, has also been planned.'

'So who has done all this?'

'I am not at liberty to tell you.'

'Well, I would like to know.'

'I think the person involved wishes to make himself known to you at some point.'

'What if I don't want to do these things?'

'It would be very awkward; however, I am led to believe these are things that you would very much like to do.'

'I know! But I would like the ordering of them myself.'

'But it is all arranged, Ma'm'selle.'

'What if I unarranged it?'

'Please, Ma'm'selle, just go and enjoy it.' His voice was almost pleading and Sarah relented. What had been arranged for her she was very pleased about, for each of the activities were ones she would have gladly chosen for herself. Still, she would have liked to have arranged them herself.

'Just one other thing, Ma'm'selle… Have you any money?'

'No, I need to change some pounds into euros.'

'Well, I have to give you this.' He handed her an envelope. 'Can you be down in five minutes?' It was a question, but said in a tone that would not brook a negative answer.

'Of course,' replied Sarah and opened the envelope. It contained €200 in a selection of notes. She was not even allowed to get her own currency! But it was no use getting petulant, for there would come a time when she would repay her benefactor.

Claude was pleased to see her, and drove her through the Paris streets giving a running commentary.

La Place de la Bastille… La Gare du Nord, pour Londres…

He turned up a side street and stopped the car at some steps.

'Ici en haut la place du Sacré Coeur. Vous pouvez vous promenez. À gauche se trouve Montmartre.'

He was holding the door open for her, making it plain that Sarah should alight. She obeyed, giving him a little wave, confident that he was going to meet her somewhere at the top.

The steps from the bottom appeared to be endless and though progress was slow and steady Sarah turned round frequently to look at the scene of Paris becoming more visible as she climbed. The Eiffel Tower was to her right looking down on everyone with its lofty superiority. She was above the trees now, and Notre Dame Cathedral could be seen. To her left were the extensive roofs of the Gare du Nord. Finally she reached the top and stood beneath the white walls of the Sacré Coeur. It was a cathedral that no one in Paris wanted built, for to do so they had pulled down many homes. Émile Zola, an eminent French writer, had a subplot in one of his books in which it was planned to blow up the building while it was being constructed. Doubtless it drew the wrath of God upon him resulting in his untimely death!

Sarah wandered around admiring the view, but dutifully she turned towards Montmartre. Here she found the square of cafés with all the artists displaying their wares. Visitors from all around the world walked between the rows of easels admiring their work. Sarah was no exception and she had a feeling of privilege. She could if she desired buy some the artwork, but there was one problem and that was that she was not sure that she liked any of it sufficiently to make an investment. One man had done a number of miniatures about four inches square of the Eiffel Tower, being symbolic of French pride. While the miniatures were priced at twenty euros, which seemed very reasonable, Sarah doubted if putting the paint on the wood had taken much longer than thirty seconds. She felt no reason to spend her money. But the square was inviting, and one soon gravitated to the café of one's choice.

Sarah sat down in a wicker chair at a table in the warm morning sunlight. A waiter appeared and she smiled, for she felt he was a typical Frenchman satisfying her mental picture of the genre. He asked her in French and it gratified her that she was speaking so much of the language. All too often her visits had been plagued by her French hosts insisting on practising their English. She took umbrage at their forthrightness, for her time in France had always been limited and she always took home a feeling that she had not made the most of her holiday.

She watched the people going past. Neatly dressed tourists contrasted with the locals, who seemed keen to show off their identity, for they stood out. Some wore the French beret complete with its tiny tag stuck on top, leaving one wondering what it was for. Many wore what she could only describe as a smock, which consisted of a denim type of cloth jacket and trousers. The women still looked like women, wearing light cotton dresses and petticoats. It gave Sarah something of a conscience as she was wearing a trouser suit and did not possess in her wardrobe a single petticoat!

A man sat down close to her. She wondered if it was because of her, but she decided that there were few places for him to sit and he was actually forced to sit there. But he leaned across and spoke to her, and she decided that after all he had sat there solely to speak to her. She was flattered only because he wanted to converse.

'I'm from Richmond, Virginia,' he said in such a fashion that it was impossible to ignore him. 'And might I be as bold as to ask where are you from?'

'London,' she replied.

'John Shample the Third.' He held out his hand and there was no point in not responding and taking hold of his. He grasped her hand firmly and shook it as if it were something that, if it were detachable, he would soon have completed the process. Sarah was glad when he released her hand and she was able to slide both her hands beneath the table and with the unharmed hand massage the circulation of the abused member to restore some life back into it.

'Ever been stateside?' he asked.

'No,' said Sarah, 'it's one of those ambitions that I still have ahead of me.'

'So if you went tomorrow where would you go?'

'The Grand Canyon.'

'Is that all?'

'No, I'd love to see the prairies and cross them by car and see the Rockies approaching.'

'What about New York?'

'I'd like to see it, but I rather think that it is a gateway to the interior.'

'Too big and too impressive? No, you'd love it.'

'So what do you think of Paris?'

'Very old and twee, and that's nice, we don't have old stuff in the States. But a bit dirty, though.'

'And what about the people?'

'So-so, I don't mind them.'

'And how long are you here?'

'I've got a stopover for three days... and you?'

'Just the weekend.' Sarah toyed with the idea that this man had in fact paid for her weekend and was desirous of meeting her, but everything about him said that it was not him. Why meet up with her in Paris? His familiarity would have held him in just as good stead in London. Yet there was an insouciance about him that suggested that he was exactly who he was – a chancer!

'Join me in another coffee?'

'Yes, why not?' she said.

He immediately turned and called out to the waiter. It was an action that none of Sarah's male acquaintances would imitate. They would sit quietly trying to catch the man's eye, and if that took ten minutes then that was how long it took; but the American could not wait any length of time at all. It must have been gratifying to the man to see the waiter trotting over without apparently a thought for anyone else.

'Two coffees,' he said abruptly, 'and some of your cake.'

The waiter nodded and disappeared. If he resented the brusqueness of the American he did not show it and returned in a short space of time with a tray of coffee and the cake. He was rewarded with a ten-euro note on top of the bill and went off with a large smile on his face.

To the American it was nothing, and he continued as if the interlude had never occurred. It was so pleasant to be sitting there eating the cake and drinking the coffee.

'What is your itinerary?' Sarah inquired politely.

'Paris, Versailles, Fontainebleau and Reims.'

Why did the Americans always think that Europe was a small place? No one could take in Paris in one day, nor in one week. Versailles and Fontainebleau both needed the best part of a day each and Reims was at least two hours of driving distance and if he was going by coach then he needed three hours. Yet he expected her to take in New York in detail!

'What have you seen of Paris so far?' asked Sarah.

'Yesterday I went to the top of the Eiffel Tower and then I took a boat trip along the Seine. I've seen the Arc de Triomphe and the Champs-Élysées.' He rambled on about what he had seen for some minutes.

'What are you doing next?'

'Versailles this afternoon. Then I leave Paris tomorrow morning for Reims, and I fly out in the evening.' He looked at his watch and rose to his feet. 'Twenty minutes to meet the coach! If you're ever in Richmond, Virginia, come and look me up. John Shample the Third, that's me.'

They shook hands and the American hurried off. Sarah was pleased that he went, as it relieved her of the necessity of making the excuses to leave. But then her mobile rang and it was Claude. He was parked up nearby and directed her to the car. He greeted her with a large grin and held the car door open for her. They drove down the hill passing the French equivalent of Highgate Cemetery. They turned through the streets of Paris and arrived at the Arc de Triomphe. Having rounded that they were bowling down the Champs-Élysées before following the bank of the Seine back to the hotel and lunch.

After lunch she was back in the car and driven to the Louvre. Claude could only point the direction to her and explain what she was to do when she had entered the building. It was a pleasant walk from the road through the gardens of the Tuileries, past an ornate lake which she could see was a superb piece of modern engineering; for it was so laid out that the lip was barely one millimetre above the level of the water. Beyond this was the heavily criticised glass pyramid that formed the canopy of the entrance. Sarah went in and down the stairs, to find it exactly as Claude had described. She crossed to the inquiries desk and told the girl there who she was.

'One moment, please,' said the girl. She made a phone call. 'Please take a seat.' She indicated some chairs on the far side of the foyer.

Five minutes later an elderly woman arrived and spoke to the girl, who pointed in Sarah direction.

'I am Madame Cruchet; I am directed to show you certain of the exhibits here.'

'Hello,' said Sarah, rising from the seat.

'Please come.' The woman led the way down a corridor. They

walked for some time down long corridors, and eventually, having crossed a gallery, Sarah was shown into a dark little room.

In front of them was a painting that Sarah instantly recognised. It was the Mona Lisa. Madame Cruchet spoke at some length about the history of the work. It seemed somewhat irrelevant, for if a work of art was a masterpiece then there should surely be something about it that spoke to the viewer. And the eyes of the painting were looking straight at Sarah with a look that seemed to say that this two-dimensional women fully understood her. It was uncanny to feel that a mere picture could dissect her more than she could dissect the picture, and the smile on the face was so positive and self-assured. No matter where one moved the face still stared at one. It pleased Sarah enormously to see it, and when they left to find the next gallery she found that she did not want other images thrust upon her but rather she wanted to keep the image of the Mona Lisa firmly in her mind.

The next gallery they visited contained works by Rembrandt, Rubens, Goya and other artists that Sarah was familiar with. After and hour and a half Madame Cruchet asked Sarah if she had anything she wanted to see.

'Maurice Utrillo,' said Sarah.

'*Mais oui*,' said Madame, clearly pleased that her charge had an interest in a French artist.

They found the gallery where most of his work was hung and wandered from painting to painting. Maurice Utrillo had painted many scenes of Paris towards the end of the nineteenth century and gave a wonderful insight into the city at that period.

Time was getting on, though and Sarah called Claude to come and pick her up. She felt a bit mean, as her hotel could not have been much more than a mile from the Louvre, but Claude was no more than a few minutes away.

After dinner Claude was back to take Sarah to the opera. He met her in the foyer, and suddenly she realised the manager was standing beside her.

'We have a little mission first,' he said, and ushered her out to the car. He opened the door and let her in and then opened the front passenger door and sat in the car himself. Claude seemed to know where they were going, and after half a mile he pulled up outside a jeweller's shop. The hotel manager was out and opening the door for her.

Inside the jeweller's shop he turned to Sarah and said, 'I am commissioned to help you buy something for yourself.'

'What about the money?' asked Sarah.

'You are not to worry about that; it is all taken care of.'

An elderly Frenchman with dark hair stood behind the counter.

Sarah found it all rather surreal. She was not a person who bothered with jewellery. Rings, she felt, were matrimonial and necklaces were for those who wanted to draw attention to their cleavage – and she was most certainly not either of those. She had never had her ears pierced and felt somewhat at a loss.

'What do you want to look at?' asked the hotel manager, and his closeness for an instant made Sarah wonder if her beau were not this man; but she could think of no reason why.

'A brooch, Ma'm'selle?'

Sarah shook her head.

'A bracelet, perhaps…'

That was more like it.

'Have you any others?' asked Sarah, for the ones being offered were quite plain, and it crossed her mind that she was supposed to choose one from among them. She remembered thinking that if it were any of the bankers she would make them pay. The jeweller pulled out another tray. The bracelets were far more expensive. It was a dilemma for Sarah. Was her benefactor testing her? Was she meant to have something relatively cheap? It did not correlate to her expensive hotel room. If it was a test then she was meant to purchase something expensive. The bracelet in the middle was the best and it also had the best price tag. Sarah picked it up and looked at it. It was made of a number of diamond-encrusted gold segments. She felt the hotel manager stiffen beside her. Was it outside his remit, or was he going to allow her to buy it?

'I'd like that,' she said.

He had collected himself and said, 'Of course, Ma'm'selle.'

Sarah smiled to herself. If her beau were a real gentleman, then he was not going to moan too much at €2,000. She tried to imagine him telling her off later for overdoing it. But what could he do? Take it off her and sell it? It was too bad if he could not afford it! But it ought to flush him out.

The jeweller had boxed the bracelet and the hotel manager seemed to be paying for it. Then they were back to the car and on to the Parisian opera. It was Poulenc's *The Carmelites*. Her ticket, which she found at the ticket office, was for the dress circle, where she sat and played with her new toy. The particular opera was not one of her favourites but the atmosphere and her surroundings were so uplifting that she returned to the hotel fully satisfied. She had given up hoping that a man was going to slide into the seat beside her, as she reasoned that he had had ample time to do so and there had been many better places for them to have met during the day. Having locked her door and placed her safety system under the handle, Sarah was soon asleep.

The following day began with a trip to the Eiffel Tower. Claude intimated that she should go to the top, and Sarah joined the queue for the lift. It took an hour of waiting but then she was whisked aloft in a cage with thirty other people. But the view was terrific, with the whole of Paris laid out. The Seine wound its way beneath them, and to the west performed some enormous curves criss-crossing a number of times before disappearing beyond the controversial building of the La Défense, a huge white structure of apparently two thin walls joined by an equally thin roof at the top. To the north were Montmartre and the Sacré Coeur, where she had walked the previous day. To the east were Notre Dame and her hotel, which she tried in vain to pick out from the myriad buildings. To the south was the thin strip of grass of the Champ de Mars running off towards the skyscraper of Montparnasse.

Back at ground level Sarah bought a snack lunch and called up Claude.

'Where to now?' she asked.

'Versailles,' said Claude, threading his way on to the *périphérique*.

The Paris ring road, which went completely round the city, led out to the motorways and out of the city.

The mention of Versailles concerned Sarah, for it was where John Shample the Third had said he would be, and she had no desire to make his acquaintance again. For moment she wondered if he were not her benefactor, but she could think of no reason to explain it. He was a man who liked to meet women and chat them up. Some obviously he could get further with than others, but he seemed a genial enough person to take the rough with the smooth and depart with his oversized smile still intact.

Versailles was more of a walk than she had anticipated, with the cobbled courtyard for inspecting the troops far larger than she expected. She tried the gardens first and wandered past the palace to the rear, where a magnificent fountain played at intervals to the benefit of the visitors. Finally she turned her attention to the palace itself and attached herself to a group of French tourists being shown around. The interior was as extensive and as magnificent as all the literature proclaimed it to be. The guide pointed out paintings and tapestries and the most wonderful furniture. Her French she found was sufficient to keep up with the guide, but her French history was lamentable. Strange how her school days had ignored French history after the Hundred Years War. France had got the occasional mention at the time of the French Revolution, but even Napoleon was discounted in favour of Wellington's exploits. From the tone of the guide it was unmistakable that the French psyche was greatly influenced by jealousy for its nearest overseas neighbour.

They were late returning to the hotel and Sarah found that she was one of the last in to dinner. But it had been a tiring day, and she was glad to find her bed and have an early night.

On the flight home the next morning she had time to reflect on the weekend. An overweight lady sat in the seat next to her and her presence alone robbed her of any idea that her beau might suddenly bow over her. But she was at a loss to understand why he had not materialised at almost any point in her stay. Nor could she decide if she was disappointed or not. Not knowing who he was was still intriguing, yet her expectations had not been fulfilled. Had she placed too much store by him? And if she had, why? Wasn't she a woman who could stand on her own two feet? She didn't need a man's arm to lean on. Yet it would have been more satisfying to have shared the weekend with someone. Was it possible that her beau had intended to join her, but he had been unable to? What could have kept him away? Would a death in his family have been sufficient reason? Yet the hotel staff had given no hint that she was due to meet anyone, and in many ways they had given her to understand that she would not be joined over the weekend. But then that might have been for the hotel only; and with that thought she gave up, for it was all unsatisfactory. She was glad when the plane landed.

The Website

It was mid-morning when Sarah arrived back from Paris and lugged her case upstairs into the office to deposit it by her desk. She took no notice of anyone in the room and it was only when she sat down and looked around her that she realised she had not seen Ms Marchbank by her desk. Then she noticed that everyone was gathered by Tom's desk on the far side. As Sarah made this observation, it seemed they all as one turned and stared at her. She returned their looks yet no one said a word. It was odder still, for Sarah could see that Ms Marchbank was one of their number and that Emma and Clemmie were there with them. Tom's browser was the focus of their attention. Yet there was something strange about the way they all looked at her.

'What's the matter?' asked Sarah rising and going to join them. They continued to stare at her and offered no resistance as she went to Tom's browser. Emma and Clemmie suddenly returned to their desks and Tom moved forward towards Sarah.

'You don't want to see this,' he said when she reached the point where she could see the screen.

'How do I know whether or not I want to see it before I've seen it?' said Sarah.

'Suit yourself,' said Tom in a resigned manner and stood back.

She could only stand and stare at it, horror-struck. She felt very angry and she wanted to cry but refused to do so in such company. A numbness crept over her and then she said, 'Good grief!' She brought her hands up to her mouth and shook her head slightly. No one moved until another person came into the room. The authority of his presence galvanised people into action and they all stood back except Sarah. He took one glance at the browser and said, 'Take Sarah into my office.'

Sarah found herself being led away. In Mr Deakin's office she stood at his desk waiting for him. Some instinct told her that she was due to lose her job, but still she could not cry. Then Mr Deakin was in the office.

'Sit down there,' he said and wheeled out the chair from behind his desk. He turned to Ms Marchbank, who was hovering in the doorway. 'Get Sarah a sweet cup of coffee, and get me one as well, but the usual sugar.'

'How could anyone do that?' said Sarah and tears began to flow. She felt a hand on her shoulder.

'I've told them to get it off the Internet or I'll sue the hosting company.'

'How did they get a photograph of me?'

'Took a picture of you! Maybe someone gave them a picture of you. They might have been through your handbag and taken one from you. Maybe someone had a photo of you and lent it to them.'

'But how did they a picture of me naked?'

'They haven't! They had a picture of your face and someone has found a model with about the same body and married them up.'

'How do you know?'

'Well, I haven't made a study of the picture but the proportions were not that good from what I could see!'

'Who would have done that?'

Ms Marchbank brought the coffees in and Mr Deakin took them from her.

'That's all thank you, Ms Marchbank.'

'Drink your coffee, Sarah.'

'I'm sorry to be such a nuisance,' said Sarah.

'Think nothing of it. That sort of thing should never be put on the Internet. I'll go and see if they've got it off yet.' He left the room.

Sarah looked round his office and realised that she was seeing it from an unusual angle, for she was almost behind Mr Deakin's desk, whereas his normal habit was to keep people on the other side of his desk. It was hardly a position from which she was about to receive notice to terminate her employment. And she found it odd what strange notions should come into one's mind when one was under stress. She found he had placed some tissues beside her, and she wiped her eyes with one. She never cried – and yet she had! She sipped the coffee and felt better for it, and a feeling that she had been very foolish swept over her. Mr Deakin returned.

'I'll get back to my desk,' said Sarah.

'Finish the coffee first.'

'Have they got it off the screen yet?'

'Michael's speaking to someone now.'

'How nasty! It was quite sick of someone to do it.'

'And those that condone it are just as sick. Tell me, though,' said Mr Deakin, 'what is going on?'

'What do you mean?'

'Well, I seem to remember giving you some time off to go to France… Presumably it was an affair of the heart, and as a woman of your age, you cannot persuade me otherwise… and now this. So what is going on?'

'I don't know,' said Sarah sadly, 'I wish I did.'

'Well, can you explain the website?'

'No, not at all.'

'It seems to me that you could at least explain some of the references.'

'I don't want to.'

'Well, virginity does seem a very personal matter, doesn't it?'

'Yes, perhaps that is my fault. I got drunk one night and that's when it became public. You see, my flatmates knew and they let it out; I merely confirmed it.'

'Well we had better say no more about it, or I'll be accused of prying.'

'This is terribly humiliating,' said Sarah. 'I wish you did not know about it.'

'Why's that?'

'Because when something happens like that you go down in a person's estimation and one's ambitions seem further away than ever.'

'I can assure you my lips are sealed. It is not something I will be going around telling all and sundry, and I certainly don't hold it against you.'

'That's very kind of you.'

'Not really, my mind is still on money. If the people out there aren't doing their jobs then I'm not making any money. So my motives are very mercenary.'

'Even so, it was still a very nice gesture.'

'I would have done it for any of the women out there. What do you want to do now? Do you want to carry on today, or would you prefer to go home?'

'I'm not sure that I could face the office, and there's no one at home.'

'Well, make your mind up; I'm out to see a client in ten minutes.' He was checking his briefcase and Sarah watched him.

'I think,' he said, 'you had better go and sit at your desk in the office. I'll have words with Ms Marchbank and Tom.'

'You're only saying that because of your profit.'

'Too true, but if there's no one at home to talk to you'll only sit there brooding on it for the rest of the day, and tomorrow you'll still have to face the office!'

'I could get another job.'

'But everyone in the city will have seen the website. Do you want every Tom, Dick and Harry to point you out as the woman in the browser?'

'No, I suppose not.'

'Back to your desk, then…'

Sarah rose and went to the door. 'Thanks for supporting me,' she said and returned to the main office.

The atmosphere there was subdued with everyone sitting silently at their desks apparently hard at work; yet Sarah knew that every eye in the room followed her steps as she crossed the floor to her desk. She tossed her head back in a gesture of defiance and switched her computer on. Emma and Clemmie were very quiet, which was quite unusual for them but it became clear why they were so diligent: Mr Deakin had crossed the landing and Clemmie at least could see him leave his room. He came into the office and glared around at everyone. Then, having said something to Ms Marchbank, he left to keep the appointment with his client. No one it seemed dare say anything until lunchtime, and then the office emptied, leaving Sarah and Michael at their workstations.

'I'll get some lunch,' he said suddenly. 'Do you want anything?'

'Just a salmon sandwich, thanks.'

'Won't be five minutes! Why don't you put the kettle on?'
'All right.'

Ten minutes later Michael was back and sitting at his desk. He looked at Sarah as if he were trying to gauge her mood.

'How did your trip to Paris go?' he ventured.

'All right.'

'Did you meet the fellow?'

'No. Actually I had a super weekend, but coming back to this has spoiled it.'

'Yes, I've never seen old Deakin angry before.'

'What did he say, then?'

'He laced into Tom and described him as the most insensitive person he knew. Millie protested and he told her that if she wanted to support Tom then she was no better than him. She was seething. Tom took it on the chin; he knew that he was in the wrong and it irked him that Millie said what she did. Ms Marchbank copped it for not intervening, while Emma and Clemmie had managed to get back to their end of the room and appeared quite innocent.'

'What did he say to you?'

'He asked me if I was part of it and I said that I was not and that I was dumbstruck by what I saw. To that he said it was typical of someone who was so complacent. Then he told me to get in touch with the Internet people who hosted it and get it off. If they refused he said I was to threaten them with being sued.'

'What did the web hosting people say?'

'They were sympathetic. It was a bit of a problem finding out who did host it, but we did. To be fair to the people hosting the site, when I told them they took one look and had it offline within about twenty seconds. But the damage had been done by then.'

'But why would anyone do that?'

'Didn't you stand a number of them up the other week?'

'I suppose I did, but that's a bit over the top, isn't it?'

'I would have thought so, but some people are very mean.'

'Who do you think did it?'

'Oh, any of the blokes in the pub! They'd think it a laugh offering a £5,000 prize to whoever took your virginity. You have to be pretty sick to think that funny.'

'Where did they get the picture of me?'

'I've no idea. But you should have seen Deakin's face! He was livid, and you can see the effect it had on the office. He even managed to switch the twins in the corner off.'

'Who? Emma and Clemmie?'

'The proverbial chatterers! I honestly doubt if they listen to what the other says.'

'Oh, you shouldn't run them down so.'

'Mention their names, and here they are! Look at them skulking to their desks! And after them come Tweedledum and Tweedledee.'

Millie entered first, casting a look of disapprobation in their direction. Tom followed stooping as he normally did but unlike Millie he did not go to his desk. Instead he came over to where Sarah was sitting.

'I really must apologise to you for this morning. It was most thoughtless of me. I never meant to hurt you.'

Sarah was forced to acknowledge him. 'I don't hold it against you,' she replied. But Tom had said his piece, and with a nod of his head he went to his desk.

It was later that evening that Sarah felt that she had been too lenient with him, for it turned out that both Cathy and Gerrie had seen the website.

'It looks like small boobs are going to become the fashion,' said Cathy.

'That'll put some plastic surgeons out of business,' said Gerrie.

'They're likely to lose their jobs anyway,' agreed Sarah dryly, 'for I see the latest treatment is like taking a bicycle pump to them.'

'But to get £5,000 for losing your virginity…'

'That's very insensitive of you, Cathy, to bring that up – and you had better note that I don't get it, only the bloke does.'

'But what I want to know is how can you prove that a particular man took a woman's virginity?'

'Is that all you two can talk about? I was very hurt by it and I don't want to hear any more about it.'

'Well, some of the girls in our office were quite jealous of you for having so much attention given to your body.'

'But they wouldn't have liked it if it had been them. Anyway, how did you hear about it?'

'It went the rounds today. How come you know about it, Gerrie?'

'Someone in the office was told and knew where to look. But you've become something of a celebrity, Sarah!'

'Well, it isn't exactly the way I'd have chosen.'

'Hey, how did your French trip go?'

'It was fine.'

'We had a bet, Cathy and I, as to where he was going to meet you. Cathy was certain it was on the plane or at the airport. My guess was that it was the hotel.'

'You're both wrong.'

'So where did he meet you? The most romantic place we could think of was the top of the Eiffel Tower.'

'I wasn't met by anyone.'

'So what have you been up to?'

'Well I've had the most amazing weekend at someone's expense, and yet I don't know whose!'

'Wow, that was a damn good challenge you issued!'

'What do you mean?'

'To have been given a weekend abroad and become famous the day after.'

'No, Cathy, let me correct you there. I did not become famous; I became infamous because I acquired a degree of notoriety.'

'Never mind that! Today, any publicity is good publicity.'

'That's because we live in a talentless world and the people who shout loudest and do the most stupid things become famous.'

'Whoa! I detect some bitterness there,' said Cathy.

'You detect what you want. And while we're talking about it, hadn't you better do some washing-up?'

'Why?'

'Two reasons – most of it is yours, and it's ages since it was your turn.'

'It's not all mine.'

'Look, I'm fed up of coming home simply to clear the kitchen up. I don't want to end life as your servant. And Gerrie, do you have to paint your toenails on the furniture?'

'What's the matter?' said Gerrie, who was only wearing a dressing gown.

'You're not decent!'

'But we're all women here, aren't we?'

'Why can't you do it in your own room?'

'You never moaned before – and why have you come home in such a temper?'

'I haven't.'

'Oh yes you have! You're never this critical.'

'Well I would have thought it's obvious why I'm upset, and no one has attempted to placate me.'

'We can't sympathise when we're quite envious of you.'

'Isn't that film about to start?' Cathy was switching the television set.

Sarah could do little else but sit with them and watch the film. Whilst Cathy and Gerrie seemed intent on it, Sarah found herself rather bored and her mind wandering. She had not told them of the bracelet. She was not a person who wore jewellery, and though she was pleased with it, she was not able to triumph as some women might, seeing problems with it, especially if the mystery man was unable to properly afford it. The cost might well force him out into the open, since he would certainly want to claim his rights, and if it were known, how many of her banking friends might attempt to say that it was theirs? If Cathy or Gerrie knew about it then by tomorrow evening half the City would also know, and she resolved to keep silent about it... But could she keep quiet?

It was a vexing question and it consumed her for most of the film. Finally, she came to a conclusion. She would be asked about the weekend and it was likely that she might let slip about the jewellery... But what if she were to say it was a ring? That wouldn't be a complete lie, since both bracelets and rings are round. It might also root out the true mystery man, since only he would know exactly what piece of jewellery she had purchased. She felt pleased with the idea. Looking up, she noticed that the film was coming to an end and she would be able to finally retire to bed.

The following day it was necessary to take some work in to Mr Deakin. So far as Sarah could see, Jonathan French had left a chunk of his book out, and she was adamant that she was not going to phone him up. She told Mr Deakin and insisted that he spoke to the gentleman.

'Why can't you do it?' said Mr Deakin.

'I would have thought,' said Sarah, 'that it was painfully obvious.'

'Don't you want to ask him why he left me to pay the bill?'

'I wasn't thinking of that. It was the way he spoke to me and looked at me.'

'What did he say?'

'You were there… I mean those extravagant compliments he paid me.'

'I thought women liked compliments.'

'Not those.'

'And how did he look at you?'

'He leered at me, and if he could he would have taken my clothes off with his eyes.'

'Well, all right, I'll deal with it.'

'Thank you.'

'And how was your trip to Paris? Did you meet your heart's desire?'

Sarah blushed at his words. 'No.'

'You told me that he would sit beside you on the plane.'

'He didn't, and he wasn't at the airport.'

'So you had a frustrating weekend…'

'No, I didn't, actually. I had a lovely time.'

Mr Deakin looked surprised. 'But if you weren't met by anyone, you couldn't have had much of a weekend.'

'But I was met, I suppose. A chauffeur came and took me to a hotel and he was around the whole weekend. Oh, it wasn't him; he only spoke French, which was nice, as I could brush up my French.'

'So not being met by this man didn't bother you?'

'No, not really. It would have been good to have the company of someone, but in a sense it was so well planned that it was almost as if someone were there.'

'I would like to hear more but I'm a bit busy at the moment.'

His words were dismissive and Sarah rose. She would have liked to have told him about her visit in detail, but she could see that he had lost interest in her and had resumed whatever it was that he was doing when she entered. Now he was engrossed in the papers in front of him; it was pointless to do anything other than leave.

The following Wednesday Sarah kept her date with Clive. She was determined to find out if it were Clive who was her mystery man. She didn't want to ask him straight out, but to deduce from some of his replies whether or not it was indeed him. They had agreed to meet at the King's Head just off Savile Row. Clive was waiting for her when she entered.

'What are you drinking?' he asked. There was a brandy glass in front of him.

'Lemon juice,' replied Sarah.

'Nothing in it?'

'No thanks.'

'I thought we would have this one and then go and meet a friend of mine.'

'Fine.' This must be the person who seemed to be behind Clive, and she wanted to meet him for she was curious. He too was a candidate for being the person who paid for her Paris trip.

Having finished their drinks they went outside to find a taxi. They were taken to South Kensington, where they stopped outside a small restaurant. Clive paid the taxi and they went inside.

It was not very busy and Sarah thought that at that time of the evening it ought to be busier. Still, it was a Wednesday evening. A man saw them arrive and rose from his seat to greet them. Clive led Sarah across to his friend.

'This is Keith Turner. Keith, this is Sarah Levine.'

'How do you do, Sarah?' Keith held out his hand and she responded, noting that he gave her hand only the briefest of shakes. Her first impressions were that he was not comfortable in the presence of women and she wondered if the evening would confirm her diagnosis. They sat down and the menu was put before them. Sarah decided to have a light meal of the king prawn salad, but she noted that the two men were having fillet of sole.

'Do you have a preference for wine?' said Keith.

'No, I don't count myself as a connoisseur, and to be honest I can't tell the difference between most wines.'

'You should try and acquire some discernment, Sarah.'

'Well, I find it laughable that a person can say that this wine came from the end of the vineyard and that came from the other!'

'I think it's possible.'

'Perhaps, but then my sex is at a disadvantage.'

'How is that?'

'Because usually the men choose the wine, and they seem to keep its secrets to themselves. Have you ever seen a waiter uncork a bottle and hand the first glass to a woman to try?'

'Now that you mention it, I have to say no.'

'I understand you wanted to meet me.'

'My dear, anyone as elegant and beautiful as yourself would grace and enhance any company.'

'That makes me sound like part of the furniture.'

'If you were here to make up the numbers you would be right, but I believe that you can more than hold your own in a conversation.'

The wine waiter came to the table. He swiftly uncorked the bottle and poured a small amount into a glass. He went to hand it to Keith but Keith indicated that he should offer it to Sarah. She blushed in embarrassment but was forced to take the proffered glass. She had watched many people assay a glass of wine and put it up to the light first to check its clarity. It was certainly not corked. Then she gently swirled liquid round the glass and lifted it to her nose. Should she sip it? Why not? It tasted like... wine.

'Is it to madam's liking?' asked the waiter.

'That's fine,' said Sarah and putting her glass down allowed him to fill the glasses.

'So I have seen a woman test the wine.'

'For the first time in your life. But you have not answered my question.'

'Which question is that, for we have passed on to other topics.'

'Why you desired my company.'

'I am desirous of meeting someone with your reputation.'
'Which reputation are you talking of?'
'Do you have two?'
'I am led to believe that I have. The one that you see and the one that you might have seen on the Internet.'
'Yes, I have heard about that. Tell us more!'
'No, because it's quite unflattering.'
'But my understanding of the situation is that I have never known so much money put on a person's virginity.'

Sarah blushed bright red and felt very uncomfortable. She wished she hadn't started this particular conversation.

'Of course, it is no shame to admit that you have not experienced sex, for I am of the opinion that women today value their virginity too low.'

'Many people today believe that it is an impediment and should be got out of the way as early in life as possible,' Sarah offered.

'Then how pleasant to meet with someone who has higher values in life.'

The meal was put in front of them.

'Are you happy in your employment?' asked Keith.
'Yes, I think so.'
'Then you're not sure.'
'I am sure in that I like what I'm doing, but there is always that feeling that if something better was to come along I might be tempted to go elsewhere.'
'So are you loyal to what you do or to your employer?'
'You're making this into a job interview.'
'No, I was curious, for you sound loyal to your present employer and yet loyalty is not a word used in business today.'
'No, you cannot be loyal on a short-term contract.'
'But you're not on a short-term contract.'
'No, but I feel more loyal to what I do; I can't see myself doing anything else and I actually like what I do.'
'That's when employers become unscrupulous. They discover that a person is happy doing his job and so they allow them to languish there. Five years later that person has ruined their CV and they are stuck in a backwater of a career.'

'What – in a period of five years?'

'Oh yes, or even shorter. When they go for a job interview the question is, "Why have you stayed at so-and-so's this long?" And your answer has to be very good or the interview is immediately terminated. It explains of course why it is so hard for women who have taken time off to have children to get back onto their career paths. How long have you been with Deakin's?'

'Nearly two years.'

'And what are your plans for continuing on your career path?'

'It had crossed my mind that Mr Deakin might make me a manager or even a partner.'

'Has he done anything or intimated anything towards that end?'

'No.'

'So it is all wishful thinking, and while it remains so, you will languish.'

'Yes, I suppose so.'

'Have you made any other contacts within your line of business?'

'No.'

'No, you wouldn't have. Deakin keeps them all to himself.'

'What is your opinion of him?'

'He's a person I can admire, for he is his own man, but he is part of a dying breed. Any business today needs to surround itself with youth and vitality, and be prepared to live in a world that is becoming more frenetic.'

'Your assessment of this world is very pessimistic.'

'Indeed, I align myself with those who believe that this world will destroy itself by its madness.'

Clive was nodding his head. It was the first time that evening that he had acknowledged that he was part of their group, having remained quite silent throughout the conversation. Sarah doubted that he went along with all that was being said, and that in his mind there was different agenda. But she knew that Keith was correct; if she were not careful her career would end in the stagnant pond that was Deakin's. Nothing, however, had been said about how she or anyone in general could avoid the pitfall that lay ahead.

'But you were giving me your opinion of Mr Deakin.'
'Yes. He is, first of all, very autocratic.'
'Didn't he have some trouble with his wife?' said Clive.
'If he did, I don't know what.'
'Yes, he did, I believe. Many years ago. He had a messy divorce or something.'
'You don't know what?'
'No, except that he's a very bitter man. He's not the kind of man with whom I'd want to do business. And he has a very bad reputation within his profession.'
'I didn't know that...' Sarah was worried about what might come next.
'Oh yes. People go along with him because he has made money, and money in today's world speaks louder than anything else.'
'And what else do you know about him?' Sarah asked.
'He's a very shrewd man. He likes to give the impression that he is listless and hasn't heard or taken in anything. Yet he is right on the ball. I have known him give a contractor the impression that he is totally stupid, and yet when it came to the crunch he ruthlessly crushed the man.'
'Tell me more about it.'
'Well, I would, but I only had the story second or third hand, and I don't feel qualified to enlighten you further.'
'So your opinion of him is that he is a nasty piece of work.'
'Undoubtedly. He will give you assurances about something and then deny it by his next action.'
'And where are we going with this conversation?'
'Well, maybe you were right with your first observation. This is, in fact, something of a job interview. How would you like to head up a new publishing company?'
'Let me say straight away that I will not give you an answer to that this evening.'
'I don't expect you to, for you need to know much more about it; but it should within five years or less make you a millionaire.'
'What's the catch?'
'The only catch that I can see is hard work.'
'What will you be doing?'

'Client liaison and accounts.'

'What have you got in the pipeline?'

'A number of smaller projects and then there are at least two big ones that might well turn out to be blockbusters.'

'What's the competition doing about those?'

'So far as I am aware, nothing.'

'So you want to walk in and make a killing. Who is the client?'

'That I cannot disclose.'

'What is it – a biography? I don't see why you need my help.'

'I have seen your work and there is no one, in my opinion, who does it better.'

'I like being flattered, but that is way over the top.'

'Miss Levine underestimates her abilities,' said Clive.

'I have no doubt of that,' said Keith.

'Look, there are plenty of people who do it as well as myself, and many of them do it better.'

'It is something I want you to think over, Sarah. There really is no hurry. Take a few days, or a week even.'

'It may be longer than that as I'm going on holiday for a fortnight this Saturday.'

'It can wait; I've said there's no hurry.'

'What would be required of me?'

'Well, apart from your abilities and your obvious qualities there is the financial side. The whole thing is to be carved up between a small number of people who will each take an equal share. Of course they will be putting up the capital, and they have agreed that since you will have the principal part the amount of capital you put up will be comparatively small.'

'And how small is small?'

'About £25,000.'

'Oh!'

'You don't have that sort of money?'

'Oh, yes, I do, but it sounds an awfully large amount. How much are the others putting up?'

'Well, all I can do is to assure you that it is much more than your contribution.'

'Six figures?'

'I'm really not at liberty to say, as negotiations are still going on.' But he was nodding.

The meal had long since finished and the coffee cups were empty. Clive had sat back and smoked two or three of his thin cigars.

'I think Sarah needs to go away and start thinking,' he said.

'You're probably right,' agreed Keith. 'Will you keep in touch with Sarah and let me know her decision?'

'Certainly,' said Clive. 'Now I think I ought to escort Miss Levine home.'

'Oh no,' said Sarah, 'just get me a taxi.'

'It will be my pleasure,' said Clive and called the waiter across. He spoke quietly to him and he hurried off again. 'He's gone to order you a taxi.'

'Thank you,' said Sarah, relieved that it was for her and not both of them. She glanced at her watch and saw that it was close to eleven o'clock. It was fifteen minutes before a minicab arrived and another half an hour before Sarah arrived home.

She was glad to get to bed that night, and postponed any decision she had to make till after her holiday.

Disillusionment

It was the girls' first evening on the Greek island of Corfu, and having dressed, they were off to find a restaurant. The first thing they had agreed to do was to look around the little shops and get the feel of the place. As they walked up the main street it was clear that they would be welcome at any of the street restaurants. The most persuasive of the waiters would stand in the street talking the clients into their restaurant. Their public relations manner was an object lesson in itself. Most relied on their personality, and usually in a quite unashamed manner they flirted with the women. The wives were easy, for despite their sagging figures they were responsive to flattery and all too often it was they who made the decision about where to eat in the evening.

For the unattached younger women, more often than not sporting trim figures, the single waiter outside was insufficient. He must have had a special signal, for all the young male waiters would be there urging them to eat in their establishment. For the local women, some of whom were the waitresses, this was par for the course. What did it matter if to get the punters in they broke all the rules of sexual discrimination?

Sarah was conscious that she was the one out of line. Her five friends lapped it up and flirted with any of the waiters, whether they were going to eat there or not. By the time they had reached the top of the street and had passed a dozen restaurants, and were due to eat at all of them. They finished their window-shopping and turned back to the restaurants, choosing the one where the waiters had been the sauciest. It was a pity, Sarah felt, that the choice had not been made on the menu or the price of the meal, but she knew that to voice her opinion would put her out of line with the others.

They were led to a table by four waiters, which was most embarrassing; at least it was for Sarah, for she could see that the waiters had left the other tables to lend a hand to their comfort.

The others clients could only stare at the favouritism being displayed before their eyes.

'Oh, that doesn't look too nice,' said one of their group, called Beatrice, looking around at the fare. 'I think I'll stick to a beefburger and chips.'

'The mixed grill looks all right,' said Gerrie.

'But I'm going to have the fillet of sole,' said Vanessa, Beatrice's friend.

'You mean it's fish and chips for you,' said Gilly, and they all laughed.

'Isn't anyone going to try the local dishes?' asked Sarah.

'No way,' said Cathy, 'or are you?'

'I'm thinking of the *kotchinisko*.'

'Oh, how could you, Sarah?'

'What's wrong with it? It's only chunks of boiled beef. If it was dished up at home you'd call it a casserole.'

The waiter came back and put some dishes on the table. He leaned over Cathy and Gilly, and Sarah had the distinct impression that he did so simply to look down their cleavages.

'What on earth has he put on the table?' said Beatrice and they all, with the exception of Sarah, agreed that it looked disgusting.

'What's wrong with that?' asked Sarah innocently, 'it's only a plate of salad!'

'We're not looking at that one.' said Cathy.

'No, we're looking at that!' said Gilly, with evident disgust in her voice.

'Oh,' said Gerrie, 'it looks like dog dos.'

'Don't be so stupid!' said Sarah. 'It's a Greek delicacy.'

'It not fit to be near the table,' said Beatrice, 'let's go elsewhere.'

'Look,' said Sarah and took one of the offending pieces, 'all it is, is rice wrapped up in a vine leaf and boiled. It's really very nice.' Sarah bit into the one she was holding and ate it.

'Oh, how could you, Sarah?' said Beatrice.

'Oh – and look at the salad! It's got black olives all over it,' said Vanessa.

Two waiters were now hovering, and the first said, 'Have you made your decision yet, ladies?'

No one had changed their minds and they gave him their orders. The other waiter asked them what they wanted to drink and the girls agreed to two bottles of wine. They were both back in no time, one carrying a tray of wine glasses and the wine. While one put the glasses round, the other opened the bottles. Then they took a bottle each and went round the table pouring it out. It was noticeable that the girls with the better cleavage were given far more attention. Sarah felt embarrassed with her small breasts, for when the waiters poured hers he sloshed it carelessly into her glass. The waiters left them and the women clinked glasses and they each had a long drink.

'He had a good look at you,' said Gerrie to Beatrice.

'He had a look at everyone,' said Vanessa. 'Well who'd cover up their assets if they wanted men to look at them?'

'Sarah only got a cursory look,' said Cathy drawing attention to Sarah's lack of assets.

Sarah went red. There was nothing she hated more than attention being drawn to her small breasts.

'Why don't you get a boob job done on them?' asked Gilly. 'Half the women who go to the consultant's room want boob jobs.' Gilly was a doctor's receptionist. Sarah was certain that she was grossly exaggerating things and did not bother to reply.

'We've often said to Sarah that she ought to have it done,' said Cathy.

'You should, you know,' persisted Gilly.

Sarah was bright red with embarrassment and feeling very uncomfortable.

'I heard a story about Sarah's boobs once,' said Cathy.

'Tell us,' said Beatrice.

Sarah stared at her flatmate in agony, trying to implore her not to say anything but; there was no way Cathy was going to be persuaded out of telling everyone and Sarah could only lower her eyes.

'Apparently, Sarah put tissues in her bra and then went swimming, and to everyone's delight they disintegrated.'

Everyone was now laughing heartily and it seemed to be the cue for two waiters to come over and check if all their needs were being met. This gave way to another round of flirting for all of them except Sarah. She knew that the waiters had overheard their conversation, for Cathy's voice carried and now they too were sharing the joke. But Sarah felt utterly humiliated.

Cathy sensed her mood and said scathingly, 'For goodness sake, Sar, when I told everyone last year about your breasts you were laughing too!'

'But you're always telling people, you never let it rest! Why is it that people I rely on so often let me down?'

'Oh, come on, Sar, we're only having a good laugh!'

'Yes, and it always costs me! All those waiters know of your joke and they're all over there having a laugh amongst themselves. Suppose I told them about the tattoo on your buttocks.'

'What about it? If they really wanted to see it I'd show them.' She looked round at the waiters as to give them an immediate invitation.

Sarah subsided into silence. Women could be their own worst enemies. Instead of closing ranks against men, they exposed the weaknesses of their own sex to ridicule. Every time women move the frontiers of emancipation forward there always seems to be another group of women moving it back again! They seem to be almost perverse in wanting to prove that men were right. She ate her meal in silence, unable to involve herself in the badinage of her friends. She had looked forward to the holiday and was left with a profound sense of foreboding that it was going to be a complete disaster.

At the end of the meal they were urged to come again. They agreed to this and walked unsteadily off down the road. They passed a bar advertising karaoke.

'That place is dead,' said Gilly, 'let's find somewhere else.'

At the next bar a group of young men called them over.

'Do you girls want a drink?' said the first man.

'Are you buying?' asked Cathy.

'Might be,' said the man.

'Where does it all happen around here?'

'Wherever we are,' said one of the other men.

'Is there a disco round here?' asked Beatrice.

'Right here, we can make it a disco especially for you.'

Sarah stared at her friends, for they looked as if they were about to be beguiled by these men and she did not want to drink with them.

'Come on, Sar,' said Gerrie, 'we're going in. Come and join us.'

'No,' said Sarah sharply, 'I'm going back to the apartment.'

'Oh, come on, we agreed to stick together.'

'Then someone should come back with me.'

'We're going in, aren't we, girls?' said Gilly, and they all agreed.

'I'm going back to the apartment; can I have the key, please?'

Cathy hunted for the key and handed it over. 'You won't lock us out this time, will you?'

'No, provided you don't come back with all these fellows… and remember, I don't want to know them.'

Sarah turned and walked off. The shops gave way to a pleasant avenue of trees with bougainvilleas flowing over the walls. The night air was very warm and she was glad of the silence. Perhaps if they had determined on a walk along the front she would have gone with them; but then she was through the gates and into their apartment complex.

Sarah lay on her bed. She worried about herself. Holidays had always been a time of fun for her and she had looked forward to them with great enthusiasm. But now she was here on this Greek island she felt that she wanted to be back home. She could not blame the company, for they were the same as last year, though their group had two more this time. Her friends had hurt her with their jibes about her breasts. They didn't realise just how conscious she was of them. Was it the reason that she was not interested in men? Did men always sum a woman up by the size of her breasts? Surely not! Had any of the men who had professed to wanting to make love to her made allowances for her lack, or would they too have persuaded her at some point to have implants? Why did she not have implants? It was a simple enough operation, and if it made her feel more womanly then why not do it?

Her only answer to that was that the thought an operation was worse than her lack of cleavage. They would not be hers! They would be just appendages under her flesh rather than in her cups.

But then why have it done? Was she after a man? She thought not, for she hadn't fancied any of the waiters. She had instantly recoiled from the sight of their sweaty shirts and their dark hair, which was so greasy that it was surely not natural.

Had the trip to France unsettled her? If she was honest, the answer was positive. She had enjoyed visiting Paris. She had enjoyed being taken around, even though she had had no say in what she was to see. Had she had control of her itinerary, it wouldn't have been as good as what she had experienced, and she wanted to meet the person who had planned it. Was she just curious about him? Or did she have some feelings for him? Was it possible to have feelings for someone you have not seen? But not meeting him was the only downside to the weekend. There had always been a feeling that someone was close to her and that his presence was benevolent and benign. If it had not been, then why go to all the expense? She had brought the bracelet to annoy him, yet someone had absorbed the cost of it with a good deal of complacency. And it was that cost that precluded it being prank by her friends. They would never have thought up something costing so much. Indeed, it was the price of their entire holiday for a fortnight. No, the choice of hotel implied that the person knew something of Paris.

She had changed and she did not know in what way. Was it a product of getting older? Was she lacking the energy to do stupid things? Was she happy wanting to be a single woman?

Despite being on her own she blushed and immediately knew that it was one of the vital questions she had to answer. Ten years ago she had made the decision that she would stay single. It had only been in the last few months that she had felt uneasy with herself. She was aware that she had made certain statements when she was drunk but she reasoned that no one listened to drunken people, least of all to the pronouncements of drunken women.

The truth was that she had been mentally challenged and stimulated by her trip to Paris, and here the last thing she was going to get was that. Up in the hills were ancient Greek ruins. But did any of them want to know? Of course not! Cathy had declared that there were plenty of ruins around them here, and it was some reference to current Greek building practices, so why go and find another... What were they reading? They had all brought magazines with them but she was the only one who had brought a book! But then they would say that she was a publisher! But why do you have to be a publisher to read a book? If they only ever sold books to individuals in publishing there would be very few sold. She had two weeks of mind-sapping boredom in front of her and she should have seen it coming.

Where were they now? Probably at a disco, and they would stay there until two or three in the morning when they would come struggling back. They would crash in regardless of anyone asleep and sit and talk in the kitchen. Someone would make a hot drink for everyone, which wouldn't be touched, and she would have to clear up after them in the morning. One by one they would have an appointment with the toilet – and that would not be for normal activities, since they always moaned, groaned and heaved! Then they would find their beds and eventually a peace would descend for whatever was left of the night. It would be unlikely that anyone would emerge before midday. They would then sunbathe in an unconscious fashion with someone appointed to go round and rub blocker into them. At six o'clock they would stir and spend the next two hours getting ready for the evening. Sarah felt ashamed that until the previous year she too had been just like that. But sleep overcame her and nothing disturbed her until eight o'clock in the morning.

She collected up the mugs of drinks that had been left and generally cleared the kitchen. There was nothing in for breakfast, mainly because no one was thinking of having any. Sarah went to the small supermarket a short way down the road and purchased a croissant for herself. Having eaten some breakfast she changed into her bikini and found a recliner by the pool. Most of the other guests had yet to rise. She tried to read her book but put it down and stared at the pool.

She was hopelessly dissatisfied with everything. There was the daunting prospect of having to decide what to do about Keith's offer. It affected her relationship with her present employer, and though she had no particular regard for Mr Deakin, she was prepared to admit that he had been kind to her, and she was not the type of person who dismissed kindness easily. It came down to a question of whether her loyalty to him was greater than her loyalty to herself, for she was ambitious and she wanted to be someone who achieved. Did that bring Keith's offer into proper perspective? For even if she took up his offer she was still not her own boss, despite the fact that she might make millions.

Was it a female weakness to feel loyalty? She was glad to be part of something and it made working that much more pleasant. Of course Ms Marchbank was a martinet of a woman; Mr Deakin had needed someone like her to run his office. Did that show him to be a weak person? Not at all, for anyone building a business has to delegate and trust employees, their duty being to keep within the rules. Ms Marchbank had to do that while Mr Deakin made up the rules; just as it had been Mr Deakin who had been angry about the website and not Ms Marchbank, who in all likelihood had enjoyed seeing her embarrassment!

Sarah sighed, for life had suddenly become very complicated. She had changed and she did not know how she had changed. Life for her until recently had been straightforward. She rose in the morning and went to work; left the office in the evening and had a drink in the pub. She went home and spent the evening watching the television. The following day was nothing more than a repeat of the day before. She had made it clear to the opposite sex that she wanted nothing to do with them, and they had all received the message without too much effort on her part.

Was it her stupid drunken challenge that changed her? No, that actually did not change her. It was merely the outward sign that she had changed. It was the small boy in the Oxford Street store who had changed her, and more specifically the mother's attitude towards her. But why should that have made any difference to her? The injustice of it did affect her, and she would readily admit that; but then there was much injustice in the world anyway. She had only to open a newspaper and read it. What she had endured in that respect was nothing compared to what others had suffered.

She looked at the pool again with its smooth surface allowing the bottom to be clearly seen. Was she looking straight through herself? Was she unable to admit certain things to herself? She had been challenged by the mother's attitude and been appalled at her lack of real concern for her child. Was it that it had offended her maternal instincts? There, she had dared to admit it!

Did she have maternal instincts? No, she did not; at least she certainly did not up until that event. Had someone suggested she might like to have a child she would have laughed at them. But now she could not say that. She could never be as bad a mother as that. She could never show so much disregard for her own flesh and blood; no, she wanted to think that she would err by pouring out too much love on her offspring.

The sun was beginning to make itself felt on her skin and she reached out for her bottle of sunblock. She rubbed it over her legs and enjoyed its cooling effect reaching the top of her thighs. She looked down at her bikini bottom and wondered if she really wanted to let her body open up and give birth. It was strange, because it had always been a thought that she could dismiss, since there was no way it was going to happen. But here she was trying to imagine it...

And in reality her body was telling her that she needed a man. That was the real change that had come about her! Her attitude towards the opposite sex had changed. She had looked at Clive and immediately seen that he was a perfect specimen of the male sex, and she knew that she was in danger with him. She could flirt with him but there would come a point when he would have his way with her, and how would she feel about that? Would she feel pleased? Or would she want to shout, 'Rape'? It was dangerous, because the result was not clear cut and would almost certainly end in her being hurt in some way. But what if he were the man who had arranged her trip to Paris? Could she yield to him? She doubted it but she could not explain why. He would never be a husband and she would spend the rest of her life nurturing a deeply wounded spirit.

But who had arranged her trip to Paris? She could go through a long list of men who she thought that it was not, but then she could see that any one of those men could have done it. Even though she had spent a lot of money on the bracelet, it was not out of the reach of any of the bankers who had been in the pub to hear her challenge, and it must have come from there. It was very subtle for it was breaking down her resistance to men, and now she had a longing to meet the man in question. If he were a man whom she could never respect then it would be easy. She could repay him and forget him and return to what she used to be. But what if he were acceptable? What if he were a thoroughly nice person? It was here that she had changed so much, for there was a time when there was never a man she would even consider. Now she was wondering if he were a man she could like. To go any further was too dangerous!

She looked across the pool again and knew that she was going to spend her holiday thinking about it continuously and never coming to a conclusion, because the man was not going to reveal himself to her. Was it something that was going to worry her? She doubted it, for she rather liked her thoughts and wanted to go through them again, but this time in more detail. She was glad her friends were still asleep!

It couldn't be the dreadful Gareth for he could not even afford a taxi. How could he have afforded the airfare, the limousine or the hotel? Then there had been the €200 for her to spend, and surely the bracelet alone would have demolished his credit card! Perhaps that was why the person had not revealed himself. The financial damage had blasted his pride, and now he didn't want to come forward and admit to it. But he would not be revealing himself publicly, for she had not mentioned it to anyone; so there was no loss of face there, although he might feel that he had lost face with her. If he revealed himself and he was in dire straits, she was not a person who could let him suffer. She could hand the bracelet back to him or even buy it from him. It was what made the bracelet so awkward and for that reason alone she could not get attached to owning such a beautiful piece of jewellery. Would she help him with the rest of the costs? There was no reason for her to do that, for it was not a course of action that she had planned, and whoever had done so had surely taken the cost into account. It wasn't something one could ignore. But Gareth was out of the question, and if at the end of the day it turned out to be him she would own up to being the first to be shocked.

The truth was that she was not wanting so much to meet this person for her sake but really for *his* sake, so that she could be certain that he was all right! She could then thank him for his attention and direct him on to a path towards a woman more worthy of his affections. But the thought made her feel very guilty, as it was clear that she considered herself superior to the male sex. Yet she had thought that she merely felt herself to be equal to any man. But why should she suffer from the feminine tendency to feel guilt when she had done nothing? She had not encouraged a man on this particular piece of extravagance, yet to yield to him in order to expiate her own guilt left her bowing down to his superiority, and either way she was the loser. And that was annoying! No, this man had set himself up for his own downfall despite what she had said the pub. He could in no way blame her for his hurt feelings and being out of pocket. She would give him the credit for having tried with her but no more. But there was one thing wrong with her logic and that was that he could be someone she could look up to!

But she had never met a man who brought those feelings out in her. She had gone to dances at university with many young men but none of them had awakened in her any sort of emotion. Never had she gone back to her room and not wanted her escort to leave, leaving her glad that the evening was finished.

Suddenly, she realised that Cathy was leaning over her.

'Do you want the cream on your back?' she asked.

'Yes please! What time did you get in last night?'

'About two o'clock. We met some guys who are going to take us to a disco tonight. It's in the next resort.'

'That'll be nice for you.'

'What about you – aren't you going to come?'

'No, I don't want to. What's the time?'

'Lunchtime, but I don't feel hungry.'

'Big hangover?'

'The worst. Gilly and Beattie are still flat out and Vanessa's sitting in the kitchen, moaning.'

'I've got no sympathy for any of you.'

'You should have, but I'm going to try the pool.'

Sarah watched her friend jump straight in. Everyone around the pool was watching and once Cathy had disappeared beneath the water all eyes seemed to turn on Sarah. She resented people looking at her. Most of the women stared because they were envious of her figure, and looked in curiosity at her lack of breasts. The men looked at her in exactly the same way, though they were motivated by lust rather than envy.

Was the man who had sent her to Paris motivated by lust? If he were, she would soon send him packing. But then he would never have seen her in a bikini, and how could he be certain that she had a good figure beneath her trouser suit? For all he knew, she wore trousers because she had deformed legs! But whoever he was he must have some refinement, for he had sent her on a very stimulating weekend.

Cathy climbed out of the pool. Some young men were now placing themselves opposite to give themselves a good view of herself and Cathy. Gerrie suddenly arrived from nowhere, and seeing the men staring across the pool began to parade up and down in a very provocative manner. Then she jumped into the pool and Cathy followed her. Beatrice and Vanessa arrived and, seeing Cathy and Gerri in the water, jumped in as well. This was too much for five young men and they found a football and all jumped into the pool. It was not long before it was men against women. The smaller children at the shallow end decided that it was too violent for them to stay in the water.

Sarah tried to continue with her book but was suddenly conscious that there were two strapping young men bearing down on her. Everyone in the pool had stopped and all eyes were glued on her. It was obvious what their mission was, and Sarah glared at the man closest to her.

'Don't bother,' she said, 'unless you want to spend the rest of your holiday in the local nick!'

Cathy was out of the pool and shouting at them, 'I told you to leave her alone!'

'It was only a bit of fun,' complained the first young man.

'It might be for you, but it isn't for me!' Sarah spat the words at him and rose to her feet. Gathering up her things she retired to the apartment.

Cathy was behind her, protesting, 'I did try to stop them, Sar, honestly I did!'

'Why is it I come out here for a bit of peace and quiet and all I get is some bloke wanting to assault me?'

'It's just fun and high spirits.'
'Yes, it is but it's the kind of thing teenagers do!'
'You were all for it last year.'
'I may have been, but things are different now.'
'How are they different?'
'Because I think I want a bit more out of life than this froth and bubble.'
'The way you're acting anyone would have thought you were in love.'
'I can assure on that score that it is not so.'
'I'm going back out there. I suggest you pull yourself together and join us.'

Sarah felt miserable, for the scene had convinced her that the holiday was going to be a trial for her. Was she in love? How could she be? She didn't know anyone to be in love with. There was Clive... Was she in love with him? She liked him well enough and she liked his manners, his bearing, and everything about him except for his familiarity. He used woman for his own gratification and he was unstable. Why should she fall in love with a man like that? What about the man who sent her to Paris? How could she be in love with him – she did not even know who he was! Surely you couldn't be in love with someone you've never met!

Why was being a woman suddenly so difficult? Was she broody? She had no desire to play with the children in the apartment across the way or the ones beside the pool. No, it was none of these things. It was simply that this man was an enigma. He was interesting, and she wanted to know him. Why? For the simple reason that she could eliminate him as a potential suitor. She did not want a lasting relationship with him, but until they met she was not in a position to tell him that she didn't want any more to do with him. That she knew was mostly true, but at the back of her mind there was a small doubt. It could be that he was a man who came close to her ideal and someone she could love in return. Feelings of guilt returned, as it was not the way she had been thinking for so long. She'd had no problems until recently with being and remaining single. Her brother had two children, with a third on the way, and she could be quite happy later in life being an aunt to them. She could have them for part of a day or longer, and when she tired of them she could send them back to their parents. But it did not answer her needs!

What was this man like? He had money, and she was glad of that. How horrible it would be to marry one of the men out there in the pool. Almost certainly they drank too much and had no money set aside for a house. They would see her salary as being necessary to live on and she would have to keep working. And what if he were a real wastrel? She would end up keeping him! It might be worth it if he had some wonderful talent, and recognition was just round the corner. No, there was something about Paris that said about this man that he wanted to live like that and that he had the money to do so. She felt that she was being invited to join him, but she did not want to be his trophy.

But what was she going to do with her holiday? She had looked forward to it, yet at that moment she wished she were back home. It was, however, a nightmare that would eventually end.

The Plan

It was a holiday from which it was a relief to return home and push the front door open. The woman from the downstairs flat had piled their mail up on the bottom of their stairs, and it seemed more sensible to the three women to leave their cases at the bottom and carry the post upstairs. It was duly sorted and they sat at the kitchen table, each with a large pile in front of them. Most of them knew that it was junk mail, but the bills needed to be sorted out. Every so often there would be a letter from a sender who was unrecognised and this was the moment they each waited for.

'It's my mother,' said Gerrie. 'Why can't she email it to me?'

'Does she have a computer?' asked Cathy.

'How do I know?'

'Because a lot of people of her age don't bother with such things.'

'I suppose not. Oh, her neighbours are cutting rough over the hedges as usual. And my sister's pregnant again.'

'I thought this was interesting,' said Cathy, 'but it's just a circular dressed up to look like a letter from a friend.'

'Or, "You are close to winning a quarter of a million, just send back the letter with the pretty stamps attached." No one ever wins the money, why do they bother?' said Sarah.

'They get you in a right tizzy about it: "You have won through to the third round, and we're pleased to inform you that you are one of the lucky people in Earlsfield who will go into the final draw."'

'Yes, Cathy, you will – along with the other 50,000 inhabitants of the same community! We guarantee that not less than fifty per cent of the population has been entered for the draw!'

'Who wants the phone bill?'

'You can keep that – it's mostly yours, Gerrie.'

'Well, in that case I'll sort out who had what and send you the bill.'

'But I use my mobile.'

'*Sarah uses her mobile*,' said Gerrie sarcastically. 'I thought mobiles hung from the ceiling and went round and round in the wind.'

Sarah pulled out another letter and stared at it.

'What's up, Sar?'

'Nothing, it's just a postmark I don't recognise.'

'What's in it, then?'

Sarah slit open the envelope and pulled out the contents.

'So what have you got?'

'It's an airline ticket.'

'What, another one?'

'Yes – to Amsterdam.'

'Who's it from?'

'Doesn't say.'

'Got to be the same fellow, then.'

'When is it for?'

'Two weeks' time.'

'What a way to conduct a relationship! Still, perhaps this time he might not miss the plane.'

'It doesn't matter to me whether he catches the plane or not, for this time I'm not going.'

'Seems a shame to miss out on a treat...'

'Yes, but I think he's taking me for a ride.'

'I wish Charles would take me for a ride.'

'I thought he did,' said Gerrie, suddenly butting into the conversation.

'You can call it what you like, but if he sent me a ticket I'd soon be off. Anyone put the kettle on?'

'No, I'd look too stupid with it on my head.'

'Ha, ha, not funny! Someone always says that. Why can't they say it would never cover everything, or something?' Cathy asked rhetorically.

'Since that's your line, you had better use it. So I'll say, "Cathy, have you put the kettle on?" And you say, "It will never cover everything," and I'll say, "But it's better than going around naked."'

'Shut up, Gerrie, you really do talk nonsense at times. Sar's looking stressed already.'

'Too true! I've never seen anyone have such an uphill fight with men before.'

'Especially with one she doesn't know and has never met.'

'Like the weather couple, when it's fine she's out and when it's not he's out. Trouble is they never meet!'

'I'm going to have a shower,' said Sarah, rising and intending to go to her room. 'I'd really hoped this guy had missed his meeting with me and given up.'

'But what if he's a real man?'

'I have yet to meet one.'

'You're much too hard them.'

'The only men I've ever met are either scheming and deceitful or stupid and nasty.'

'You have only met a narrow section of the population.'

'Sounds like she's disappointed,' said Gerrie in a low voice that Sarah heard clearly.

'I'm not disappointed, as some of you would be; I'm just upset that I feel someone is stalking me.'

'I wish someone would stalk me with brilliant weekends, and drop money and trinkets into my hand!'

'And I suppose, Sar, you would go to court and say, "Milud, I'm being stalked by persons unknown, could you put an order on them to stop!"'

Sarah left her flatmates and went to sit on her bed. Her holiday had given her plenty of time to think things through and she had hoped for certain conclusions. In many ways her conclusions had served to ease her mind over the whole matter. If a man was interested in a girl it meant there was emotional upheaval ahead whether she wanted it or not, and whatever the outcome. One could argue that testing emotions was all part of life, but in many respects it was what she had opted out of. The ticket had ruined her thoughts and removed the little pleasure she had had from the holiday and also the pleasure one derives from coming home. She simply wished that she had not returned.

Whoever he was, he was still interested in her. No longer could she argue that the bracelet had ruined his credit card balance, though it was just about possible that he had not received the latest statement and did not yet know the cost of the bracelet.

But she doubted that. The manager when she purchased it would never have let her have it if the man had not agreed in advance to a sum of that size. And almost certainly he would immediately have been in touch with the man to check that he had done the correct thing. Which meant that the man's credit with the hotel was very high. An idea flashed through her brain. What an idiot she was! She should have checked the guest book and seen if there were any names in it that she knew. She could not remember seeing it and guessed that she had asked to see it the manager would have told her that it was not available.

She should be pleased, as the man was not without funds and the fact that she had spent so much of his money was acceptable to him. What was worse was that it showed that he put a value on her. Nor was he without taste, for the hotel was excellent and could not simply have been picked from a travel brochure. And how did he know about her? The weekend he had planned was to her liking and in many ways she could not have improved upon it. But that meant the whole thing was serious. She had accepted his largesse and was therefore to some extent beholden to him, so that getting out of the situation was going to be more painful than she had originally envisaged.

It was Wednesday afternoon before she could talk to Mr Deakin. He had been away on both the Monday and Tuesday and had then been too busy to see her until four o'clock.

Sarah entered his office.

'Take a seat, Sarah. I'm sorry not to have been able to see you sooner but I have been rather busy.' She pulled a chair up and sat down.

'What has Jonathan French been saying to you now?'

'Nothing, why?'

'Oh he's always talking about you on the phone.'

'I wouldn't dare go out for a meal with him again, as I might find myself paying the bill.'

'So what is the problem?'

'Look at this,' said Sarah, and handed him the airline ticket she had received in the post.

'It's an airline ticket made out to you.'

'Yes, I know it is, but it simply came through the post to me. I don't know who it is from.'

'Are you going to Amsterdam, then?'

'I don't know.'

'So what you want is my advice.'

'Yes, please.'

Mr Deakin creased his brow and said, 'Why ask me? I don't see how I can help you.'

'I'm asking you because I don't know who else to ask. Everyone that I know of would laugh at me or tell me how lucky I was. If I mentioned it in a pub they'd all be talking about it and I'd be so embarrassed.'

'So you think my advice would be better... I'm not so sure, since I'm a different generation to you.'

'You may right, but at least you listen and you've never said anything stupid.'

'Really you want a confidant.'

'Yes, I suppose so.'

'All right, presumably this ticket has come from the same person.'

'I presume so.'

'Why shouldn't it have come from someone who knew about your previous exploit and is hoping to cash in on it?'

'I never thought of that.'

'So who knows about your last trip?'

'My flatmates, some of the people in the office.'

'Would Tom know?'

'He might. Why Tom?'

'He has connections in the City.'

'It was Tom who invited the bankers to the pub that evening.'

'What evening?'

'When I made a complete fool of myself.'

'Have we spoken about it before? You'll have to remind me.'

'Everyone in the office went to the pub and we were joined by these bankers and other men. They got talking about virginity, and then Cathy told everyone that I was a virgin.'

'That sounds a stupid thing to say.'

'Yes, but I managed worse than that.'

'Really – how?'
'I challenged them all.'
'Challenged them to what?'
'I offered my virginity to any of them who could show he was worthy.'
'So this is what this ticket and the website are all about.'
'Now you know. I hadn't meant to tell you that.'
'How do you expect me to be a confidant if you are going to tell me only part of the story?'
'You're right, but now I have told you. I haven't before because I don't want to lose your respect. I don't want you to think I'm an odd person. I've always been very down-to-earth and I get drunk once in a blue moon and I've never mouthed off before; it was quite out of character. And it's very unfair. I know people who make fools of themselves all too often, but no one seems concerned about their behaviour.'
'I haven't condemned you for saying it, have I?'
'Not yet.'
'I'm sorry that you think so little of me.'
'No, I didn't mean it like that. If you were in my position you would know how I feel, and with my friends I'm now on edge.'
'Right, let's forget that you said that. We haven't spoken about how you got on in Paris.'
'I was expecting this man to meet me on the plane flying out but he didn't. I didn't know what to do when I got to Paris, and when I walked out I was met by a chauffeur. He took me to a really nice hotel and I was put in one of the best rooms. Someone had planned had a whole weekend for me and it was really very enjoyable.'
'Then why have you got any problems?'
'Because getting this ticket means that he's serious about me.'
'And you're not serious about him?'
'How can I be? I don't know who he is. But anyway I don't want a relationship, however nice he is. I tried to put him off by buying a piece of jewellery.'
'What did you buy?'
'A ring. It was rather expensive,' said Sarah, aware that she hadn't told her confidant the truth. She thought about correcting

herself, but decided against it. She knew that telling one person and not the others would make life difficult.

'Really?'

'Yes, it was €2,000.'

'Ouch, he won't enjoy that!'

'Then why has he sent me another ticket?'

'I see your point; if he didn't like it the first time, why go for a repeat...'

'Exactly.'

'So should you go to Amsterdam? That is the question. You went to Paris out of curiosity, I think you said.'

'Yes.'

'But now it is an affair of the heart.'

'No, I just want to meet the guy to tell him where to go!'

'I was going to advise you not to go, but I don't see how you can get to meet him otherwise. Yet by going, you are somehow giving him the green light – at least that's the way he'll see it.'

'I hadn't thought of that. It makes it worse.'

'What about this as a solution?'

'Go on tell me!'

'Why not go on this man's ticket and take a friend with you. One of your flatmates!'

'But what do I do when I get to the car and the chauffeur says he will only take me?'

'Tell him that you both go or no one goes, and you take the next plane home.'

'Do you think this man will pay for two?'

'I doubt it; you'll have to make sure that you've the money on you for her. There is another point. If you tell everyone what you are doing then maybe this man will hear about it and cancel the weekend.'

Sarah brightened up and said, 'Do you think he would?'

'I don't say that he would, but only that it is a possibility.'

'Then I'll have to do that.' Sarah brightened and rose. 'Thanks for your help.'

Later that evening Sarah put it to Cathy.

'I really don't understand you, Sar. He gives you a wonderful weekend, buys you some jewellery, and you don't want to see him.'

'I am consistent. I have never wanted to go out with anyone.'

'But you made all those men put the bit between their teeth; you're only reaping the consequences of what you started.'

'I never expected any of them to have the guts to do anything.'

'But one of them has. What if he claims his prize?'

'Well, he can't.'

'In many respects he's done enough to claim it now, and you're very lucky that he hasn't. The truth is, Sar, that you have a sneaky liking for him.'

'I haven't.' But her face was reddening.

'I think you would be very pleased if he turned out to be your perfect male. And let's be honest, he hasn't put a foot wrong yet. So I don't understand why you want me to go with you.'

'I'd just feel safer. In Paris I made sure the door was locked and that I had a chair under the handle so that no one could move it.'

'So why bother to go?'

'Because I feel I ought to go.'

'So you really want to meet him.'

'I think so, if only out of curiosity.'

'Then I had better come with you.'

Having got Cathy's agreement to accompany her to Amsterdam, Sarah set about telling various people in the office what she was doing.

'You remember I had a weekend in Paris, Michael,' she said, to which he nodded. 'I've received another to Amsterdam.'

'That's nice for you.'

'I've decided that I ought to go with one of my flatmates.'

'I thought you liked being alone.'

'Most of the time, but I have a feeling of a foreboding about this.'

'So why go? Why get your friend involved?'

'No, my foreboding's about the person who has sent me the ticket. He seems to be serious about me.'

'Lucky you!'

'Not really, I have plans to remain single.'

'Oh, I see! Moral support for when you give him the elbow.'

'Exactly.'

'I thought he bought you some jewellery in Paris.'
'He did.'
'I heard that it was rather expensive.'
'That's right.'
'I heard that it cost over £1,000.'
'It might have done.'
'I can't see why you're quite so keen to give him the heave-ho.'
'He will want marriage, and I don't.'
'What about just living together?'
'That's even worse. Anyway, I must get on.'

Emma was the next person to speak to Sarah.

'I hear your new boyfriend is taking you for a weekend in Amsterdam. You're so lucky; I've never been to Paris or Amsterdam.'
'How can he be a boyfriend, Emma, if I've never met him?'
'Stands to reason that it's a boyfriend.'
'Well, I'm going to disappoint him by taking a friend of mine.'
'Oh, you shouldn't do that.'
'Why not?'
'Well, I don't go on a date with a girlfriend.'
'I'm going with Cathy, my flatmate. Ms Marchbank is watching you, by the way.'
'I'd better get on then.'

On her way home that evening she walked some of the way with Tom.

'Millie heard from Clemmie that you were taking a friend to Amsterdam, is that right?'
'Yes, it is,' said Sarah feeling pleased that the grapevine was working.
'May I ask why that is?'
'I didn't know that you were concerned about me. But if you must know, Tom, I found Paris a bit lonely on my own.'
'I suppose one would. It can't be easy for an attractive woman like you.'
'Why can't it be easy?'
'Don't men look at you?'
'Yes they do, and I find it quite hateful at times.'

'Why don't you come and a have a drink with me?'

'No thanks, Tom. I appreciate the offer, but I want to get home.'

She crossed Piccadilly to the Underground station and left him standing watching her. It would be awful if the man were Tom for she could never look him in the eye. Still, enough people now knew about Amsterdam, and it ought to make whoever it was do something!

It was later in the week Sarah ran into Clive. He was wandering around Piccadilly and she again had the impression that he had been waiting for her.

'Why is the most attractive woman of my acquaintance looking so glum?'

'Just problems.'

'And what is the nature of these problems? Are you going to enlighten me?'

'The office is one.'

'So take up Keith's offer! At least you become your own boss.'

'I'm inclined towards it, but I need more time.'

'Keith has made it plain to you that Mr Deakin is not a man to be trusted, and he ought to know.'

'Why should he know?'

'He and Mr Deakin used to be in business together.'

'I didn't know that!'

'Mr Deakin wanted out and managed to stitch Keith up.'

'What evidence is there for that?'

'The fact that Mr Deakin kept all the best titles. He also kept the Mayfair address, which is so prestigious.'

'That sounds pretty conclusive! How do you know this?'

'It's just one of those things one knows. You need to bear in mind that it's Mr Deakin who won't speak to Keith, or even myself.'

'Well, never mind that. I must tell you that I'm going to Amsterdam.'

'That will be pleasant for you. Business?'

'No, a bit of a holiday. I'm taking Cathy with me.'

'You won't be lonely, then.'

'No, neither of us has been there before.'

'I'd like to ask you if you will have dinner with myself and Keith next week some time.'

'It will have to be next week.'

'Next Wednesday?'

'All right, next Wednesday. Where?'

'My club?'

'I'll go straight there... seven thirty?'

Amsterdam

Sarah and Cathy were sitting together on the plane for the short flight to Schiphol.

'That was nice of the stewardess to let me sit with you.'

'They couldn't do anything about it until we'd taken off.'

'So do you think this man might have bought the seat beside you?'

'He might have, or he might have reserved it for a small fee and he would then lose his right to it at some point before take-off.'

'So you don't think he's on the plane.'

'No, he's not on the plane, nor was he at the airport and I doubt he will be waiting for us at Schiphol.'

'Are you excited about seeing him?'

'Not excited, interested I think. What sort of man has taken a fancy to me?'

'He might be as ugly as sin.'

'True.'

'But would that matter if he was really rich?'

'It won't matter to you but it will to me.'

'So if he's no good, you will let me have first refusal.'

'Certainly.'

'But what kind of man would you really like to meet?'

'I don't know, I've never quantified it.'

'Do you want him to be drop-dead gorgeously handsome?'

'It's not necessary.'

'Do you want him to have a wonderful body with strong arms and huge pectorals?'

'Makes him sound like the circus strongman!'

'Well, you watch enough television. Do you watch boxing?'

'I can think of nothing worse in a man than flabby ears, a flattened nose and slurred speech.'

'But you watch the boxing to see these people knock each other into oblivion.'

181

'If I watch any boxing it's due to that fact that there nothing else on.'

'More likely it's due to you not being bothered to get up and switch it off.'

'There is that, of course.'

'Well, you tell me what you want in a man.'

'I can't answer that as I've always wished to remain single.'

'Come off it, Sarah, that's nonsense! If you were determined to remain single you wouldn't be sitting on this plane now.'

'Then let's say he would have to be very special.'

'So he would have to be cleverer than you.'

'He would have to be mentally stimulating, yes.'

'Right, narrows life down somewhat, considering you've had a university education. So I shout out to all the men on the plane for anyone one of them who has a good degree and is not married.'

'I do hope that you'll do nothing as embarrassing as that.'

'But you don't want an academic kind of person.'

'No.'

'Do you know any men like that?'

'Oddly, I know at least two.'

'But you had to think about it.'

'Yes, but they're both out of the equation because they're too old.'

'I'm quite fascinated! Who are they?'

'I can't say, I've already said too much.'

'Come on, Sar, you've got to tell me now or shall burn with curiosity.'

'You'll have to burn.'

'Then I will sit here and talk about the men in your life.'

'There aren't any.'

'There's your father and your brother.'

'I can discount relations.'

'You must tell me, I'm desperate to know. Who are these two men?'

'Three, perhaps! But I don't like Keith.'

'You're a sly one – you've never mentioned him before. Who are the others?'

'There's Clive.'
'What's he like?'
'He amazing! He has everything – looks, physique, manners and education. He's the kind of man who makes woman go weak at the knees.'
'I'd love to meet him.'
'But I can see another side to his character: incontinence!'
'What – he wets himself!'
'Don't be stupid! It means unable to curb his passions.'
'Why is this a bad thing?'
'Because he's a man who will seduce a woman, and having had his way will treat them with utter contempt.'
'Has he done this to you?'
'No, I haven't allowed him to.'
'Wow! I didn't know you met such people. Who's the third man?'
'Oh, he's my boss!'
'What's he like?'
'Surly, unsmiling... Life seems a bit of an effort to him. But I had dinner with him some time ago and he was really charming.'
'So what if it's him?'
'I can't see that it's him. I spoke to him before I left and he advised me not to go. Well, he told me not to go to Paris.'
'So you're hoping it's a younger version of your boss.'
'Or Clive, before he was corrupted.'
'But then you'd be his wife while he went through his corrupting period!'
'How true! So we're back to the point where we should not bother.'
'But you have to admit, these trips are changing your view of men.'
'I disagree there. They serve only to strengthen my views on avoiding marriage.'
'You've undertaken this trip with surprising eagerness.'
'Because I lead such a drab life, Cathy.'
'But you've still got the notion that Mr Perfect might be waiting for you.'
'That is just the romantic side of your nature. Consider what

marriage really boils down to. Having a child, to begin with. Why is it a woman's lot is to have to go through such a degrading and undignified procedure?'

'Because if it was down to the men then they'd be the women.'

'Yes, but in a man's world we become unpaid servants. We look after his house, his children and his well-being. Men expect us to do their washing, prepare and clear up food, do all the housework. The list is endless. Then he comes home and puts his feet up and goes to sleep.'

'So you think you've got problems! My Charles doesn't earn enough to own a house! With our combined salary we're still thousands short of buying a one-bedroom flat!'

'So you would happily settle for that sort of life.'

'Too right I would! I worry that I shan't get married until I'm into the menopause. It's all right for people like you! You've got brains and talent, and a decent job! There are many people like me who've put their ambitions on hold because they can't financially realise them. I think there's going to be a generation of very disgruntled people.'

The plane was lining up for its final approach to Schiphol. From the window Sarah could see the Dutch countryside spinning towards her underneath the plane and allowed herself to feel excited. Instructed to fasten her seat belt for landing, Sarah obediently complied.

Once inside the terminal, it was a question of collecting one's case off the carousel. After two minutes, Sarah's case was coming serenely towards them. She pulled it off the carousel.

'What I don't understand is that both cases went on together, yet mine is nowhere near yours,' said Cathy. They waited for ten minutes before her case finally emerged.

'It does annoy me when all those people stop my case to check that it is not theirs!' she complained.

'You would have thought that they knew which their cases were without having to check the label.'

'Now where? This is the interesting bit, isn't it?' Cathy asked.

'Yes, what does the chauffeur look like? But we have immigration to walk through.'

'What's left of it...'

'Nice of him to wave us through.'

'It was, I'm usually stopped so that they can have a good look at me.'

'This takes us out to the main concourse.'

'And now we look for a chauffeur.'

'Look, that man over there has a placard with your name on it,' Cathy pointed out.

They went over to the man who had a woman standing beside him. The man introduced himself as Nicholas, the woman was his wife, Giselle. Sarah introduced herself and then Cathy, who was given some very peculiar looks. After the introductions, Sarah and Cathy were led off to the car park, with Nicholas and Giselle putting their heads together and talking in Dutch.

'Do chauffeurs normally bring their wives?' asked Cathy.

'No, but then I don't think he's a chauffeur.'

'I'm getting a bad feeling about this weekend.'

'Already? You can't leave me now! They were expecting only one person, after all. Maybe they will actually insist on you going home.'

They reached the car park and were led to an old Volvo estate car.

'Where's the limo, Sar?'

'Just put your case in, Cathy, and get in the back.'

'But aren't we going to go to a top hotel?'

'I don't think so somehow.'

Twenty-five minutes later they drew up at a smart house deep in the suburbs of Amsterdam. Nicholas spun the car into the short drive and stopped just before the garage doors. They got out of the car and Giselle led them in. Cathy was left in the hallway, and Sarah was taken up a flight of wooden stairs and shown into a bedroom.

'Your friend,' said Nicholas, bringing Sarah's case in, 'we were not expecting her.'

'No, I must apologise for her presence. It's just that I did not want to come on my own. I trust that it does not put you out too much.'

'It was you who was to come to us and we were going to look after you this weekend.'

'I'm sorry, but I didn't want to feel lonely.'
'I understand, but we have no bed.'
'Then make her a bed on the floor in here.'
'If that is all right with her.'
'It will be, I'll see to that!'

A minute later Cathy joined Sarah in the bedroom. 'They're going to make you a bed up on the floor.'

'Fine five stars this is turning out to be! Even a youth hostel had beds!'

'You'll be all right. You don't snore, do you?'
'No one's ever complained. Do you snore?'
'I don't think so; I've never heard myself snore.'
'How can you hear yourself snore? You're asleep!'
'But I have only myself to refer to.'

Giselle appeared and motioned for them to go down.

'I thought all the Dutch spoke English!' hissed Cathy.
'I don't think she's Dutch. He is, but not her.'

They were led into a dining room where the table was laid for a meal. Giselle fussed around laying another place. It was noticeable that there were three extra places. One was a high chair set near the head of the table. Another chair had two cushions on it.

'This looks likes real domesticity to me,' said Cathy.
'It does, doesn't it? Still, you never know what you're going to get.'

'Don't you think there's a message here?'
'Yes, I share your sense of foreboding.'

'This fellow of yours first gives you a good holiday, next he sends you to someone's home. So as I see it, he says, "I've got money," and then he says, "This is the life I would like."'

'Your powers of observation today have excelled themselves,' Sarah remarked.

'But you can't want to stay here! Let's get a taxi into town and find a hotel.'

'No, we can't change the plans.'

'What are you playing at, Sarah? Has this fellow really gone to your head?'

'No, but it's a lovely house, and the people here have put

themselves out for us; they would be very upset if we upped and left them.'

'But what about my image back home!'

'If you told all your friends that you were going to live it up in Amsterdam for a weekend, it's your tough luck.'

'You could find it in yourself to be sympathetic.'

'I don't think so.' They were alone in the room. 'It may be that I don't much like the weekend so far, but the last thing I'm going to do is to say so in our host's house.'

'So we just go along with it.'

'Yes! These people are putting themselves out for us and we should show some gratitude. I see it that we're having a weekend of rest and relaxation, and we should be thankful for that.'

'You really want to meet this fellow, don't you?'

'Here comes dinner.'

Giselle carried a large casserole pot in and placed it on the table. Two small children appeared from nowhere, followed by a girl of about twenty years old. Nicholas came in, having presumably rounded everyone up.

'Meet Tricia. She's two, and this is Piers; he's four. Now this is Anneka, she's our au pair.'

Nicholas proceeded to assign everyone a place at the table and they all sat down. One by one the plates were passed to Nicholas, who filled each of them.

He grinned at Sarah and Cathy and said, 'Don't worry there's plenty there.'

'Your wife is not Dutch?' asked Sarah.

'No, she is from Finland. She speaks some English but now she has to speak Dutch. When that improves she will learn English again.'

'Does Anneka speak English?'

'Yes, but she is shy.'

'Where is Anneka from?'

'Mainz, in Germany.'

Tricia had eaten as much as she could be bothered with and had discovered that if she flicked her spoon then little bits of brown gravy sprayed over the table. Giselle looked embarrassed and fed the little girl with another spoon.

'We are hoping that she has finished with putting the plate on her head,' said Nicholas. 'Don't try and copy Tricia, Piers!'

Anneka, who was sitting on the other side of Tricia, also lent a hand feeding the girl.

'There is some left,' said Nicholas, looking first at Cathy and then at Sarah. Out of politeness Sarah handed her plate over. Cathy shook her head.

Tricia decided that she would like her plate on her head and started to do so, but Anneka moved a little quicker and took the plate from her. The little girl howled at being deprived of her self-inflicted agony. The plates were cleared and a large iced cake brought in. The sight of it stopped Tricia wailing and it seemed very unfair to give her the first piece.

With the meal over, Nicholas suggested to Sarah and Cathy that they might like to see Amsterdam. They collected their coats and met in the hall. Nicholas took the two women around the side of the house where there were three bicycles propped against the wall.

'You've got to be kidding!' said Cathy.

'Oh, come on, Cathy, they all cycle round here.' Sarah was starting to get frustrated with Cathy's constant complaining. 'It's the best way to see the place.'

'I haven't been on a bike for years.'

'It's one of those things you don't forget how to do.'

It took twenty minutes of easy pedalling down various paths to reach the outskirts of the city. Nicholas led the way and suddenly they were cycling beside one of the canals. Amsterdam in many respects was laid out for the cyclist, with plenty of cycle lanes and even their own lights at the traffic lights. Nicholas told them to be careful of the tram tracks, as it was possible to snag the tyre of the bicycle in the track. They passed Anne Frank's house and continued on to the railway station, where the buses and trams all met together. Then they went into the centre to be shown the sights there and in particular the diamond shops. Finally they returned by a picturesque route, taking in some of the other canals.

The children were in bed and asleep when they returned. Nicholas took them into the lounge where Giselle was sitting with Anneka. After a chat and a cup of chocolate Sarah and Cathy retired for the night.

'I'm exhausted,' said Cathy, finding a bed laid out on the floor for her. 'Are you sure there aren't some television cameras following us?'

'I haven't seen any.'

'By the way, don't rope me into any more of your blind dates!'

'You wanted to come! Now go to sleep.'

The morning was a slow start, though the children had been up for ages. By the time everyone else was up for breakfast they were ready for a nap! After breakfast, Anneka took charge of the children and Giselle and Nicholas took Sarah and Cathy out in the Volvo. They drove through Amsterdam and then turned north passing villages with Dutch names such as Durgadam. Twelve miles on they made their first stop at a small fishing village called Marken. It was one of those places laid out especially for the tourist. Having pulled up in the large car park. Sarah and Cathy traipsed into the village.

'Oh look,' said Cathy, 'a cloggery!'

'They make clogs still,' replied Sarah.

'But no one would be seen dead wearing clogs today.'

'It's part of the Dutch national costume.'

The village was based around a square-shaped harbour and was composed of wooden houses. The houses were tiny inside, yet people had at one time been happy to live in them.

Nicholas and Giselle caught up with them and showed them a lot more, finishing at a small restaurant where they had some lunch.

'Now,' said Nicholas, 'Giselle is going to take you across in the ferry to Volendam, while I take the car round.'

They crossed the southern end of the Zuider Zee and disembarked at the next tourist village. They looked around the shops until Nicholas found them. Sarah still had euros left over from Paris and shared them with Cathy. Then it was back to the car and they drove on to see Edam a few miles to the north.

'I thought Holland was full of windmills,' said Cathy.

'We will see them tomorrow,' said Nicholas.

The following day they drove south towards Rotterdam, finding their way through to Alblasserdam, where they parked for Kinderduik. The windmills stood sentinel in the flat landscape. They were impressive not just for their size but their age, and were probably the most photographed windmills in the world. The four of them took a boat trip down the stream passing the windmills and then went and explored one of them. Lunch was late, and after a roundabout drive back through Delft it was time for some tea. Later Nicholas drove them to the airport for their flight home.

The Drab Life

'I really don't see what you do in this bloke, Sar,' said Cathy as the North Sea passed beneath them.

'I don't know who he is, so I can't say anything.'

'But you've changed recently, Sar. You used to be a person who was asked out in the pub at least twice a night. And without fail you put every one of them down. Some of them were really nice guys.'

'But I didn't want to go out with them.'

'I was lucky if I got asked out once a fortnight.'

'If you want a few tips then you need to get rid of Charles, because he hangs around you so that any bloke can see you're with him. Next you ought to play hard to get.'

'That's easy for you, Sar! They make a beeline across the bar for you.'

'No, they don't, that's silly.'

'But we're missing the point, and that is that you've changed. When we went to the pub and all the bankers turned up, you were different.'

'No, I wasn't.'

'Yes, you were! When they teased you, you took them on and played them at their own game. You used to put them down quite quickly and firmly.'

'Well, so many of them are stupid – quite idiotic, really.'

'So you feel superior to them.'

'No, I don't think so. I have certain standards and I expect my friends to have the same standards.'

'So these men should all remain chaste for you.'

'Yes. If they really wanted to know me, then yes.'

'But you won't find many men who are less than sexually experienced.'

'It's a sad thing and I don't know why, but if I were to get married I would like to say that I have kept myself for him; that's how I would want to say that I love him.'

'And you expect the man to be the same!'

'Yes.'

'Oh, you are so idealistic!'

'I know, but I can at least try. I suppose I missed out on the bit where all the girls at school lost their virginity. I never went for a quickie behind the bike sheds or under the bushes on the playing fields. Where did you lose your virginity?'

'Took this guy home one afternoon when I was in the sixth form. My parents weren't in and we listened to a record and then got down to it.'

'Just like that?'

'Well, it didn't seem much of a deal at the time. Everyone else I knew had had sex, so why not me? How come you missed out?'

'Too busy with exams and things.'

'What if this bloke turns out to be a Lothario?'

'It does worry me, but it will simply confirm that I want nothing to do with men.'

'So if Mr Perfect had had, say, two partners before you, what would you do?'

'I don't know. I would like to think that were I to marry it would be for all time. So what guarantees do I get if he's had a number of women?'

'Why do you want a guarantee?'

'It's not so much a guarantee but an assurance. Imagine going to bed with your fellow and he had spent the afternoon with another woman...'

'So what?'

'But if he says he loved you he wouldn't do that!'

'But if he sleeps around, why shouldn't you do so as well?'

'Then the marriage has become pointless.'

'So you think that this fellow who been sending you away is a bit chaste.'

'Considering the amount of money he has spent so far, he certainly ought to be! But I can't see him, having spent this money and meticulously planned two weekends, as someone who keeps jumping into bed with any floozy that comes along.'

'Any of your acquaintances come up to this standard?'

'Not that I'm aware of.'

'You're a bit of a sad case, wanting a man to be so perfect.'

'I know I would like perfection and I am a realist, but does he have to fall so far short?'

'Surely one reason for you not wanting to go with any man is that you might be frigid.'

'That has crossed my mind, and I do worry about it at times; but, assuming that I've no problems in that department, I would like to think that if I married I would be able to service him.'

'And what if you couldn't?'

'It would be heart-rending to let him go with another woman because I was incapable: I would be on the road to losing him.'

'Have you ever been in love?'

'I had a crush on a teacher at school but apart from that I don't think I have ever been in love.'

'And this fellow gets the elbow if he does nothing for you!'

'Definitely.'

'So you admit to an interest in men.'

'A passing one, but no more. I suppose I want to satisfy myself that I didn't want even the most persuasive of men. Then I needn't look back in old age and feel that I've missed out.'

'So this man is the most persuasive of men?'

'What do you think?'

'I think the time has come to flush him out.'

'What do you mean?'

'What if Mr Perfect were suddenly to see you go hand in hand with another man?'

'You think he would have to reveal himself?'

'Yes! No lover wants to be supplanted.'

'But what if I settle on the man who is Mr Perfect?'

'Then when no one revealed themselves as being him, you know who it is.'

'Maybe, but I wouldn't want to antagonise him. And there is a flaw in your plan.'

'There would be, if I thought of it.'

'This man knows some of my activities. If it is at the office then it would be known and he could act accordingly. The same if it is the pub and so on. If it's none of these people, then it is someone just outside of that scenario. I think it could be one of the authors we deal with and there's enough of them. Any number of them are lecturers.'

'That's a whole section of men I hadn't thought about. You'll have to make out a list of them.'

'Since we're about to land I'm not going to bother. I don't know about you, but I've had a very pleasant weekend.'

'It's not been bad.'

'I've not felt under any pressure. They were just nice people though somehow there has to be a connection with Mr Perfect. What I don't understand is why children today seem to want to throw their food around; my brother's little girl was doing exactly the same thing.'

The Monday progress meeting passed off and everyone filed out. Sarah glanced at Mr Deakin, for she wanted him to ask her about the weekend. She needed an excuse to talk to him but her mind went blank and she felt herself being swept out of the office with everyone else. She sat at her desk and pondered why she wanted to talk to him. One reason was that he understood the rules of a confidant and she knew that anything she said to him would not be passed around the office for all and sundry to mull over. But more importantly she liked his intellect, as he seemed to enjoy a deep conversation and it was what she wanted. She settled reluctantly into her work and did not notice that Ms Marchbank was standing over her until she spoke. Startled Sarah looked up.

'Oh, it's you... What is it, Ms Marchbank?'

'Mr Deakin wants to see you with the Sutton file.'

'Yes – right now?'

'Now!' Why did she have to sound like a schoolteacher?

Sarah went to Mr Deakin's office with the appropriate file.

'Mr Sutton wants some changes made to his manuscript,' said Mr Deakin.

'Has he notified us of the changes yet?'

'No, he says he's rewriting certain chapters.'

'Which chapters?'

He handed Sarah a piece of paper.

'They are listed on there,' he said.

'Right, so you want me to continue without bothering with these chapters.'

'What else can we do? It's very unsatisfactory, and I don't like putting you out like this.'

'Is that all?'

'Yes.'

'I just wondered...' Sarah ventured.

'What did you wonder? I think you need an object in your statement.'

'I went to Amsterdam at the weekend.'

'Oh yes, you did say something about it. How was it? You had better take a seat, as you obviously want to talk about it.'

'It was a strange weekend.'

'What? Was the hotel was completely awful?'

'No we didn't go to a hotel.'

'How can you stay in a place unless you go to a hotel?'

'That's what so strange. We stayed at this couple's home!'

'Why should you have done that?'

'That's what I've been speculating about. One answer we had was to see domesticity.'

'Why?'

'I suppose that if the message in the trip to Paris was financial, then with Amsterdam the message is family!'

'There could be another explanation. Suppose the first trip was arranged by this man who likes you, and like most of these bankers he couldn't keep his mouth closed. Then, after he's told his mates, someone else sends you to Amsterdam for a totally different weekend.'

'Would anyone do a thing like that?'

'Since they managed to put you on the Internet with a naked body, I should think anything is possible with them.'

'Put like that, then, the whole thing is a waste of time.'

'I tend to think that it is, but you did say that you lead a very drab life. So if that's the way you want to pep it up, then who am I to stop you?'

'I must be a very boring person...'

'No, you're no different to the rest of us. We're all stuck in a rut. We get up, come to work to earn a crust, go home and back to bed.'

'Let's get back to the man,' said Sarah. 'Assuming it is one man, what kind of person would do it?'

'Difficult! I wouldn't put him in the category of a stalker.'

'No, I wouldn't, either.'

'Perhaps he overspent on the first trip. Remind me, how much did the ring cost?'

'Around £1,500!'

Mr Deakin managed a smile and said, 'There is someone out there licking his financial wounds and nurturing a very unhealthy bank balance.'

'Should I give it back to the person?'

'If you don't know who to give it to, how can you? But having said that, I don't think you should. A man who lets a woman loose in a jeweller's shop with a free hand is either mad or quite willing to take the hit.'

'Yes, I suppose so.'

'But you seem to want to have a conscience about it. Why did you buy a ring?'

Sarah reddened slightly. 'I liked the look of it.'

'But you're not wearing it.'

'No, it was a bit expensive to put on my finger.'

'Perhaps you ought to bring it in one day.'

'But you were saying about the type of man who would do such a thing.'

'To be honest, I don't know about the character of such a person. I would prefer to try and understand why he was doing it,' said Deakin.

'I can understand his ultimate reason.'

'And what is that?'

'To impress me!' said Sarah.

'With what intention?'

'Marrying me, I should think,' said Sarah.

'Why marriage? I didn't think it was the in thing!'

'Well, if he wanted less, why not ask!'

'Ask for what?'

'To cohabit I suppose.'

'Are you up for all this?'

'No, none of it at all.'

'So he's ploughing a long furrow with no hope of reaching the end.'

'Quite; he's wasting his time and money.'

'He certainly is, and he wouldn't want to know that at this moment.'

'Why not?'

'With his credit cards at their limit, that would be a facer. He would feel that he's been quite asinine and is now wallowing in a slough of despond. But you were saying, why shouldn't he just ask? And that takes us to the reason he's doing it.'

'I don't see what you mean.'

'Well, why not simply ask you straight out?'

'I think he should! It will save him a lot of bother in the long run. I could tell him to his face to get out of my life.'

'But you see, this is exactly what I mean. If he came to you and asked you to your face, you would immediately send him packing. And my guess would be that in the process you would flatten his manhood and belittle his ego.'

'I suppose you're right,' said Sarah slowly.

'I once saw a television documentary about a lion and a lioness mating. It was something the lion had to do with a lot of circumspection because the female was very temperamental; she could have lashed out at him at any moment and wounded him badly. Clearly a young lion or a weak one stood no chance; only the biggest and fittest would take her on.'

'So you think I'm like a lioness?'

'Yes, I do.'

'I don't know if that is a compliment or not.'

'It depends on what you want from life. I'm simply glad of the immunity that age confers upon me.'

'The only thing is that you've likened me to an animal, I always thought that human beings were above the animal world.'

'In what respects?'

'In all respects.'

'So that we have perfect control of ourselves?'

'Yes, that's exactly what we should have.'

'Leaving the man who fancies a woman as some lower order creature.'

'Yes!… No!'

'Make your mind up.'

'Yes, I think men do stoop to lusting,' Sarah declared.

'And women are nothing more than victims of men's carnal lust?'

'Yes.'

'So a woman rises above any sexual desire, and thus never wants a man,' Deakin suggested.

'Yes.'

'And she can't have any carnal desires?'

'You're trying to make me say things that I don't mean.'

'Yes, because women do have sexual needs, and just as men can succumb to carnal desire, so can women. It is given to man to start the process and for the fulfilment to reside in woman.'

Sarah blushed furiously and said in a strangled voice, 'I ought to get back to my work.'

'I should wait a moment or two, or the rumour mill out there will crank itself up.'

'Perhaps you're right,' said Sarah, for she could feel the heat in her cheeks. She paused for a moment and then changed the subject. 'Why is Mr Sutton rewriting chapters six, nine and thirteen?' she asked.

'I don't know, Sarah.'

'I'll have a read of it and see if I can see why.'

'Now you're looking more like yourself! You had better hurry along now; you've spent far too long talking to me.'

It was Wednesday evening, and Sarah sat in the lounge of Clive's club with Clive and Keith sitting facing her. She was pleased, for she felt she was getting an entrée to part of London that she would not otherwise have seen. Her flatmates and most of their friends were quite envious of her and wanted to know how she had done it. But with the meal ordered and the dry sherries in front of them, the pleasure was all hers.

'Even in her trouser suit Sarah looks wonderful.'

'I like her naturalness,' said Keith.

'What do you mean?' asked Clive.

'I mean simply that Sarah looks stunning without masses of

make-up or any of the adornments that most women prefer.'

Sarah blushed in return. She liked their compliments but she was not sure that she liked them talking about her as if she were an inanimate commodity. She was too polite to object even if she had a mind to, for the novelty of exaggerated praise had yet to wear off.

'I'm looking forward to making her a millionaire,' said Keith.

'How fortunate beautiful women are,' mused Clive. 'Every man wants to know them and desires their bodies. She could if she wanted to marry anyone and never have to lift her hand to work again.'

'But Sarah is not like that and wants to be her own person.'

'Which adds to her attractiveness and mystique.'

The waiter was hovering to tell them that their table was ready. The interlude made Sarah determined to change the subject. She need not have worried for once seated Clive asked about her trips abroad.

'So who has been sending you to Paris and Amsterdam?' he asked.

'I don't know,' said Sarah, 'I had expected whoever it was to sit beside me on the plane but he never did. And then I thought he was going to pop out of the woodwork at any moment.'

'So you have no inkling at all as to who it might be.'

'None.'

'And none of your male acquaintances has dropped even the slightest hint.'

'No, and I've not been able to eliminate anyone on the same basis.'

'Have you eliminated anyone at all?'

'Yes, I think I have. Since it has cost someone a deal of money I can eliminate a large number of people.'

'Why should anyone be eliminated on financial grounds?'

'Because I estimate that it has so far cost the person over £4,000.'

'So a man who only just has that amount of money would not throw it away so recklessly.'

'That is my reasoning.'

'I don't understand,' said Keith; 'why has it so far cost so much?'

'Because he bought me a ring.'
'What, an engagement ring?'
'No, just a ring.'
'And how much did that cost?'
'Around £1,500.'
'That would be something of a facer for a man with small pockets.'

'I had hoped,' said Sarah, 'that by buying something so expensive it might have made the person reveal himself.'

'If he can only just afford it, he would be opening himself to ridicule – and deservedly so.'

'Exactly, and he won't reveal himself to anyone until he has revealed himself to me.'

'Does this man mean anything to you, Sarah?'

'Nothing at all. I admit to some curiosity, but nothing more.'

'So after repairing his finances, this man's due for a massive let-down.'

'Oh yes, there's no way he's going to make me cower before him.'

'What if he turns out to be a millionaire, though? Will you still reject him?'

'Maybe I would give it some thought, but after one minute I'm sure that I will hand out the same treatment.'

'But what if he is everything you could want in a man?'

'I would have to stop and think hard for maybe two minutes, but I've never met anyone who comes remotely close to my ideals.'

'Clive was hoping that he might, Sarah.'

'Then he won't be disappointed later, knowing my answer all ready.'

Keith was smiling in a superior fashion at Clive and said, 'The lady has your measure Clive.'

'But she makes herself even more alluring,' said Clive, allowing himself the luxury of speaking.

'I have never seen Clive so restrained; you have done a remarkable job on him, Sarah!' Keith suddenly changed the subject and said, 'Have you made up your mind yet whether you want to head up our company?'

'You know my answer to that.'

'I can be fairly certain that I do, but I need a positive confirmation one way or the other.'

'Since my present job is going nowhere, my answer has to be yes.'

'Excellent, Sarah! Let's raise a glass to that.' Keith reached for his wine glass and waited while the other two picked theirs up. 'To a profitable partnership.' They chinked glasses in pleasurable agreement.

The evening was very satisfying for Sarah. She could see a picture of herself just a few years into the future as a rising star in the publishing world; someone who in their sphere was the person everyone wanted to know. There would be invitations to parties from people outside her acquaintance but they would be desirous of meeting her. They would place a value on her opinions and she would find that it motivated other people. And it would be even more gratifying to find herself amongst people of real power and influence, and discover then that her opinions were weighed and received in the corridors of power. Even the thought that she was being presumptuous did not dent her euphoria, for it was not that she specifically wanted to change anything but just to have the feeling that she might have done.

She was convinced that it was Clive who had sent her to Paris. For in the course of the conversation there had been one moment when Keith had shot a peculiar look at Clive, and that was the mention of Paris. There really could be no other reason for it and that was the instant that Keith had discerned who it was. She did not mind if it was Clive but she was saddened that he was such a womaniser. It didn't do her ego much good, either, if Clive was treating her as the highest pinnacle he had yet to scale. Against him, even Tom's brother had more going for him, in that she would have much preferred a man of limited experience. She worried that she might want it to be a younger man but she was sure that none of her male acquaintances came anywhere near to Clive's standard. But the worry was enough to make her determined to hold Clive at arm's length for as long as she could.

The Theatre

It was no surprise that later that week another letter arrived addressed to Sarah. She hoped it was a letter from her mother with the envelope typed by her father's latest computer. He would have insisted on doing that for the price of the stamp, and her mother would have yielded to keep him happy. But the envelope did not feel like a letter and when she opened it a single ticket fell out.

'What have you got now, Sar?' asked Gerrie.

'One ticket for the opera.'

Gerrie picked it up and looked it over. 'Well, it is at least the show that everyone wants to see, and it's quite an expensive ticket.'

'I wouldn't expect anything less… Saturday week.'

'Busy, are you?'

'No, I can't get out of it that way.'

'You don't want to go?'

'I want to see the opera.'

'But you would prefer to have your hand held.'

'No, I wouldn't.'

'But you don't want to go on your own.'

'I just feel that I'm being pushed around.'

'I wouldn't mind being pushed around by a guy who bought expensive theatre tickets for me, and they would be wasted on Ted; he couldn't sit still for long enough.'

'I couldn't see either of you there.'

'But then it might be just the place to meet your Mr Perfect.'

'I think he's much less than perfect, otherwise he would have revealed himself to me by now.'

'Yes, but be fair, if you knew who it was by now he would be history.'

'That's true.' It occurred to Sarah that she could hand the mystery man back his jewellery. The thought that he could not afford it so embarrassed her that she hadn't had the heart to tell Cathy and Gerrie about it.

'Oh, Cathy,' said Gerrie, as Cathy into the kitchen, 'Sar's got her next assignment.'

'Oh good! Where are we going this time?'

'Well, I am, but you're not. There's only one ticket for the show at… the theatre.'

'Oh, drat it!' she said, looking at the ticket. 'And that's the show everyone at the office is talking about. Can I have it, Sar?'

'Only if I decide not to go.'

'Then decide not to go now!'

'She's got no intention of not going, Cathy, so don't waste your breath.'

'Desperate to meet him, is she? You know, Gerrie, I never thought I'd see the day that Sarah was going to keep a date.'

'No, it's not bad going for a confirmed female bachelor!'

But the bantering could not last for long as there was a train to catch.

On Wednesday it was difficult to avoid meeting Jason, Tom's brother. Tom insisted that everyone went for a quick drink after finishing in the office. To Sarah it was an excuse for Jason to draw her to one side for a chat.

'Haven't found out yet where the website came from,' he said.

'Oh, I didn't know you were looking.' Sarah wished she hadn't been reminded of it.

'But we'll find out sometime.'

'And what will you do then?'

'Blacken whoever did it.'

'That will only create factions.'

'I don't know why you stay in publishing,' he said.

'I like it.'

'I like money, and I wouldn't do something that made so little.'

'And suppose you were utterly bored.'

'If the money was good enough it wouldn't matter.'

'I would have difficulty in coping with it.'

'No, you wouldn't, you would soon find something to put your mind on.'

'Writing my own book?'

'You see – you've got it in one! On the one hand you make a million and on the other you become a famous author!' He continued talking but Sarah was taking very little notice. She observed him closely and found that she pitied him. True, he claimed that he could get her a wonderful job in the City but his own job was not that wonderful. He was shy and did not want to commit himself. While he could hold a good conversation he was prone to taking long pauses and staring at her. And that was the kind of man that he was, one who was forever looking at a woman and wishing she were his, but always feeling that she was much too good for him. One day he would find a woman but she would be tame and insipid.

Did she feel anything for him? She already had the answer to that without exercising any brainpower! Yet the worst thing for her was that she couldn't dismiss him as her possible suitor, though to discover that he had orchestrated her trip to Paris and Amsterdam would be nothing short of a nightmare.

'I'm for another drink,' he said, cutting through her thoughts for once. 'What are you having, Sarah?'

She looked at the pint glass that he held and decided that she wanted nothing. Why did men drink so much? It seemed completely mindless! But then they have so little, she reflected.

'Nothing for me, thanks,' she said, 'I'm going in a minute.'

'Have one for the road.'

'No, I really don't want one.' There was only one way out and that was to say goodbye and leave. She slipped out of the bar before Tom and the others realised what she was doing.

Saturday evening arrived and Sarah had half a mind not to go to the theatre, but it was a show that she had wanted to see so it seemed silly to pass up the opportunity. But the downside was that she was the monkey dancing to this man's tune. He could just as easily say that she owed him, for she had spent a large amount of his money, even though it had been at his behest. The theatre gave him cover in which to hide and watch her, though on the other hand it afforded her at least a chance of seeing him! She decided to go.

The ticket she had been given was for the stalls, and when she arrived at the theatre and saw the seating plan she discovered that it was only six rows from the front. Having located the row containing her seat she found that the seating was in three blocks across. The second aisle showed that she was in the middle block, and to her embarrassment there was a lone seat left in the middle of a group of people who were already sitting down. The man on the end must have realised where she was going to sit and rose up from his seat to allow her to pass. Everyone else did so in turn until she was able to reach the seat. Finally she was able to sit down and make herself comfortable. To her left was a young couple who seemed all over each other. He had one arm behind her and they kissed every now and again. To her right was an older couple who had got past that stage in their relationship. Sarah settled in for a tedious evening. She hoped the show lived up to its early expectations.

The first interval arrived and the lights went back up. Sarah rose, ostensibly to have a good look round. But the middle-aged woman got up as well and for a moment stood beside her.

'Are you on your own?' she asked Sarah.

'Yes, I am.'

'Would you like to join us for a drink?'

It was a bit unexpected and Sarah's natural politeness took over. 'No, I couldn't...'

'You're not on your own, then.'

'I am on my own.'

'Then come and be sociable with us.'

'Yes, do come and have a drink with us,' said the man adding his entreaties to the woman's.

'Well, if that's all right with you,' said Sarah.

'Of course it is! Come with us,' said the woman as they eased their way along the upturned seats to the aisle. It was simplest for Sarah just to follow them. They reached a bar.

'I'm Connie,' said the woman, 'and this is my husband, Curzon.'

'I'm Sarah.'

They all shook hands rather formally.

'What are we going to drink?' said Curzon.

'Mineral water, please,' said Connie.

'I'll have the same,' said Sarah, looking in her bag for some money.

'Don't worry about that,' said Curzon, 'one extra mineral water won't break the piggy bank!'

'How are you liking it?' asked Connie, as Curzon left them to push his way to the bar.

'I'm enjoying it very much. I've never sat so near the front before; isn't that odd?'

'Not if you don't go very much.'

'Well I'm not a frequent goer – once or twice a year. I'd go more often if my friends were like-minded.'

They talked about the performance until Curzon returned and handed their drinks round.

'So you're not meeting anyone tonight,' he said amiably.

'No, but I had thought that I might.'

'How come?'

'Well, someone sent me a ticket, so I thought I ought to come.'

'And you expected that person to meet you?'

'Yes.'

'I hope we haven't drawn you away and left some young man running round the theatre looking for you.'

'I haven't a young man running after me; whoever sent me the ticket did not reveal his name!'

'That's not much good, surely, sending a girl to meet you and then not turning up! Very poor show. I'd give him the elbow when you do meet,' said Curzon.

'You're right there. I certainly shall, at least I've every intention of doing so.'

'I think Sarah would like to meet him first,' intervened Connie.

'But what's a good-looking lass like you doing going anywhere without a young man?'

'I'm not too bothered about it,' said Sarah. 'You know, he'd have to be wonderful man, because in many ways I'd much rather remain single and unattached.'

'So what made you take up his offer?'

'Feminine curiosity.'
'So what are you planning for the big put-down?'
'I haven't planned anything yet.'
'Is this the first ticket that he's sent you?'
'In a way yes, as regards the theatre, but he has previously sent me airline tickets.'
'Really! What a strange fellow? And where have you been?'
'Paris. It was a super weekend.'
'Was he there?'
'If he was there then I wouldn't know. No, it was meticulously planned, and I really did enjoy it.'
'Would it have been better if he had joined you?'
'No, I don't think so. I punished him, though.'
'And how was that?'
'He allowed me to go to a jeweller's shop. It was bit like a supermarket dash but I could have only one item!'
'And what did you buy?'
'Oh, er, a ring... very expensive.'
'So he can't actually afford to take you out now.'
'I did think that it might have flushed him out. Some of the men I know would have rushed round to get it off me and try and get their money back. But no one has.'
'So he wants you to have it?'
'He must do!'
'Are you wearing it now?'
'No, I didn't think to. Anyway, it's my proof!'
'How is it your proof?'
'I have the ring and he should have the invoice! So we'll be able to put them together and I'll be able to prove that this is the man who deserves the biggest put-down any woman can give him.'
'But what if this man just happens to meet all your expectations?' said Connie.
'It's very unlikely, I'm afraid.'
'Don't you know any men you might possibly like?'
'No.'
'None at all?'
'I know a man called Clive, he's very handsome and he

definitely has something, but I think he has known too many women.'

'Do you see much of him?'

'No, but his friend has offered me a position in his new venture.'

'What sort of position?'

'He wants me to run it.'

'He's got his tentacles around you, then.'

The five-minute bell now sounded and they moved slowly back towards their seats. The musical continued until they reached the second interval. Sarah made up her mind to stay by her seat this time. She liked the couple who had spoken to her and she had been pleased with their company, but she felt that it was imposing on them to talk with them in the second interval. When the final break came it was what Connie and Curzon were expecting.

'Come and have a coffee,' said Connie to Sarah.

'No, I can't join you again.'

'Of course you can!'

'Well, I need to go to the ladies' room, and I wanted to see if I could spot this man.'

'Could I suggest, then, that you meet us at the bar in ten minutes? We'll get you a coffee.' Connie moved out of the row of seats, leaving Sarah who had no time to refuse, to watch them disappear.

A minute of looking around the tiers of seats and Sarah came to the conclusion that she was not going to be met. Four minutes later she arrived in the bar and looked for her new friends. Connie was standing on almost exactly the spot that she had been during the first interval. Curzon was still getting the drinks but he finally dragged himself out of the press of people with a tray laden with coffee cups.

'Nice to have you joining us again,' he said to Sarah, 'Connie was saying just now what a pleasant chat we had.'

Connie smiled and said, 'It was like talking to an old friend, not someone we had only met that evening.'

'So you're a career woman, are you, Sarah?'

'Yes, I'm in publishing.'

'Is it rewarding?'

'Oh yes, I wanted to go into something that was creative. I keep getting offers of jobs in banking but it's too boring – and where's the satisfaction in scraping money out of people's overdrafts? You haven't created anything; it's just legalised robbery!'

'Most people would have interpreted my question in the financial sense.'

'Oh, I see.'

'No, it's very refreshing to hear someone put their work before remuneration.'

'Actually, the man I work for is quite generous. It is his best point; he's quite a dreary sort of person.'

'What do you mean by that?'

'Oh, smiling seems to be an effort to him. He works too much and seems to do little else.'

'He sounds rather dull,' said Curzon.

'He is, although I did have dinner with him once. It was a most curious evening, for this author wanted take the boss out and he also wanted me to go because I had been working on his book. It was just the three of us. Halfway through the dinner the author started paying me some extravagant compliments, and then he suddenly disappeared without paying the bill and left my boss to settle up! He didn't seem too put out and reckoned he could make the chap pay later.'

'Sounds very embarrassing.'

'It was! Then I was left, chatting to my boss, though it was quite amusing… until he took my femininity apart.'

'No wonder you don't see eye to eye with him! Did he bask in his triumph?'

'No, it was all done very subtly, and left me feeling angry afterwards.'

'To change the subject, I was very interested in your comments earlier on about you heading a new venture.'

'Why?'

'It's nice to hear of people with great opportunities coming their way.'

'Yes, I'm looking forward to being my own boss.'

'So you'll be moving on.'

'Oh yes, you have to, really.'

'Nobody seems to have any loyalty these days.'

'You can't afford to.'

'But it does concern me that loyalty has all but disappeared.'

'Well, it has. It doesn't look good on a CV. The employers don't ask for it because they aren't going to be loyal to you.'

'When we were at school you were taught to be loyal, and employers required you to be loyal; but it was the sixties that knocked all that to bits. For instance, married women always wore a wedding ring and you didn't them chat up – at least not openly. That's what changed then; people thinking it was clever and fashionable to boast about their amorous conquests.'

'Isn't it more honest to be open, as we are today, then to be secretive about these things?' Sarah posed.

'I personally don't agree. Is it moral to boast of one's adultery? Surely the morality ends when you commit the act. Being open about it does not remove the offence.'

'But what if you have real feelings for a person, shouldn't you be honest and open about it?'

'To claim one has feelings for a person's spouse is to have no control of your feelings. If a man had amorous feelings about my wife and made himself open to me, I would want to do something really nasty to him,' said Curzon.

'But haven't you succumbed to animal instincts if you do that?' answered Sarah quietly.

'I speak,' said Curzon trying to redeem himself, 'not as one who would do a man harm, because as much as anything there's the question whether I could actually hurt him! My point is to express my feelings in the matter; I can think of nothing that would make me more angry! You see, I should never have to be put in such a position, yet it is happening all around me, to the point where I fear even for myself.'

'Perhaps you worry too much.'

'I sometimes think so. Tell me, do you flit from one relationship to the next?'

Sarah reddened at the directness of his question, 'I've never had a relationship in my life.'

Curzon blinked in astonishment and said, 'So you live a morally upright life, and yet support the immoral.'

'Yes, because I realise that it is so easy to become like that.'

'Leave Sarah alone, Curzon,' said Connie suddenly.

'Why?' said Curzon, grinning. 'She's a strong-minded woman and it's clear that she likes a good argument.'

'But you've taken advantage of me,' replied Sarah.

'And how is that?'

'By trampling all over my natural politeness!'

'Up the girls!' said Connie.

'You see, Connie, I haven't misjudged Sarah.'

'Yes you have, dear; you thought you could have the last word. And the bell went a few minutes ago!'

Back in their seats, Connie turned to Sarah and said, 'So typical of a man to want to always be right.'

'We women must stand together.'

'Absolutely. Trouble is, I don't know where I'd be without him!'

'What – you want to leave him?'

'Oh no! I'm still very much in love with him; I just cannot imagine life without him.'

'You could have had ambitions and desires without marrying.'

'What is ambition in this world? Money? No, it boils down to the fact that I wanted a family, and to love and to be loved.'

The lights dimmed and the final part of the evening's entertainment began. An hour later they stood outside the theatre.

'Well, Sarah, it's been a very pleasant evening,' said Curzon.

'Yes, I've enjoyed it too.'

'Can we take you anywhere?'

'No. I'm going to Waterloo.'

'Can we get you a taxi?' Curzon was hailing one down and already the taxi was crossing the road to them. The door was opened and Sarah felt it would be undignified to refuse. She obediently climbed in and, to her surprise, Connie and Curzon followed.

'Oh,' said Sarah.

'We want the taxi home, so we'll go by Waterloo.'

At Waterloo, Sarah started to get out, but Curzon shook her

hand in a mannish fashion, then Connie embraced her and said, 'It would be nice to think that we could run into each other again.'

'Yes,' said Sarah, 'I work at Deakin's.' She waved to them and disappeared into the terminus to find her train.

The Confidant

The evening left Sarah feeling very pleased and it was somewhat depressing that when she arrived home that her flatmates were not in to tell them. Nor did she see them until very late Sunday, by which time the event had lost some of its piquancy. But they sat down and chatted about it before they were off out again for the evening. Little was said about the matter until one morning later in the week, when Gerrie revealed that she had some profound thoughts on the whole episode.

'I've been thinking about what you said Sunday evening about the show you went to see on Saturday.'

'What about it?' said Sarah.

'These people you met – you said that you ran into them. Isn't it possible that this man sent them to look you over!'

It took Sarah so much by surprise that the tea she was drinking went down the wrong way. She coughed and spluttered but recovered to say mournfully, 'I never thought of that!'

'I mean, wouldn't it be funny if you'd been talking to his parents!'

In that instant, Sarah wished she had never gone near the theatre. It was too humiliating to think about it, and that it should come from Gerrie seemed to heap further humiliation upon her. How was she ever going to face Connie and Curzon again? And there was Curzon, gently lecturing her on loyalty and morality! Oh, what a fool she had been!

Cathy came in and tossed the post on to the kitchen table.

'Bills, nothing but bills!' she groaned, as one who was a confirmed bad riser. Sarah reached out and checked through them. Her eye was drawn to a plain envelope with her name on it, and mechanically she slit it open. From inside she pulled out what was obviously an airline ticket.

'Oh no!' she moaned.

'Now what Sar?' said Gerrie.

'He's sending me to Venice now.'

'So you've met his parents, and finally you're going to meet him.'

'Hey, what's this I'm missing out on?' said Cathy.

'When Sarah went to the theatre on Saturday she met his parents!'

'No, really?'

'You don't know that, Gerrie,' said Sarah, aggrieved at the suggestion.

'It stands to reason that you did.'

'Venice… now that sounds romantic. Imagine him proposing to you in a gondola!'

'It's one place too far,' said Sarah and flung out of the kitchen. She wanted to hide in her room but decided that the better place was behind her desk at the office with her work to take her mind off things.

It was just gone eleven when Ms Marchbank came to her and told her that she was required in Mr Deakin's office. Sarah felt a certain relief that her boss wanted to speak to her.

'Have you done those changes yet?' he asked.

'Yes, but I told Ms Marchbank that some of it did not make sense. She was either going to tell you or phone the author herself.'

'Why didn't you?'

'I'm worried about who might be on the other end of the phone.'

'You look upset about something.'

'I had something said to me which disturbs me.'

'Someone in the office?'

'No, my flatmate.'

'What did she say?'

'It's a bit of a long story.'

'Should I be wearing my confidant's hat?'

'Please don't laugh at me!'

'No, I shan't, I promise.'

'I was sent a ticket for the theatre last week so I went there on Saturday evening. I met two very nice people and we got on really well, but Gerrie this morning suddenly suggested that they were his parents.'

'His parents? Who is he?'

'This mystery man who has been sending me to various places. He must have sent me the ticket.'

'This man – is he the invisible lover!'

'You *are* laughing at me.'

'Forgive me, but I do find it slightly diverting.'

'Please don't, this is serious.'

'He must a very shy person not to want to meet you.'

'I think he's planning a grand entrance into my life.'

'How's that?'

'Just after Gerrie said her bit, the post came and there was another ticket in it.'

'To the theatre?'

'No, to Venice this time.'

'And this is where you think he will make his grand entrance.'

'Yes, but it worries me.'

'If it worries you that much, then put the ticket through the shredder.'

'Not yet, I haven't made up my mind about going.'

'Then I must ask you a question which I have asked before, is this down to feminine curiosity still, or has it become an affair of the heart?'

'How can it be an affair of the heart? I don't know who is he is!'

'No, but suppose he turns out to be a perfectly acceptable man, are you prepared to look at him seriously? Because we both know that that is what he is going to ask of you.'

'I would have to say yes to that possibility, but two months ago it would have been a definite no.'

'Do you feel you are being stalked by this man?'

'Yes and no. If I went down to a police I think they would laugh at me when I told them how much he had spent on me.'

'You don't know who he is, and you've never seen him to know who he is.'

'No. But I shall know him when we meet.'

'You've set a little trap for him!'

'No, he'll be able to prove that it is him.'

'But you appear to have met his parents!'

'Yes, I wish I had thought of it at the time, for I would have asked some awkward questions that might have elicited the truth.'

'How does this fit in with your theory of all the salient words beginning with "f"? As in, "father-in-law"!'

Sarah winced and replied, 'I hadn't thought of it and certainly not that. But it seemed to be "finance" and "family". "Father-in-law" is not right because there were two of them and the word is too specific. It ought to be "friends".'

'To think of them as friends might improve your mood.'

'All right, suppose it is "friends" – then they are not his parents.'

'Could it be that he sent some acquaintances along to meet you.'

'That's more likely.'

'And you've given them your whole life story, and now you're embarrassed.'

'No, but I did say some things which I should have toned down. The man was called Curzon, and he had a bit of an argument with me. I put him down, of course.'

'Naturally, you would.'

Sarah flashed a guilty look at him and said, 'It was very rude of me but he needed a put-down.'

'So the mystery man is now sending you to Venice. And how does the "f" theory relate to Venice?'

'Well, a word that comes to mind is "fate". Yes! That's what Venice is – *fate*. Destiny. Cathy said how romantic it would be; to her, it was decision time.'

'Perhaps "future" would be a less emotive word.'

'That's true; then three "fs" point to the fourth.'

'So we've reached the part that really does worry you.'

'Yes, because what is being planned has never been on my agenda.'

'You're not under any obligations.'

'No, I just don't know.' Sarah stared at the window mournfully. Suddenly she brightened and said, 'I must go and get on with my work. Thanks for talking to me; I'd have gone scatty without someone I could trust to talk to.'

'You were with Deakin a long time,' said Michael when she returned to her desk.

'Yes, this stupid author makes more problems than he solves.'

Michael stared at her with his eyebrows raised for a few moments and then continued with his work.

On Friday night Sarah met up with Clive, as she had planned. Together they went to a small restaurant in Earl's Court where Keith was waiting. Meeting with them was not to her distaste as they made her feel important and necessary to their project.

'You favour me with your loveliness,' said Clive, 'and I am not unappreciative of it.'

'Yes, you are,' said Sarah teasingly, 'you were looking at that woman over there.'

'I regret that I did indeed perceive the presence of another woman.'

'But you looked at her too!'

'It was just that she's wearing a torn blouse and a tear in the buttocks of her jeans which, when she leaned over, was most revealing. I argue that I would have been a poor sort of male not to have looked.'

'What about you, Keith?'

'I was luckier, for the woman was straight in my line of vision.'

'So you weren't staring, you merely had your eyes open.'

'I am in the habit of only closing them when I go to sleep.'

'There is the consolation,' said Clive, 'that the woman's attire is designer clothing. It's just that by taking the scissors to them she has made her clothes trendier.'

'I didn't think you subscribed to such nonsense.'

'I don't unless it shows off the female form to its advantage.'

'That's very sexist.'

'Why? If the woman didn't want myself as a red-blooded male to look at her, she should have worn clothes that were less revealing.'

A change of topic was called for.

'So, how's the business plan coming on, Keith?' Sarah asked.

'Very well. I've two more contacts lined up and I have to say that I believe we should take on some staff as soon as possible.'

'Do we have enough money behind us to do that?'

'Oh yes. I calculate that our turnover on the first year alone will be just short of one million and by the end of three years well in excess of five!'

'That's quite scary.'

'Not at all. We wouldn't have approached you if we thought that you couldn't handle it! How is your share of the money coming?'

'I locked it up on a forty day deposit to get the extra quarter per cent.'

'Pity. May I suggest that you unlock the rest of your assets…'

'Why's that?'

'Purely because a new venture like this does have heavy outgoings at its inception, and if no one has instant cash available then everything slides a bit. It's a safety valve.'

'Oh, I see.'

'And when will your money be available?'

'About three weeks' time.'

'Good.'

'When will you want me to start?'

'We will have to sort that out, as you will need to give Deakin two weeks' notice.'

Sarah nodded, aware that the wine had already gone to her head. The mention of the name Deakin worried her a little bit.

'We've had this conversation before,' said Keith, sensing her sudden hesitancy. 'There is no such thing today as loyalty. The biggest pot is always won by the strongest. Deakin is yesterday's man, and what may seem to be nasty is actually a kindness to him. He has money and will never go short. I expect he will be living in the South of France soon, very happy, and pleased that something made him see the light.'

'It does seem a bit cruel.'

'You have to be cruel. Sometimes it's the kindest thing to do. Get some more wine, Clive.'

'No more for me, thanks,' Sarah put in.

'Come on, Sarah, you can manage another glass.'

Sarah had eaten well and now felt light-headed. In this serious conversation she was becoming a bystander. She had a mental picture of Curzon with his bald pate preaching on morals, and she wanted to laugh.

'I think you should go and get the rest of your savings out,' said Keith.

'Of course,' said Sarah, 'I'll do it on Monday.'

'Could you put your notice in as well?'

'Looking forward to that.'

'That's settled then! Coffee everyone?'

'A brandy for me,' said Clive.

'What about you, Sarah? Are going to join us in a brandy?'

'Oh, why not... but I would like a coffee as well.'

'Oh, let's have both!'

Sarah was past caring and gingerly sipped the brandy letting its fiery taste sear her lips. She only had one problem and that how to get home.

The next day only Cathy knocking on her bedroom door succeeded in waking Sarah up.

'It's gone midday! Are you getting up?'

'No, I feel awful. Go away.'

'Got a hangover, have we?'

'Don't go on about it so much.'

'She who never drinks too much... Fine state you were in when you arrived home last night! I've got you a glass of water.'

'Thanks. Bring it in.'

'Taxi driver brought you home about twelve o'clock. He wasn't too pleased to have a drunk in his cab.'

'Thanks, but now let me suffer in peace.'

It was late in the afternoon before Sarah felt able to rise from her bed. The memory of the previous evening came back to her and she lay against the pillows running through it. But when she reached the brandy stage she found that she could not remember any of the rest of the evening. What had she done between ten thirty and twelve o'clock? The cab would have taken twenty minutes from Earl's Court. That left an hour! Had Clive touched her in that time?

She was still fully dressed and her knickers were still on. How could you tell if a man had interfered with you? Could a man have sex with an inert woman? She slipped her underwear off and felt herself. She was no more wet than usual and certainly wasn't sore.

She went to find Cathy.

'Cathy? Suppose I was out last night, how could I tell if a man had touched me?'

Cathy laughed at her and said, 'You'd know if someone had had sex with you.'

'Yes? Well, there's an hour of my life to account for. What time did I actually get in last night?'

'Oh, about ten to twelve.'

'Who brought me home?'

'Just the taxi driver.'

'Did he say anything?'

'Nothing, except that two men had paid him well over the top to do it.'

'How was I dressed when I arrived?'

'As you are now, only slightly less crumpled.'

'Did I have my underwear on?'

'Yes, I did notice, and you were decent.'

'What a stupid thing to worry about!'

'If anyone had had sex with you you'd be sore underneath and they'd have had to force your legs apart. If you're really worried then nip round to the chemist before he closes and get a morning after pill.'

'Could you do that for me?'

'No, I couldn't! Do it yourself.'

Fifteen minutes later Sarah was back.

'This is just precautionary,' said Sarah to Cathy.

'Aren't you on the Pill?'

'No, I've never taken it in my life.'

'You do like walking a tightrope, don't you?'

'Why? I don't expect to find a man at every street corner.'

'Common sense these days. Who were you out with?'

'Two men I know.'

'I didn't think you were like that.'

'No, I'm not sure why I went now.' But the question brought back to Sarah the reason why she had gone. She felt ashamed of herself and returned to her bedroom. She could no longer be sure of Clive and Keith and she began to worry about the money she was going to put into their venture.

Yes, she was bothered. Clive and Keith wanted her to put her notice in at Deakin's, yet sitting in the office in front of her workstation it all seemed so different. She did feel loyalty towards her present job. To hand in her notice also gave her a guilty conscience. In Clive's presence it was all so different. It was as if he hypnotised her and removed her thought process. She could agree with him and accept that everything he said was so right. Yet away from him she was racked with doubts. It would be better if Deakin fired her, though she doubted if he would. How did one contrive to be dismissed? No, she would resign her job when Keith had finalised the investment. Would it be too awful to work for two employers for a short while? It was something that was going to worry her for some time.

A few days later, after finishing for the day she made her way to the Underground and to her dismay saw Clive waiting for her. He fell into step beside her with a conciliatory manner and assumed that she wanted him to walk with her. But his manner seemed to be deliberate and calculated, and she sensed that he was pressurising her. She was annoyed, and decided that he lacked the subtlety to be a man who sent her off to distant places.

'I trust I did not make too much of a fool of myself the other night.'

'No, you seemed to switch off and just sat there before suddenly going to the ladies' room. You didn't come back but sat out in the foyer, where we found you and put you in a taxi.'

She was relieved at his words but he still vexed her.

'Keith is close to completing the contract,' he said.

'Oh good,' she replied, trying to hide her feelings and sound enthusiastic.

'And how long before your bank releases the money?'

'Two or three weeks.'

'Enough of banalities. I would rather pay you exquisite compliments.'

'Naturally.'

'Have you ever realised how perfect your face is?'

'No, but you're going to tell me.'

'Your eyes are the colour of sapphires, and wonderfully set. Your complexion is like peaches.'

'What show have you been to recently to become so poetic?'

'Isn't that cynicism? I prefer to draw upon the wonderful mosaic that is life itself.'

'So you have no time for the theatre.'

'None. The theatre is artificial reflecting the accidents of life for the edification of its patrons. Life means not reflecting on what has passed; we'd do better to anticipate what is to come.'

'I think you have more than made your point.'

'My dear, it is a subject on which to wax eloquent.'

'But time is limited, unless you are joining me on the Underground to Waterloo.'

'No, I have an appointment shortly.'

'I trust it is in furtherance of your future and not one of these accidents that so unexpectedly befall the rest of us! Goodbye!'

If Clive had the words on his lips to cap what Sarah said, he was too slow for her as she tripped light-heartedly down the steps and out of sight. Clive had a problem; he met too many compliant women and not enough lively women!

Venice

On the day before Sarah was due to go to Venice, Michael approached her in the office.

'You're not the only one off for the weekend.'

'What do you mean?' said Sarah.

'I hear Deakin's off to Geneva.'

'What for?'

'Some publishers' conference. Got it up on the website.' He reeled off the activities for the weekend and then said, 'Would you pay a thousand pounds for such a weekend?'

'No, I wouldn't.'

'And doesn't even cover the cost of the airfare. Strange what makes the world go round.'

Michael disappeared in the direction of the kitchen, leaving Sarah to her thoughts. After a minute she rose and went to Mr Deakin's office. She found him on the telephone and she started to leave but he waved her back, leaving her standing facing him. His conversation was finishing, but like so many of Mr Deakin's clients the person at the other end of the line had another point to make. Finally Mr Deakin insisted that he had to go as there were pressing matters requiring his attention. He put the phone down and turned his attention to Sarah.

'Sorry about that,' he said in his soft low voice, 'but I've a car coming in a moment. How can I help you?'

'I came in to say that I have made up my mind.'

'In what respect?'

'I've decided to go to Venice tomorrow.'

'Was there any doubt?'

Ms Marchbank pushed her way in unceremoniously and said, 'Your car is here, Mr Deakin.' She flashed a look of loathing at Sarah before leaving.

Sarah turned back to Mr Deakin, who was pushing papers into his briefcase. Michael had assumed that he was going to a publishers' conference in Geneva, and she wanted him to say so to her now. But watching him on the phone and seeing the looks he gave her jolted her instincts, and with no apparent thought process involved she was certain that the man she was going to meet in Venice was most likely to be Mr Deakin himself. He had the money and the opportunity! Other thoughts flashed into her mind, and an instant afterwards she was horror-struck that she was planning his ruin. Then she felt anger that he had played with her, suggesting that he was a confidant and yet gratifying himself at her expense. She felt, as the woman involved, that he was very shortly going to get his just desserts; but then she felt gratitude for his manner towards her.

Her jumble of thoughts left her detached from any natural inclination. She could not grasp hold of any one of her emotions, finding it odd that she was very pleased yet at the same time very angry, but aware that she could not instantaneously sort out the turmoil of her emotions. Other odd thoughts pressed in on her. Why hadn't she given more credence to it being him before? Why couldn't he admit it to her? Why did he continue to play on? In reality she did not want him to admit to it. But then she didn't want it to be Mr Deakin! It couldn't be him! Her mind was totally confused and full of contradictions that she was incapable of articulating.

Mr Deakin rose from his desk and locked his briefcase. In a hypnotic trance, Sarah watched him until he was standing close to her. She felt him clasp her wrist gently.

'You had better go with my blessing,' he said. 'Be happy and don't do anything stupid.'

Sarah nodded numbly and wondered if he had any idea of what she was thinking. The warmth of his hand seem to permeate her flesh and suddenly she felt very bad about everything, and it seemed that all her logical arguments went out of the window. The colour was rising in her cheeks and she knew that she was being very disloyal and had badly treated him as her employer. She stood accused of being a Jezebel and she felt trapped. She wanted him to stop and give her an opportunity of explaining herself. Her only response was to manage a nod again.

'My car is waiting,' he said, and before she could respond he kissed her gently on the cheek. Then, releasing her arm, he was away along the landing and down the stairs followed by Ms Marchbank, who took it as her cue to leave as well. Sarah was left standing miserably in Mr Deakin's office wondering what to do next. Her thoughts were so jumbled and fraught that it seemed best just to get on with being busy with something.

She picked her papers up from where she had placed them on the side and in doing so she noticed the manuscript written by the cabinet minister's wife lying by the telephone. Out of curiosity, Sarah picked it up and opening it began to read. The cabinet minister's wife name was Rosalind Cudman, and the work was titled *Secrets of Stately Homes*. Sarah read the first page and gasped.

'This is rubbish,' she said aloud, 'we can't publish this.'

She rifled through it and found nothing to make her change her mind. The woman might have a good story to tell but she was certainly no writer! Her basic English could be improved upon by anyone who could pass their GCSE examinations. Just to have put it on a word processor and run a spelling check through it would have improved it enormously, but even that tool could not make up for the deficiency in basic grammar. Nor could any computer put in the structure that was so necessary to make a book readable. What was Mr Deakin thinking to have a deadline of less than a month for such garbage? The book needed to be totally rewritten – and that could take weeks! Really, the deadline ought to be a minimum of ten weeks, as it was for most books; but for this work a deadline in a year's time would hardly be unrealistic. In truth, it should have been rejected out of hand! It was utterly ridiculous. This was a prime example of what Clive was talking about. Presumably Mr Deakin had some favour in mind, and so he imposed on his staff, who got no extra remuneration or credit in the book – thus proving that he used people. What favour could he expect from a cabinet minister's wife?

Sarah felt her anger rising, for there was only one favour he could be expecting and that was a mention in the next honours list! What was Mr Deakin after? An MBE – or was he after something better, such as a knighthood! That was it, since a peerage was over the top! Sir Philip Deakin!

How could he appear as a father figure to her and yet at the same time be as scheming as this? Her hand went to her cheek. She rubbed it as if it were possible to erase the kiss she had received from him. She determined that he deserved everything that was coming to him and stormed from the office.

Michael was still at his desk shutting down the workstation. He saw her and said amiably, 'What's the matter? You look very upset about something.'

'Yes, I am,' said Sarah, 'You know that cabinet minister's wife whose book has been shoved in front of others?'

'Yes,' said Michael.

'Well, have you read it?'

'No, I haven't seen it.'

'It's in Deakin's office! I've just had a look and it's garbage!'

'Is it that bad? I guessed it might be awful.'

'It needs to be completely rewritten.'

'Oh dear.'

'Don't be too complacent about it, because it falls to either you or me to do the rewrite.'

'Then how do we manage that in three weeks?'

'Only by working most evenings.'

'What if both of us did it?'

'It would probably give us an evening off every now and again, but whatever hours we put in we would never get paid for!'

'And Charlotte isn't going to like it.'

'But what really gets me is that, having rewritten it, neither you nor I will get any credit for it, but Mr Deakin gets all the plaudits!'

'How do you make that out?'

'Well, who is the book for?'

'Rosalind Cudman.'

'And she's the cabinet minister's wife.'

'So?'

'Use your imagination, Michael!'

'I don't quite understand what you're getting at.'

'What I am getting at is that Mr Deakin has expectations from the next honours list!'

'Really?'

'Don't you think so? It can't be a peerage, as that would be too much; but what about a knighthood? Mr Deakin elevated to a 'Sir' for services to publishing, a patron of the arts and bootlicker to the government.'

Michael was laughing. 'Well, most titles are given to people for doing such things! Can you really condemn a man for cutting corners? I rather admire him for taking his chances – best of luck to him.'

'But you might have to do all the hard work! Then how will you feel?'

'Probably like you. At the end of the day, very angry.'

'It really is too bad! I've heard a lot about his double-dealing and I'm really quite disgusted.' Having said that she thought that it might be a good idea to resign immediately, but then she saw Mr Deakin's face close to hers saying, 'Don't do anything stupid,' and she realised that her response would have to be far more rational.

'Mr Deakin is a hypocritical con-man who deserves his come-uppance!'

Sarah took her temper out on her desk and, throwing her paperwork into a drawer, slammed it shut. She had been close to tears when she left the office but she prided herself on being a woman who did not succumb to such degrading emotions.

Sitting on the train back to Earlsfield, Sarah thought of her revelation about Mr Deakin. She touched her cheek with her fingertips, as if she could still feel the sensations that she had when she had been kissed. She had never let a man apart from her father kiss her like that before and she felt ashamed that she had now! Had any other man done that to her she would have she would have slapped him as hard as she could and lashed him with her tongue as they left the room. She would have made sure that they went with their tails between their legs. But Mr Deakin had caught her at a moment when she had felt disloyalty towards him, and her response had been that of a penitent person. She had felt more like Judas or Brutus, who, having accepted the accolade of their respective masters, had gone on to betray them. But as Clive said, she shouldn't feel any remorse, for it was all part of business. The weak go to the wall and the strong take over. Every business eventually goes down or undergoes a metamorphosis such that the original cannot be seen in the new. She should feel no remorse for someone one day would be plotting her downfall! But how did she come to be thinking like this? No, she had seen her boss as an impediment to her career and ambitions, but she had not seen her boss as Mr Deakin. She had seen Mr Deakin as a father to her and as a man who for reasons she had not understood was being more than unusually well disposed towards her.

Clive and Keith changed her views, for they talked of Mr Deakin in impersonal tones, dissociating her from her real feelings. Every time she talked with them they split her world in two such that she could live in either part. But she could not blame them, for she was a willing partner, and if anyone had deceived her then it was herself. Yet what a revelation for her to realise that the man she saw as a father figure was a potential lover! The kiss he had given her was not paternal but real, and stemming from his heart. His little strictures were not just to say that she should be careful but he was telling her to be there for him. She was gratified by his emotion and she could not deny it. She had shared intimate things about herself with him and accepted his assurances that he was merely a confidant, yet he had been nurturing his feelings for her without her being party to it.

Didn't that show that Clive was right about Mr Deakin's character? She couldn't deny to herself that she had been drawn to Clive, and that meant she was drawn to older men. Indeed, she was disdainful of the younger men and had preferred the company of Clive. Also, she had enjoyed the company of Mr Deakin; in fact she enjoyed going to his office for a chat with him. Did the two men compare in any ways? Mr Deakin did not have Clive's looks, nor did he dress quite as well, but of the two he was the more intelligent and the more interesting. The real revelation she'd had was that Mr Deakin had feelings for her, and that did not make him the prime candidate for being her suitor. It was far more likely to be someone else who had arranged her trips and was now planning to meet her. It had to be someone else!

Her anger towards Mr Deakin was not going to go away easily, for his motives were too transparent, and to get an honour in the way that he was intending was to her outrageous. Michael might admire him for but she could not. If that was how people obtained honours then they had degraded the honour before they had received it. Honours should be given to those who deserved it; it was not something one could deliberately earn.

She was meeting Clive that evening and she knew that he would put her under a lot of pressure to complete the contract for setting up the business, and she was still angry about her missing hour. She decided to feign a headache and not see him. The trip to Venice would take her mind off things, though it would bring her back to wondering who was behind it all, and she wished she could understand the person's reasoning. She had been through everyone it might be, including Mr Deakin, and the only other person who had denied anything was Clive – though that was not a complete denial. Could it have been a slip of the tongue, and he'd nearly revealed himself? Mr Deakin kept on denying things. He had accepted that the bracelet she had bought in Paris was a ring. He had taken delight that a young man had ruined his credit card balance! He claimed he was too old! It simply could not be him.

Logic demanded that it be someone else, and her own peace of mind could only be satisfied knowing that it was another. It had to be one of the authors whom she knew, and they also had a reason for doing so. When they eventually had the meeting that had been planned they would be writing copious mental notes, and doubtless it would form the basis of their next book. But how would she feel? She did not know, though she had a strong desire to box their ears.

She tried to imagine Jonathan French meeting her, but was unable to and reflected that he had no money. She grinned to herself at the thought of the bracelet, since, had it been Jonathan, he would have been licking his financial wounds with the cost of it. But she had been through the arguments and personalities and never came to a conclusion, always arriving back at the beginning – merely to start again! She had to go to Venice and find out exactly who was behind it, and maybe they would give her the answers she needed!

The train had reached Earlsfield and Sarah alighted. She let herself into the flat and, going into her bedroom, flopped onto the bed. She was still angry with Mr Deakin, for he had shown his true colours. He used people to further his own personal ambitions and was quite unscrupulous about how he achieved his ends. Worst of all, he gave himself the appearance of a person who cared. Yet he had finally betrayed himself and revealed a despicable nature. But how did it fit in with her revelation that it was Mr Deakin himself who might be her pursuer, though she still wasn't sure; her revelation was merely that he could be the man, and perhaps he should be on the list. But how could she have been so taken in by him? He had let her enjoy his company and he had made himself agreeable. The air of sadness he always assumed had lifted and he had begun smiling more. She had thought he was simply becoming more human! And certainly she had seen him as being paternal. He had talked to her without her feeling that he was going to share what she said with the rest of the office or her friends. She saw his counsel as being good, and she had sought it and accepted it. He had helped her with the disgusting website, and that had surprised her; for he had not only been the person who had cared for her but he had been quite vehement in his condemnation of the inaction of everyone in the office. Did that show that he had designs on her? But then he said he would have done that for anyone one in the office: would he? It seemed that he took her insult on the website very personally! But then he had suggested that she continued in the office, so he still got a day's work out of her!

He could certainly have afforded to send her to Paris, and of all the people she knew he could have afforded the bracelet; but why hadn't he corrected her when she told him she had bought a ring? Had he foreseen it, and been prepared for something like that? Had it been a good piece of acting? He would not have wanted to give himself away too easily. If it was good acting then he was cleverer than she thought. But it couldn't be Mr Deakin, for he could never have thought up such a scheme. He published geographical and historical textbooks. None of them required any inspiration or imagination! And anyway, he was going to a publishers' conference that weekend in Geneva. Could it be that he was the man who was going to emerge in Venice? Surely not! He lacked the romantic zeal to do anything like it. But what about the kiss? She had accepted it in the paternal spirit in which she thought it was being given. But what if it was a lover's kiss, and he had seen the opportunity and planted it on her, knowing that it would be received. Had she welcomed it? Had she wanted it? Had she wanted him to take her hand? If she was strictly honest with herself then it had not been disagreeable. She had never allowed a man to kiss her before and yielded herself to the kiss so willingly. It meant that she was wrong about Mr Deakin's romantic streak, and if that were so then he could be meeting her in Venice.

And this was where the real worry came in, for she was going to go into business in direct competition with him and she had been determined to see him go out of business. It was so easy when Clive was speaking to her. He seemed to cast a spell over her, protecting her from all normal thoughts, and that stopped her worrying about the consequences. He could pull Mr Deakin's character to shreds and she'd sit there believing him. When she had sat in Mr Deakin's office chatting quite amicably with him she never gave a thought to what she was planning and she had no qualms about it. Even when discussing loyalty she never put two and two together. No, it took a kiss to drag her out of her complacency, and now she had a dreadful conscience about Mr Deakin. Even if he were not the man she was going to meet, how was she ever going to face him again? But if it were him, how could she meet someone romantically, with her conscience?

But why was she meeting anyone romantically? She wanted nothing to do with the opposite sex; she was happy with just being a person and she had no needs in that direction. She had spent the last ten years being glad that she was not going in and out of relationships and she did not want one now... or did she? For some time now she had wanted to see this thing through and had always said to herself that there was nothing in it. Yet it had been Mr Deakin who kept asking her if her heart was involved or if it was feminine curiosity, and she had been forced to admit that the curiosity was slowly taking second place. If it was him, how pleased he must have been with her answers! What pleasure they must have given him! Did he get any pleasure from buying her the bracelet? He must have done, when he suggested that there was a young man out there with a badly dented credit card! How awful to be giving some middle-aged man such satisfaction. And who was it who talked to her about loyalty? It was Curzon, at the theatre! What if Mr Deakin was their friend? She had given them her opinion of her boss! How dreadful! How awful! How was she ever going to face him?

It just couldn't be Mr Deakin who was going to meet her; it simply must not be! How was she going to look him in the eye? She would sooner die on the spot. How could he ever forgive her for being so rude? How could he forgive her for being so presumptuous? How could he forgive her for being such a hypocrite? She had been so looking forward to seeing Venice, and now her hopes were crushed. How was she going to enjoy the weekend? The only chance she had was to believe it was not him and push him to the back of her mind.

In the morning she prepared for the trip to Venice as one who was unwillingly obeying a strong sense of duty. She wondered about not going, but having prided herself on being a strong-minded woman, it seemed somewhat cowardly not to go. Was it fate? Could she accept fate unemotionally? Yet why was it an onerous fate? None of the trips she had undertaken had nasty connotations about them, so there was no reason to suppose that this was going to be different. If the person who met her was going to propose to her, she only had to say no! That was not beyond her, and she was well practised in getting rid of potential lovers.

At Heathrow she looked round the terminal for the sight of a familiar face but as usual she decided that it was impossible in a crowd of milling people. Then she was through the various checks and into the departure lounge. Finally she made her way to the boarding gate and onto the plane.

Sarah gave up looking for anyone she knew, as she had no expectations of being met on the flight. She was not disappointed when a large woman sat beside her, who kept talking across the aisle to some other people. It was clear that she was with a large group of fellow travellers. They were all in high spirits and it looked as if it was going to be a noisy flight. Soon they were in the air, with the noisy group surprisingly settling down. Below them it was cloudy the whole way across Europe, and even the northern plain of Italy was covered in cloud. Then they were down and taxiing to the terminal.

Having collected her case from the carousel, Sarah went outside. Sure enough, there was a young man standing in the hallway with her name on a placard. She introduced herself and he led her outside, turning left, and after a short walk brought them to the Venetian equivalent of a taxi. Sarah was taken aboard the launch and then they were speeding across the lagoon. Venice seemed grey and grim in the distance and it left Sarah wondering why people went there. But gradually the buildings grew closer, and then she was amongst them as the boat nosed through the small canals until they emerged onto the Grand Canal. But before Sarah could take anything in, they had drawn up outside a hotel. The boat was moored and Sarah was ushered inside.

The Meeting

It was nine thirty when Sarah ventured outside on the following morning. She was almost loath to leave the sanctuary of the opulent hotel, and only the thought that later on she would be coming back to it spurred her on to see the magnificent city that was Venice. Once through the hotel doors she found herself in a narrow street. Having seen some of it the previous evening she knew what to expect, and with the sun shining down presaging a hot day to come, she felt pleased that she had dared to explore so early.

She saw some restaurants overflowing onto a wide piazza and determined that she would eat and drink at one of these. To the right-hand side there were a multiplicity of shops selling goods in a manner that was surely banned under European law. One shop sold loose tea with the window piled high with different teas. Every other shop sold the locally made glassware, and Sarah decided that she would take some back with her. On her left were stalls selling fresh fruit and fresh fish. The fruit was piled high and looked delicious, from ripe peaches and nectarines, black plums and succulent apricots to exotic fruits such as mangoes and large pineapples. Always the ubiquitous bunches of grapes were there, tempting the palate; but Sarah had less than twenty minutes ago finished breakfast and could not be drawn. The fish stalls were not the slightest bit enticing, and the sight of a little old lady buying white squid rather put her off. She had never found squid appetising at the best of times, and it was even less so that morning with the creatures lying in their black ink that in their death throes, they had squirted out at their unseen enemy. Other shops were selling trinkets for the tourists.

She walked on, absorbing the hustle and bustle of life that was perfectly intermingled with the tourist trade. Then, to her right, Sarah could see the Rialto Bridge rising up above the crowd of people before her. She moved past barrow stalls selling scarves and belts among their other bric-a-brac until she was on the bridge itself, with the little shops huddled up close to each other, the floor of each being three or four feet higher than the last. Nor was she disappointed with the shops, for their windows displayed hundreds of items, some in gold and silver, many drawing on Venice for their theme. There were shelves stacked with glittering glass and china, and Sarah knew that she could spend a fortune in such places. Almost reluctantly she dragged herself away and took the route that was sign-posted via San Marco.

She marvelled that the buildings were so old and little had changed from the days when Canaletto had painted his busy scenes of Venice. The streets had ancient buildings piled upon even older buildings, producing tiny alleyways that always seem to end in a piazza. Sometimes it was small, yet at other times it was wide with cafés and restaurants crowded together trawling for the passing business. Having crossed one piazza, another alleyway led Sarah deeper into the maze of buildings. Each alleyway was so different; rounding a corner ahead of her she found a hump which could only be a bridge crossing one of the smaller canals that criss-crossed the city. Sarah reached the bridge and having waited for a knot of tourists to disperse she found herself looking down the canal with two gondolas moored waiting for customers. It was a sight she had always assumed would be tacky, but while it was very much part of the tourist scene, in reality she found that it was not at all tasteless, and the desire to take a gondola grew in her.

She sighed as her instinct told her that it would be more satisfying if her beau was sitting beside her. He had after all paid for her to come, and would doubtless be paying the fare! She stood at the top of the bridge looking wistfully down the canal. The sight of two gondolas bobbing gently on the canal water strengthened her conviction that she would soon meet her benefactor. If she had any doubts about him surely a trip in a gondola would dispel them, and she was back wondering what he looked like. Was he tall, dark and handsome? Maybe he had hidden himself from her because he was short, fat and balding. It was Gerrie who had been determined that he would be a let-down and that he had chickened out of accosting her in either Paris or Amsterdam. She had declared that he probably had a big nose or a massive wart on his face. Sarah dismissed her friend's thoughts, banishing them from her mind. She could be certain that he was here and was going to make himself known to her! She looked round and wondered if any of the faces of the men in the crowd close to her belonged to her admirer. And then she decided that she was angry with herself for setting so much store by their meeting.

Across the bridge the path turned to the left alongside the canal for some ten yards before turning sharp right back into the narrow streets. Sarah dawdled for she was in no hurry. She was delighted with everything around her and yearned to know it better. Surely, she thought, one could never tire of such a place? Each corner brought new sights. The tourist shops were full of glassware, and many sported masks. She stopped to look at some and decided that they were not for her.

The alleyway opened up and Sarah was standing in a very large piazza. Instinctively she knew that she had arrived in St Mark's Square. She drew her breath in and decided that her first impressions were better than her hopes. She walked out into the piazza determined to fall in love with the place.

Suddenly Sarah was aware of a figure close to her looking intently at her and she knew that it was him. It was the moment she had been anticipating. Here was the man who had given her tickets to Paris, Amsterdam and Venice. Her heart was full of gratitude towards him and her mind could only think that he had at last come. She turned slowly with her eyes averted for she was determined not to let him see her eagerness. Then they were face to face.

Sarah was not disappointed, for before her stood a handsome man perhaps four inches taller than her. His countenance was dark with black hair combed neatly back. Two piercing brown eyes beamed at her, and his smile was urbanity personified.

She was pleased and overjoyed. She could see herself telling her friends of the moment when they met. Their envy would be almost palpable. She laughed within herself.

'Madam,' he said in perfect English with a hint of a Latin tongue behind it, 'I am so charmed. You're from London?'

She loved his voice and knew that her reserves were at their lowest. If only he knew how much she wanted him and how much she was prepared to give herself to him! But it was not the moment to tell him of her innermost secrets.

'Of course,' she replied.

'And you like our city?'

'It's magnificent,' said Sarah fascinated by his eyes.

'Better than London?'

'Yes,' she whispered, and now her heart was so full she was beginning to think that it might burst.

'Better than Paris?'

'Oh yes,' she breathed, 'and Amsterdam.'

'May I have the privilege of showing around Venice?'

'Please do,' said Sarah and she did not resist when he took her hand and drew it through his arm. His sheer presence was threatening to overwhelm her and she was glad of his arm to hang onto.

'Amsterdam…' he said, 'you know the Dutch call it the Venice of the north, but it is nothing compared to this. This,' he said expansively with a grand wave of his hand, 'is unique.

'Napoleon came here,' he continued, 'and called this piazza the finest drawing room in Europe.'

They walked slowly round in a circle taking in the buildings around them. Finally they faced the Basilica, which made up the fourth side and the focal point of the whole square. They walked slowly towards it and Sarah fancied they were a couple walking towards their marriage destiny.

The queues were forming outside the main door of the cathedral. It was impossible to take in all at once the form of the building, with its onion-shaped domes above, the superb stone carving on the exterior and the wonderful golden mosaics that formed the outside ceiling above the entrance. Sarah could only marvel.

They turned to their right and saw the tower of St Mark standing sentinel not just over the square but over the whole of Venice and the surrounding lagoons. Then to their left they came to the breathtaking Doge's Palace.

At such a sight of beauty Sarah thought her heart had stopped and she stood staring at it, oblivious of the man a few yards away who was selling corn from a barrow for the visitors to feed to the pigeons. They walked on towards the front and stood beneath the two columns, one with a lion atop and the other with a crocodile. Before them was the wide sweep of the Giudecca Canal with the entrance to the Grand Canal to their right, and across the Grand Canal stood the Church of Santa Maria della Salute. Sarah recognised it from her history, for it was the church that Christopher Wren had visited shortly after it had been finished and the story went that it gave Wren the idea for St Paul's in London. The difference between the two was that the Venetian church had massive stone pillars to take the outward forces generated by the weight of the dome, but Wren had seen that if he put chains in the walls to take the bursting forces he could build a far lighter structure. Sarah wanted to go there and see it for herself.

Her happiness was complete, and she felt it could not be bettered until her companion ushered her forwards and spoke to one of the gondoliers. Suddenly she found herself being helped aboard a gondola. Her mood was one of compliance, and she all but welcomed her companion into the seat beside her.

In an easy manner the gondolier got the craft underway with his single oar. She could only marvel at the action. They moved away from the front and onto the water of the main canal. It should all have been ridiculous, and ordinarily Sarah would have derided it, but if she had been told at that moment that they were going to heaven she would have believed it. Then she felt his hand slide across her shoulders. Such attention back home would have attracted her instant condemnation of the man's conduct, but she was surprised that she wanted and expected it.

Then they were turning under a bridge with tourists streaming across it to go down beside the Doge's Palace. Some of the crowd were waving at them, and it was as if they had become part of some tremendous living tapestry. It gave Sarah pleasure to think that she would appear in people's photographs or videos. Ahead of them was the Bridge of Sighs. Her companion said, 'You see the little windows in the bridge? When the judiciary had finished with a man he was handed to the inquisition and taken from the palace across the bridge to the dungeons and his fate on the other side. It is said that those little windows gave the man his last sight of sunlight.'

Sarah shuddered at the thought and was glad of the comforting arm around her shoulders.

They slipped along the canal, passing the houses of the city dwellers. Every bridge had its little knot of people with their cameras at the ready. Proudly they went under each bridge with barely a ripple on the green water. Some of the houses had hung out the washing. It was draped between two windows and gave Sarah a wonderful feeling of being part of it all. Each house had a door at canal level, always shut but presumably leading to the inner sanctums of the house. It added to the wonderful mystery of the whole. It took nearly twenty minutes, but suddenly they emerged on the Grand Canal close to the Rialto Bridge.

They paddled steadily down the canal until, on what seemed like a whim, the gondolier turned right between two dark buildings. This surprised Sarah, for none of the other gondolas had gone that way. A hundred yards down and they stopped at some steps. Her companion jumped out and helped her to dry land. With much ceremony they parted company with the gondola, and then they were walking through the west side of Venice.

Up until this moment Sarah had been carried along by the tide of events and her assurance that she had met her man of destiny. But on finding herself turning from another narrow alleyway into a campo, she realised suddenly that she was lost. It disturbed her and set her mind thinking. She had assumed that this was the person who had sent her the tickets. He had been everything that she could have desired, and it had all been so perfect – yet who was he? Why had he asked if she came from London? He should have known full well that was where she had come from, and if he were the mystery man he would have known all about her! But then he had only made the point to extol the virtues of Venice. Why had he mentioned Paris? Was it just a lucky guess? Or was it purely coincidental? Why had he mentioned Amsterdam? But he hadn't, of course; she had volunteered the information. Was she mad to be wandering around a strange city with a total stranger? Gradually the conviction grew that she had made some kind of mistake. Her instincts when the gondola had turned away from the others were correct. The feeling of euphoria that had threatened to overwhelm her evaporated to be replaced with a feeling of desperation. Somehow she had to get out the situation.

Perhaps her companion saw her doubt for he suddenly said, 'I am taking you somewhere special. When you see it you will agree it is the most wonderful of things.'

She sensed his enthusiasm but it now had the opposite effect on her. She was certain that she had compromised herself. She felt very foolish and determined to tell no one about it at home. She could feel them laughing at her. They turned another corner and she knew that she was hopelessly lost, but every step was bringing them nearer to whatever her fate was to be. She had to do something fast. His hand had tightened on her arm and he seemed to propel her round the corner. She kicked her shoe off.

'Oh drat!' she said as lightly as she could. 'Look, my shoe has come off.'

He tried to pull her on but she feigned helplessness by hopping on one leg. He was forced to let go of her to pick her shoe up and with a marked lack of grace brought it back to her. There was a small restaurant few yards from them with chairs and tables outside. She hopped up to a chair and, sitting down, held out her foot for the man to put her shoe on for her. But her mind was working overtime. Across the campo was an old man shuffling along. It was pointless to call out to him as he would not understand English, and, even if he did, in all likelihood he would shuffle hurriedly on. An old woman came into view. An appeal to her would produce the same effect. Indeed, the woman would think she was stupid trying get away from a handsome young man!

'I'm parched,' she said, 'let's stop here for five minutes and have a drink.'

'Yes,' he said, 'it is a very warm day.'

The waiter, a fat little man, hovered into view. His surly looks made Sarah feel that he was quite capable of dishing up any disgusting fare and it was pointless to think of trusting him. The dark stranger who held her in his power was one of their own. If it came to taking sides it was clear whose side he would take. She was in total despair. She had made one decision in her whole life and now it had utterly humiliated her!

The Rescuer

She neither heard nor saw the person approach.

'If it isn't Miss Levine,' said a man's voice.

At the sound of the familiar English words Sarah looked up. She knew the voice and her eyes filled with tears of gratitude. 'Mr Deakin!' she said. 'How come you're here?'

'I'm staying a short distance from here and I have a meeting shortly.'

Sarah understood what he was saying but before she could speak her companion had risen from his chair and accosted Mr Deakin. The exchange was short and very clear, but Mr Deakin did not seem to understand what was required of him and there was one punch thrown. It landed flush on Mr Deakin's left eye, knocking him straight to the ground, where he lay on his back with his hands on his face. The man turned back to Sarah and made a grab for her; but Sarah, who had risen from her chair as the man assaulted Mr Deakin, had foreseen what was to come. As the Italian turned and lunged at her she dodged his outstretched hands, throwing her chair at his feet. The man went sprawling. Mr Deakin was recovering and had endeavoured to reach a sitting position. The man was quicker getting to his feet but he must have appreciated the futility of his situation, for he suddenly went running across the campo to the far corner where he disappeared.

Sarah went to help Mr Deakin to his feet. He still held one hand over his eye.

'What were you doing with that man?' he gasped.

'I thought he was the man who had sent me all the tickets,' she said sulkily, for the last thing she wanted was to be told off by him. Her gratitude towards her saviour had vanished, since Mr Deakin was the last person she had wished to see, and that he had found her so compromised only seemed to add to her humiliation. But Sarah was not so cold-hearted as to leave a wounded man to fend for himself and she helped him into a seat.

The café owner had been watching from inside and even now refused to come to their aid, preferring to retire deeper into the back of his little restaurant.

Mr Deakin sat in a chair looking very dazed. 'I waited for you come out of your hotel this morning and I followed you to the piazza.'

'Do you make a habit of following people?' Sarah flung at him.

'No, but I saw you meet with that fellow and I could only watch. You seemed to know him and you seemed very friendly, as if you had known each other for some time. So I didn't come up to you. Then you both went off in the gondola... I decided to follow.'

'So you *did* follow me.'

'Oh yes, and when I got to the Rialto Bridge I was not too far behind you, but I lost sight of you. Then I saw the gondola you had been in come out from that side canal and I went down it. It took a while to find you, since I took a wrong turning back there.'

'This is so humiliating,' said Sarah, 'everyone back home will now know!'

'Why should they?'

'Because you do.'

'Why do you presume that I should be the originator of gossip?'

'Most people do.'

'Miss Levine, it is hardly in my interest to tell the world of your mistakes. Your friends would speak of your humiliation because they would think it a great laugh. But I feel more responsible for you. I take no pleasure in saving you from a situation where you were almost certainly going to be raped.'

'You think that was to be my fate?'

'Oh yes, and there would have been little you could have done about it legally, for even I was a witness to the fact that you had gone off with that man willingly.'

'Why should you feel responsible for me?'

'I thought you might have guessed by now.'

'I did guess that it was you but to be honest I was hoping it wasn't.'

'Have a look at my eye, will you?'

Sarah stared at his face. 'You're going to have black eye.'

'I think so too. Can you help me back to the hotel?'

'I really have no option,' she replied, but as he rose to his own feet, Sarah was shocked that her boss should look so unsteady and went to his side. He draped an arm around her shoulders and slowly they made their way back towards the Rialto Bridge.

'Go down here,' he said suddenly. Sarah turned and after hundred yards found herself back at the Grand Canal on the opposite bank to her hotel.

'We've gone the wrong way,' she said.

'No,' he said, 'take the *traghetto* across.'

'The what?'

'The ferry. Ring that bell and he'll come across.'

Sarah did as she was told and a minute later a man in a small motorboat crossed towards them. They climbed aboard and a few minutes later they stood on the other side beside Sarah's hotel. Sarah led Mr Deakin round to the front of the hotel, where she expected to leave him, but when she looked at him she saw that he needed some help.

'Come up to my room,' she said, 'and I'll bathe your eye, maybe we can stop some of the swelling.'

They went in and Sarah led the way upstairs to her room where Mr Deakin threw himself into the armchair. Sarah left to find some ice and had to go downstairs to the bar but she returned a few minutes later with a large glass of ice cubes.

Mr Deakin was sitting very still and took no notice of her as she began to apply the ice, though he grimaced as the first cube touched his cheek. The melting ice ran down Mr Deakin's face and onto his shirt.

'Hold that there,' said Sarah conscience-stricken, pressing a flannel full of ice against his eye. 'I'll go and fetch a towel.' She returned from the bathroom to find Deakin lying on her bed.

'Sorry,' he said in a small voice, 'but I must lie down for a minute or two.'

Sarah continued to minister to him but after ten minutes she decided that there was little more she could do. If the cold compress had been administered earlier it might have been possible to stop much of the bruising. She cleared the things up and looked down at the man whose position on her bed looked somewhat settled. She peered at him more closely and saw that he was asleep.

It was two o'clock in the afternoon, and not having had any lunch, Sarah was feeling hungry. Reluctantly she left her room and went down to find that the dining room was almost empty, with waiters clearing away the last of the dishes. But they seemed to understand her need for a sandwich and cup of coffee.

'I'll have them sent to your room,' said one of them, and Sarah felt that she had been dismissed; but she returned wondering if she should have ordered anything for Mr Deakin. When she entered her room she found that he was still asleep.

'So much for your couple of minutes,' she said softly.

The sandwich arrived twenty minutes later and Sarah received the tray at the door, not wishing the waiter to come into the room and see a man sleeping on her bed. Slowly she ate the fare, allowing herself to get lost in her thoughts.

Her suspicion that it was Mr Deakin who had been pursuing her had proved correct. He had always managed to put her off the scent, and even when she heard that he was going to be away at the same time as her, she still gave no credence to the possibility that it was indeed him. But then she had hoped that it was not him at all, as she had a thoroughly guilty conscience about him. She had been harbouring thoughts of wrecking his business and installing herself as the overlord of his destruction. The memory of the way she had bad-mouthed him on the day before departing for Venice was still strong in her mind. Even as she had spoken, she had known that what she was saying was not true and the knowledge that she was slandering him had not stopped her.

Now that he was close to her she wished that she had remained silent. She shouldn't have read the manuscript and she should have used language that was more moderate, but she had been determined to compound her misery. It was the knowledge of her duplicity that stopped her admitting her gratitude for his actions. True, she had been pleased to see him, but that was because his presence had intervened in what was going to be for her a very embarrassing episode. She could have wished it were anyone else, since she could find no sympathy for his injury. He had really asked for it, and she considered his intervention to have been completely foolhardy. Mr Deakin should have known what would happen and he should have been ready to get out of the man's way. Instead he had virtually asked to be hit! He really was so naïve and stupid!

Sarah just sat and stared at her rescuer with contempt. Then it occurred to her that perhaps the whole thing was a put up job. Had Mr Deakin paid the man to abduct her? Had he waited hidden close to the agreed rendezvous point, so that he could come upon the man and make a heroic rescue and appear as her knight in shining armour? For his pains he had received a black eye, which he richly deserved…

For some time nothing disturbed her train of thought, except that the man lying on her bed began gently moaning. It made her feel uncomfortable with her reasoning for it was becoming increasingly illogical to her that a man would pay a fellow human being to punch him, and not just punch him but to punch him hard enough to be badly hurt. It would not be in the man's plan to spend the next few hours asleep in front of the woman he had saved. Maybe it had gone wrong, and the man while he was required to hit Mr Deakin had gone and overdone the job. That satisfied her for another ten minutes.

Perhaps Mr Deakin's strategy was sympathy. Was he lying on her bed waiting for her to come to him? No, she could not see what he was hoping to gain by that ploy, and out of curiosity she went over to the bed. She bent over the prostrate body of her boss and gave him a sharp prod in the ribs. She got little response apart from a moan, and turned her attention to his eyes. His good eye was underneath and out of reach. She reached for the bruised eye and ruthlessly pulled his eyelid up. It was clear to her that Mr Deakin was out cold, but she was horrified at the sight of his bloodshot eye. She wondered if he had been injured more severely than she thought and that he needed to see a doctor.

It worried her. She did not want to draw attention to his plight by getting a doctor to him, and she was certain that he wouldn't thank her if she did. But if he were unconscious she ought to get a doctor, and she satisfied herself that he seemed to be asleep. She decided to keep an eye on him and returned to her chair.

The thought that no man would put himself in the way of a serious injury came to her. Mr Deakin would never have paid anyone to hit him that hard. No, if he had paid the man anything it would be for them to have a scuffle and Mr Deakin to emerge as the victor. That, for his assailant, would be easy money. There was also the fact they had only stopped because she had shed her footwear, so it could not have been planned.

She felt mean and stupid for even having considered that Mr Deakin had brought his troubles on his own head. No, Mr Deakin, whether she liked it or not, was above such base thinking. He had said that he had followed her and she had no reason to disbelieve him. He had followed her because he was the man who was going to meet her in Venice! He was the invisible man! It must have given him great satisfaction to say that. He had planned to meet her in St Mark's Square. He had wanted her to melt into his arms, just as she had with the Italian. Yet how could she? Despite having a premonition that it was Mr Deakin she had set her heart on it being someone else.

But why had she been taken in by the Italian? And Sarah felt a flush come to her cheeks as she thought about it. When he materialised by her side she had been pleased and even thrilled to see him. Why had she been taken in by him? She had never let a man slip his arm around her waist before and lead her off so easily. No, she was a woman who took delight in seeing men humbled! Had she not seen off her flatmate's lecherous friend? She was a woman who had made a habit of turning men away; indeed, Cathy would say that she had made an art form out of it. Yet for the first time in her life she had been bamboozled by a man. Never before had she been so taken in, and it was mainly her naivety and lack of expertise in dealing with the opposite sex that had caused her to make such an error of judgement. Was it because she had not wanted it to be Mr Deakin and the subsequent embarrassment of confessing what she had done to him?

What would have happened to her had she continued with the man? At the time she had merely understood that she was in a serious predicament without having defined just what it was.

Would he really have taken her to a quiet house and raped her? Yes, that had been her fate; she could see it now. The Italian was expecting sex and had assumed that she was ready for it. Would he have listened to her entreaties when she arrived at the house? She doubted that, and could see herself being thrust unceremoniously indoors. Once his anger was aroused then anything could have happened, so she would have submitted with apparently good grace and gone into the house. There would be no one there to whom she could appeal and she would have been pushed upstairs to a bedroom.

Would he have locked the door? That probably depended on how willing she seemed to be. If she angered him then it was likely that he would have torn her clothes off, leaving her the embarrassment of wandering back to the hotel in a state of semi-undress. So she would capitulate to maintain her dignity. What would he have required from her? It would not have taken him long to realise that she was sexually naïve, and that alone would have angered him. He would then have forced sex on her and she would have been badly hurt. Would sex just once have satisfied him, or would he want it two or three times before he released her? Only then would she have crawled back to the hotel to face Mr Deakin. How would he have taken it? She shuddered to think, for he had seen her go off willingly with a laugh on her face.

She could not have faced him. She would have had to bear his condemnation and she would have lost every vestige of his respect. Much as he might have wanted otherwise, he could no longer have retained that much sympathy for her. At best he would have treated her with total disdain, adding to the hurt that she would have felt. And how she would have hurt! She would have been battered and bruised and the sex would have left her raw; but at least the physical injuries would have healed, unlike the mental injuries that she would have sustained alongside them. The embarrassment would be the least of her worries. The indignity of it she might get over in time, but what about her loss of self-respect and self-esteem? As for other considerations, such as sexually transmitted disease or pregnancy, they did not bear thinking about. It would have shattered her.

No, Mr Deakin's intervention had been most fortuitous and she owed him a lot, too much. She owed him her sanity.

What about Mr Deakin? If she believed him, he had followed her and been lucky in finding her. Perhaps he expected the Italian to be more reasonable when he was approached, or maybe Mr Deakin simply hoped that he would run away at his arrival. Perhaps he thought that she was not necessarily in trouble and was just giving her the option of saying so. No, she thought none of those things could account for what happened. Mr Deakin had come up to her without a thought in his head as regards his own safety. It was very doubtful that he could have overcome the man in a fair fight, unless he had some qualities that she knew nothing about. Had he been a judo expert he might have overcome the man, but then he would have seen the blow coming and reacted accordingly. It would have been the Italian lying on the cobbles feeling very hurt. No, Mr Deakin had intervened knowing that he was going to get hurt, though he did not know how. And the viciousness of the way the man treated Mr Deakin convinced Sarah that he would have had no respect for her finer feelings.

She was loath to admit it but she knew in her heart that Mr Deakin had been very brave, and whatever he had done he had done it for her. She knew of no one else who would have done the same for her. He was now carrying what should have been her injuries.

She went to the bed again and stared at Mr Deakin. He looked hot and very agitated, with his breath coming almost in gasps. He moaned somewhat and made little movements with his hands. Sarah wondered that she had not noticed it before, for she could see that he was running a temperature. She debated again whether or not she ought to get a doctor and decided against it, as she was convinced that it was the heat of the room. She felt him and found that he was dripping in sweat. The room was stifling but Sarah couldn't see how to open the windows. She hadn't realised but she too had sweat running down her. But her first thoughts were for the suffering of the man lying on her bed.

She reached out and loosened the collar of his shirt, but it seemed a prosaic gesture and she felt she could do better. His feet were encased in his shoes and socks and Sarah felt silly in not having taken them off before. She went to his feet and removed his footwear. She sighed and went back to his shirt. Having undone the cuff on his exposed arm she peeled his shirt off one side of his body. Carefully, she worked it underneath him until she could pull it from his other arm.

Still he seemed hot, and she set to work on his trousers, hoping that he was decent below. It was a struggle but finally she had Mr Deakin's trousers off. He lay before her in just his underpants. However, she could see beads of sweat bursting out on him, and went to the bathroom for a wet towel. She wiped his body carefully, feeling oddly pleased with herself, and had the further satisfaction of hearing his breathing ease and much of the fretting disappearing. It took half an hour before she could be certain that his temperature was down.

She found that she needed a drink of water and returned to the bathroom for a glass. It occurred to her that if she needed a drink then the invalid also needed one. She returned with a glass of water, slid an arm behind his neck and pulled his head up.

'Wake up,' she said gently, but received no response.

She put the glass down beside her and shook him violently. Mr Deakin moaned and stirred. He opened his eyes and Sarah felt for the glass.

'Drink this,' she ordered and brought the glass to his lips. He sipped it slowly with no thought that she was pulling his head up, and she felt her patience running out; but after what seemed an age the glass was empty.

'Do you want any more?' she asked in a very firm tone.

He shook his head and made it clear that he wanted to go back to sleep. Sarah returned to the armchair, glancing at her watch. It was seven o'clock and she felt hungry. Once again she checked the man lying on her bed and deciding he was comfortable enough for the time being, she went down to the dining room. At the sight of the fare laid out before her she felt she was not really that hungry and selected a piece of chicken breast and a roll. She ate quickly and then returned to the bedroom with a cup of coffee in her hand.

She sat in the armchair and looked at the sleeping man. She felt a lot of admiration for him coming to her aid, and upon reflection she wouldn't have been surprised if he hadn't bothered to pursue her in the way that he had. For he had seen the enthusiasm that she had poured out on the Italian, treating him as her beau, and it would have deterred a less than ardent lover. She couldn't have blamed Mr Deakin if he had turned away in disgust and buried his grieving heart. Her fate would have been resolved justly there and then, but he had determined otherwise. That he had found her was extremely fortunate, and she was sure that he would be the first to admit it. Yet he had approached her sitting outside the café merely as a person who had come across a friend in the street. He must have known that his reception would not be greeted with any pleasure, and in all likelihood realised that he was going to get hurt. Yet despite everything he must have felt, he had played his part, and she was thankful for that. She wished she did not feel so guilty about her dealings with him, and she wanted him to wake and talk to her about it. She could only hope that he wouldn't be angry, though if he were like any other employer she would shortly be receiving her cards and looking for another job. She would have to rely on his desire for her to forgive her. But it made her feel very mean-spirited towards him, and she worried about it. She now felt naïve for never being more serious with the opposite sex. She was aware that she had had no practice in dalliance, and for her any relationship that had got underway was of a short duration and very one-sided.

She thought of the kiss she had received in the office from Mr Deakin, and she knew that she had wanted it and welcomed it. She had wanted him to touch her, yet it had been him walking out of the room that had promoted her anger. She had wanted him to admit there and then that it was him and to have taken her out for a meal where they could have got to know each other better. True, she would have had to confess her disloyalty towards him, and that could have provoked difficulties; but at least Venice would have become unnecessary. Would she have wanted him? She wasn't sure, but she was open to persuasion, for there was her guilty conscience to contend with. And what if Connie and Curzon were Mr Deakin's friends? She had made some quite injudicious remarks about Mr Deakin when they met at the theatre.

Why had she not seen him as her lover before now? Surely she should have done! Why had she let Clive speak so badly about him? Why did she let Clive persuade her to go into business with himself and Keith? How could she have been so taken in? Or was she merely proving that women were the illogical creatures that men believed them to be? No, she was not illogical, and had always thought of herself as being rational. If she was honest, Clive exerted an almost hypnotic effect on her just as he did with most women. Usually he wanted sex with them, after which he cast them aside like garbage. But she had prided herself that she could hold him off from that. And there was an attraction in being so close to such a dangerous man. But of course she had deluded herself, because he was not interested in having sex with her – at least not at that moment! He was interested in her money, and she had promised him over £20,000 to start a business. He and Keith were already working on her for the next £20,000, and presumably once having got that Keith would have let Clive off the leash to collect the interest on his investment and finally gratify his physical desire. And he would have hunted her down before she realised just how much money she had lost. Could she have resisted him?

Bitterly she shook her head. To think that she could have done would have been to continue the delusion. Yet she still had to get out of her promise to Clive. Her bank would eventually have the money ready... and then what? Her best hope lay shattered on her bed. Did he know of her predicament? She had all but told Connie and Curzon, and surely they must have told him. What would he say when he knew the full extent of her dealings with Clive? Was his love for her strong enough to survive a black eye and the knowledge that she had spent weeks plotting against him? *Loyalty*! That was what Curzon had tried to get across to her. He had seen through the whole business despite having little to go on, and had tried to puncture her illusion.

She made Mr Deakin drink some more water. Though he opened his eyes and drank the proffered drink, she couldn't see him getting up and finding his own hotel. She found herself feeling oddly contented, and concluded that her heart had for once completely overruled her mind. Her arguments had drained away and given her a different perspective on things, and she found that she could think positively of a future with Mr Deakin. He had not been in the pub that fateful night but she had told him about it. He had won her challenge and shown himself to be worthy of her. He had laid siege to her citadel, beaten down her defences and overrun her ramparts. She had yielded to him and wanted to exult in his victory. But the general seemed to know little of the victory, and did not know that his flag had been hoisted aloft! She willed him to wake and feast on her, but he remained lost and forlorn in the oblivion of sleep, with his breathing steady and rhythmical.

The cooler evening temperature suited him and she found a sheet to put over him. But the evening was slipping away and Sarah had to make plans for the night. She could hardly leave the room and had no idea where Mr Deakin was staying. The armchair was not comfortable enough for her to sleep in, and the floor, despite being carpeted, did not look at all inviting. But the bed was wide, and with Mr Deakin lying on one side of it there was room beside him.

She stripped down to her bra and pants and climbed in beside his inert body. She leaned over him and, being close, she was appalled at his eye for it looked rawer than ever and was turning purple. She kissed him and wished that she could kiss away his wounds.

She lay back for a while staring at the ornate ceiling, which she had not noticed before, thinking that she had never spent a night in the same room as a man before and certainly never in the same bed! She wondered what her flatmates would say if they knew, and she concluded that they would tell her to go for it! Their idea of life was to have a good time all the time – and they meant sexually; but Sarah could not see that sex was possible with the man lying inert beside her. She felt very comfortable and at ease, apart from her career worries, which persisted; but despite that she was tired and knew that she would shortly be asleep.

The Proposal

For how long she slept she did not know, but she became aware of a tightening around her chest. She half woke to check what it was and found that Mr Deakin had pushed her bra up and was lying with his face against one of her breasts. His free hand was over her other breast. She was surprised that she did not feel annoyed. She should have been annoyed but the emotion was not there for her to dwell on and work into a frenzy, and the more she thought about it she realised that she felt a certain pleasure. She moved and released her bra, throwing it onto the floor for good measure. Her actions partly woke Mr Deakin, who began muttering. She slipped back beside him and felt him once again rest his hand on her breast. He continued to mutter and then said something audibly. It sounded like Caroline, but she could not be certain.

Sarah stared back at him wondering if she had heard him correctly and to whom the name belonged. She knew no one in or connected with the office who had the name and he had never spoken of another woman in his life. And he did not seem the type of man who took lovers, for it had always struck her that he was wrapped up in his business. Should she be angry and throw him off the bed? No self-respecting woman would let him continue in the same bed. But her curiosity got the better of her and she determined to find out in the morning what he was on about; besides, she felt too comfortable.

The sun was streaming in between the gaps in the curtains when Sarah woke again. However, it was not the light that awakened her but the pressure she felt on her bladder. Becoming more conscious she realised that Mr Deakin's hand was inside her panties and pressing on her mound. Carefully she put her hand down to double check that it was his hand, but her touch caused him to moan. She wondered if she had awakened him, but he seemed to be half asleep, like someone having a dream. His hand moved on her and she could not be sure whether it was deliberate or just one of those movements a person makes when asleep. But his finger touched her most sensitive part and she moaned softly with pleasure and tensed her hips as the sensations inflamed her senses. His hand moved again and his finger seem to increase the sensation that she felt, causing her to move her legs with a small jerk, and her knee caught Mr Deakin's leg. The action did not wake him but roused him sufficiently to say, 'What's the matter, Caroline? Go back to sleep!'

The name during the night had been garbled so that she could dismiss it, but it was clear enough now! Her anger rose quickly and she pulled his hand from her panties and thrust it away from her. She threw off the sheet that covered both of them and leapt out of the bed, stopping only to find a dressing gown, and dropped angrily into the armchair. Mr Deakin lapsed back into sleep, and Sarah could only sit and glower at him. But he rallied again and sat up in the bed, blinking at his surroundings.

'I thought Caroline was here,' he said and looked around as if he expected to see another woman with that name.

'You owe me some sort of explanation,' said Sarah, but she was not sure that he heard her. He continued to look at her and then round the room. His actions only served to increase her anger.

'Who is Caroline?'

'Yes, of course,' he muttered, 'how stupid of me.'

'Are you going to make sense?' she asked, raising her voice so that he should hear her.

He was looking at her but he did not seem to be pleased to see her.

'Are you going to tell me who Caroline is?' she persisted.

'She is my wife.'

Sarah felt anger, for it was not nice to be compared with an ex-wife and she had no plans to share Mr Deakin with another woman. She decided his divorce must have been messy and was one that Mr Deakin had not sought or wanted, leaving him still very much in love with his wife. Presumably his wife's love for him had been sorely tested while he had built a business, and it was her infidelity that caused the split.

'Why did you go with that man yesterday?' Mr Deakin demanded suddenly.

She was silent and refused to meet his look.

'If it had been me who met you in St Mark's Square, as it should have been, would you have greeted me in the same manner as him?'

'I don't know. I had convinced myself that it was not you who was going to meet me.'

'Oh? And who were you expecting?'

'I don't know.'

Mr Deakin climbed off the bed and started dragging his clothes on.

'You didn't seem very pleased when you found out.'

'I had a conscience about certain things.'

'Such as?'

'I was very rude about you to someone before I left.'

'Everyone is rude about their employer. What else?'

'I was considering leaving and starting a similar business to yours.'

'I know; these things cannot be kept a secret.' He had put his shoes on and stood up. Sarah thought that he did not seem too steady on his feet.

'Why didn't you tell me that you knew?'

'I wanted you either to tell me or discover for yourself that it would be a wrong move.'

'That's a bit conceited of you,' she said with asperity, but managing to keep her temper.

He seemed to shrug and turned to the door. She expected him to look back at her but he opened the door and left without another look at her, pulling the door closed behind him. She could only stare as the door and for a second remained stunned. Then she was on her feet.

'Don't walk off!' she shouted at the closed door. On reaching the door and swinging it open she realised Mr Deakin was out of sight on the stairway. The impropriety of running after him came to her, as she was barely decent. She hesitated, wanting to shout again, but she was suddenly fearful of creating a spectacle of herself. With nothing to vent her anger on, she shut the door and stood leaning against it. She was angry with him for leaving her. She was angry with what he had said and she was angry with herself for not defending herself properly and for being outsmarted. Finally she managed a breath and allowed the tears to flow down her cheeks. She had always despised certain types of women for their weakness, and considered her emotional level far superior to theirs. Now she suddenly found herself in sympathy with them and she had no reason to stem the flow. Then she felt the pain of rejection and the tears flowed faster still.

She saw herself as one who was on top of her relationships and always had the last word. The few men who had tried to come into her life had been rejected, thoroughly browbeaten and glad to escape the lashings of her tongue. She knew they had suffered, and now she knew what they had endured. It was not the simple rejection of a friendship, for her heart had become inclined towards Mr Deakin, and because of that it was far worse. She felt as if she were being torn apart, and the severity of it was such that she felt physical pain.

For half an hour she wept before gradually her mind began to reason how much she was better off without the man, and though loath to listen, her heart finally gave way to logic. She had spent the night with him and let him feel most of her body – how humiliating it was to be told that he thought she was someone else! Didn't he know that she had spent the previous day nursing him? Couldn't he see that she had wanted him and that she had lowered herself to gratify him? Wasn't she the prize that he had fought so gallantly for? Hadn't she taken him back to her hotel and bathed his wounds? Was she to be so despised because she had been rude about him? Why continue the charade, if he knew of her business dealings?

The worse thing was that she was going to go home feeling a failure and depressed. Tomorrow morning, Monday, she would hand in her resignation and start to look for another job. Doubtless Mr Deakin had bought tickets with adjoining seats for the flight home and she would meet him then. He would make small talk and she would spend the flight being as nasty as she could, but at Heathrow they would go their separate ways. But she had to admit to herself that it had been something of an adventure to be sent to places for the weekend, and her life had surely been lacking in adventure hitherto.

She dried her tears and, like any woman with self-respect, she started planning her revenge. It was very unlikely to happen but it relieved the emotions and gave her mind something positive to work on. Perhaps she should re-book her flight for that morning, but decided that to completely avoid the man was not real revenge. Better to sit beside him and say absolutely nothing, then spill a hot cup of tea over him and just say 'Tough!' Perhaps she could open the little pack of cheese and get it all out on her hand and then at an appropriate moment slip it down his collar. She enjoyed the thought of that. It was strange how a woman could plot an assault on a man and get away with it, whereas if a man plotted such a thing on a woman he would find himself in court on a charge of assault, or even attempted rape! Her problem was that her mind could determine some things but her heart was going a completely different way, for if he were to suddenly come back to her room and straighten everything out she would want it. And her heart would never let her mind take revenge while there was even the slimmest of chances of a reconciliation. Perhaps it was why women were known as the weaker sex!

She had to do something with her day, though she did not know what. She hated Venice; for all its beauty and history, it had turned against her. Had she lived in a different age she could see herself being led from the Doge's palace and across the Bridge of Sighs to spend her last days being tortured in a deep dungeon, and the thought of such a fate suited her mood.

Finally Sarah went downstairs to the lounge. A waiter brought her coffee and she sat reading an English newspaper from the table in front of her. Having finished that she picked up a magazine and gave it a thorough perusal. She glanced at the clock and noted that it was well past midday. She had another cup of coffee.

Then the waiter was hovering over her again, and she turned to him irritably and said, 'What now?'

He was holding a telephone and said unnecessarily, 'Miss Levine? There's a phone call for you.'

It could only be one person, and she would have liked to make the waiter suffer by saying awkward things such as, 'Who is it?' or, 'I'll take it in my room.' Any delay would make the man suffer! But her hand went out eagerly to take the phone.

'Yes,' she said, hoping that she had not betrayed her eagerness and sounded serious.

'It's Philip,' said the voice. For a moment she was stunned as she did not know a Philip... Oh, but of course, that voice belonged to Mr Deakin, and her heart leapt.

'I'm sorry about this morning, Sarah,' said the voice, 'but I felt ill and wanted to sort myself out.'

'Oh, really...'

'I'm phoning to ask you to do me a favour.'

'What is it?'

'Well, could you come to my hotel with some make-up, I've just seen my eye and I really can't go out with it. Anyone seeing it as it is would wonder what I've been doing.'

The thought came to her that he was apologising just sufficiently to her to get the favour off her and nothing more. But her professionalism got the better of her, and she was not going to refuse her employer, even though it was likely to be the last favour she could do him.

'Of course,' she said demurely, and he told her where he was staying.

It was an hour later that Sarah knocked on the door of Mr Deakin's room. Almost immediately it opened and he seemed to sweep her in closing the door behind her.

'I'm sorry,' he said again, 'but this morning when I left I just wanted to feel part of the day. And I thought that if I went back to my room and had some breakfast and showered and put on some clean clothes I'd feel better.'

'How did you feel?'

'Not brilliant... I seem to have a hangover that won't go away. At least that's what it feels like. I think I was a bit dehydrated and when I got back here I drank a lot and went to sleep for a couple of hours, and then I remembered I had left you in the lurch.'

'You did rather,' she said drily.

'Did you bring the make-up?'

'Yes, of course I did.'

'I'm sorry but I took one look in the mirror and decided that I could not go about with such a black eye. Do me a favour and put it on for me.' He sat in a chair and stared anxiously at her.

She put the make-up on a small coffee table nearby and turned to his eye. It looked very sore and she flinched from having anything to do with it, but he was expecting her to help him and she could not let him down. She applied the make-up and from the movements he made she knew that it hurt him a lot. But after some minutes she was able to stand back and admire her handiwork. One could no longer see the bruising, and the only visible sign of anything untoward was his bloodshot eye. There nothing she could do about that.

Mr Deakin went over to a mirror and having inspected his face closely announced that she had done a good job.

'Now I want to take you and show you Venice,' he declared.

Sarah was reluctant to go with him but she had nothing else to do, and to refuse him would merely be petulant.

'Why are you staying at this hotel?' she asked once they were outside.

'It was the first hotel I ever stayed at in Venice, and I keep coming back to it. My parents brought me here a few times when I was a boy; they always stayed there. Father liked it because it was small and they had an excellent chef.'

They turned towards the Rialto Bridge, passing the hotel where Sarah was staying.

'You see that alleyway there,' said Mr Deakin suddenly.

Sarah obediently looked where he pointed and said, 'Yes.'

'When I came down from university I was lucky enough to stay here for a month, and I lived in lodgings down there. A little Italian lady ran the digs. They were amazingly cheap and she was just like a mother. But the house is all part of a hotel now.'

'How do you know that, if it's somewhere down there?'

'I looked it up the last time I was here. She must have passed on, as the place did not exist. It had been swallowed up by the hotel next door.'

'What were you doing here then?'

'Having an extended holiday and brushing up my Italian.

Those were days! All the girls wore dresses and showed their legs. They were magnificent!'

'You don't like women in trousers, then.'

'They don't seem very feminine, do they? There was an art to being a woman then and the game was played openly.'

'How can there be an "art" to being a woman! That's total nonsense!'

'Is it? Women in trousers plonk themselves down on a chair rather like dumping a bag of potatoes on a shelf. Now, when a woman wore a skirt, she had to sit properly.'

'I won't have that! What does "properly" mean?'

'Well, if you threw yourself in a chair then your skirt would blow up, revealing your underwear. And not only that, if a woman wanted to encourage a man then she showed him a bit more of her leg.'

'So you don't think much of me wearing trousers!'

'I think you wear trousers because you want to look dowdy.'

'So it doesn't matter where a woman is or what a woman is doing – she has to look sexy!'

'Do you see that window up there?' Mr Deakin pointed to a window in one of the houses that rose out of a backwater off the main canal.

'Yes.'

'Well, a couple of friends and myself knew the girl who lived there, and we used to go to her room and listen to records there.'

'But you ignored what I just said.'

'What did you say?'

'I took issue with you about a woman always having to look sexy.'

'You don't have to take issue with me! I'm a man, and I've a different point of view to you.'

'No, you can't dismiss it like that. That's not fair! Why should women look good all the time purely that men might have a continuous fantasy?'

'Funny how one can still remember the interior of her bedroom so clearly...'

'Should you be speaking to me like this?'

'We were just friends enjoying the latest hits. She liked it, as the Italians were always miles behind our hit parade.'

'Where are we going? The Rialto Bridge is to our right.'

'Let's go through to San Marco.'

Sarah gulped for it brought back the memories of the previous day. She thought he was being very insensitive, and not just over that one matter but in his views on women in general. He was hardly endearing himself to her.

They walked down the next alley and emerged into another campo.

'We used to come here in the evenings and drink wine at the bar over there. I didn't tell you, but I had ideas of writing a book on Venice – not your usual sort but out of the ordinary. Before I left I took hundreds of photographs and they're still at home somewhere.'

Sarah was becoming bored with his memories and raptures about Venice. She found it was rather like walking with a museum guide who could not stop talking.

They crossed a number of canals on wonderful little bridges that simply went up and over, and each bridge gave them a new vista between the buildings. They passed some shops, and Sarah remembered having come that way the day before and decided that she did not much care for it. She hoped Mr Deakin had a genuine purpose in dragging her that way, as she felt it would have been more diplomatic as regards her feelings had he taken a different direction. But then they were in St Mark's Square with the red-brick tower of St Mark straight ahead and the Basilica with its onion domes to their left. To their right was the square, with its colonnades round its three remaining sides. Pigeons wheeled over head giving it a frantic atmosphere. But Sarah was unimpressed, as the memory of her error was still too fresh in her mind. She worried that the man might suddenly appear and take on Mr Deakin again. She would rather that they were anywhere else than here. But Mr Deakin seemed unconcerned about what she thought, and propelled her towards the very spot where she had been standing when the Italian had approached her. She shuddered and could not bring herself to look up.

'You stood here yesterday,' said Mr Deakin, 'and you thought that the Basilica was magnificent, didn't you?'

'Yes,' she agreed, 'but I don't want to be reminded of it.'

'But don't you see that, despite yesterday, it is still magnificent?'

She was forced to look up. 'I know, you're right.' She listened while Mr Deakin gave her some of its history.

'Do you know,' he said, 'they still require woman to enter the Basilica with their arms covered.'

'A last bastion of the male-dominated world that we used to live in.'

They moved on to view the Doge's Palace just beyond the Basilica. She listened to Mr Deakin without hearing him and suddenly realised that he had his arm around her shoulders. She sighed, as it would have been so perfect the day before and now she did not care for it. She contemplated telling him to take his arm away. Her duplicity came to mind and she felt embarrassed. She had wanted to talk to him about many things but he seemed wrapped up in himself and did not appear to have much time for her.

They wandered round the square and paused by an outdoor restaurant. Beneath the arches a small orchestra was playing.

'Let's have a coffee,' said Mr Deakin, and they sat at one of the tables. A waiter came into view and took their order.

Sarah looked around her and felt pleased. She was glad that Mr Deakin had forced her back to see the square. There was a constancy about it, giving it an air of a grand stage where the actors came and went. People came onto the stage from surprising angles, each with a purpose, each wanting to absorb something of the constancy and yet each adding in some small way to the mosaic of life. She was feeling more agreeable with everything, and the coffee when it came was delicious. She wished that she did not feel so guilty about Mr Deakin. She turned to him and smiled wanly. He smiled back.

'Sarah,' he said suddenly, jolting her out of her reverie, 'there something I've been meaning to ask you.'

'Yes,' she replied, 'what is it?' She expected him to ask her some mundane question and looked surprised when he took hold of her hand. Perhaps it was because she let him do it or perhaps her renewed pleasure had simply dulled her senses, making her appear agreeable, she never knew; but Mr Deakin was kneeling before and had taken her other hand.

'No!' she said, aghast.

'But will you marry me?' he asked.

'No,' she said, her anguish turning to misery.

'Please, Sarah,' he persisted. 'Please marry me, I love you so much.'

Sarah became aware that some of the nearby people were taking an interest in them. It was becoming embarrassing.

'Please get up,' she hissed at him.

'Just say yes,' he said. There were now at least two Japanese tourists pointing their video cameras at them. Lights flashed. She felt hot all over and she was sure that her face was bright red.

'*Yes*, then,' she gasped.

'Are you certain?'

'Of course I am.' It was a very unfair question.

Mr Deakin rose to his feet and bent and kissed her. The surrounding crowd began clapping, and a number of them came over and congratulated them both. Many more cameras flashed at them. One man had his arm across Mr Deakin's shoulder and his friend took two or three photographs of them. Then it was handshakes all round, and with little bows the Japanese men left. Gradually everyone else went their way and the people sitting at the tables close by resumed their conversations. Sarah was glad that they were no longer the centre of attention. Mr Deakin still held her hand and to her astonishment he was slipping a ring onto her finger. She looked down at it and gasped at the diamonds that sparkled on it. Fear took hold of her. She could see that it was Mr Deakin's moment, and she could not say what she wanted, as it would spoil it for him.

The waiter and a few of the other waiters came over and they too added their congratulations and waived the bill, though the tip that Mr Deakin left amply rewarded them. Together they moved off across the square, Mr Deakin's arm around her waist. Sarah knew that he was very pleased but she was not able to share his pleasure. They passed out of the square and walked along one of the alleyways back towards the Rialto.

Finally she could go no further and stopped.

'What is it, Sarah?'

She pulled his ring off her finger and handed it to him.

'I'm sorry,' she said, 'I know I said yes, but in all honesty I can't marry you.'

'But you did say yes.'

'Only because you wouldn't get off your knees.'

'You accepted my proposal.'

'I actually said "no" twice, if you were listening.'

'But you didn't mean it.'

'I did, I wanted you to get back on your chair.'

'I don't see why.'

'Because it was so embarrassing! I have never been made to look such a fool in all my life.'

'I'm sorry,' he said holding the ring. He looked crushed and Sarah felt bad about it.

'It's a beautiful ring,' she said to mollify him, 'and your proposal was gratifying. I am very flattered by it, but I cannot accept.'

'There's no reason that you can't accept it.'

'Do I need a reason when I was unaware of what you were planning? You surely must have realised that I might have said no – you can't have been ignorant of the possibility.' She felt sorry for him standing before her looking so dejected. It was as if she had blacked his other eye for him. But she chided herself, for there had been a time when to see a man cast down would have given her pleasure.

Reluctantly he pulled a little leather bag out of his pocket and dropped the ring into it. It was shoved into his inside jacket pocket. They continued their way back towards their respective hotels, both of them lost in their thoughts and a good yard between them.

They stood outside her hotel; he made no attempt to join her.

'May I have the pleasure of dining with you this evening?'

Sarah tried to smile and finally said, 'Yes, that would be very nice.'

'Then I'll see you at seven in the foyer here.'

'All right.' She was close to crying, but he turned and carried on to his hotel. She managed to reach the sanctuary of her room before she burst into tears.

How could he have expected her to marry him when she hardly knew him? He had spent the day being remarkably insensitive to her and there had been times in the afternoon when she had felt she was alone. He had walked out on her that morning and she had yet to receive a proper apology for it; and as for him calling her Caroline... it looked as if she was just going to have to accept it. And now she felt so guilty for having refused his proposal of marriage. But why should she? She hadn't asked for it or solicited it, and her acceptance seemed to be taken for granted. She had been made to feel very alone in a teeming city. She wanted to go home and in the quiet of her own room make some sense of the weekend.

It was quarter to seven when she rose and dressed for dinner, choosing nothing more than her trouser suit that she wore for work. She slapped some scent on to cover up her lack of a shower and threw some make-up on her face. Her eyes were bloodshot, and it was too bad if it were noticeable. She arrived at the foot of the stairs leading down to the foyer at five minutes past seven.

Mr Deakin was waiting in the foyer and seeing her came across to her. He was trying to smile, and yet he looked his usual severe self. She sensed the cloud they were under and could not respond to him in any way, so her reactions to him were merely mechanical.

'We'll eat here,' he said somewhat peremptorily. He seemed to propel her towards the dining room, though she offered no resistance.

They sat at a table with hardly a word passing between them. A waiter brought the menus over. Mr Deakin ordered a bottle of wine.

'I think I'll have the soup tonight,' he said at length.

'I'll have the same,' said Sarah taking the safe route. It was a toss-up between the soup and the melon.

'The white fish, I think.'

'I'll have the same,' said Sarah.

'You don't have to have the same as me,' said Mr Deakin irritably.

'But I don't really want anything else,' replied Sarah. Though she would have preferred the seafood salad, she didn't want to eat anything different to him. She felt bad about everything again and her desire to go home grew stronger. Tomorrow morning could not come soon enough for her. Here, she decided, was the bit where all men tend to dominate and she had allowed him to control her. It showed her feminism in stark contrast and she wondered that she had been so beguiled by a man. The pleasure she had felt in his company the previous night had vanished and he had shown himself to be arrogant, pompous and selfish. He wanted her for one thing and one thing only, and she was glad that she had denied him.

'What are your plans?' he asked as the wine arrived.

'I'm going home tomorrow morning,' she replied.

'I had wondered if you would stay the rest of the week with me.'

Not a chance! But she did not say so aloud.

'Is there anything to be gained by my staying?' she asked.

'As your employer, I'd say it would be best if you stayed and did the make-up on my eye.'

'You seem to have done a pretty good job on it yourself.'

Their conversation ceased, for the soup was brought to their table. Sarah found that once she had started she did have an appetite but halfway through hers she noticed that Mr Deakin had hardly touched his. She decided that he was too busy trying to sort out his next strategy. She finished and pushed her plate away. Mr Deakin did the same with his plate.

'Not to my taste,' he said by way of explanation.

'I thought it very nice,' said Sarah and she sipped her glass of wine. If nothing else, she liked his choice of wine. It brought a glow to her cheeks and she felt in a better humour. But Mr Deakin seemed even more taciturn and they sat in silence. Their main meal was placed in front of them and Sarah set to on hers quite eagerly. It was a few minutes before she looked up and saw that Mr Deakin was sitting staring at his meal. He had made no attempt to touch it.

Suddenly he rose from his seat.

'Don't mind me,' he said, 'finish your meal.'

'What's up?' she said, hoping that she sounded concerned.

'I don't feel very well!' He began walking towards the door.

Hurriedly she put her knife and fork down and followed him. But he had moved faster than she expected and was out of the main doors and into the street beyond. She debated whether to follow him to his room or not, but returned sadly to her meal. The bottle of wine was going to defeat her but she felt no remorse about it. If she had a hangover in the morning she would probably miss her flight home.

She left the table with one last thing to do before retiring, and that was to inform reception of her early start.

By six thirty in the morning she was ready to leave for the airport. Her chauffeur was waiting at reception and took her down to the hotel's launch. To Sarah's surprise, Mr Deakin turned up. He followed her onto the boat and sat down beside her. He had brought no luggage and she presumed he was not going on her flight.

'I want you to stay,' he said. She could not decide if his tone was tenderness or whether he was pleading. But she was adamant.

'No,' she said, 'my mind's made up.'

The launch was nosing its way along still canals and between the silent houses. The early morning was overcast, making the scene gloomy. They turned into a larger canal and a few minutes later reached the open lagoon. Then they speeded up, crossing the lagoon to the airport in what seemed to be minutes, though it was nearly twenty. It was only a matter of yards into the airport terminal. Mr Deakin took her arm while the chauffeur carried her case.

He waited for her while she checked in. But with her boarding pass in her hand Sarah at last felt she was in control. She turned to passport control without a glance at Mr Deakin, but he followed nonetheless. She handed her passport to the immigration officer who gave it a cursory glance and handed it back. But before she could move to go through Mr Deakin took her arm. She wished he had not come, for it made it so difficult for her.

'Then it only remains for me to wish you a good flight home.' His eyes betrayed his sadness and Sarah was not untouched. She expected him to make one last stand and claim her in front of many returning holiday-makers. It was going to be very embarrassing, and she faced him with fortitude.

'I just want to say,' he said, maintaining an outward appearance of calm, 'that we can remain the best of friends.'

She heard his words and immediately thought that he was saying them so that he might get another chance to ask her to marry him. She bit her tongue to make sure that she said nothing that would annoy him.

'Please stay,' he urged, and he genuinely seemed to want her to stay.

'No,' she said confidently, 'I'm going home.'

'I would never,' he continued, 'want to think meanly of you. I know what you have said, but you have yet to give me a reason. Would it be too much to ask for one?'

She looked at him and felt a certain contempt.

'You ought to look in a mirror,' she said, 'you've smudged your make-up.'

'Never mind that, just tell me!' He was holding her arm tightly and she doubted if she could push him off without creating a scene.

She had a desire to put him firmly in his place. She found that she could not, though the use of his wife's name still rankled with her.

'You almost won my heart but you didn't win my mind!' Sarah was conscious that they were becoming noticed and that more and more people were stopping to look at them. But her words to Mr Deakin had the desired effect and he released his hold on her. She immediately turned and went straight to the passport control counter again before he could gather his wits. She had a certain sense of triumph and hoped that he was sufficiently humiliated. She didn't dare to turn and look at him. Even when she was past the passport check she did not look back but found her way to the departure lounge.

Her flight was already boarding, and once through the security check she found the plane was waiting right outside. It was just a climb up the steps and into the plane, where she was shown to her seat. She sat down by the window, thankful that the seating arrangements on a plane gave one a degree of privacy. No one sat in the adjoining seat and she was glad of it. Perhaps she thought it had been reserved for him, but the plane was far from full. In what seemed like no time at all they were taxiing out to the runway. Flying had always been fun, but that day it was the worst thing she had ever experienced, for suddenly the plane was airborne and she could no longer hold back the tears.

Her thoughts were just a jumble. One moment she could see the look on his face and feel guilty that she had caused his injury, the next she could feel his warm hand holding hers, but the good moments were quickly offset by the anger she had felt when he used his wife's name. Then she saw him walk out of the room with no explanation, leaving her to experience the feelings of rejection. Just to think of St Mark's Square made her squirm with embarrassment as he knelt before her, but it was followed by the sight of his face when she told him that her real answer was no. Why did she feel so guilty about hurting him? He had set himself up to be hurt. Her thoughts were more like the pieces of coloured plastic in a kaleidoscope that made wonderful patterns and pleased the eye but had really no meaning. Perhaps she should have put him truly in his place, and she'd had the opportunity to do that with people looking at them. She could have publicly accused him of having his hand in her knickers and getting her name wrong. Had she said that, his humiliation would have been complete and it would have crushed his spirit; but it would also have humiliated and hurt her. She was glad that she had not.

The Office

After Heathrow it seemed reasonable to go straight to the office, as it would give the impression that the journey was over. But at Green Park Sarah wished she had gone home first, for getting the case to street level was hard work, and once in Piccadilly she hailed a taxi for the short trip to the office.

At the door she met Michael, who carried her case in with an ease that annoyed her. At the top of the stairs Ms Marchbank eyed her with animosity and did not respond to the equable greeting that Sarah managed. As she arrived in the office, all eyes turned to watch her as if she were an alien dropping in to do a day's work. But ignoring the stares she sank thankfully into her seat. Michael put her case in the corner and said, 'You look as if you could do with a cup of coffee.'

'That would be brilliant,' she managed. He disappeared from the office towards the kitchen. Sarah looked at the door and wondered if Mr Deakin was going to follow her in, but only Ms Marchbank filled her vision.

Michael returned with the coffee.

'How was Venice?' he asked.

'Oddly,' said Sarah, 'it's one of those places that looks just like its pictures.'

'I suppose it would,' he agreed amiably. 'Who went out to meet you?'

The question was a shock to Sarah, for she hadn't thought about it at all. Should she or should she not reveal that Mr Deakin had met her?

'I don't know what anyone was playing at,' she said, 'but it was just like Paris and Amsterdam.'

'He didn't turn up?'

'When he sends me a ticket to the next exotic place I'm going to tear it up.'

'Oh, sorry to hear that – but why not give it away?'

'Because the tickets I've received have been non-transferable.'

'Of course. Look, Ms Marchbank is on your case. She's been moaning all morning about your lateness.'

'Oh, let her. I did have Mr Deakin's permission to go.'

'Ms Marchbank thinks you should have come back last night.'

'But my ticket was for this morning, and I've come straight in.'

'That was a mistake.'

'Yes, I'm beginning to think so.'

Sarah switched her workstation on and Michael resumed his seat. Having found where she had left off last Thursday, Sarah put her mind to her work. She had little inclination to do so, but felt that she had to force herself to, otherwise her mind would travel back to Venice. Her mood was calm enough for her to concentrate on what was in front of her, but soon she was aware of someone standing over her. She did not want to look up, but when someone is standing that close to you it is very difficult not to look, if only to see who it is. Sarah looked up and stared into the face of Ms Marchbank.

'I'll make no bones about it, Miss Levine – I'm upset with your behaviour,' she said, 'and in consequence I have to give you this.' She handed Sarah an envelope.

'What is it?' she asked.

'A written warning for lateness! I cannot have people wandering in whenever they feel like it. It is bad for office morale.'

Sarah looked across the room at Emma and Clementine, who were smirking and nudging each other. Emma presumably had had the job of typing it out and knew what was in it. Clementine knew as well, for she would have looked over Emma's shoulder. They would have debated fervently whether or not Ms Marchbank had the nerve to give the letter to her and now they were enjoying Sarah's discomfort.

The warning was very unjust and quite unwarranted and Sarah felt she ought to make a stand, but she was conscious that a major row between her and Ms Marchbank was what everyone in the office was expecting. And she claimed only the pleasure of denying them their due by accepting the envelope with a nod and shoving it straight into her drawer. Even Ms Marchbank was taken aback, and did not seem to know what to do; but gathering her wits and the shreds of her self-respect she retired to her desk. Emma and Clementine renewed their conversation, while Michael could only watch out of the corner of his eye.

It ruined Sarah's good intentions. She had ruthlessly suppressed all thoughts of Mr Deakin and had determined to do her work. At first she was inclined to believe that Mr Deakin was at the bottom of it and had phoned Ms Marchbank tell her what she should do. Ms Marchbank would be only too happy to oblige, but Sarah could not reconcile the action with Mr Deakin's last words to her. He had spoken to her sincerely, almost too sincerely, and it showed moreover a meanness of attitude to which she did not think that he would stoop. No, Ms Marchbank was acting on her own impulses. She had the authority to do it as office manager, and she was not capable of leaving aside her personal animosity.

Now everything that happened at the weekend flooded back and demanded her attention.

What was he doing now in Venice? Was he still there? Or had he caught the next plane home and was about to enter the office? She glanced at the door for the umpteenth time and saw that Ms Marchbank was sitting there glowering at her. If Mr Deakin was around she would be a different person.

So Mr Deakin must still be in Venice, learning to do his own make-up... She chided herself for having such a mean thought. When would anger take over? When would he realise that his pride had been thoroughly trampled on? While she had been with him, he had been passive and pliant, but there would come a time when he would realise that she had left him and then reaction would set in. What would he do? Would he act like most men of her acquaintance and hit the bottle? Was he now at his hotel room with a bottle of his favourite spirits, drinking himself silly? She hoped that he was not, but she felt guilty that she had possibly put him in that position.

But why should she feel guilty? What had she done to feel guilty about? Was it a crime for a woman to refuse to marry a man? How many women actually married men because they faced the feeling of guilt if they did not marry him, yet they knew in their hearts that the relationship had no future, and they should never have married? So a woman agrees to his proposal just to please the man but in doing so takes on his guilt, and when the relationship ends she feels doubly guilty for she knew that their marriage had no future before it started. And she feels even worse because she knows she has been dishonest with herself. Surely it was one of the injustices that women have suffered for centuries! Women have taken the blame for many things when they were actually blameless. Men were so often the villains, and to maintain their moral standing they had deposited blame on others. Mr Deakin had only to blame himself.

It angered Sarah and she was angry with herself for finding excuses for Mr Deakin. Had he in fact been complicit with Ms Marchbank? Hadn't Clive and Keith spoken of Mr Deakin being devious? Wasn't he mistrusted by the whole of the industry? He sat at his desk looking as miserable as someone who could not care less about his fellow beings, yet it was a facade so that his piercing eyes could look into everything nook and cranny of human nature. Behind the eyes was a very shrewd mind probing for a weakness so that he could manipulate others and profit from their failings. Yes, on that score he surely helped Ms Marchbank.

Why should she be sad for him? As far as she was concerned, for once he had got his just desserts. And she was well out of it! She had never wanted anything to do with marriage, and she had never wanted anything to do with the opposite sex! But this man had moved her in a way she had never experienced before. He had allowed her to glimpse a whole spectrum of emotions and feelings that she had not appreciated. The worst part of the whole affair was that there had been a time when she not only cared for him but she *wanted* to care for him. There had been a moment when, had he turned over, he could have claimed her, and she had no arguments to repel him, wanting only to return his kisses. But to her consternation the feeling was still latent, and when she thought about it, though she wanted to deny it for the first time in her life, she could not!

Sarah continued with her thoughts running along similar lines for the remainder of the day. Her conscience had made her work through her lunch hour, and as four thirty approached she should have been glad to be going home – but she was not! She had managed the day in the office, but the greater problem was ahead of her. She had said too many things to Gerrie and Cathy, and now they were going to probe her. She dreaded them for they did not know when to leave something alone and they would press her until they were satisfied on every point.

She wondered about going elsewhere but could not think of anywhere to go. She knew of no one she could talk to. Keith or Clive crossed her mind, yet they were tainted people, and their ministrations had cost her during the weekend. Mr Deakin had known of her disloyalty towards him, and while he had seemed indifferent she was certain he had been hurt by it. But then she chided herself for thinking positive things about Mr Deakin, and remembered that it was only a few hours ago that she had been happy to totally denounce him.

The truth, she argued with herself, as she dragged her case back down into the Underground, was that she was a mess! She had not reasoned anything out and she had not searched out the areas of truth. At that moment she was a victim of her emotions.

At home she felt safe. She could breathe without worrying about others. She was alone, and having made herself a cup of coffee she fled to enjoy the relative sanctuary of her room.

Gerrie was home first and it became immediately clear that she wanted to know all the gossip. She was in no mood, either, to wait for Cathy to get home. She knocked loudly on Sarah's door with no thought for the neighbours.

'Are you going to tell me what happened?' she shouted, giving the bedroom door a good thumping.

'I was just having a nap,' Sarah called out.

'Oh, come and tell me about your weekend.'

'No, leave me in peace until Cathy gets in, and then I'll tell you both together.'

'What was wrong with it, then?'

'Nothing – why?'

'Oh don't be an idiot, Sar! I can always tell when you're hurt.'

'Then just leave me alone.'

'You're stubborn... but I'll wait until Cathy gets in!'

Gerrie left her and went off towards the kitchen area. Sarah was left to work out what she should tell to them, for it was patent that to say a lot about a particular part of the weekend would mask the need to talk about the rest. She decided what she would tell them and waited with anticipation for Cathy to come in. Cathy did not disappoint either of them, arriving some ten minutes later.

Both women were at Sarah's door.

'Come and tell us, Sar!' called Cathy.

To their surprise, Sarah opened the door and emerged. They sat round the kitchen table.

'Who was it, then?'

'Did you like him?'

'What was he like?'

'Tell us, Sar.'

'Well, first of all, guess who it was?'

'So we know him?'

'Yes, or at least you ought to, for I'm sure that you've met him.'

'Mr Deakin!' said Cathy without hesitating.

'Yes, it was,' said Sarah, feeling very deflated.

'Told you so, Gerrie! And that's five pounds you owe me!'

'Why, did you think it was him?'

'Stands to reason, doesn't it?'

'I didn't think it was that obvious.'

'Oh, really, Sar – are you blind or something? How could it be anyone else?'

'Gerrie thought that it might be someone else. What made you so certain?'

'Nothing,' interposed Gerrie, 'she just had a guess and it happened to be right.'

'Well, how many people do you know with money?'

'Not many – why?'

'He was the only one who has pots of money.'

'How do you know he has pots of money?'

'Were you born yesterday, Sar? He *reeks* of money!'

'I don't know how much money he has, I've never seen his bank account.'

275

'Believe me, he's got money.'

'In comparison to any of the men you go around with, I suppose he has. But it did cross my mind it was him, and there was a moment I was positive it was Mr Deakin.'

'Where did he meet you in Venice?'

'In St Mark's Square.'

'And did he declare his undying love for you?'

'Sort of.'

'You can't sort of declare undying love. You either do or you don't!'

'Did he propose, Sar?'

Sarah blushed. She had hoped to avoid the question and she knew that the heightened colour of her face had given her away.

'Yes, he did,' she admitted.

'Brilliant,' said Gerrie. 'And when's the wedding day?'

'And where's the ring, or haven't you bothered with one?'

'It's not that easy,' said Sarah.

'But you can't say yes to a man with conditions attached. "I will marry you,"' mocked Cathy, '"provided I don't have to do all the housework, washing and cooking."'

'I refused him,' said Sarah miserably.

'You can't have refused him!'

'Well, I said yes at first, and then I changed my mind.'

'Are you nuts, Sarah! You can't not marry a man like that when he's a meal ticket for life!' Both women looked shocked.

'Why shouldn't I refuse him?'

'I'd never considered stupidity as one of your faults,' admonished Cathy, 'but that is just madness!'

'I suppose you in the same situation would simply have said yes!'

'Oh course I would have done, and so would Gerrie. Do you think I'd have a rich man chasing after me with his tongue hanging out just for the satisfaction of saying no? No way!'

'So you'd marry him despite not loving him.'

'Yes, I would,' Cathy replied fervently.

'Me too,' said Gerrie, with less conviction.

'And I'll tell you something for nothing, Sar, that if all I had to do was to keep him sweet then I'd do it.'

'And how would you keep him sweet?'
'By studying the ceiling every now and again.'
'By doing *what*?'
'Oh, Sar, you're so innocent it's unbelievable!'
'She means lying on your back with your legs apart...'
'It's what keeps a bloke hanging around! Just let him climb Mount Everest once in a while, and let everything come up roses until he wants to put his mountain boots on again!'
'Well, whatever you feel about it, I don't. If I ever marry it will be because I do love the person and not his money.'
'And you don't love Mr Deakin.'
'No.'
'I don't believe you! You've come home many evenings and all you could talk about was Mr Deakin! There's a man any girl would have. Take those two dumbos in your office – Emma and Oranges and Lemons – they'd think nothing of sticking their tits out to attract him, and had Mr Deakin gone in the office and ogled them they'd have been reeling him in!'
'You sound as if you'd do the same.'
'Too right I would! Ask yourself another. What did God give you tits for?'
'Feeding your offspring, I thought.'
'Don't be stupid! Tits aren't for tots, tits are magnets for getting a man.'
'Sarah hasn't got a pair of tits.'
'Oh, I was forgetting.' Cathy could be very hurtful at times.
'I'm sorry I told you,' said Sarah, rising from the table.
'But you're such a total dipstick, Sar. As they say, there's one born everyday.'
Sarah fled from the room, close to tears, and did not hear Gerrie castigating Cathy for her complete lack of tact.
It was a miserable week for Sarah. The flat was no home, with Cathy and Gerrie unable to keep silent on the matter. One of them was always starting on the subject by beginning on another aspect.
'Where did he propose to you?'
'In a gondola?'
'Was he romantic about it?' They laughed because they could not see Mr Deakin being the slightest bit romantic.

'Some men,' pronounced Gerrie, 'fall naturally into the romantic mould, the rest are just losers.'

But at least at the flat she knew what to expect and she could normally escape to her bedroom, leaving the sound of their laughter in the distance; but the office proved to be very different.

Michael intuitively knew that she had had some sort of bad experience and maintained a silence on the matter. Others knew that there was a fair amount of tittle-tattle involved and sought to find out about it. It worked to their advantage that Sarah had said nothing, for as each morsel came along it could be thoroughly chewed over, and the old rumours were dug up to be chewed for a second or third time. Clemmie and Emma were in their element. But gradually some of the truth leaked out.

Gerrie had told her friends at work and some of them knew members of the office staff. At first Gerrie had let slip one or two bits of news, and once the rumour mill had got a whiff of it, it demanded more.

Tom heard about it and came to Sarah. He apologised that he had heard a rumour and promised Sarah that he was no party to its propagation.

'I made one mistake,' he said, 'and I'm not going to make it again.'

'Thanks,' said Sarah. 'What is the rumour?'

'That your beau made you an offer and that you refused.'

Emma was not so circumspect and sat on Sarah's desk one morning asking all sorts of questions.

'Who was he?'

'What was he like?'

'Was he rich?'

'Why aren't you wearing his ring?

'Surely you didn't refuse him!'

It took Michael to get her back to her desk. It was odd that no one had yet put Mr Deakin's name to the story, but she guessed that it would not be long coming.

Though this was all enough to depress Sarah, the worst thing for her was watching the door, for she anticipated Mr Deakin coming in every time there was a flurry of activity from that direction. But a quick glance at Emma and Clemmie was usually sufficient to assure her that it was not him.

She had planned to resign from Deakin's on returning but now she had her doubts. Despite her worries, she was comfortable in her job and she could no longer bring herself to throw it in because of a fit of pique. She felt a certain concern for Mr Deakin and wanted to be sure that he was all right, and that meant staying until he returned. Yet there were other considerations, Ms Marchbank's attitude had offended her and Sarah did not want to give Ms Marchbank the satisfaction of seeing her off the premises. Then she had the problem of Clive and Keith. Seeing Mr Deakin lying in her bed had shown her that the two men were little better than vultures wheeling over some weakened animal, waiting for the moment when they could feast. She doubted if any business they set up could be successful, and did not want to put her money in a position to prove it. But she had virtually promised them the capital and she didn't know how to get out of it. She wondered if she should just give them the money. But this all brought into question the issue of loyalty, and she didn't want Mr Deakin to think that she was disloyal. It had became a matter of pride with Sarah. If Mr Deakin wanted to dismiss her, he would have to do so because their relationship had broken down!

But as the week progressed Sarah found herself thinking about Mr Deakin, and she felt concerned as to his whereabouts. She sat at her desk chiding herself for her feelings, but she wondered what he did after he left the airport for he did not appear well. At first she pushed the thoughts to one side but she could not rid herself of the idea that he might be unwell. Given that, she worried that his condition might be worse. Still she could not rouse herself to be concerned; but then she had a picture of him in his hotel bed desperately in need of medical attention. If that was so she could never forgive herself, especially if one phone call could help him. That decided it, and she went through her bag looking for the name of her hotel. She found their card and decided to phone there. They would be able to give her the phone number of Mr Deakin's hotel.

There was one problem! What if the hotel told her that

Mr Deakin was in, and did she want to speak with him? It was easy to say no, but they might go and tell him that she had rung anyway. So if she did speak to him, what impression would that give? Would the sound of her voice stir his crushed feelings? Would it renew his hopes? How should she respond if it did? No, she had crushed his hopes, and his pride alone would not let him renew his pursuit.

It took five minutes to obtain the required phone number and less than a minute later she could hear the phone ringing at Mr Deakin's hotel. Then it was answered.

'Do you speak English?' she asked, and received an Italian version of English in response.

'Has Mr Deakin left the hotel yet?'

'He leave on Monday at midday.' His turn of verb was excruciating.

So Mr Deakin had returned to his hotel and paid the bill. Then he must have gone back to the airport and flown home. So where was he now? Presumably at his house, and it was likely that he would not surface until the bruising left his eye. But at least he was all right. Why, though, did she feel that he was not well? Could his slightly eccentric behaviour on Sunday be put down to the fact that he wasn't quite right? The punch he had been felled with had all but knocked him out. She had assumed on Sunday that he was well. But it was doubtful that he was, for there were too many signs to the contrary. He had hardly listened to her, and for him to argue with her was something he had never done. Then there was the meal he failed to eat in the evening! He was merely someone who had remembered his mission and knew what he had to do and had simply done it. That he needed tact and a far more romantic disposition wouldn't have seemed necessary to him, as he had never countenanced her refusal! No, she was being weak! She should not sit at her desk making excuses for him!

Yet the thought persisted, and by Friday Sarah's feelings had undergone a seismic shift. At the beginning of the week she would have agreed with anyone who wanted to deride his character, but no longer. She was worried about him now, and when he did not appear that morning the worry became worse.

She was convinced that he hadn't been himself on the Sunday and had forced himself to say the things that he had. She could not see that he was then the mild-mannered man whom she respected sitting behind his desk. Had he asked her stay because he still felt unwell, she was sure that she would have done, but her anger had dissipated her feelings of sympathy for him. If he felt better they could have discussed things, and she was sure that there was a logical explanation to everything. It was grasping at straws but she felt guilty for not staying with him.

Ms Marchbank had disappeared, and Emma and Clemmie were chatting as if it were a tea break. Sarah could only presume that a client had come and she was dealing with him or her in Mr Deakin's office. But a minute later she was surprised to find Ms Marchbank bearing down on her, and she could not dismiss the thought that another warning was coming.

'Would you come through to the office,' she said abruptly.

'Of course,' said Sarah and obediently followed her tormenter. Her heart was pounding, for it could only be that Mr Deakin had come! What did he want her for? What was he going to say? What were his feelings towards her? Had he had a change of heart, and now wanted to see the back of her? But why was she bothered about him? Why did it feel as if her heart was in her mouth? I shouldn't be, if she had no feelings towards him. Or did being dismissed arouse the same emotions?

Ms Marchbank pushed open the office door and went in. Sarah followed and saw that Mr Deakin's chair was empty. She had expected him to be sitting there, and a wave of disappointment swept over her; but then she was conscious of someone else, partially obscured by Ms Marchbank, who turned to Sarah.

'I told Mr French not to bother to come in until Mr Deakin came back from his holiday, but he insisted. He wishes to speak to you about his book.'

Sarah's heart was immediately deflated. She had finished Jonathan French's book, but only because she had to. She could not forgive him for making a fool of Mr Deakin. She stood before him silent and somewhat aggressive. The phone rang in the main office.

'Mr French has brought in a few changes; I must go to the

phone.' Ms Marchbank was out of the room. Sarah faced Jonathan French.

'What is this?' she said. 'Have you come to repeat the exercise, or gloat over me?'

'Not at all,' he replied, stung by her attitude. 'But what are you doing here?'

'I work here. Why do you ask?'

'You're supposed to be in Venice!'

'What makes you think that?'

'Philip was hoping to stay the whole week with you in Venice!'

Sarah closed the office door.

'Do you have to go blurting it all out for everyone to hear? Why are there so many tactless people like you around? You invite Mr Deakin to a restaurant and then walk out on him in the most bizarre fashion, leaving him to pay! Now, I'm rather busy at the moment, so...'

'Hang on a minute! Didn't he tell you?'

'Tell me what?'

'All I can say is that he did a very good job on you!'

'Don't talk in riddles. What do you mean?'

'Philip Deakin and I cooked up the stunt at the restaurant. He wanted to have dinner with you!'

'What? So you didn't stand him up!'

'No, Philip wanted to take you out but he didn't know how to ask you. You were always a bit forbidding, and he didn't want to be rebuffed, as he felt it would alter the professional relationship between the two of you – and you'd end up leaving!'

'That's another black mark against him.'

'No, it isn't! He's talked about little else in the last few months except you.'

Sarah blushed.

'He told me that he was going to meet you in Venice.'

Ms Marchbank came into the room.

'Have you settled everything yet?' she asked. 'I know these changes are awkward to make at this stage, but they seemed straightforward enough to me.'

'No,' said Sarah, 'we haven't finished discussing the changes.

They are quite extensive and I'm trying to get Mr French to reduce them! I think it would be best if you left us alone while I sort it out. It shouldn't take above an hour.'

'This is most irregular, Sarah! Be sure that Mr Deakin will hear of this when he returns.'

'He will,' said Sarah, 'for I will tell him myself. Oh, and two coffees, please! Send Emma in with them.'

Ms Marchbank turned on her heels and walked out.

'That told the old bat!' said Jonathan admiringly, as Sarah closed the door. 'Now, where were we?'

'So the restaurant was a trick!'

'Well, I wouldn't call it that. A ploy, perhaps, but it was a means to an end.'

'Why did you tease me with all those extravagant compliments?'

'I wasn't teasing you, I was teasing Philip!'

'Oh – then I've been very stupid in not seeing things sooner.'

'You're too severe on yourself. Philip was ecstatic about the meal after I left. You were perfectly natural, and only seemed worried that you would not be left doing the washing-up.'

'So that hair on top is a toupee!'

'No, it's not – it's my own! Look!'

'All right, I can see that if I pulled it your hair would come out by the roots. I still can't see why he had to do it. Couldn't he have asked me?'

'He could have done, but I think he was right. You are very difficult a woman to please, and Philip certainly sensed that. He could have gone straight up to you and asked you out, but he felt that it would be a confrontation with the result that it would have done nothing but bruise his ego and damn his chances. So he needed to be circumspect.'

'You've made me feel a terrible fool.'

'And you have spent the last couple of months hating me intensely.'

'Are you suggesting that that was worse?'

'No, just that we ought to call a truce on the matter.'

'Perhaps it would be best. What do you know about Venice?'

'Let me start earlier. He told me that he had heard about the challenge you made one night in a pub and that set him thinking. It confirmed his existing opinion and he didn't dare approach you straight out.'

'I knew it would all come back to being my fault!'

'I don't think so, but he's one of the nicest men I've ever met.'

'But that's from a man's point of view.'

'True. But I've never heard him speak ill of anyone. And he often talked about you. He was distraught one day because he had told you off.'

'I deserved that, for I was rather rude to him.'

'And he couldn't see how a direct approach would work, so he took up the challenge.'

'Was I that unapproachable?'

'Oh yes, especially when it came down to a male-female relationship, and he felt he had to break that down before making himself known. And he was right, for you came back from Paris pleased and more than a little curious. Amsterdam – you were not so pleased. After the theatre I gather that you guessed that Connie and Curzon were friends of whoever had sent you.'

'Yes, but I wasn't pleased about Venice.'

'Why was that?'

'I had guessed it was Mr Deakin and then he denied it. He didn't lie about it or anything but just made it seem that it couldn't have been him.'

'What would that have done?'

'Nothing, except that I think I would have preferred to have been taken out for a meal, followed by a show. I would have welcomed his confession. I think I wanted him to court me properly.'

'So you're not playing the hard woman; you do have some feelings for him.'

She shrugged. 'I'm very confused. You see, he proposed to me!'

'I thought he might.'

'Why only *thought*?'

'Because we discussed a number of approaches but he refused to discuss what he was going to do in Venice. What happened?'

'I refused him.'

'May I ask why?'

'I hardly know him.'

'But he's your boss!'

'That's as may be, but when two people start to get things together they talk about much deeper things than the workings of the office or the gossip that goes around.'

'But he knew plenty of things about you!'

'He might have done, but there are many things I don't know about him. I don't know where he lives, for a start!'

'I see what you mean. Do you want his address?'

'No! Oh, I don't know…'

'It's very nice house, just off Wimbledon Common.' He wrote down the address and handed it to Sarah.

'Do you know why he's never told me?'

'No, but I guess he wanted you to love him for himself and not for anything else.'

'I see… I think.'

'I had better go. The changes to my manuscript are in the envelope. Just one thing though: where is he?'

'I don't know,' said Sarah as she saw him down to the door onto the pavement.

Rumours

Sitting back at her desk, Sarah found herself annoyed with Mr Deakin. It would seem that his hand had been on most things and while she was ignorant of his intentions everything went smoothly, yet when she knew about it his plans it all deteriorated into farce. It could only mean one thing, and that was that they were not compatible. His planning and his schemes grated badly with her feminist outlook and she was not going to have it. He wanted her to love him! He really wanted her solely as a woman whom he could dominate, someone who would put his comfort and well-being far above anything else; and that was just what the modern feminist was against: men ruling the roost.

The thought pleased her and for some time she basked in its apparent moral sense. But gradually a feeling of guilt came over her. Had she not cared for him when he was asleep? Had she not leaned over and kissed him? Had she not wanted him to roll over and return her caresses? What would she have done had he wanted to go further? Would she have let him make love to her? How would she have felt afterwards? Why would she have continued to kiss him when he would have hurt her? Why did she want to allow it? Her reflections at that moment did not relate too well with her thoughts that night in Venice. She could only reconcile the position by the fact that he had ruined things! She should really feel pleased with his faux pas, for it had saved her from a life of meek acquiescence and submission.

Now she could turn her anger upon herself. She who saw herself as being so strong and self-confident had allowed herself to be blinded by the designs of a man. That his schemes produced nothing but confusion for her demonstrated the wrongness of them, and for being thus duped as a woman she was deserving of the severest condemnation from herself.

Sunday morning Sarah took the train to Chichester, and from there a taxi to her parents' bungalow at Bracklesham. She knocked on the front door and it was opened almost immediately by her mother.

'Oh, hello, Sarah,' she said, 'I wasn't expecting you. I thought it was Mrs Ridgeway come to take me to the bowling club.'

'Hello, Mum,' said Sarah, 'I've come down for a chat.'

'Well, I haven't got long, and your father's there already. You'd better come in.'

Sarah was led into the front room where she sat down on the sofa. Her mother remained standing. 'Do you want a cup of tea?'

'No thanks,' said Sarah who actually did want a drink; but she wanted to unburden herself first.

'So how are things in London?

'Fine?'

'How's the job going?'

'Quite well.'

'So what brings you down here?'

'I think I've done a very silly thing.'

'It's most unlike you to come and admit such a thing to me!'

'I know but I've run out of confidantes.'

'You must have done to come and tell me. So what it is that you've done?'

'I've had a proposal of marriage.'

'That's nice! Will I like him? What's he like? You know, after all the things you said about marriage, I really thought you'd remain single.'

'Yes, well, I refused him.'

'Oh, that's typical of you, Sarah. Still, if he had no money and no prospects, what does it matter? You're father will be disappointed, though.'

'But everyone seems to think I should have taken up his offer.'

'What bad points did he have?'

'None that I know of.'

'How old is he?'

'I'm not sure; he's middle-aged and going bald!'

'Not lively enough for you, is he? Has he any money?'

'He has a house and quite a bit of money.'

'So he's really well off!'

'I don't know. I've never seen his bank balance and I don't know where he lives.'

'He sounds a bit dodgy to me.'

'He happens to be my boss.'

'You're always having problems with men at the places you work.'

'Not like this!'

'But there was that nice Neville who came down to see us.'

'He was a complete wet blanket! And I never went out with him or anything. To this day I don't know where he got your address from.'

'But we thought he was very nice!'

'Well, you would! You only saw one side of him!'

Her mother rose summoned to the front door by the imperious ringing of the doorbell. She returned with a sprightly old lady.

'Have you met Mrs Ridgeway, Sarah?'

'No, I haven't. How do you do?'

'Sarah's had a proposal of marriage from her boss. Isn't that nice?'

'Oh yes, that is nice. You don't hear of people getting married as often as you should.'

'No, people today do it in such a roundabout fashion.'

'Most of them don't bother. Shame, really! In my young day everyone got married. You didn't shilly-shally about it; you just got on with it.'

'That's right. The girls all wanted to start their own home, and it was just a matter of finding the right man.'

'And they didn't do that very well,' interposed Sarah.

'Well, you say that, dear, but in my day there wasn't a lot of divorce. Most people got married to stay married.'

'But Sarah refused this man!'

'Oh, dearie me! He couldn't have been worth much, then.'

'It was her boss.'

'But no one's making any money today. Are we going, then?'

'Why don't you come and see your father, Sarah?'

'I hadn't planned to do it this way. I just wanted to talk to someone.'

'Come and sit on the veranda, and while we watch the bowls you can chat.'

'It's not that kind of chat that I want, Mother! I want a private chat. I want a mother and daughter chat.'

'Your mother is due at the bowls club and we've got to lay out the lunch.'

'I'll go for a walk down the seafront and then go home.'

'Oh, won't you come and see your father?'

'No, he's playing bowls and he'll be full of that.'

'No he won't. He likes to see you.'

'Mother, if I know my father he will not be in a talking mood until the bowls has finished, you've had lunch and he's had his afternoon sleep!'

'I don't think so, dear.'

'You carry on. Maybe I'll walk down in a bit.' Sarah went to the front door and wished her mother goodbye.

The sea was only two minutes from their gate, and a strong breeze was blowing off the sea making the air feel damp. The tide was up, covering the shingle beach and reaching almost to the sea wall. While the sea was not rough it was whipped up by the breeze and it had a green-brown look that made it quite uninviting. With no one around there was an air of desolation about the seafront, and Sarah found herself reaching for her mobile phone to get a taxi back to the station.

If the rumour mill had run out of steam on Friday it was back in full swing by Monday lunchtime. It was Ms Marchbank who inadvertently gave rise to the further rumours. She had the task of manning the phone and meeting the visitors. Her answer to everyone was that Mr Deakin had taken a week's holiday. But when he failed to materialise at his usual hour, the jokes started that he was late and would fall foul of Ms Marchbank's wrath. By lunchtime his absence was most marked and Ms Marchbank was telling people that he had had to take an extra day. By now people wanted to know where he had gone on holiday. Did he drive there? Did he fly? It was Emma or Clemmie who suggested that he had gone to Venice, and then everyone had looked in Sarah's direction. It was followed by shrieks of merry laughter.

Both of them came and sat on Sarah's desk.

'Did Mr Deakin go to Venice?' asked Emma.

'How would I know?' replied Sarah.

'Because he didn't go to Timbuktu.'

'I thought he went to a publishers' convention in Geneva.'

'But we think he didn't.'

She was saved by the intervention of Ms Marchbank insisting the two girls get back to work.

Then, on Thursday, there was a surprise visitor. Sarah was sitting at her desk and had seen the woman come in but had taken no notice, as she was not expecting any visitors. But soon she became conscious that the person was coming towards her, with Ms Marchbank hurrying behind her. Then she was at the desk and Sarah was forced to acknowledge the woman. She looked up and recognised Connie, the woman she had met at the theatre with her husband.

'Hello, Sarah,' she said, 'I wondered if we could talk.'

Ms Marchbank was now trying to intervene, saying in her clipped accent, 'You cannot just come barging in here like this. I must ask you to leave!'

'I don't think this is the time or place,' said Sarah tentatively.

'It will have to be now,' said Connie speaking as one who usually had her way. 'I've had to put myself out just to come here.'

Sarah appealed to Ms Marchbank.

'Ms Marchbank, would it be all right if I took a break for ten minutes?'

'No, it would not, Sarah; I've had to give you one written warning this month.'

'Well, Connie, I'm so cheesed off that another warning would be welcome.' Sarah picked up her coat.

'You cannot just walk out of here like this.'

'The work will keep,' said Sarah. 'I'm well ahead with it.'

'I order you to sit down!'

'Come on, Connie,' said Sarah. 'Let's leave Ms Marchbank to her typing.'

'If it means losing your job, Sarah, perhaps we'd better not.'

'I'm past caring,' said Sarah, and walked to the door. Connie followed and they left the building.

'Where to?' asked Connie.

'There's a little café down the way, let's go there.'

It was two hundred yards and the walk gave Sarah time to think. She was sure that Connie had come from Mr Deakin and was rather pleased. She had liked Connie and her husband, for they had presented themselves to her as people she could trust. She hoped it would be possible to talk to Connie and try and explain herself to her, though she was aware that it was possible she had come purely to put Mr Deakin's side of the story and berate her for making him so unhappy.

They sat down in the café and Connie began talking before a waitress hovering in the distance had time to come over.

'I came to the office this afternoon to see where Philip was. We know he went to meet you in Venice, and we expected him back last weekend at the latest, but we haven't seen or heard from him.'

She let her words sink in.

'We knew he was due back then because he had an arrangement to dine with us on Monday evening.'

Sarah could only nod.

'He did promise us that he would come and he said he was bringing you!'

'I knew nothing of this,' said Sarah.

'When did you get back?'

'Monday morning a week ago.'

'So you last saw him ten days ago, and he's not been back to the office or to his house in that time. And he did return with you, didn't he?'

'No,' said Sarah.

The waitress arrived and two coffees were ordered.

'But you did meet him there, surely?'

Sarah paused; her mind was on the time she had spent with Mr Deakin. 'Yes, we did meet up!'

'Then I fail to understand why you didn't come back together.'

'Perhaps we agreed not to.'

'That was never his intention.'

'I was not privy to his intentions.'

Connie was staring at Sarah. 'Have you any idea where he is?'

'No. Anyway, apart from missing a dinner date with you, why are you so interested in him?'

'Well, luckily I'm happily married, or I might take umbrage at that. No, my interest is sisterly. He's not my brother, but he and Curzon were best friends at school together and when we married he was our best man. Curzon reciprocated the compliment when Philip married. But more importantly, he confided a lot in Curzon and me. The day before he went to Venice he was in raptures about going, though he didn't say why – except that he was going to meet you. He wanted to show you Venice, for it's one of his favourite places.'

'We saw very little of it together.'

'He didn't say so, but we suspected that he was going to propose to you.'

Sarah looked down at the table like someone seeking inspiration and finding none. The slight shadow across her lowered face was unable to hide the redness of her embarrassment. But the last thing Sarah wanted to do was to admit to this woman what had happened over the weekend. How much of it Mr Deakin wanted to make public was up to him. And while Connie was clearly a good friend of his, she was almost a stranger to Sarah. She had wanted to confide in Connie but now realised that she could not. The coffee was placed before them. Sarah remained silent.

'You have refused his offer of marriage, haven't you? He was not expecting you to.'

'You seem very sure that he was going to propose to me. If you knew his thoughts, why don't you ask him about it?'

'I would ask him if he were around. But did he propose to you?'

'How could he propose to me? I hardly know him.'

'Is that why you refused?'

It was becoming a battle of wills.

'You know how well he knows me.'

'It seems to me that you're embarrassed about something. I'm not really interested in what you both did, I just want to know that he's all right.'

'I've phoned the hotel and I understand he left Venice at midday on the Monday.'

'So it's reasonable to assume that he flew home.'

'I would think so, but I can't confirm that.'

'I find it very odd that he should come home and not contact me.'

Across Connie's shoulder Sarah saw a man staring at her. She refused to catch the eye of Clive Brunswick, but Connie had seen the look she had given and perceived that Sarah had seen someone behind her. She swung round but Clive had ducked out of sight.

'Who was that?' asked Connie.

'Just someone I recognised. Mr Deakin's been to his house, then.'

'No, by home I meant rather loosely "this country". I have seen his housekeeper, and she hasn't seen him.'

Sarah blinked at this bit of information. 'That's odd; I would have thought he would have gone home.'

'Was he well?'

'I thought so.'

'You seem to hesitate, Sarah. Are you sure?'

'He seemed all right. He came with me to the airport and returned on his own. He packed his things, paid the hotel bill and then returned to the airport.'

'The inference being that if he could do that he was quite well. I wish, Sarah, that I didn't have this feeling that you're not telling me everything.'

'I think if there was anything to tell, then he ought to tell you. I would like to be friends but I don't think we've reached the point where we can swap confidences.'

'I had hoped that you would be more responsive. I wanted to extend a hand of friendship.'

They had both finished the coffee. Connie stood up and said, 'Well, thank you for telling me what you have. It hasn't put my mind at rest. Perhaps we will meet again.'

Sarah replied, 'I'm sorry it's not what you wanted.'

Connie left her sitting at the table. The meeting had left Sarah depressed. Connie should have had news of Mr Deakin but instead she had come to glean news. She might have left in a better humour had she been told more of the details of the weekend and she, Sarah, could have pretended to use her as a go-between, which was probably what Connie wanted. But she would have to go home and draw her own conclusions.

Suddenly she was aware that Clive was standing close to her.

'May I?' he said, pulling the chair out that Connie had vacated.

'Of course,' said Sarah.

'You're looking a bit glum this afternoon.'

'Yes, life's not been treating me too well.'

'Then it's time to get a new one.'

Sarah smiled and said, 'You're right.'

'Has the money arrived?'

'I'm not aware that it has.'

'It is the key to unlock the door to your new life!'

'You didn't come over while Connie was here. I thought you might at least have said hello.'

'It is not to my taste to speak to one woman in front of another.'

'Do you know her?'

The question was so direct that it caught him off guard.

'I do know her, but only slightly.'

'Why only slightly?'

'We have met and been introduced.'

'I must get back to the office.'

'I take it your overlord does not know that you're here.'

'No, he doesn't,' said Sarah, watching to see his reaction.

'Would you like to dine out with me this evening?'

'I have a prior engagement,' said Sarah, smiling at him.

'Is this with the man who met you in Venice?'

'No.'

'He did not meet with your exacting standards.'

'No, he didn't.'

'You're a very hard woman to please.'

'I thought I was too easy!'

'Not a bit of it. Severe on the opposite sex, and in reality no less severe on your own.'

'You paint a very bad picture of me; it makes me sound very disagreeable.'

'You're the first woman I've met who doesn't suffer fools gladly.'

They were walking towards the office and stopped on the corner.

'Tell me something,' said Sarah.

'What do you want to know?'

'Women are supposed to love easily, but surely it's men who love even more easily.'

'I think both sexes can be equally stupid.'

'So would a man still be smitten by a wife he divorced eight years ago?' She saw a querulous look pass across his face.

'Nothing surprises me,' he managed to say.

'So, speaking from a man's point of view, do you think it possible that Mr Deakin should still be bothered about his ex-wife?'

'I can't judge that,' he said, and he appeared ruffled by her question.

'But you should be able to say yes or no.'

'Then I would have to say yes.'

'I must go, but the money will be here sometime next week.'

Sarah walked up the road and entered the office. Ms Marchbank was waiting for her and the envelope had been sealed for her already.

'I have told you before about your behaviour and this is your second warning.'

'That's very kind you, Ms Marchbank, I shall look forward to reading it when I have time.'

Sarah went to her desk and deposited the envelope in her drawer.

'What's going on, Sarah?' asked Michael.

'To be honest I've no idea.'

'Well, this place is disintegrating around us.'

'Is it?'

'Of course it is, and you know it.'

'It could be that I couldn't care less.'

'Well, take care! Because those two girls over there are not above discussing that you and Mr Deakin are having an affair.'

'How can we be when he's not even around?'

'I wasn't born yesterday, you know! I know he's been paying you more attention than he should, and with him not being around you've become very moody.'

'Mr Deakin means nothing to me!'

'I wish I could believe that.'

Sarah ignored him. It was bad enough having the two girls on the other side of the room speculating about her, but it came to something when a man whom she thought of as one of the least discerning of people should be busy with his own musings on the subject. Still, he had given it as a friendly warning, and he was right! But surely she was not thinking that much of Mr Deakin. Connie had given her cause for concern, as she had been certain that the one person Mr Deakin would have told was Connie. If he had told just Curzon, then he would have had to say something to Connie, if only to stop her having the very sort of meeting she had had today. How could she tell Connie that Mr Deakin had a black eye! She hadn't thought that he would keep it to himself for as long as he had. It was odd that Mr Deakin had not been in touch with anyone. First Jonathan French had come to ask her, and then Connie. Both felt that they were very good friends, but she couldn't tell them that he had a black eye; that was surely up to him!

But then, why had she asked Clive about Mr Deakin? And why had her question disconcerted him so much? She had never managed to get under his smooth exterior before, and suddenly he had looked shifty, giving the impression that he had told a lie. It all had something to do with Mr Deakin getting his divorce. How did one check on a person's marital status? It was easy enough to find out about their marriage. One could also find out about births and deaths and that, she decided, was what she would do on Saturday.

But there was a matter pressing equally heavily on her mind. She was unhappy with the business arrangement being offered to her by Keith. She had had a bad time with her conscience and her disloyalty to Mr Deakin. She should have set it straight with him, but not having talked about anything it had been left. The City might think that loyalty counted for nothing, but when it came to personal relationships it was paramount. From the very beginning she had known what Clive's character was like and she should have avoided him, but she had felt the danger and had naively wanted to sample it, like a moth flitting around a candle. For

Keith she had less respect, and the picture they had painted of her future had obscured her legitimate reservations. Their arguments had always sounded so good, yet Venice had shown her that they were up to something, and she did not know what. She was certain that Clive was covering up something, and she needed to know what it was. But first she needed to check on just who Mr Deakin was.

It was ten thirty when Sarah entered the Family Records Office on Saturday morning. She had decided to start looking for Mr Deakin's marriage certificate. On entering the main hall she found it somewhat daunting, with rows upon rows of large books. But 'Marriages' in green covers were straight ahead of her, and she began her search there. She had only an approximate date for their marriage and guessed that it was some twenty-six years ago. She started at four years before that and checked each book. There were books were for each season. But finally she found the entry. Philip Myton Deakin married Caroline Jane Cressing on such-and-such day in Wimbledon. See checked the full entry and saw Mr Deakin's age when he married. He was twenty-four, so he was now forty-seven! The next question was, did they have any children?

'Births' were red-covered books stacked in shelves around the corner. Sarah started at the date of their marriage and worked through several books until a year later there was an entry for a Tamzin Deakin, born to Philip and Caroline (Cressing), which seemed pretty conclusive that they had had a daughter. She dodged the next two books and continued, but over the following six years she could find no other reference to any children.

It was now a question of finding out about divorces, and she decided to ask about that at the desk. But since it had taken her less time than she imagined, Sarah felt she ought to have a good look round first. She checked her own birth and then went back to the marriages and checked for her parents' wedding. Across the way were shelves filled with black-covered books. Sarah shivered at the thought of them, but then remembered that her grandparents were both in there somewhere. Odd that life came down to a date for one's birth, marriage and finally death!

Suddenly, she knew instinctively that she had to check for eight years ago. With some reluctance she drew out a large black-bound volume and checked the name of Deakin. It took twenty minutes, but there in front of her was what she suspected: Caroline Deakin's death. That explained Mr Deakin's use of Caroline's name. Had he simply divorced her he would not have been bothered, and surely would never have blurted out her name, but if she had died tragically he would have spent the next eight years getting over her. Why hadn't he told her? What a stupid man he was! She had quarrelled with him over something that must have really hurt him. Her indignation at his actions turned to guilt. She looked at the entry again to see if any more information could be gleaned from the entry. Why did she die in Newbury, Berkshire? They must have lived in that area! There was no reason given for her death, and if she wanted to know more then she would have to buy a copy of the certificate. But with the knowledge she had just gained she could pump Connie for more. So there was a daughter somewhere around! She would certainly like to meet her! Why had Mr Deakin not introduced her to his daughter? Why hadn't he even mentioned her!

Sarah glanced back down the list of names and discovered to her amazement that there was an entry underneath for another Deakin in Newbury. Her astonishment was immense, for the entry was for a girl called Tamzin! It was the same day in the same place! And the girl's age was right – it had to be Mr Deakin's daughter! Sarah felt tears on her cheeks. So both Caroline and Tamzin were dead; there could be no doubting it. He should have told her. He really should have done! She would have understood what he said in Venice and she could have made allowances for it. Why had he doubted her sympathy? Why couldn't he trust her? Was he so hurt by it all that he couldn't talk about it?

She closed the book and returned it to the shelf. Two minutes later she was outside in the cool of the street. All her mind would say to her was, if you are going to snoop then be prepared for the worst! She was suffering now from the shock of learning about the deaths of two people. Why was it that the awfulness of one's own mortality crept in?

She returned home and sat on her bed with a cup of coffee in her hand. If what she had found out was correct, Mr Deakin's family had been wiped out. She was amazed that he had kept going and managed to build a business.

Clive came to her mind. He knew what had happened and yet he wanted her to think that Mr Deakin had got divorced. Why? Was it just to paint the worst picture possible of Mr Deakin? Had they told the truth, her sympathies would have lain with Mr Deakin. But Keith had told her in Clive's presence. Technically, they had told her lies, and if that was so then what did it mean for their business plan. Furthermore, she had yet to receive the promised details! She was being pressed for money, but they could string out their promises on the business plan. She could see it all now! They were starting a business from scratch. Maybe they had some contacts, and perhaps Keith had an old desktop publisher. With her money, they could easily fund the office and telephone. In other words she would be one step further down the line than if she left Deakin's and started her own business. Yet to go along with them she would be £25,000 down, and take only a third of the profits!

How could she get out of it? Perhaps she ought to spend the money! But how did one spend that sort of money in one morning? No, she would have to say that she had changed her mind; but if Clive turned the charm on she had no idea how she would treat him, and she'd have a feeling that she had no immunity against it. Once he knew that she had the money he wouldn't let go.

Could she just give them the money and forget it? But that would look as if she was still going to go in with them and it left her appearing as a disloyal person in Mr Deakin's eyes. Why did it always come back to him? Before she did anything she had to resolve her problems with him. If he no longer wanted to know her, then she was a free agent and could do as she pleased. But what if he renewed his campaign to win her? She had tasted life with him and it had not turned her off him. Instead, if she was strictly honest with herself, she had found it alluring. She wished she knew what love was! If only her mother had sat down and talked to her, but the bowls club had become more important... But why did Mr Deakin not get in touch? Was his eye taking longer to heal than she thought? Was he more badly hurt than she realised at the time?

Sarah's feelings were still mixed, for she felt angry that he had not told her about his family, and her anger increased for she knew so little about him. He should have spent the Sunday in Venice persuading her to stay with him for the rest of the week, and then he should have wooed her. His proposal then towards the end of the week might even have been expected, and had he put himself out she might even have found it agreeable!

But he should be in on Monday morning. He had to be in – it was just too dreadful without him!

The Printer

It was Monday morning, and two full weeks since Sarah had returned from Venice. Of Mr Deakin there had been no sign, and she assumed that he would appear in the office that day. Two weeks seemed long enough for his wounds to disappear, though she suspected that his bruised ego would take longer to heal. She was not looking forward to him sitting in his office and holding the weekly progress meeting. She could see that his eyes would roam around the people sitting before him but always finish looking at her. They would plead with her or demand to know why she had refused him. Each time it happened she would colour and everyone would look at her. Tongues would wag and there would be those who in their ignorance would cruelly accuse her of fancying Mr Deakin. For how long would she bear it? She didn't know but she resolved to go to as few such meetings as possible before she resigned. Should she have resigned already? She didn't know, but she felt concern for him and wanted the assurance that he was all right before she did anything which she might regret; though Ms Marchbank's efforts might catch up with her before she had time to make up her mind. That was a bridge she would cross when she got to it, for it was easy to doubt that Mr Deakin would ever endorse the written warnings she had received.

Today, Sarah was sure, was the day when all such things would sort themselves out. She imagined him arriving at the office. Would he come straight in to see her and stand before her desk to greet her, as the true friend he wanted to be? Or would he be in some towering rage, spitting revenge? How would she really feel with him glaring at her? In fact she doubted that she would be his first port of call. No, he would go to his room and Ms Marchbank would start to look busy. There would be a large smile on her face, as she could relax in Mr Deakin's presence. She was there to do his bidding, whatever it was – whether making him a cup of coffee or digging out some long lost file. Emma and Clementine would see him from their vantage point facing the across the office towards Ms Marchbank's desk and the landing. Their heads would go down as if they were busy, and they would be giving sly glances upwards to see what was going on. Gradually everyone in the office would become aware of what was happening and there would be an increase in activity, with many nods in the direction of Mr Deakin's office. But now, though people would glance in that direction, they still showed the unconcern of people for whom the event that they were expecting had yet to come about.

What would happen after he arrived? Would he call her into the office? He had the excuse of the written warnings from Ms Marchbank, and they were most certainly somewhere on her list of things that needed to be brought to his attention. Or would he sort out the rest of the list first, leaving Sarah to stew in her worry? The latter course was most likely! And eventually she would be called to his office. She could see herself being invited to sit in a chair facing him. Ms Marchbank would lay out the charges against her and then she would be asked to leave. When she closed the door on them, would he open himself up to her? And how did he think of her? Would he be true to his words when she left him at the airport? Or did her parting shot damn her for good? Would his feelings have undergone so complete a change that he would go along with Ms Marchbank?

Sarah couldn't see that, since she could think of nothing that Mr Deakin ever said that he would not honour. What would he say to her? What did she want him to say? She wanted to hear his voice. She wanted him to break down the barriers that separated them. She wanted him to sweep her off her feet. Would he find the arguments to satisfy her? She did not want him to come straight out with everything but slowly to woo her; offer to take her out for a meal or a show, and allow her time to respond properly to him.

But her feminine will began to rear itself, as it normally did. How could she allow herself to be tugged down into the situation she rebelled against? Surely she didn't want to sit in a house waiting for her man to come home and become the next neglected woman. Her mind would continue to rage, but her heart, when he touched her arm or her hand, would be the stronger, and she cursed herself being a weak woman! And still he had not yet come.

By eleven o'clock Sarah was having doubts, for Mr Deakin was always in by ten, and the Monday meeting was usually over within the hour. No one seemed bothered, least of all Ms Marchbank. As the senior person she should be making much more effort to keep the place running, but all the staff knew that anyone who had phoned had been told that Mr Deakin was out, and that he would be in touch when he returned. She made no allowance for matters that needed immediate attention and considered them irrelevant and trivial concerns. The business was not yet suffering but a month or two down the line and one would inevitably see the result of the rising administrative inertia. Sarah had been there longer than anyone else and took it upon herself to tackle Ms Marchbank.

'What is happening about future manuscripts?' she asked.

'I don't know,' said Ms Marchbank forcibly. 'It is up to Mr Deakin to sort it out when he decides to come in.'

'But what if he doesn't come in this week?'

'It is not up to me to worry about it. Now, I believe you have finished the project you were on. Mr Deakin will complete it when he returns.'

'Well, I've done the basic layout of the blocks, checked the wording and illustrations. It needs a few decisions made and the frontispiece added. I suppose there's the best part of a week's work there.'

'That's not for you to decide.'

'Yes, it will have to wait for Mr Deakin,' said Sarah sarcastically.

'I don't like your tone, Miss Levine. Now take that and sort it out.'

Sarah took a fat folder of papers from her and returned to her desk. Michael watched her.

'You seem very put out. Have you had your third warning yet?'

'Not quite. I wasn't rude enough.'

'You did try, then.'

'Of course. Oh, look what she's given me!'

'What's the matter now?'

'She's given the manuscript belonging to the cabinet minister's wife! Oh no – the deadline's for this coming Friday!'

'You're going to be busy, then.'

'Not with this rubbish! It needs to be totally rewritten, apart from being laid out. There's easily six weeks' work here. No, she can have this back. It would be better to finish the other that I've just given her.'

Sarah took the folder back to Ms Marchbank.

'This needs to be rewritten,' said Sarah, 'there's no chance of doing it by Friday.'

Ms Marchbank frowned. 'I understood that it had been started. I wonder where I got that impression? Isn't there is disc in the file?'

Sarah put her hand in the envelope and pulled everything out across Ms Marchbank's desk.

'Yes, there it is,' said Ms Marchbank, jumping on it. 'Have a quick look and give me some estimate of the time it will take.'

'Yes,' said Sarah with great reluctance and returned to her desk.

'Why can't people see that this minister's wife is a con artist? Mr Deakin obviously thinks he can get a knighthood out of it.'

'Good luck to him,' said Michael.

'Hey, you can't possibly support such actions!'

'Why not? Everyone does it.'

'Does what?'

'Well, you reach a point on the social scale where you're in line for such things and all you have to do is give someone a nudge.'

'A nudge?'

'Well, you have to do something, and if currying favour isn't good enough I don't what is. I'd do it if I had the chance.'

Sarah pushed the disc into the drive on her computer. 'I can tell you that this is an imposition.' She stared at the screen and Michael, glancing at her, saw she was looking at the screen intently.

'Looks like the frontispiece is done, then.'
Sarah tapped some keys and the screen rolled on.
'Well, it looks as if it has been started. That's not bad either.'
'And it's been rewritten! Look, the screen does not agree with the manuscript at all.'
'Run through it, then.'

A quick search of the disc suggested that it was complete. She returned to Ms Marchbank's desk to tell her, but it was as if she had seen Sarah coming, for she went over to speak to Emma. Sarah waited for her to return.

Then the telephone on her desk stared flashing and making a low buzzing noise. Ms Marchbank remained immune to its summons and kept her back to Sarah. It could not be left indefinitely, so Sarah picked it up.

'Is Mr Deakin in yet?' said the voice of a man on the other end of the line.

'No,' replied Sarah, 'he's been ill and has not come back in yet.'

'Then I need to talk to someone in authority. Who is there?'
'Ms Marchbank.'

'Don't be stupid, she's as much use as an electric kettle with no plug!' He spoke so loudly that Sarah wondered if Ms Marchbank had heard and she had to stop herself from laughing. The man spoke again.

'Who am I speaking to?'
'Sarah – Miss Levine.'
'Ah! I've heard Mr Deakin speak about you, and I could not remember your name.'
'Who am I speaking to?'
'Mr Bashley at the printers.'
'Oh, haven't we met?'
'We might have done.'
'Yes, we did once, and we were introduced in Mr Deakin's office. About a year ago,' said Sarah.
'Were we? I honestly don't remember. I've got a problem I need looked at.'

Ms Marchbank had seen what was happening and was storming over.

'What are you doing, Sarah?' she said sharply.

Sarah covered the phone and replied, 'Trying to sort out a problem with the printer.'

'I have told Mr Bashley that he'll have to wait until Mr Deakin gets in.'

'Then I hope Mr Deakin turns up in the next few minutes, because it sounds as if it can't wait.'

'I'll be the judge of that,' said Ms Marchbank curtly.

'No! Put the call through to Mr Deakin's office and I'll deal with it there!'

It was a battle of wills. Ms Marchbank glared at Sarah who simply glared back.

'If you take the call you'll be dismissed immediately.'

'That's a great threat, isn't it? Take the call and get fired, or don't take the call and lose your job!' Sarah was becoming conscious that other members of the staff were watching them with a keen interest.

'Put the call through to the office *now*!' said Sarah handing her the receiver. She walked across the landing to the office.

Ms Marchbank had little option. Sarah picked up the office phone and was pleased to hear Mr Bashley was still there.

'What's going on?' he demanded.

'Ms Marchbank was throwing her weight around. Now, tell me, what's the problem?'

'Well, I'm not sure that you can help me...'

'Of course I can't, until know what the problem is.'

'It would be so straightforward if Mr Deakin were in.'

'But he isn't! Are you going to tell me or not? You do know the book is ready for tomorrow?'

'Oh, good! But the problem is this: I've a client who's going to go bust. He owes me a lot of money, and I was expecting a cheque from him last Friday but it never came.'

'How does this affect us?'

'It doesn't really. What I was wondering was, could I have some of the money Mr Deakin owes me? I just need it a bit sooner than it is due.'

'Why does he owe you money?'

'On the monthly account. He owes three months' worth. I

had a cheque last week from you, but that had been arranged before Mr Deakin went away.'

'How much are you looking for?' asked Sarah.

'£20,000. But it's only a part of what Mr Deakin owes me.'

'And what is the downside, if you don't have this money?'

'I'm not sure. If I can't pay the wages then everyone will know and I'll be squeezed. That at least means all my schedules will slip. Then I'll lose customers and finally I'll go out of business. You might be able to reschedule with one or more of the other printers, but you'll have a severe dip in your accounts. It affects you too, you see.'

'Why don't you ask your bank for some money?'

'They're the last people one goes to in my situation! If I ask them to cover a hole in my cash flow they'll want their overdraft repaid immediately, and then I'll be right in shtook.'

'Look, ring me back in twenty minutes and I'll speak to the woman who looks after out accounts as she's in today. At least I can see if we can help.'

'Brilliant! I'll ring back in twenty minutes.'

Sarah put the phone down.

'What is it, Ms Marchbank?'

'What gives you the right to go into Mr Deakin's office and speak on his phone?'

'The necessity of doing something,' said Sarah glaring back.

'I'm giving you your notice this very minute! I suggest you resign, or it will look bad on your record.'

'I think I have more right to be in here than you,' said Sarah gently.

'And what makes you think that?'

'Well, I don't know where Mr Deakin is at this very moment, but I do know where he went three weekends ago.'

'That is entirely irrelevant.'

'Oh, I don't think so. Who is Mr Deakin going to support? You – who right now are presiding over a company that is sliding downhill – or me?'

'Mr Deakin left me with the authority.'

'Mr Deakin left me with the authority to overrule you,' retorted Sarah.

'Don't be so stupid, woman! You don't know what you're talking about.'

'Oh, I think I do! You see, three weeks ago I was in Venice with Mr Deakin, and we were having what's called a dirty weekend!'

Ms Marchbank was visibly shocked. 'How can you say such things?'

'Easily, because it's true. Now, you gave me a written warning about being late, isn't that right?'

'Yes!'

'Well, Mr Deakin put me on the plane back to London that morning. He knew perfectly well I would be late back.'

'But he's not here to corroborate that.'

'No; and secondly you gave me a warning because I left the office one afternoon – correct?'

'Yes.'

'The woman who came round here was a very good friend of Mr Deakin's. I had met her only once before and she came round because she wanted to find Mr Deakin.'

'I did not know that. And I've still only got your word for all this.'

'Then I'll put it calmly to you. In my drawer are two envelopes. I suggest you go there and take them out and destroy them. Also, go and erase the text from the computers. If, when Mr Deakin gets back, he supports you, I shall resign immediately. However, if he supports me, you won't look so big a fool as you do at present.'

'I'll do no such thing!' Ms Marchbank was as white as a sheet.

'Well, you can go from here and think it over, but I'll not be responsible for his wrath and subsequent actions. Oh, and one last thing before you go, I want all telephone calls put through to me here in Mr Deakin's office.'

Ms Marchbank stormed out, slamming the door behind her. Sarah wanted to sit down and think through what she had done, but she knew that Mr Bashley would be phoning back any minute.

Their accountant, Ms Arboth, did the books on a part-time basis. Monday was one of her mornings in to oversee the day-to-day accounts, so Sarah called her into Deakin's office.

'I need to pay some monies out,' Sarah told her. 'Is that possible?'

'No, not at all. Mr Deakin only left me cheques for certain accounts and a couple of spares. They've all been used up.'

'So it's not possible to write out another.'

'Not at all. Only Mr Deakin can sign a cheque, and they've all been used.'

'So what are we going to do if someone urgently needs a cheque made out?'

'Rest assured, at the moment we have nothing that must be paid, so there's no one dunning us for money.'

'So we ask them to wait a week or so?'

'Nothing else we can do.'

'And how much do we owe the printers.'

'Bashley's?'

'Yes.'

'I'm really not at liberty to tell you this.'

'I think for the sake of your job you ought to.'

'Is that some kind of threat?'

'Not at all, but a situation has arisen that might well jeopardise every job in this office, and that would include yours.'

Emma had come over wanting to speak to Sarah.

'Mr Bashley's on the phone, Sarah.'

'Tell him to ring back in ten minutes.'

'Yes, I'll tell Ms Marchbank.'

Sarah turned back to Ms Arboth.

'Now tell me how much we owe the printer.'

Sarah received a very sour look, but the woman was already pulling out a file. It took a minute for her to find the account and the necessary figures.

'The outstanding amount for the three months is £108,000.'

'Have we received any of that money yet?'

'No, it will be coming in from various places over the next six months.'

'When the books are sold, I presume. If it were possible to write out a cheque for £20,000 would we have the money in the bank to do so?'

'Oh yes.'

'Would it give us a cash flow problem?'

'No, we should be able to ride it fairly well. But in any case, you can't have a cheque!'

'I know.'

'And even if you could I wouldn't allow you to write one that size.'

'Why not?'

'Because it would have to be done by Mr Deakin.'

'But he's not here!'

'Then it will have to wait. Tough, but there it is.'

Sarah could see that there was nothing to be gained by arguing the point and Ms Arboth went back to the main office. She sat down and rang the telephone number of the printers.

'John Bashley here. Is that you, Miss Levine?'

'Yes.'

'What can you do, then?'

'Well, I have spoken to the woman who does the accounts and she can't do anything. The money is there in the bank account but we can't touch it.'

'Then what am I going to do?' He sounded quite distressed.

'Are you sure that Mr Deakin would advance you the money?'

'Well, ninety per cent sure. I'm only asking for my money a bit sooner. And I've known Mr Deakin for years.'

'Then I'll have to lend it to you.' Sarah was surprised at herself and felt a certain thrill at offering such a large sum of money to a man she hardly knew; but it also got her out of a hole.

'No, don't be stupid. I can't take twenty grand off you.'

'I thought you were desperate.'

'I am, but I can't do that.'

'Why not? I'll get it back off Mr Deakin.'

'The only reason I don't want it off you, Miss Levine, is pride!'

'So with your pride we all might have to suffer…'

'Put like that, I don't have much of an option.'

'I'll get the cheque couriered down today.'

'Well, I can only say thanks! I hate to stand in your debt like this, but believe me it's for the best. Many thanks.' He rang off.

Sarah sat back and contemplated what she had just done. She decided that she was utterly mad and a great fool. Surely he could have found someone else to help him? But then he might have to rely on two or three of his customers to bail him out. And again, despite the fact that what she had done was foolish, she felt very good about it. It was money sitting in her bank account waiting for her to hand over to Keith. She was due to give it to him sometime that week and she did not want to. Now she had the excuse that she wanted. She felt pleased with herself and sat at Mr Deakin's desk, smiling. There was also another side to it! It would also go some way towards soothing her conscience over being disloyal to Mr Deakin.

Then the phone rang. Mechanically she picked it up.

'Miss Levine speaking.' It was a literary agent who had been trying to reach Mr Deakin for the last week. Sarah told him that he was not in and then invited the agent to talk to her. It took ten minutes before she could put the phone down, but he was recommending that they looked at a book with a view to publishing it, and since that was their business she invited him to send it along.

She went out into the office and was surprised to see everyone staring at her. It was patent that Ms Marchbank had said something to someone and the rumour mill had swung into action again. Emma was staring at her with her mouth open.

'Get on with your work, Emma,' said Sarah as she passed.

'I haven't got anything to do, Sarah.'

Sarah stopped. 'Then start clearing that rubbish behind your desk.'

'There's just one thing, Sarah. Did you really spend the weekend with Mr Deakin in Venice?'

'Get on with that clearing up!'

Everybody else in the room put their eyes down to their work. Sarah checked that the two envelopes had been removed from her drawer before returning to the office. On her way past Ms Marchbank she stopped.

'We need a courier as soon as possible. Can you get one?'

'I cannot agree with your high-handed ways, Sarah.'

'And I cannot agree with sloppiness.'

She returned to Mr Deakin's office with her bag and took out her chequebook. She made a quick phone call to the bank and was pleased that everything was in order. Once the cheque was off to the printers, she set herself to find out what else they had on. By the end of the afternoon she could only find one manuscript that had not been started. That, plus the one that was coming in, was not enough to keep everyone in work. Still, she decided that she would keep at least Emma or Clementine clearing the office, for it had always irked her that things were simply piled up all over the place. Much of it was never looked at and never likely to be looked at. She could get it boxed and archived at the warehouse. It was just too bad if people didn't like it.

Outside she ran into Clive, who fell in beside her.

'Sarah! You are looking lovelier than ever,' he said. Sarah was immune to his compliments now that she knew that he had at least gone along with a lie, bringing into question the rest of his judgement. But it was not yet time to tell him that she knew, and she let his words bring a smile to her face. Clive saw her smile and took it as a sign of encouragement.

'Mr Deakin seems to be taking an extended holiday.'

'He does.'

'Ms Marchbank is out of her depth.'

'Yes, she is.'

'He only took her on to run his sales office. Six years ago all the books were delivered to the office and lugged upstairs. Ms Marchbank's job was to package them and send them out.'

'And presumably she collected the money in.'

'Yes, but he only kept her on as a favour. She's a millstone round his neck.'

'You seem very well acquainted with our office.'

'One keeps one's ear to the ground.'

'But you had led me to believe that you and Mr Deakin were barely acquainted.'

'Well, we've hardly spoken in the last eight years.'

'And before then?'

'He was a rival in business.'

'So you had a business eight years ago... What happened to it?'

'This is something I never wanted to tell you, but your erstwhile boss saw to it that it could only lose money.'

312

'How could he do that?'
'Somehow he got hold of the best authors before I did.'
'That's no excuse.'
'He always had better backers than I had.'
They had reached the top of the steps going down to the Underground station.
'Won't you join me for drink or dinner tonight?'
'No, I'm very tired and I want to get home.'
'You must know, Sarah, that I'm deeply in love with you.'
'I might have guessed.'
'You are by far the most perfect woman I have ever been privileged to meet.'
'That's very sweet of you,' she said and tapped his hand, 'but I must go.'

She descended the steps and only looked back when she was round the corner to check that he was not following. Was he really in love with her? There were people like him who loved women easily but once they had sampled the goods they grew tired and moved on to the next person. Clive was like that; once he had had a woman in bed, boredom would set in. He liked laying siege to a woman. As long as she resisted him he would continue to be charmed by her.

The Cabinet Minister's Wife

What sort of business did Clive have? If Mr Deakin was busy in his office, where did he find the time to wreck someone else's enterprise? And what was the business relationship between the two men eight years ago? Did Keith fit into this anywhere? A thought occurred to Sarah: was it possible that they were getting at Mr Deakin through her?

She spent the rest of the week in Mr Deakin's office sorting out his company's affairs.

Friday brought her first shock. A letter in an official-looking envelope arrived, and it was addressed to her at the office. Warily, she looked at it, debating whether or not to open it. Strange how she could open the letters addressed to Mr Deakin without a care in the world, but it was different when her name was on the envelope. But she slit it open and pulled a single sheet of paper. The heading was official enough and it came from a City bank that she had never heard of. She read the letter and felt annoyed. Why should she take her passport to a bank? She read it again and realised that she was required to take it to be a signatory on an account. This was surely a new ploy to get people to take out loans and so forth. She had reached the point where she wanted to throw it away but her eyes were drawn to the bottom and she was stayed. Understanding began to crowd in on her. The account for which she was being invited to become a signatory was Deakin Publishing Ltd. She read the letter again and nearly burst into laughter.

It could only mean one thing. Mr Deakin had gone to his bank and told them that he wanted to make her a signatory. He must know of the money she had sent to the printer! Was he about to entrust his company to her?

Sarah called Ms Marchbank in.

'I have to go out this morning. Some urgent business has cropped up. Everyone has their instructions.'

'Yes, Sarah,' said the woman sullenly.

'If anyone phones, tell them I'll ring them back this afternoon.'

Sarah hurried home for her passport. So Mr Deakin was still playing games with her. Would he meet her somewhere? Was he watching her right now? She didn't mind for she felt very excited that he still held her in his affections.

She arrived at the bank an hour later and was shown into a side room. A young man came out with a folder.

'Miss Levine?' he asked. 'Now, that is Sarah Levine, I take it.'

'Yes, that is correct.'

He checked her address and then picked up the passport. For a full minute he scrutinised the passport photograph and then put it down on the desk.

'Do you have a driving licence?'

'No, I've never learned to drive.'

'Do you have any other identification on you? A bill, perhaps?'

'I have a credit card statement.'

'That will do.'

'You have no objection if I photocopy them.'

'No, none at all.'

He disappeared for five minutes and on his return handed the passport and statement back. He pulled some more papers out of his folder.

'First you need to sign these that you agree with everything. Now you need to put your specimen signature there, and there, and sign the bottom.'

Sarah did as she was required.

'When can I sign cheques?'

'From today. We have all the necessary paperwork.'

'Is there any limit on the cheques that I write?'

'None has been specified, but you are expected to work within the current balance at the bank.'

'So I shall be able to look at all bank statements and so forth.'

'Oh yes.'

'Anything else?'

'No.'

Thirty seconds later Sarah stood on the pavement feeling

totally bemused. She could rush back and write herself out a cheque for any amount she liked! What a wonderful feeling! But she did not want her money out yet, since it was safely tucked away. It probably meant that Mr Deakin was not going to be in for a while yet. She wandered back to the office. The wages would have been done and sent in by Ms Arboth, as per the agreement with the bank, and should Mr Bashley need any more money she could now give him that; except that if Mr Deakin knew about that money, as she supposed he did, why didn't he give it to Mr Bashley? And why didn't Mr Deakin give him the money to begin with? The conundrum bothered her for the next half a mile. There was only one answer, and that was Mr Deakin knew about it in the first place! So why use her money? Did he actually want her to run his company?

If that was so, then her future went one of two ways. Either she took control of Deakin's and married Mr Deakin or she left and remained single! Had Mr Deakin forced her to the crossroads? But Clive had made him out to be quite a nasty piece of work! If that was so, why hadn't she seen any of it? She had been around for two years and she had never heard a malicious rumour or a bad thing said against Mr Deakin. Was it possible that both Clive and Keith were imagining things? Or was it more likely that the pair of them had failed, whereas Mr Deakin had not? Clive's attitude to working was completely wrong. He was a person who seemed to live for the moment; he was someone who was idling life away.

Back at the office, her first visitor was Ms Arboth.

'I've prepared the cheques that need to go out next week,' she said, 'But I have no idea when Mr Deakin will be in to sign them.'

'That's all right,' said Sarah, 'I'll sign them myself.'

'Don't be stupid, Sarah; Mr Deakin has to do it.'

Sarah took out the letter from the bank and showed it to her.

'Why should you get a letter like that?' asked Ms Arboth.

'These things happen.'

'No, they don't. This rumour about you sleeping with Mr Deakin must be true, then.'

'There are always rumours like that going around.'

'So where is Mr Deakin?'

'He has had an accident and is recovering.'
'So you've seen him recently.'
'We've been in contact. Now I really must get on.'
Ms Arboth left and Sarah was glad to see her go.

Sarah was just settling down to a sandwich at lunchtime when the office door was pushed open. She looked and Connie came into the room. She looked stern, as if she was angry about something. For once her politeness deserted her and she launched straight in to what she had to say.

'Where is Philip? You must tell me what has happened!'
'Hasn't he been in touch with you?' asked Sarah.
'No, he hasn't.'
'Well, he's sort of been in touch with me.'
'What do you mean?'

Sarah pulled the letter from the bank out and showed it to Connie.

'But this is a letter from a bank, not from Philip.'
'Yes, but don't you see, the only person who can authorise such a change is Mr Deakin.'
'I see... and why should he suddenly make you a signatory?'
'That I don't know precisely, but I have had to use my money to help the company, and it's why I have assumed control of it. Mr Deakin – Philip – must know about that and has made me a signatory.'
'But this doesn't explain why he's disappeared.'
'Well, why didn't you tell me about Caroline?'
'I rather think that that is down to him.'
'It should be, but for some reason he's not told me. I had been told that Philip was divorced. However, I have found out that his wife Caroline is dead. Also that his daughter is dead.'
'I really can only say that they were killed in a car accident. You must ask Philip for other details. He has never spoken about it. I thought once he might have talked to Curzon, as they were quite close, but he hasn't.'
'I'll tell you a bit more about Venice. Philip and I went to bed together! In the morning he called me "Caroline". You can imagine that I was very angry, and he wouldn't talk about it. Later he proposed to me and I refused.'

317

'I didn't realise you had a relationship like that with him, I'm sorry.'

'You're not prying. I want to tell you. I haven't told anyone, but you must not talk about this. You see, I made a huge mistake in Venice and went off with the wrong man. Anyway, Philip chased after us and managed to catch up. This man hit Philip and gave him a massive black eye. I took him back to my hotel room and gave him first aid, but I think I should have called a doctor. Anyway he slept all day, and late that night there was nowhere else for me to sleep but in the bed beside him. He was out of sorts the next morning, and that's when he called me Caroline. I didn't know who she was.'

'Well, at least we've a reason why Philip's not around.'

'You're not to tell him that I told you.'

'Would it have made any difference if he had told you who Caroline was?' Connie added.

'Of course it would! I'm not that stupid.'

'Then what happened?'

'I was angry with him and he just walked out on me. Later he phoned and half apologised. Then he took me out in the afternoon and proposed to me. He pressed me to accept and had a really nice ring to give me, but I refused because he had given me no explanation, nothing.'

'And had you known about Caroline, would that have made any difference?'

Sarah could no longer maintain eye contact with Connie. 'Yes, I think so,' she said quietly. 'At least, I would have stayed the rest of the week with him. It might have made a difference.'

'Are you still angry with him?'

'I don't know. When I look back I think he was much more badly hurt by his assailant than I realised at the time. He was not himself, and when we sat down for a meal on the Sunday evening he ate nothing and just suddenly got up and went back to his hotel.'

'How did you come to go off with the wrong person?'

'Because I did not know for certain that it was Philip. You see, I didn't want it to be Philip because of something I'd done, and I couldn't face him at that moment. Then this man came up to me as if he were the person who had sent me all over the place and the relief that it was not Philip was overwhelming. He was so handsome I went weak at the knees, and it was half an hour later when I realised that he was not the man. Philip found us and came up to me and this man hit him.'

'I see,' said Connie slowly. 'I came to give you a piece of my mind. I didn't realise that you had been so badly hurt.' She moved forward and embraced Sarah.

Sarah smiled wanly. 'I'm only able to tell you that because he's made me run his business.'

'So one of us should be seeing him shortly,' said Connie, stepping back.

'I would have thought so. I'm surprised he's not been in touch with you.'

'Pride, Sarah, male pride! Doesn't want to be seen around with a black eye.'

'It ought to have healed by now.'

'I must go.'

Sarah was pleased with Connie's visit. She had wanted to be friends with her and now she felt she could be. It just required Mr Deakin to make himself known. Who would he see first? If it were Connie then he was sure to get a lecture; but if Connie was right about his pride then he would want to secure her first before speaking to Connie.

She decided to leave early that afternoon and do some shopping. In fact she had a more pressing reason, and that was to avoid Clive, who was beginning to make a habit out of waiting for her. At three o'clock she left and went up to Oxford Street. It was uncharacteristic of her to want to spend money but she felt a need to. She wanted to feel feminine, and if Mr Deakin had doubts she could dispel them by looking the part. Trouser suits were all very practical and were the uniform of the working woman but they did very little for a woman. One noticed that men rarely looked at a women dressed in a trouser suit, at least not in the sexual sense; but the skirted woman who crossed her legs on a train had most of the carriage looking at her. Then there was the cleavage, and Emma flaunted hers to perfection, for she rarely wore clothes that did not reveal that part of her body. She wanted men to gawp at her! To her, any man who did not was queer! Which meant that she must have a poor opinion of Mr Deakin; but Sarah doubted that, and guessed that he was sufficiently under Emma's gaze that had he so much as swivelled his eyes at her cleavage she would have been over him like a rash. No, Sarah wanted Mr Deakin to gawp at her. He did not expect her to show her cleavage, and he must have noticed that she was not endowed in that direction; but he had never had the insensitivity to mention it. However, he did know that she was a virgin; but then he would need to be illiterate not to know about that! And that was where he departed from all her male friends. He did not embarrass her about it. In fact, the website episode had been embarrassing because of the way Mr Deakin had reacted. He had taken it as a personal insult and had refused to share the interest and mirth shown by the male sex. And there Clive and Keith had been tactless, for they had both laughed and joked about it, as if it was a natural thing for a woman to be embarrassed in that way.

She found some skirts to wear in the office in shades that matched her jacket. Next she went the blouse section and discovered that she enjoyed browsing through the racks. Having made a choice she went to the lingerie to buy tights or stockings, and reflected that she had not worn such things for ages. She felt very pleased with herself as she went home.

She put her purchases in her room and did not reveal them to her flatmates until Monday morning as they all went to the catch the train.

'Where are you off to today?' asked Cathy staring at her.

'Just the office.'

'Something special happening?'

'No.'

'Oh, you're expecting Mr Deakin to come, are you?'

'He may, but I'm not anticipating it.'

'So what's happening to Deakin's?'

'Well, I thought it might have been obvious.'

'What! He's not left you in charge, has he?'

'Yes, if you want to know.'

'You'll have to marry him, then!'

Sarah remained silent for they had reached the station and

were climbing the steps to the platform level. She noticed the men looking at her and felt pleased. She began to understand how Emma felt about it. A train to Waterloo pulled up at the platform and they got on. As always it was crowded, but Sarah noticed that some of the men moved to one side for her while Cathy seemed trapped by the door. A youngish man suddenly offered her his seat. It was most unusual, and she almost refused since Waterloo was only a few stops down the line; but then she realised that the man expected her to take his seat. She bestowed a smile on him and took the proffered seat. He received a few strange looks from other men sitting close by but Sarah guessed that it had given him a lot of pleasure, and the looks he was now getting gave him a feeling of superiority over the rest of his sex.

As they walked down to the Underground at Waterloo, Cathy turned to Sarah and said, 'That's a turn-up for the book. I've never been offered a seat before!'

'I've never had so many men look at me,' said Sarah.

'And you, an arch-feminist!'

'Perhaps if you wore better clothes more men would look at you,' Sarah replied.

'What's wrong with what I've got on?'

'Jeans with holes in them, buttons missing on your blouse... And as for those trainers!'

'There's nothing wrong with them.'

'Nothing at all if you're slopping around, but why your employer let's you get away with it I don't know!'

'Oh – management now, are we!'

'I suppose so.'

She reached the office and stood by Mr Deakin's desk, which was fast becoming hers. There was something odd about it. If it had merely been cleared by Ms Marchbank she could have understood it, but the mail had been tossed on the desk by her. It seemed inconceivable that someone should tidy the desk and then throw the mail onto it. But the neat pile on her right contained a large folder of someone's manuscript that she had never seen before. The desk looked as if it had been arranged.

Sarah began opening the mail. Emma came in and, noticing Sarah's skirt, stood before her glowering. She saw herself as the most desirable woman around and she did not like Sarah taking her mantle. It was all too obvious that she did not like being upstaged.

'I never saw you, Sarah, as being a person who wore smart clothes,' she remarked. 'I mean, you always wore nice clothes, but never *smart*.'

'Did you clear the desk this morning?'

'No, I didn't.'

'Then have you finished the invoicing?'

'Not yet, Sarah.'

'Then I suggest you go and do it.'

'Can I ask where you got the skirt from?'

'No, get on with what you're paid to do.'

'I only asked,' said Emma, very sulkily, but she went anyway.

Ms Marchbank came in and, after looking Sarah up and down, said, 'I presume you're waiting for a certain person to arrive.'

Sarah was surprised, as she never thought Ms Marchbank was capable of a cutting remark, but she replied with a blunt, 'Yes.'

'There are the papers you wanted.'

'Thank you.'

'Nothing else?'

'Just one thing. Have you moved the things on the desk here?'

'No I haven't.'

'Then that will be all.'

It seemed that her dressing up had put everyone on edge, especially the women. But everyone now assumed that she was dressed to the nines in anticipation of Mr Deakin's arrival. But her desktop worried her more as someone had rearranged it, and there was a manuscript on it that she hadn't seen before. The only person in the office who could have put it there was Ms Marchbank, and she had denied doing so. That meant that someone had been in over the weekend and arranged her desk. There could be only one explanation, and it meant that Mr Deakin would not be coming in that day.

It was an hour later that Ms Marchbank put her head round the door and said, 'There's a gentleman to see you.'

Sarah's pulse rose and she pushed back her hair. 'Show him in, please.'

The door was opened and Clive Brunswick came in.

'I have heard certain whispers,' he said, 'so I've come to see for myself.' He looked round the room and then at Sarah, a smile crossing his face. 'You're looking very elegant this morning! May I be so bold as to ask the reason?'

'Well, I was not expecting you, Clive.'

'Evidently, since you've spent last week hiding from me.'

'Have I?'

'You know full well that you have.'

'So you've come to ask me for the money.'

'If you wish to put it in my hand then I will deal with it.'

'No, I've changed my mind!'

'Of course you have! Isn't it a woman's prerogative?'

'It may be, but I don't like giving my word and reneging on it.'

'And yet you do! How do you think Mr Deakin will react when he hears of your disloyalty? Do you believe that he will be won over by your feminine charm?'

'I do hope so!' said Sarah fervently.

Clive was forced to smile at her artlessness. 'I do know that one of his dislikes is people who are disloyal. He demands his employees to be obedient and faithful to his cause, and when they are not he never takes them back.'

'I should hope not.'

'You look as if you've spent the money.'

'No, I haven't, actually.'

'Then you still have it.'

'No, I haven't got it now.'

'Back up on deposit and locked up?'

'No, I lent it to a friend, if you must know.'

'I see. I don't know how Keith is going to take it, as he was relying on your money.'

'You told me a lie last week, Clive.'

'I beg your pardon, but I did not.'

'You may not actually have told a lie but you went along with a lie and in doing so gave credence to it.'

'You'll have to be more explicit.'

'I shall. Keith let me believe that Mr Deakin had divorced his wife, but I have since discovered that she is dead! I think you know more about Mr Deakin's affairs than you let on. I'm going to make an educated guess, and you can tell me if I'm wrong!'

'I'm not going to play such stupid games with you.'

'Oh yes you will, Clive! I think that both you and Keith were in business with Mr Deakin. For some reason you all split up and today, out of the three of you, there is only one who is successful!'

'You don't know what you're talking about.'

'It's true that I'm only guessing, but when Mr Deakin returns I shall know the truth.'

'You will only know the truth that he wants to give you.'

'Possibly, but are you a betting person?'

'I never bet with women.'

'But I have bet all my money on Mr Deakin!'

'He really does have his claws into you, doesn't he?'

'He certainly seems to be pulling all my strings at the moment. Now, if you don't mind, I have things to do.'

At the sight of the anger in Clive's face Sarah felt a strange pleasure. It was likely that he had never been worsted by a woman before and it hurt him. His face contorted slightly and he clenched and unclenched his fists, not knowing quite what to do. But it was plain to him that he had been dismissed, and all he could do was retreat as gracefully as possible, taking whatever pride remained intact with him. He stood at the door glaring at her.

'And please close the door behind you.'

Clive slammed it as hard as he could, and though it seemed that half the room and the door frame moved in response, it only served to confirm his anger, giving Sarah a corresponding frisson of pleasure.

In the afternoon Emma entered in the office, having become Ms Marchbank's messenger.

'There's a Mrs Cudman to see you, Sarah.'

The name rang a bell but Sarah could not place it.

A woman came into the office and she held out her hand.

'I had hoped Mr Deakin was in.'

'I'm afraid he has been ill, and is still convalescing.'

'I'm sorry to hear that about the dear man. Nothing serious, I hope!'

'No, it just laid him low, and he did not seem to recover very quickly.'

'Well, do give him my best wishes for his recovery. Lovely man. So delightful... and we did have some moments!'

'How can I help you?' Sarah asked politely.

'I popped in to see how my book was coming on.'

'Which was it?'

'The one called *Secrets of Stately Homes*.'

Immediately, Sarah realised that she was the cabinet minister's wife. She felt her hackles rise towards the woman, for she disliked the fact that Mr Deakin had rewritten her book, and now she could see that the author was also good-looking. What 'moments' was she talking about? Had Mr Deakin been attracted by her qualities? Sarah had never felt such anguish before. Why should it hurt so much that he might have gone off with this woman? She had never felt such an emotion before, and she knew that she loathed Mrs Cudman and would gladly do her an injury. She had always considered women who fought over a man to be rather pathetic, but that was exactly what she wanted to do to this woman; in some way or fashion she really wanted to hurt her!

Her mind wanted to dwell on the form of retribution she should employ but she forced herself to be polite. Her real fight was not with this woman but with Mr Deakin.

'It's finished,' replied Sarah controlling her voice well, 'and it went to the printers the week before last.'

'Oh, that's wonderful,' Mrs Cudman said. 'So good of dear Mr Deakin to put himself out for me like that. He always took such care of me!'

'I doubt if kindness comes into it; Mr Deakin would have been thinking of the profit it will make.'

'Oh, you think it will sell well...'

'From what I've read of it, I would have thought so.' Sarah did not tell her that she thought it was full of the kind of sleazy rubbish that always seems to sell.

'Well, I do hope he gets better soon, it will be so nice to see him again.'

Sarah could only stare at Mrs Cudman. The emphasis in her voice and the way she was looking at her confirmed that there was more in the conversation than had actually been said. Sarah had a great desire to go with her to the stairwell and throw her down it, but she was saved from further conversation by the phone ringing.

'I must go,' said Sarah. 'It's been nice meeting you.' She shook hands formally and then picked up the phone. The matter was unimportant and Sarah was soon putting the phone down, but Mrs Cudman had gone.

Sarah thought over the meeting. She was rash in presuming that there was anything between the woman and Mr Deakin. Perhaps it was a state of the heart that one felt that every woman who also knew your man was a rival. But why had he rewritten the woman's book? Her writing was dreadful and way below publishing standards. How had the woman forced him to rewrite it? Was it some sort of payment? The thought hurt her badly, just as she was just beginning to think so well of him. Should she write out a cheque for herself and leave? She was close to tears and leaned with her back against the door. How ironic for her to want to give herself to this man, and then discover that he was spoiled merchandise! She couldn't stop the tears rolling down her cheeks.

It took half an hour for her to regain some equilibrium. The meeting left her low, having quite ruined her day. Could she blame Mr Deakin if he had availed himself of the favours of this woman? He was a free agent, and if he wanted or needed to do it she should not worry about it. In truth, she was free to do the same, and that she had not was because she had exercised her own choice. She determined to put it out of her mind and get on with the matters at hand. It was going to be a late evening for her.

The Fright

It was well past six o'clock, and with the autumnal darkness settling rapidly over the city Sarah sat at Mr Deakin's desk in his office. She was used to late nights and found that she rather enjoyed them. But suddenly she heard the click of a door latch, and knew that someone had opened the street door that she had purposefully locked earlier. She froze in her seat with a paralysing sense of fear taking hold of her. In the evening stillness she could hear the sound of footsteps on the treads of the stairs and the peculiar squeak of the handrails. She ought to have gone to the door to see who it was but instead slid deeper into the chair. For an instant she wondered about hiding under the desk, but the office door was now opening.

'Hello,' said a familiar voice, 'anyone about?'

Sarah wept with relief at the sound of Philip Deakin's voice.

'Hello,' she said rather demurely, 'you really frightened me, coming in like that.'

'Sorry! I didn't mean to frighten you, but I don't see how else I could have come in.'

'You should have called from the bottom of the stairs.'

'Yes, I could have done, but I didn't. I'm sorry.'

They both knew it was a bad start. She was vexed at having been so frightened and he was annoyed with himself for being so thoughtless. She should have been so pleased to see him for she had wanted to see him and talk, but he had stayed away from her. She was angry with him and now he had burst in on her, her anger had the upper hand.

'I've not picked a good time,' he said, trying to start a conversation.

'No, you haven't.' Sarah bit back a rebuke while at the same time chiding herself for being so ungracious.

'How are you getting on?'

'You should know, since you've been in here a number of times.'

'I thought you were doing very well as managing director...'

'But you had to spy on me, didn't you?'

'I don't really call it spying; that's a bit strong. I have checked on you because it was politic. Suppose the train was heading at high speed for the buffers, shouldn't I be allowed to ask for the brakes to be applied? What would my creditors have said if I told them that I didn't have a clue why my business collapsed?'

'Do you have to be right all the time?'

'I certainly don't walk around being right every moment of the day. I've apologised for coming in on you at the wrong moment and I apologise again, because I have made the mistake of thinking that you would be pleased to see me.'

'Where have you been?' said Sarah.

'After you left Venice I went back to my hotel and I was very upset. I was angry and very bitter. I believed that I had done enough to win you, and it was a shock to realise that I had not. Later I calmed down and began to think a bit straighter. I could see that my anger was not with you but myself. I don't think I was too well on the Sunday, and I was doing things without really thinking. I had worked out how I wanted to propose to you and I rather jumped the gun. So I blamed myself for that. I also don't think that we had spoken enough together – I mean we have, but not so much of the things that a courting couple should talk about. And as I pondered on this I began to realise that one of things you did not want to be was simply a housewife. Or at least you didn't want to marry and be expected to do all the household chores while I went out to work. Having returned to the hotel I packed up and came back to London. But first I went to see my doctor for a check-up. He suggested that I had some tests done and I spent three days in hospital. They decided that there was no real damage but told me that I needed to rest for at least a week. So I booked myself into a hotel in Torquay, and I've spent ten days there doing nothing. When I came back to London I went to see the printer, John Bashley. He and I have been good friends for many years and we worked out a simple ploy for getting you to put money into my company.'

'You used me despicably.'

'Well, I'm not going to apologise for that, as to be a real part of a business you have to commit your own money. You have felt rightly that Ms Marchbank should now obey you. Try and imagine telling her what do to if you had not put any money into the business! You've started decorating the office, and if you had not put your money into it you would never have done so, for the simple reason that if I belly-ached about the money, you have only say that you were only spending yours!'

'I still feel that you are bribing me into marrying you!'

'It's not a bribe; all I have done is to put an opportunity before you that has challenged you. You could have said, "This is not for me," and walked away, but later you would be very angry with yourself for having missed the opportunity. You might think that you could have the position without marrying me, but that would require an extraordinary amount of tolerance on my side. Imagine you and me working close together. You would always be thinking that this man wants my body! And you would be right. That Italian in Venice certainly wanted your body. Clive Brunswick wants your body, and both those men would have taken it whatever you might have said. In both cases it would be rape.'

'And how come you're any different, then?'

'Because I don't want to take your body by force, I want you to give it to me!'

'You've accounted for two of the five weeks. Where have you been for the other three?'

'I went to a hotel for most of the time.'

'And what have you been doing?'

'I've been doing all those things that one never has time for.'

'Such as?'

'I haven't visited any of London's museums in twenty years. I've visited a lot of the tourist attractions that I've never bothered with and I've been on the London Eye!'

'That sounds fun.'

'Oh, I've done some other things. I've been looking up the records of my family. Then I took a train down to Southend.'

'What on earth for?'

'I remember my parents taking me there when I was a little toddler and I had all these memories which I've never been able to place. I walked the length of the pier and back and on the way home I broke the journey at Leigh, and there were the cockle sheds that I remember!'

'That must have been thrilling for you.'

He ignored her sarcasm. 'Yes it was! I've had these memories and I've never known where they were and I saw the place as the train went through and decided to check it out on the way back. Don't you like finding these odd memories, and filing them in your mind properly?'

'I've never thought about it.'

'No, in the normal run of things we don't have time. I've been privileged to have someone look after my affairs for me.'

'So I haven't driven into the buffers yet.'

'No, not by a long chalk. You've made one or two decisions which I would not have done, but since the issues are open to doubt, your ideas may be just as good as mine, and I suspect that at the end of the day there won't be much difference – at least not in monetary terms.'

'So I have done all right?'

'Better – and I doubt if you would have done it had I been sitting at the other end of the office watching you. You would have every decision referred to me. You would not have been your own person and you would have grown to resent me.'

'There are other things we need to talk about.'

'What are they?'

'Caroline, for one.'

Sarah watched as Mr Deakin's face fall. He recollected himself and then said, 'Yes I must tell you about her.' He paused. 'Sarah, it's very hard for me to talk about it, and I have never talked about it to anyone. But I see now that I have to tell you. And it had been wrong of me not to say anything about it.'

'Perhaps you don't remember the night we spent together in Venice.'

'Not really, I was quite ill with my fever.'

'Then you won't remember calling me "Caroline" in the morning...'

'Did I? Then that explains your attitude, I'm so sorry.'

'And then you walked out of the room and left me.'

'I can only apologise, but I didn't really know what I was doing.'

'I know now that Caroline died and that your daughter also died.'

'Yes.' His voice was very quiet. 'They were killed in a motor accident. Caroline and I were very much in love; so in love that it adds weight to your argument about not getting too involved with another person. You cannot conceive what it is like to have a family one minute and the next moment they are gone. It's dreadful!' He paused again before taking a deep breath.

'You see, I killed them!'

Sarah blinked at him in astonishment. Here was a woman's worst nightmare! Her man admitting to being a murderer. What should you do? Do you live life with him knowing of his guilt, or do you go to the police? Can you live with a murderer? She did not know, but she didn't want to find out. Her mind was numb with shock but she forced herself to think and said, 'So you were driving, and it was your fault.'

'No, I wasn't driving, I wasn't in the car.' Sarah could only think that it was getting worse.

'At the time it happened I was in business with Keith Turner and Clive Brunswick, who were both intent on breaking up the business, and we had reached the point in the negotiations where it was being carved it up. Lawyers and accountants were involved and I needed to be beside the phone. Well, Caroline wanted to go down to see her parents in Wiltshire, since we had an arrangement to go. I refused to go and we had a row about it. In many ways it was the first disagreement we had ever had in fifteen years of marriage. Of course Caroline was right; I should have gone with them, for in the event no one phoned. The police said there was no reason for her to swerve off the motorway, and there was nothing wrong with the car, but she had – and killed herself and Tamzin. I have always felt that if I'd been in the car it would not have happened. Probably I'd have been driving, or if I was in the passenger seat, I might have been able to grab the wheel and steady the car. I think she wasn't looking because of the row, and came up behind a slow lorry at speed. When she saw she was too close and couldn't stop she panicked and lost control. Had I have been in the car, it would not have mattered if I'd been killed too. For ages after I wanted to be dead.'

'Do you still feel guilty?'

'I will always feel guilty.'

'And what happened about the company?'

'Well, the break-up of the company was completed on very disadvantageous terms for me. I was left with the present offices because they couldn't be bothered to unravel the terms of the lease my father had signed. They removed the entire cash flow and left me with the dross of the business. It was ironic but what brought about my family's death gave me life. I became so angry with the outcome that I was determined to make a go of it. As you can see, neither Keith nor Clive could make a go of it. Some years ago, in fact, Keith came in and insisted that I took him on as a partner again. I soon showed him the door.'

'And what about the cabinet minister's wife?'

'What about her?'

'Well, what favours did you expect for doing her book?'

'None why?'

'Then why did you do it?'

'Because I felt that despite her lamentable grasp of spelling, grammar and construction what she was relating was a story that would sell – and sell well.'

'But that's not why you did it?'

'No, I had two reasons for doing it. The first I thought you of all people might have understood.'

'How could I if I did not know what it was?'

'You could have worked it out!'

'I doubt it.'

'Well, I took pity on her.'

'*What?*'

'I saw her as a bored housewife. Her husband was out playing government with his friends all day, and she was shut up at home. She visits a lot of stately homes as one of the perks of her position, but the wives are rather left to themselves, being the unimportant half. So our friend collects stories about the servants and so forth and tries to write a book. Now, because the book has potential it ought to be published, but it needs to be rewritten. And I did it for her, so that she might feel that at the end of the day she has in fact achieved something.'

'I thought that you did it for the knighthood.'

'What knighthood?'

'Well if you did a favour for a cabinet minister's wife might you not get in the honours list?'

'Well it might improve my chances, I suppose, but not by much. Her husband is hardly the most influential man in the cabinet. In fact I think if he suggested it the rest of them would take great delight in frustrating any ideas in that direction. No, I did it solely because I saw that she was a bored housewife waiting for her husband to come home – which he hardly ever did until late at night, and then he was off again in the morning. It was all right for him, he had his friends to go and play with; but she had to wait around. I thought you might see that.'

'You had another reason for doing it.'

'*You!*'

'How can I have anything to do with her book?'

'Easy! I was courting you from afar. I knew that if I made a direct approach then you would reject me, but you gave me the means of attracting you, and over that period of time you were going to France and Amsterdam, I needed something to get my teeth into to stop me going mad with desire. There were times when I had to force myself to do it. I wanted to go out into the office just to talk with you. I knew that I would merely end up making a fool of myself.'

'She made a suggestion to me that you and she had had relations...' Sarah's voice tailed off.

'Relations? What are you talking about?'

'Did you or did you not have sex with her?' Sarah had raised her voice.

'No, I did not!' said Mr Deakin quietly. 'I have had a sexual relationship with only one woman, and that was my wife.'

'I'm sorry I had to ask.' She looked as she was going to burst into tears, but before Mr Deakin could move to her side Sarah continued.

'And was Jonathan French one of your stunts?'

'Yes, he did it for the price of a meal, but he wanted to meet you and for some reason he had never done so. That meal was the most pleasant I've had for a long time. For you had no suspicions then, and talked to me perfectly naturally.'

'But you kept putting me straight.'

'No, I made some little remarks to deflate your ego. I was never going to win you at that moment, for your views were much too entrenched.'

'How did you hear what was said in the pub that night?'

'I was there!'

'You couldn't have been!'

'But I was! I know that I wasn't invited, but I heard about it, thanks to Ms Marchbank. She had been invited and she told me. So I thought I would go and buy everyone a drink and then I could sit and watch you. But things didn't work out like that.'

'Why not?'

'Because I worked late as normal, and then the phone kept ringing and that made me later than I wanted to be. When I arrived all those fellows were surrounding you and I couldn't get near you. No one saw me and I stood behind a pillar listening. Then you told a joke, and finally that stupid idiot had you all going about virginity. Then you issued your challenge to all the males. I went shortly after, as I really can't stand drunkenness.'

'Then you reasoned that you had to send me to France.'

'Quite. I thought that a frontal attack, and excuse the pun, was out of the question, and once I'd piqued your curiosity you were determined to go. I had great pleasure in telling you not to go as I was certain that you would, though there was a moment that I thought you were about to take my advice.'

'I wish you had come clean before Venice. I had a suspicion that it was you and I wanted you to say so.'

'Perhaps I should have done. In hindsight it might have been best. But then I was never sure how much you were inclined towards me.'

'But you don't know how much I was hurt by the cabinet minister's wife! I wasn't imagining her insinuations and I feel very used.'

'Then let's go and have a meal and talk about it.'

'No, I'm too upset and confused. You have made me very angry and I just want you to go away.'

Mr Deakin stood staring at her without moving a muscle.

'Please go,' said Sarah sharply.

'I'm afraid that I don't understand, Sarah! What has gone wrong?' He creased his brow.

'Everything! How can I believe that you didn't have sex with her? I've kept myself for whoever I marry and I expected them in turn to have as much decency.' She was conscious that her voice was raised.

'But I haven't!' he said evenly as if that was the end of the matter.

'You've hurt me and used me abominably. I don't want to see you again,' said Sarah, betraying her anger.

He stared at her with a bewildered look on his face. Then he shrugged his shoulders and left the room. He was at the bottom of the stairs before she recovered her wits, and when she reached the top of the stairs the street door had closed.

Anger was her primary emotion since she had expected him to come to her and plead and cajole her into a good humour. He had misunderstood her.

She returned to the desk and slumped down. Once again she had forced him out of her life. When she had refused his offer of marriage she felt guilty for no reason other than that she had refused. Yet it had been he who had sprung it upon her. But now she had hurt him because she had wanted to and now she felt guilty for having done so. She could no longer justify her position. And she was worried because he had left so quickly. Had something snapped in him? Had he walked out of her life at that moment? She felt herself sweating and was more angry with herself than ever before. Then she wept.

It was late when she arrived back at the flat and her flatmates were on the point of going bed.

'You're late, Sar. Been anywhere interesting?'

'Only at the office.'

'Aren't you taking this managing thing a bit far?'

'No.'

'It's very late. Have you eaten?'

'No, I'm not hungry.'

'You should tell Mr Deakin that he ought to return and look after his own company.'

'He came in this evening.'

'And he's gone and sacked you!'

'No, I was angry, and rather let loose at him.'

'Oh Sar, you are so stupid!' Cathy could see that Sarah was close to tears and put an arm round her.

'I've had a horrible day, Cathy. This woman came and made me think that she and Mr Deakin had slept together, and that's why I let loose at him.'

'Did he have sex with her?'

'He says he didn't.'

'Then why not believe him?'

'I should have done.'

'So you got mad at him.'

'Yes, and I think I might have gone too far!'

'He hasn't walked out on you, has he?' Sarah could only nod. 'So what's going to happen about the job?'

'I don't know, we never spoke of it.'

'Have you decided anything between you?'

'Nothing! He just went and I was so shocked I let him go.'

'Mind you, it's a bit rich, suddenly coming in on you and hoping that everything was all hunky-dory! You were right to give him some grief – he deserved it!'

'He might have done but I shouldn't have done it.'

'Why not? You've said all along that you didn't want to get hitched. What more did he expect?'

'I should have more gentle with him.'

'You can never be too gentle with a man who wants to drape himself over you like a wet blanket.'

'Well, you've changed your tune! I thought you wanted me to marry him.'

'Of course I did, and I still think you're nuts to reject him; but if that's what you want then it's what you get. At least you're consistent. I'm off to bed.'

The following afternoon a visitor pushed her way into the office. It was someone Sarah had not wanted to meet at that time, but there she was standing on the other side of the desk with the door closed.

'Well,' said Connie, 'you are a one!'

Sarah flushed. 'What do you mean?'

'You're sitting in his office, doing his job. Do you know how much you have hurt him?'

'Have you come to tell me that?'

'I thought you ought to know.'

'I have guessed as much.'

'Why did you do it? He's given you what you wanted and he's been so pleased with you. I've never seen him so animated – until yesterday evening, when he came to us. Do you know, he was nearly in tears?'

'Well, perhaps he should have come back a bit more circumspectly. He bowls in here like someone who's never been far away, exuding the attitude that nothing has changed.'

'He was presumptuous?'

'Too right he was. I was not prepared for him.'

'Tell me what happened.'

'Yes, I'll tell you what it was about. I had a client in here yesterday afternoon who intimated that she and Philip had had a relationship.'

'Oh,' said Connie, looking slightly deflated. 'Who was that, or is it better that I don't know?'

'It was a cabinet minister's wife. Philip rewrote her book, and I thought he'd done it to get a mention in the honours list.'

'Good for Philip!'

'What – you would approve of that?'

'It's not the best way to do it, but does it really matter how you do it?'

'Yes, but that's beside the point; after she spoke to me I thought he had done it for her.'

'So what explanation did he give?'

'That he had had no relationship with her.'

'I'm not an authority on Philip's sexual proclivities, but I would have said that he was as straight as they come, and given the way he talks about you it really is inconceivable that he would look at another woman.'

'What has he said about me?'

'He glows about you and hasn't a bad word to say. I never thought after he lost Caroline and Tamzin that he would look at another woman, let alone find love. You won't know, but you've transformed him.'

'That's embarrassing.'

'Why? If you had seen him over the last few years, as Curzon and I have, you'd be very pleased for him. Could you not find it in yourself to put him back where he was?'

'What do mean?'

'Well, give him some hope... at least be good friends.'

'I can try. But usually if people have fallen out it's better that they don't see each other.'

'I don't believe that's the situation. My understanding of it is that Philip has not courted you sufficiently. He has seen plenty of you, as one who is in love, but for you it's a novel idea. No, he should have taken you out and dined you. Instead he's left you festering in his office. Now the question is, what is to be done about it?'

'I don't know, I've not given it any thought.'

'Well, Curzon and I are going to the opera on Thursday evening; we would like you to come with us.'

'Will he be there?'

'It's not up to you to worry about that. We would like to you to join us.'

'I'm not sure...'

'No, let me rephrase that. I would very much appreciate it if you joined us on Thursday evening. The opera is *Carmen*, by the way.'

'I can't refuse that,' said Sarah. 'Yes, I would love to go! Thank you.'

Connie brightened up. 'Well, that's settled then. It's at the Coliseum; come at 7.25 p.m. and I'll meet you at the door.'

Sarah stood up and said, 'Then I'll see you on Thursday evening.'

Connie moved to the door. Sarah followed to hold the door

open but Connie turned and allowed their eyes to meet. 'Cheer up,' she said and reached out and gave Sarah a hug. 'You know, we all have our ups and downs. The trick is to have more ups than downs.'

Sarah managed a weak smile and watched Connie descend the stairs to the door. Her mind was made up and she went back into the office.

The Opera

At ten minutes past seven Sarah stood on the north side of Trafalgar Square outside the National Portrait Gallery. The opera house was less than five minutes' walk away yet she was early. She rued the perversity the railway system. When you needed the train to hurry it invariably arrived late, or the connection to the Underground delayed, leaving barely enough time to get your engagement. Yet when one wanted to arrive at a specific time and a few minutes of tardiness was quite acceptable, the trains excelled themselves. Having timed her journey to arrive at 7.20 p.m., both the train to Waterloo and the Underground to Charing Cross had come with perfect timing, and she now had to stand around for fifteen minutes before making her entrance. She felt very exposed leaning against the iron railings and she knew she looked strikingly feminine, having spent most of the day in her preparations.

She had never spent so much on an outfit. Then she had decided on a new coat, and had finished up buying everything she needed for the evening. The new shoes pinched a little and she felt guilty, never having worn 2½-inch high heels before. That afternoon she had spent at the hairdresser's, and this time she had not had a cheap tidy-up cut but had indulged herself with a restyle and the full treatment. She had left home feeling very confident, but waiting outside in the street was unnerving, and the looks she was getting were sapping her morale.

Young men walked past and leered at her and she found it very upsetting. They must think that she was some sort of loose woman, and she wondered what to say if she was confronted. A group of young men across the road whistled and Sarah knew that it was for her. She was glad of the fast moving traffic between them, for it kept her unwelcome admirers on the opposite side of the road.

A young woman moved close to her, leaning against the railings as well. She gave Sarah a nervous smile and moved closer still.

'Are you waiting for someone?' she asked Sarah.

'Yes,' replied Sarah, 'and I hope he arrives soon.'

'Me too,' said the girl. 'I think it's the last time I'll arrange to meet him like this.'

'I know what you mean, especially when they all seem to be drunk.'

'I'm glad it's not later, I'm sure it gets worse as the evening gets on.'

'I would think so. Are you going to a show?'

'Yes, in the Haymarket, and we're going on to a disco afterwards. Where are you going?'

'The opera at the Coliseum. It's *Carmen*.'

'Oh,' said the girl, as if it made a lot of sense to her. 'Look, here he comes with his mates.' She waved at a group of young people and was off with the briefest of goodbyes. The girl's friends all looked at Sarah and made admiring kinds of noises. Sarah felt sorry for the girl, for she was good-looking, and it seemed so wrong of the men not to give their compliments to her. Indeed their words were demeaning to her, just as they were demeaning to Sarah as the recipient. How strange that a girl should spend hours on her make-up and buy fashionable clothes just to go out with men who were so unworthy.

Sarah resumed her thoughts since there was still eight minutes before she needed to go. She was certain that Philip Deakin would be there. Connie had tried to make it sound as if she had been invited to join just her and Curzon, but her body language had suggested someone who was barely suppressing excitement. No, he would be there! And she wanted to meet him. She almost hoped that he didn't want to return to his business and that during his absence he had found other avenues that took his attention. She had discovered to her satisfaction that she enjoyed running the business and that it had taken her mind off him. He was right when he said that had he been around it would not have been the same, for she would always have been referring things to him and never making decisions for herself. He had been in the background, and though she felt it had been an intrusion she had noted that none of her decisions had been overturned. She had been miffed at first having paid the printer so much of her money but gradually she had seen the reason for it, as she could sit in the managing director's chair, and if her decisions were bad it put her money at risk! And had anyone tried to challenge her assumed position she could demonstrate her superiority. No, she had known he was in the background when the bank mandate arrived. At first she was vexed that he was looking over her shoulder, as if she were a little girl who needed help; but then she appreciated it, for it allowed her access to the company's money and she had been able to run the business properly.

She smiled ruefully to herself. She would have to stop thinking of him as her boss, if she now saw herself as his equal. And she still thought of him as 'Mr Deakin', though she realised that she now ought to call him by his Christian name, Philip.

But now he was close she found that she missed him.

It was now 7.25 p.m. exactly and she turned towards the opera house with some trepidation. The pedestrian crossing held her up but she had allowed for it. Once across, it was two minutes' walk to the doors.

Sarah stood in the foyer, as it was there that she was due to meet with Connie. Then she saw her and smiled, for Connie had looked past her. But she caught her eye and soon Connie was smiling with pleasure.

'I love your hair,' she enthused, 'you look stunning!'

Sarah smiled back; she hoped very much that she looked stunning, for if she didn't then it was all a waste of money and two hours at the hairdresser's; and that evening she wanted more than anything to be seen as a woman.

Connie gave her quick hug.

'We must hurry,' she said heading the stairs, 'for they are about to start.' And she looked as if she were about to start running. Sarah smiled; the last few weeks had changed her, and she was not going to hurry. Connie glared at her for her more leisurely pace, but as they passed the door to the auditorium they could see that the opera had not started. Sarah felt that there was plenty of time. The door to the box was hardly any distance away and the time saved was not worth bothering about, and Sarah had no intention of entering the box out of breath and sweating profusely. Apart from that, she felt it was embarrassing to be seen running.

'Do hurry,' urged Connie.

'But we won't miss much of a three-hour opera,' Sarah protested.

'That's not the point.'

'I ought to go to the ladies' room,' said Sarah provocatively.

'You haven't time,' gasped Connie.

'But suppose my hair is out of place?'

'It isn't.'

'What about my make-up?'

'That's fine, and anyway you don't use that much.'

'I don't want to appear like someone who has been rushing.'

'Here we are,' said Connie, reaching a door in the cloth-covered wall. She was forced to wait for Sarah.

'Don't go in yet!' Sarah hissed. 'I want to be sure I look all right.'

She pulled a mirror from her bag and stared into it and was conscious as she did so that it was a gesture that was alien to her. Never in her life had she bothered to check her make-up, and she put it down to her nerves. She wanted to look her best for him and she did not want him to think that she had come straight out of the office and popped in at the opera house in a casual manner. She wanted to create an impression and she wanted him to be impressed. She had disappointed him for a second time and she was not going to do it for a third. He had been angry after her refusal in Venice, yet he had wanted to make her a partner in his business. Now she was worried that he might take it all back and want her to sit at her old desk. And she was conscious that somehow she had to thank him for his generosity.

Sarah pushed the mirror back into her bag and pulled out something else.

'Now what?' said Connie.

'It's a bracelet I bought it in Paris. Philip hasn't seen it yet.'

'Do come on,' hissed Connie.

'All right, let's go in,' said Sarah, feeling her heart pounding away.

Connie seemed to be running the evening, and she now had the door open. Sarah went through. Before her was the rail around the front of the box with the auditorium opening out

343

beyond. The two men were standing waiting for her. Curzon was closer, and he took a step forward to greet her with a large smile on his face.

Sarah held out her hand to him, which he grasped, but instead of shaking it as Sarah expected he carried her hand to his lips.

'You look wonderful,' he breathed, 'if I wasn't married, I'd be running after you myself.'

Sarah blushed at such a compliment. Connie looked decidedly pained, and Sarah felt the evening had already deviated from her well-laid plans. Curzon still held her hand as if he were unwilling to let it go. Philip Deakin was standing behind Curzon with a stern look on his face, like someone who didn't know what to expect from the evening. Sarah was sure that he was acting under Connie's orders.

She looked from Curzon's face to Philip's face. He had managed a slight smile and waited for his cue that he might greet her. Giving Connie a nervous glance, he stepped forward and took the hand that Curzon had released. Unlike Curzon he did not kiss her hand but shook it gently and then released it. It occurred to Sarah that the two men were like little boys who had been ordered to be on their best behaviour on an outing or else they would not get their ice cream at the end of it! Connie, she decided, had had a few words with her boss and cowed him into submission. Clearly she was worried that the potential lovers might find more to fall out over, and she was going to ration their intimacy for a bit. Philip stepped back from Sarah, but she noticed that his eyes did not leave her face.

'Now,' said Connie in her best schoolmistress voice, 'Sarah, you sit at this end and I'll sit beside you, with Curzon to my right and Philip on the end.'

Her time behind her boss's desk had taught Sarah to sum up a situation very quickly, and she had found that one's first impressions were rarely wrong. She did not want Connie assuming leadership of their little group. It was not something she resented; she just felt that Connie was treating them all as children and not grown men and women. The two men had yielded to her entreaties and it was all right for them. They could go and have a laugh about it later but for her it was not so easy.

'No,' said Sarah, 'I'd like to sit at the other end with Philip beside me.' She hoped she had spoken regally and there would be no argument.

Curzon caught her eye. His eyes brightened and his smile had broadened. At the corners of his mouth there was a slight tremor.

'Of course, Sarah,' he said, and moved to the chair that Connie indicated was for her. Philip moved his seat, leaving the far seat vacant. Connie's arrangement had left Sarah as far as possible from Philip, and had she wanted to say anything to him she would have had to reach across Connie, who had wanted to be the centre of everything. Perhaps in the second half Philip would have moved a seat nearer, and in the third part – for it was a long opera – if Connie felt that all was well she might have allowed the lovers to sit together; probably, guessed Sarah, with Connie on one end and Curzon on the other. Sarah smiled to herself, for the thought came to her that it would be akin to a gooseberry sandwich. Connie was going to be very miffed about it all; but she, Sarah, had come with different plans.

Sarah moved to the end seat and sat down. Remembering that she was wearing a skirt she brushed it down and found some pleasure in seeing her knees sticking out before her. It was perhaps the first time in her life that she had felt so feminine and found real pleasure in the sensation. Having arranged herself she took in her surroundings. The seat was positioned with a good view of the stage, which was almost straight in front her. To her right and behind was the vastness of the auditorium. Below her were the stalls and behind were the dress circle and upper balcony, with hardly a vacant seat in the house. However, there was little time to survey the scene, as the lights dimmed and a hush descended on the audience. Then a man dressed in black stepped down to the orchestral pit and the people at the front started clapping, for it was the conductor. He gave the briefest of bows to the audience and got the entertainment under way.

The novelty of the situation gripped Sarah and she felt great pleasure as the familiar strains of the overture rose up from the orchestra pit. Bizet's music seemed to gather pace and then the curtains opened on the first scene. For a time she was entranced by it all, but once the Habanera was over her thoughts turned more to the reason why she was there that evening. She stole a glance at Mr Deakin's face silhouetted by the stage lights. He seemed absorbed by the opera and had his serious air about him, but he became conscious that he was being looked at, and turned slightly towards her. He smiled reassuringly and then turned back to the opera. Sarah was impressed with the effectiveness of Connie's strictures. Mr Deakin was following her script admirably.

However, Sarah had not come that evening with the sole intention of having pleasure. She had come specifically to meet with Philip Deakin. She had no plans about what she was going to say, but she knew what she had to achieve. Since returning from Italy she had become aware that in giving him a negative answer it had hurt her. Naturally it had hurt him and she had not wanted to cause him pain; but proposals of marriage do tend to produce one of two reactions, depending on the answer. Having fled from him, she had felt alone on the flight and alone in the office. She had assumed that once in the midst of her friends any attachment that she felt for her boss would have disappeared. Yet the effect of being back in familiar surroundings among the faces she knew was the opposite, and the more she had thought about things the more she had felt that she had made a great mistake. Her loneliness had increased; her sense of attachment did not go away. She wished she had stayed with him for the rest of the week in Venice and sorted everything out. But she was grateful to him for recognising her needs, and she could see that it was why he had been quite benevolent over her disloyalty. It had told him of her determination and ambition, and he had responded to that. And now he probably had no idea where he stood with her. Of course, her entrance had given him some idea, but Connie had left him under a constraint of testing her affections. So it was down to her! She had to tell him of her real affections. But with Connie so close, Sarah felt trapped. She could do very little, and she also felt that she didn't yet want to give Connie the satisfaction of a perfectly orchestrated evening.

Sarah looked down and saw that Mr Deakin's hand was on the arm of his chair. She would have liked him to reach out and touch her but was aware that it was unlikely to happen. Perhaps if

Connie and Curzon were not there he might, but they were and Connie had put a restraint on him. Should she touch him? It seemed a momentous thought, and she could only sit back and muse over it. It went with her other thoughts that she owed him something, and she wanted to touch him. She reached out gently and slid her forefinger underneath his little finger and had the satisfaction of feeling him start. But he seemed to understand, and after giving her a quick look had resumed staring at the stage with the slightest of smiles on his face. She played with his little finger and then felt his third finger join in. After a while he intertwined his fingers with hers and held them still. The feelings it engendered Sarah had never experienced before. Her arm tingled with sensation and her whole body responded – and as for where the opera was, she had completely lost track. She hoped it was the same for him.

Suddenly the orchestra was into the finale, and with élan brought the first part to a stunning conclusion. It was time to clap, and they both released their hands to applaud as the curtain closed. The lights came up and people moved towards the doors to find refreshment.

Curzon leaned across and said to Sarah, 'There's no hurry, ours is booked and waiting for us.'

Mr Deakin stepped away, allowing Sarah to pass, and she guessed that he understood the game she was playing with Connie. Connie was looking at both of them, trying to work out what was going on between them; but she must have concluded that it was very little and resumed the leadership of their group.

The refreshment area was only a few steps from the box and Sarah suddenly realised that a waiter was showing them to a small table on which there was an ice bucket with a bottle of champagne.

'I hope there's no cause for celebration,' said Sarah.

'No, I just choose champagne because I like it,' said Connie. She placed herself to one side of Sarah and Curzon stood on the other. Sarah thought the idea was to keep Philip Deakin at arm's length, yet it allowed him to stand opposite and look at her. And though he gave the impression that he was looking at the ground, his eyes were taking in the whole of her body. It thrilled Sarah to think that he might be enjoying her but he showed no sign, except he had relaxed with a smile hovering on his lips.

Connie must have told him to say nothing and she took it upon herself to run the conversation. Since it was mostly about the opera, Sarah found that she could not add much, as her mind had been occupied elsewhere. Philip remained silent, confirming that his mind was hardly on the opera either. Curzon kept nodding and agreeing with his wife. His actions were akin to winding up a clockwork motor, for Connie continued, regardless of anyone's finer feelings.

But suddenly a bell sounded and Curzon spread the last of the champagne around. Having finished that, they began to make their way back to their seats. Curzon moved forward and offered Sarah his arm. She could not refuse and Philip could not take offence, though it left him to offer his arm to Connie, who suddenly seemed to have something in her shoe. Curzon, seeing his wife delayed, continued and when they were out of earshot said, 'Is everything all right?'

'Yes,' said Sarah, 'it's a lovely evening. Thank you so much for inviting me.'

'Thank you for your kind words,' he replied with his characteristic little bow, 'but what I mean is: is everything between you and Philip all right?'

'What do you think?'

'But the pair of you haven't said a word all evening.'

'Well, we're rather being watched, aren't we?'

'This is true, but Philip is very quiet tonight.'

'I think he's under orders not to say much.'

'True! You are so observant, Sarah. I told Connie to let the pair of you get on with it, but she wouldn't have it.' He glanced behind at his wife. 'My guess is that she's giving Philip another lecture.'

'Well, you will be able to see if we get any closer in the second part.'

'Yes, well... I'm not looking for that.'

'What are you looking for?'

'To be honest with you, Sarah, I think you and Philip would make a super couple.'

'Curzon – you make it sound as if I'm about to run away!'
'Connie would worry about something like that.'
'But you're not far behind.'
'Yes, these things get so aired that it does get to one.'
'If it is any consolation, Curzon, I am working to a positive conclusion. I have worked it out that I want to continue in my present position; there are certain things that are required of me. Don't tell Connie what I've just told you.'
'Why not?'
'I want to tease her a little bit more. She will forgive me.'
'They say that women will rule the world in the future and there will be no place in it for men, but my guess is that women will never get it together because between them there's too much jealousy!'

He led her to her seat and Sarah sat down. She smiled at him and he grinned back, suddenly looking very boyish. Philip Deakin and Connie came into the box. Connie was clearly not too happy about where they were all going to sit, but with Sarah already seated she gave up the struggle to have everyone where she wanted them to be.

Philip leaned over to Sarah as he went to sit down and whispered, 'I've been told to try and talk to you more.'

Sarah smiled at him aware that Connie watching was her but that she could not see whether Mr Deakin was speaking to her or not. Then the lights dimmed and they all settled back for the second part of the evening's entertainment. Philip's arm hung down by his chair and Sarah slid her hand slowly down his arm until she found his hand and then they spent ten minutes playing with each other's fingers. The second part was shorter than the first and it seemed to be over rather quickly. They returned for some more refreshment, but this time it was Connie who fell in beside Sarah.

'Is everything all right?' she hissed.
'Yes,' said Sarah.
'But you've hardly said a word to each other; in fact I haven't yet heard you say anything to him.'
'Do you think I've dressed all right?'
'Don't try to change the subject! But I've never seen you look so good.'

'Does he like my outfit?'

'I haven't asked.'

'But what did you talk about when you came back to the box earlier?'

'Oh, er... I've forgotten.'

'And I wanted to look stunning for him, and he hasn't even noticed.'

'No, no, I'm sure he's noticed; we were talking about other things.'

A pot of coffee with a plate of sandwiches awaited them. The conversation was even more stilted, and though Connie tried, it was an uphill battle. Sarah wanted to speak to Philip and he with her. Curzon was trying to hint to his wife that she was in the way of the couple.

At last it seemed that Connie was prepared to throw in the towel.

'You will have to excuse me,' she said suddenly, 'a call of nature.'

She turned to her husband and made some gesture before disappearing out of the door. It seemed that he was to stand over them.

Curzon glanced after her. 'I'm afraid,' he said, 'that I will have to follow my wife's example. Can you look after yourselves?' He went without waiting for a reply.

Philip took a step towards Sarah and took her hand.

'I hope you're not teasing me!'

'No, I've come tonight to say that I should never have doubted you.'

He stood even closer.

'I wanted to make you angry the other day and I wanted you to fight me.'

'I didn't think, Sarah, that you gave way to such basic instincts.'

'It was due to severe provocation.'

'Then I'm sorry too.'

'No, you don't have to be, Philip. I just want you to kiss me.'

'I'm sure that I can oblige there.' He gave her a crushing embrace and then released her.

'I asked you a question, Sarah, some time back, and my affections and resolve are unaltered. Are you likely to change your mind?'

'Yes, Philip, I have changed my mind and if your offer was still open I'd say yes to it right now!'

'You will marry me!'

'Yes, if you want me to.'

'There's nothing I want more.' He glanced at the door and pulled something from his pocket. 'I've carried the ring with me ever since... Can I put it on?'

'Please do,' she replied and held out her hand. He found her finger and slipped it on.

'They'll be back any minute,' she said. 'Did you see that I am wearing the bracelet you bought me in Paris?'

'Yes. Are we going to continue teasing Connie?'

'I want to, because she's treated both of us like little children. But it would be better if we told her, then we could sit closer.'

Curzon came in first.

'How is everything?' he asked looking at his two friends standing a yard apart. 'I thought you might have wanted to be alone for a bit. Connie is just behind me, she was caught up in the press by the Ladies.'

Connie came in. 'This has not been much of a party with your two glum faces! I had hoped that you might have spoken a bit to each other by now, and at least been civil.'

Sarah had kept her hand with the ring on it out of sight. 'Well, actually Connie, we have had a few words.'

'Doubtless you wish to continue to torture me with your infighting.'

'No, we've taken the negotiations further than that. Look!' Sarah pulled her hand out from her side and showed Connie the ring on her finger. Connie shot a quick glance at Philip and saw that a smile lurked on his lips.

'Oh, you pair of teases! But let me be the first to congratulate you.' She reached forward and grasped Sarah in an embrace. 'I'm so pleased for you. When we first met you, Sarah, I knew you were just right for Philip and I so much wanted you both to get together.'

Curzon stepped forward and added his congratulations to his wife's.

'What gives me the greatest pleasure,' he said, 'is that Connie can now stop worrying me about it all.'

The bell for the final part of the performance sounded. They returned to their box, where Philip moved their seats close together. They sat down with his arm around her and she leaning slightly towards him. Once the lights had gone down and the music started Sarah sat back giving half an ear to the music while feeling the ring on her finger and every now and then looking at him. He would become conscious of her gaze and look back at her. She could not doubt the depth of Philip's love and felt slightly in awe of him. Despite her caprice he had not deviated and let himself become resentful. He had maintained hope and continued to carry a ring on his person in the hope of an opportunity to give it to her.

Mr Deakin brought his other hand across to find her hand and on taking it felt for the ring on her finger. Once he found it, it seemed to reassure him, and he took her fingers in his hand. She gently rubbed the back of his hand, feeling his warm skin and brushing the small hairs that adorned it. The pleasure she had felt earlier was still there.

For once she was glad when the opera finished, and rose with everyone to clap simply because it was over. In the street Curzon phoned to find out where his chauffeured car was. Ten minutes later it drew alongside them. Curzon took the front seat and Sarah found herself sitting between Philip and Connie.

Twenty minutes later they drew up by the house in Earlsfield. Philip got out to hold the door for her. Sarah moved to the door and turned to Connie.

'I must thank you for this evening, in fact it is something I shall never stop thanking you for.'

On the pavement she faced her boss.

'I'm loath to let you out of my sight,' he said.

'I know, but I'm a modern woman. Trust me!'

'I have,' he grinned, 'with my company!'

'Tomorrow evening at six – I want to be taken out for dinner.'

'Just the two of us?'

'Just the two of us!'

They kissed, and when he released her she went to the front door and let herself in. Mr Deakin was still standing at the gate watching her. She gave him a little wave and closed the door.

Cathy and Gerrie were still up when she arrived in the sitting room.

'How did your evening go? Was he suitably impressed?'

'I think so,' said Sarah, 'because he gave me this.' She showed them the ring.

'Oh look, Gerrie! Sarah's taken the plunge.'

'And for a person who swore she would never do it she really has let the side down.'

'Don't be rotten,' said Cathy. 'I'm really pleased for you, Sarah. I just wish Charles would do that for me.'

Two for Dinner

At 4.50 p.m. the following evening Philip arrived at the office. Sarah was preoccupied with Emma, sorting out the last of her work that afternoon and ensuring that she had work to start with on the Monday morning, and she was not aware of him until he was standing beside her. It was a perfectly natural thing to swap a kiss in the office, even though it was in front of Emma.

'Can I have one?' asked the girl of her boss. Her manner was such that it did not annoy but Sarah turned to her.

'You would get one if you wore that.' She held out her hand with the ring on it, having managed to keep it from everyone for the whole day.

'Are you really engaged?' squeaked the girl. 'Are you engaged to Mr Deakin?'

'What do you think?'

'Well, congratulations! I must go and tell Clemmie!' She scrambled out of the office.

'Haven't you told anyone?' asked Philip.

'No,' said Sarah, 'I told my flatmates, because I could not avoid it, but I didn't know what to say to people in the office. It seemed a bit like boasting, but I was going to tell them as they left this evening.'

Ms Marchbank marched in. 'What is this that Emma's talking about?'

'We're going to get married,' said Sarah.

Ms Marchbank shot a look at Mr Deakin, who grinned sheepishly and said, 'It's quite true.'

The news deflated her somewhat and Sarah thought that there was a tear in her eye, but she collected herself and said, 'I must congratulate you both, I do hope you will be very happy.' She left the room immediately.

'You do know that she fancied me,' said Philip. 'She saw herself as my wife and has done for quite a long time.'

Sarah grimaced. 'I should have seen it coming.'

'Possibly, but she sees herself as more of a mother to me, and thinks ironing my shirts perfectly would be a virtue. She would look after me wonderfully, but with one thing missing.'

'How do you know?'

'I never thought that your imagination was deficient.'

'But you think I can.'

He smiled at her. 'I have no doubts there.'

'There's a touch of arrogance.'

'No, people don't get this far in a relationship if they know the other person is incapable.'

'But I might be frigid.'

'You might be, but I don't think so... though I must remember to call you by your real name next time.'

The office had finally emptied as everyone left for home and their weekend. Sarah was remained behind with Philip.

'Are you happy with what you're doing?' he ventured.

'Very,' she replied. 'I do hope you're not going to terminate my contract.'

'No, seeing you work so hard is much better punishment! But seriously, we have to decide where we're going.'

'You seem to have thought about it.'

'Well, an Internet connection through to the house attached to a workstation there would seem logical.'

'For what purpose?'

'I could work at home, or you could work at home in the evening rather than spending hours down here.'

'I had hoped that we could share the load.'

'Me too, but all too often I ended up working until nine o'clock.'

'But you had nothing to go home for.'

'True – but how awful if I had. And what about you? I only mention it because it would make things more flexible for both of us. For instance, suppose you want Wednesdays off so that you could go shopping and have your hair done, you could at least see what was happening in the office from home if you wanted to.'

'All right then, I take your point.'

'Where do you see the business going?'

'I haven't thought about it,' said Sarah.

'I was wondering about moving into another area of publishing and expanding gently at a controlled rate. That would leave you with the day-to-day running, roughly what you are doing now, and me overseeing the expansion.'

'That sounds reasonable.'

'We can only expand within the constraints of our present finances.'

'That's settled then, partner.'

'In more ways than one.' He drew her to him and kissed her passionately.

After a time she withdrew, saying, 'Let's go for the meal.'

'We have time for a show afterwards.'

'Possibly.'

They sat at a table in a small restaurant just off Piccadilly.

'I didn't know what to expect at the theatre last night,' said Philip. 'Dear Connie had laced into me and made me quite nervous of the meeting.'

'I did notice. She treated both of us as little children.'

'She was frightened I was going to make some loud demonstration to win you.'

'I thought so too.'

'She had arranged it that you sat with her on one end and I was on the other, and she was only going to let us move closer together if we looked as if we might be civil together. Curzon was in on the plot too. We were both on tenterhooks waiting for Connie to bring you in.'

'Why?'

'Because I didn't know what to expect. I know what I was hoping for, but after our previous meeting I didn't know how to cope with your anger. And when you came! Well, you've always been good-looking, though your trouser suits are somewhat unflattering, but you were wonderful last night.'

'I made a big mistake last night! I waited outside in Trafalgar Square and I must have been the object of every creep that went past.'

'And I'm thinking to myself, Is that really the woman I'm desperate to marry?'

'Curzon looked as if his eyes were going to pop out of his head.'

'But I had another odd thought when I saw you, and it crossed my mind that you had come to utterly devastate my emotions and my life – with the added irony that you were dressed up to the nines!'

'You didn't see yourself as a victim, did you?'

'No, but after the anger you had displayed, and Connie's strictures, I thought it best to keep silent and see what was going to happen.'

'She had both of you under her thumb. You were just like two little boys out for a treat.'

'I know. That's exactly what it felt like, and they say that women are the weaker sex! But you should have seen Connie's face when you said you were going to sit by me.'

'I saw Curzon's, and his expression said it all. I wanted to tease Connie a bit.'

'When I felt that you weren't playing with me I still didn't dare look at you.'

'Connie was afraid of us having another row.'

'Sarah, I thought I'd lost you, after you were so angry with me.'

'Weren't you hurt about the business?'

'Very, but that would have run its course. I couldn't see why you were angry; it was so unreasonable.'

'It's a bit of a story. Do you remember me telling you about my views on life and that I thought we as human beings were meant to rise above natural instincts and animal behaviour?'

'Yes.'

'I allowed my animal instincts to take over! I was angry, very angry. I wanted you to beat down my objections, to fight for me, even holding me against the wall and insisting you had done no such thing. And then I wanted to yield to you.'

'You wanted to feel guilty!'

'Yes, because I did in Venice, and I should not have done. After I had refused your proposal I felt very guilty, but I reasoned that I should not have done. I had been led to some extent into a trap, and by refusing you, I had hurt you and slighted your manhood. I didn't see why I should feel guilty when I had done nothing. Then I got home and my flatmates declared that I was totally stupid. If they'd been in my position with a man of money and means, they would have had no hesitation in accepting. That made me feel jealous, and I felt that really whatever my position I did at least have first refusal on you.'

'But you had refused me!'

'I could still grasp at straws until the time came when you wanted nothing more to do with me. And I really thought Ms Marchbank giving me written warnings was your doing. But there was a meanness behind them that was unlike you. Anyway, I was miserable and only bucked up a bit when I started taking your calls. Ms Marchbank seemed happy to let the office run down. After you tricked me into putting money into the company I felt it was a terrific compliment to get a chequebook, and I also knew that you were around keeping an eye on things. But then that woman Mrs Cudman came in and insinuated that you and she had had a relationship! I was so angry with her I could have scratched her eyes out – I've never known a feeling like it.'

'I'll tell you about her. She did actually try it on with me shortly before I finished her book, and it left me wishing I'd never rewritten it. But did you read the part where she found the couple in the greenhouse having sex? In the book she mentioned it and states that she promptly left them to it! She told me that this was not, in fact, the case. This is all confidential, of course! But she joined in and the three of them had sex together! Before I could catch my breath she offered me the use of her body straight out!'

'What did she say?'

'"Philip," she said, for she had found out my name, "I am available if you want me!"'

'Just like that!'

'Brazen! I really felt that I should have binned her book, but I didn't have the heart to as I had put so much into it.'

'Well, she implied that you had taken up her offer, and it made me very angry. I have never felt emotions like it before. You were my man, and I didn't want another woman to touch you! And after she had gone I seemed to become more angry with you, as it seemed so ironic that having determined never to get married I had changed my mind, only to find that the goods were damaged.'

'I suppose it's how one would feel when buying a new car only to find that the garage had dented it. Did your anger last until I turned up?'

'That was bad timing, for she came earlier in the afternoon and I was simmering. I never thought it through, and when you came in, well, I simply boiled over! But it was odd, because I was so angry and I felt out of control, yet I knew what I was doing. I wanted you to be angry with me. I wanted you to defend yourself against my accusations. I wanted you, in a way, to punish me, because it was unrighteous of me and I felt properly guilty this time and I deserved everything you gave me. You see I wanted you to dominate me and have your way! But you just walked out.'

'Sorry, I'm a bit mild mannered.'

'No, that's not the point. Your reaction had little to do with it! The point is I've never been so subject to basic animal responses before. I thought I was above them. I thought I was immune to such things.'

'Did you think you had lost me at that moment?'

'I wasn't sure, but I did know that when we met again it was up to me, and I had no idea when or how that was to come about.'

'You have to thank Connie for that.'

'I know, and I've been very mean to her, but I'll try and make it up.'

'I shouldn't worry. In many ways you have.'

'What, by taking you on?'

'Yes, from the moment she first met you she decided that we were well suited.'

'So how much of Venice do you remember?'

'I remember what happened almost to the point where I was hit, but I don't remember that. I came round and told you off and then everything is hazy. But I gather I spent the night in your bed. How come I had nothing on?'

'I took your clothes off to cool you down.'

'Why? Was the air conditioning not working?'

'I didn't know it had air conditioning.'

'There was a switch by the door.'

'Oh dear…'

'Anyway, in the morning I couldn't manage anything and left you and went back to my hotel.'

'You remembered where that was, then.'

'Habit, I've always stayed at that one and I just knew that I was in the wrong hotel. I felt a little better in the afternoon and I had to go through with what I'd planned. I wish I hadn't now, but I did not appreciate how much I had hurt you. And I realised later that I deserved what you said to me at the airport.'

'Did you think I might have resigned by the time you got back?'

'Yes, I did, and when I phoned Jonathan I found that he had been to the office and had words with you. I was so relieved that you had not resigned and he gave me reason to hope. Then I conceived the idea of getting you to run the business. I didn't know what you'd done with Keith and Clive. I thought I might persuade a few thousand out of you but when you came up with £20,000 I knew that you hadn't given them the money.'

'Were they starting a business?'

'I think so. You would have had to work pretty hard at it for very little reward.'

'Were they getting at you?'

'I don't think so, though you would have known most of my authors, and anyone in your position would have to go to them. Clive might have seen you as a wasted asset, but then he was always a ladies' man.'

'How did you come to be in business with them?'

'They worked for my father, who started the business back in the fifties. He got a cheap lease on the office. They were working for him when he died. I came back from Italy and took over the business. They showed me what to do! So I made them equal partners, but then they got too big for their boots and decided to break the business into three. By then Clive did all the client liaison, Keith ran the office and I was the dogsbody. Had we stayed together I think it would be a very large business today.'

'Don't you think that they are partly responsible for Caroline's accident?'

'You may be right, but it's not in my nature to shift blame like that.'

'Why weren't either of them able to make a go of it?'

'They didn't put enough effort into it. Clive thought he could hire people to do the donkey work but they ran him out of money before there was anything to show for it. Keith made a better stab at it, but so far as I know he took too much money out without reinvesting any.'

'So where did your talent lie?'

'Easy! It was in guessing how many of one title one was going to sell. Keith always overestimated. Clive never had a clue. I suppose it was the one thing I got off my father. He told me what did and did not make a good book, and he didn't pass that on to many people.'

'What made you think I could do it?'

'Nothing, really, except you are a very level-headed and capable person. Of the three books you've sent to the printers, you ordered about the number I'd have done. If you hadn't, I'd have got John Bashley to nudge you, but I didn't have to.'

'You trusted me, then.'

'Certainly! You could have run off with the cash flow and that would have been embarrassing... but you'd have to marry me to see my real assets.'

'So you had better tell me something of yourself.'

'I went to the same boarding school as Curzon, and we were the best of friends. Do you know who he is?'

'No.'

'He's actually an hereditary peer! His father never bothered with his seat in the House of Lords and Curzon was looking forward to taking it up. His father had been ill for many years and could have gone at any time over the last ten years, but he died ten days before they removed the hereditary peers from the House. Curzon never took his seat, and was naturally amongst those cast out.'

'Why did you employ me in the first place?'

'You were good-looking, you carried yourself well and I liked your voice.'

'That's not a very good reason to employ someone.'

'No, but it helps. I was pleased that someone like yourself wanted a job with me.'

'Why didn't you ask me out before then?'

'The one way to scare a woman away from a job is for the boss to start coming on to her the day after she starts. I didn't at the time want a relationship, and it was last Christmas when you were mentioned to me.'

'Who was that?'

'Curzon. I had told him and Connie about you when I employed you and casually said that if I ever married again it would be to someone like you. We were having a glass of port after a wonderful Christmas dinner when he asked what I had done about you. It set me thinking, but I had learned from Ms Marchbank quite a bit about you. According to her you were haughty, self-centred and held feminist views. She had found out your views on marriage and the opposite sex, so I knew that to approach you straight out was risky. I didn't really know what to do until you had a go at me one day and called me sad; but I took what you said to heart and tried to smile more. Then I rebuked you rather severely and I worried about it for some time. Later I devised the restaurant ploy, and that went off really well. You were so natural and didn't suspect anything. It was the most enjoyable evening I've had for years.'

'You teasing me was the only bit I did not like! Why didn't you ask me out after that?'

'Because I still felt that you would have bitten my head off. I wanted to and I nearly did, but the pub had shown how necessary it was to be circumspect. When you threw out the challenge, I had to pick it up. I thought that it was the first chink in your armour, because if nothing else I could claim that I tried.'

'I didn't expect anyone to pick up the challenge, and before I looked at them they would have to be better than Clive.'

'Was I?'

'Not then; but later, as I got to know you, you were. But remember, it was Clive who made me look at older men.'

'I don't think I shall be thanking him. It was clear that I had to do something for you, and that's when I devised the trip to Paris. I knew the manager at the hotel so it was easy to set up, including buying the bracelet.'

'Oh? How did you manage to keep a straight face at the time?'

'A certain amount of luck. I actually didn't know what you had purchased; I only knew the amount, so when you said it was a ring I went along with that. Later I read the bill and then I knew what you were playing at.'

'What happened with Amsterdam?'

'There, the hotel I was going to use had changed management and they didn't want to know. Then this Dutch friend suggested some friends of his and they were the people you met. With Cathy going, I could only hope for the best. The Dutch friend phoned me to tell me what had happened and I told him just to get on with it. I gave them a painting in the end for their effort. And as for your "F" theory, that was merely coincidental, I was wondering just how many of the letters of the alphabet could have been used in the same fashion. Now, the theatre was something of shock, because you were so honest with Connie and Curzon! After you gave them your opinion of me I didn't dare reveal myself to you. Connie stuck up for you saying that it was perfectly true! So it had to be Venice, and that was such an awful weekend I wished I had never sent you!'

'But I guessed it was you just before you kissed me in the office.'

'Why didn't you say something?'

'I felt so guilty about trying to ruin your business. I must have stood in your office and felt every emotion it is possible to have all at the same moment.'

'I thought I was taking a risk touching and kissing you.'

'I've never let a man do that to me before. But you see, I hoped it was not going to be you I met in Venice. And when that man spoke to me I was just so pleased that I got carried away. What would you have done if you hadn't found us?'

'I'm not sure. I would have been very hurt, and my instincts would have been to cast you aside, but then I felt partly responsible for your predicament. I think after a period of reflection I would have offered to marry you but I expect I would have had to do it on the basis of wealth and connections and so forth. I want you to marry me for myself not for my house or money or the business. But then if I had offered to marry you, I'm sure you would have rejected my offer.'

363

'Why do you think that?'

'Your instincts would have been to revert to what you were. You'd have found another job and been a bitter person for the rest of your life. I would have been racked with guilt and filled with the bitterness that comes from losing one's heart's desire.'

They had finished their meal and had coffee in front of them. Sarah stirred hers and then laid the spoon back in the saucer, but before she could withdraw her hand Mr Deakin had taken hold of it at the wrist and started stroking the back with his other hand. Sarah sat smiling for she could feel his finger tracing over the back of her hand and she could read the letters he was slowly tracing out. They were doing something which had she seen other couples doing and she had poured scorn on them. To any outsider she too must have appeared ridiculous, with a soppy look on her face, but she found it too gratifying to want to withdraw her hand and assume a more respectable pose.

They left the restaurant with her arm tucked firmly in his. The traffic around Piccadilly Circus was as bad as ever and the pavements were choked with humanity. Sarah did not mind where Philip took her, she just wanted to be with him. A thought nagged at her, and having crossed the end of Regent Street to where the press of people was heaviest, she pulled on Philip's arm. He stopped and turned to her.

'What's the matter?' he asked, standing close to her.

'There is something I haven't told you, Philip.'

'What is it?' he said, his face becoming serious.

Someone pushed him in the back and swore at him because he had stopped partly blocking the pavement. 'Tell me!'

'I've never told you, at least not in words.'

'What?'

'I do love you,' she said, 'I really do.'

She felt his arms envelop her and his lips find hers. People still pushed past them, some staring at the couple unashamedly embracing in public.

'Let's go somewhere,' she said, 'and finish what you started in Venice.'

Philip signified his agreement with her sentiments by promptly hailing a passing taxi.

Printed in the United Kingdom
by Lightning Source UK Ltd.
120610UK00001B/1-21